JG FAHERTY

THE WAKENING

This is a FLAME TREE PRESS book

FLAME TREE PRESS
6 Melbray Mews, London, SW6 3NS, UK
flametreepress.com

US sales, distribution and warehouse:
Simon & Schuster
simonandschuster.biz

UK distribution and warehouse:
Marston Book Services Ltd
marston.co.uk

Publisher's Note: This is a work of fiction. Names, characters, places, and incidents are a product of the author's imagination. Locales and public names are sometimes used for atmospheric purposes. Any resemblance to actual people, living or dead, or to businesses, companies, events, institutions, or locales is completely coincidental.

Thanks to the Flame Tree Press team, including:
Taylor Bentley, Frances Bodiam, Federica Ciaravella, Don D'Auria, Chris Herbert, Josie Karani, Molly Rosevear, Will Rough, Mike Spender, Cat Taylor, Maria Tissot, Nick Wells, Gillian Whitaker.

The cover is created by Flame Tree Studio with thanks to Nik Keevil and Shutterstock.com.
The font families used are Avenir and Bembo.

Flame Tree Press is an imprint of Flame Tree Publishing Ltd

flametreepublishing.com

A copy of the CIP data for this book is available from the British Library and the Library of Congress.

3 5 7 9 8 6 4 2

HB ISBN: 978-1-78758-593-5
PB ISBN: 978-1-78758-591-1
ebook ISBN: 978-1-78758-594-2

Printed and bound in Great Britain by at Clays Ltd, Elcograf S.p.A.

JG FAHERTY

THE WAKENING

FLAME TREE PRESS
London & New York

SIGNS OF POSSESSION

(from *The Roman Ritual of Exorcism*)

The following are symptoms of possession as described in *The Roman Ritual of Exorcism*. In most cases, a possessed individual will have one or more of the symptoms listed.

Victim speaks or understands unknown languages without any prior knowledge thereof.

Victim clearly knows things that are distant or hidden.

Victim can predict future events.

Victim has an intense hatred for holy things.

Victim shows a physical strength far beyond what the individual should be capable of.

Fear or loathing of the name of God, Jesus, Mary, or any of the saints.

Pain or physical discomfort in the presence of holy objects, upon hearing prayers or Scripture read, or witnessing sacraments being performed.

Supernatural activity, including but not limited to levitation, the appearance of unusual objects, and the presence of ectoplasm.

STAGES OF POSSESSION

1. Oppression: When a demon plagues an individual. This can include physical torment, health issues, and even paranormal activity in the victim's vicinity.
2. Obsession: This encompasses mental, physical, and emotional torment. Often a person will act irrationally and show signs of abuse.
3. Infestation: When a demonic entity takes residence inside a person. This can include all the above signs, plus speaking in tongues, levitation, stigmata, and psychic phenomena.

SECTION ONE
OPPRESSION

Los Angeles, Present Day
Excerpt from **Good Morning with Josh and Jenny**

Jenny Durso: "Tell me, Mr. Graves, what made this such a difficult case for you?"

Stone Graves: "I could name a dozen things, Jenny, but really what it came down to was information and interpretation. The Catholic Church actually has a list of signs, what they call symptoms, of possession. You can find it in *The Roman Ritual of Exorcism.*"

Onscreen behind Graves, a list appears.

Josh Black: "That's some list!"

Graves: "It is. And usually it's very accurate. But what they don't take into consideration is that the presence of a supernatural being is a lot like getting sick in the winter."

Durso: "How so?"

Graves: "Because you can't always tell what you've got. A cold, the flu, a sinus infection. A lot of the symptoms are the same."

Black: (points at list) "Ectoplasm and physical discomfort? Sounds a lot like my last flu!"

Audience laughter.

Graves: "Trust me, Josh. Having a demon or poltergeist in your house is no laughing matter. We learned that the hard way."

On the screen, a picture of a covered body being taken away by two EMTs appears. The audience goes silent.

Durso: "When we come back, Stone Graves will tell us more about his new book, *A Town Possessed.*"

CHAPTER ONE

Guatemala, fifty-five years ago

Evil lives here.

Father Leo Bonaventura shivered as he entered the remote village of Tapajo. Satan's presence lay across the tiny settlement like a malevolent blanket, woven between the scattered huts like a deadly miasma. Darker than the jungle night, more oppressive than the cloying, sulfur-tainted mist rising from the nearby river, it lapped at skin and clothes with an oily, invisible tongue.

"This way, *Padre.*" Benito, the native boy who'd met the boat at the dilapidated wooden dock, tugged at Leo's sleeve. He wore a ragged tie-dye t-shirt and cut-off denim shorts. Despite his preoccupation with the coming task, the priest still managed to feel more than a small measure of discomfort at the boy's knowledge of both English and Spanish. Not to mention his clothing.

Hundreds of years later and the handiwork of the Church is still evident everywhere, both good and bad. We brought them new languages, gave them education and clothes, and showed them the path to Heaven, but at what cost? Their identity, their culture.

Ahead of them, someone – or *something* – cried out, a long, animalistic howl that raised gooseflesh on Leo's arms despite the stifling tropical humidity and heat. Hoarse shouts followed, a barrage of words in no language Leo recognized.

"*Venga, Padre.* Come."

Leo realized he'd stopped walking. He forced his body to move forward, fighting the instinctive urge to turn and flee. Around them, the jungle sat silent, as if the birds and animals had gone into hiding or fled the area to escape the unnatural presence that had invaded their territory.

Benito led him to a large thatch hut on the far side of the village. *A communal hall, perhaps,* the priest thought. A group of about twenty villagers stood nearby. Waiting.

Waiting for me. Their last hope.

Their savior.

Although he kept his face impassive, Leo grimaced inside. He came not as a savior, but as a warrior. A big difference.

Unlike saviors, warriors didn't always triumph.

Leo paused at the entrance to the hut, wiped sweat from his face and neck, and whispered a short prayer for safety.

"Gracious Saint Joseph, protect me and those around me from all evil as you did the Holy Family. Amen."

As he crossed himself, he noticed the villagers repeating the gesture. More evidence of the Church's subjugation of primitive cultures.

We force them to change their gods and promise them a better life, but we also bring diseases for which they have no resistance, and medicines that half the time don't work as well as their own.

"*Gracias a Dios que venites, Padre,*" whispered an older woman. *Thank God you came.*

I hope her faith isn't misplaced.

Leo nodded to her, took a deep breath that filled his lungs with oppressively moist jungle air, and then pushed through the vine curtain that served as the hut's doorway.

The low roof magnified the humidity to almost sauna-like conditions, and Leo found himself mopping more sweat from his face before his eyes finished adjusting to the dim, green-tinted interior, where the only light came from two small candles atop a wooden crate.

"Leo. Thank God you're here," someone said in a wheezing voice.

Halfway across the circular dwelling, two men knelt next to the prone form of a boy, the child nude except for a ragged towel covering his private area. The man who'd spoken, Father Jorge Sanchez, rose to his feet, the cracking and popping of his ancient joints audible to Leo from ten feet away. Sanchez wore the purple silk stole of an exorcist over the customary black shirt and trousers. His clothes clung to his thin shoulders and round belly, plastered on by sweat. It was the first time Leo had ever seen him without the traditional black cassock. As he approached Leo, he removed his thick glasses and wiped uselessly at them with a stained handkerchief.

Time has not been kind to him. Leo watched his old mentor's stiff movements. *Ten years since I last saw him, but he looks like he's aged twenty. Is that one of the hazards of the position? Will it happen to me as well?*

The idea of growing old and losing his faculties disturbed Leo deeply, which surprised him. He'd only recently completed his studies in exorcism and been assigned his first Church posting, in Guatemala City. Until now, he'd never contemplated his own mortality. He quickly pushed the thought aside to focus on the matter at hand. The matter he'd trained the past five years for; that had, in fact, been his sole reason for joining the Church.

To rid the world of Evil.

Behind Sanchez, the boy on the ground let out a loud moan and his body went into convulsions, legs and arms shaking, heels drumming against the dirt floor, head whipping back and forth. Even in the badly lit confines of the hut, the child's eyes stood out, wide and white against the darkness of his skin and the surrounding gloom.

"*Ay, Dios mio.*" Sanchez hurried back to the boy.

As Leo followed, he felt the gaze of the boy's parents, who stood near the back of the hut. Ignoring their pleading looks, he set down his traveling case and knelt while Sanchez whispered passages in Spanish from a tattered Bible.

"You must be the doctor," Leo said to the other man, who gripped the boy's arms and attempted to hold him still. "I'm Father Leo Bonaventura."

"John Zimmerman." The doctor was thin and pale, with close-cropped hair almost the same carrot red as Leo's. He looked a few years older than Leo's twenty-four. Leo guessed he'd recently graduated medical school and had to complete some kind of foreign service in return for a reduced tuition. A black medical bag sat next to him, closed. That simple fact indicated the man had already done everything in his power for the boy.

Which was why Jorge sent for me.

The idea of his mentor needing help worried Leo; it had, in fact, led to many hours of lost sleep during the four-day trip from Rome to Guatemala.

If things are so bad the teacher has to turn to the student....

The boy screamed again, the same primitive cry Leo had heard while walking through the village. Without warning, the boy sat up, easily breaking free from Zimmerman's grip even though he couldn't have been more than twelve years old and all of seventy pounds.

"You!" the boy shouted and pointed at Leo, who fell back in surprise. "I will see you dead, Leo Bonaventura. Your heart will boil and I will devour your soul!"

The child stood, the cloth falling away to reveal an erect penis. He waggled his hips in a crude, suggestive manner. Leo wondered how he could have thought the boy was short, seeing him tower over their heads. Then the doctor gasped and Leo looked again. The boy floated a foot above the ground, hovering in the air like an angel.

Or a demon.

Leo didn't doubt the existence of demons. He'd read too many tomes, heard too many stories from Sanchez and the others at the Vatican, had seen too much himself in his young life, for there to be any doubt.

However, he hadn't been a hundred percent sure about the native boy's condition until now.

"Jesus, Mary, and Joseph," he whispered, making the sign of the cross with his thumb.

"Fuck your God!" the boy screamed, his face contorting into a mask of rage.

Leo reached for his bag, which contained his Bible and exorcism paraphernalia, but Sanchez was faster. Standing with surprising speed, the old priest cast a handful of holy water at the child, who shouted in pain and fell to the dirt floor.

"*Nāṉ uṉṉai narakattil pārppēṉ!*" the boy cried, and then his frail form began to shiver uncontrollably, as if he lay naked in a snowy field instead of a sweltering jungle. The doctor looked up at Sanchez, who nodded once and then motioned to Leo.

"Come with me. We must talk."

"But the boy...?"

"The demon will not return for an hour or so. Anibal has been like this for more than two days. He has...spells...but in between he is mostly delirious with fever."

"Spells?" Leo held the fiber curtain aside so Sanchez could walk through. "Is that what you're calling them?"

"Yes. What words would you prefer? Manifestations? Fits? Seizures? Haven't you learned words mean nothing? Things are what they are, regardless of what you call them."

Sanchez led them to what appeared to be a gathering place. Groups of logs had been peeled, notched, and fitted together to create crude benches. They took seats and Leo sighed. Although the temperature still sat well into the nineties, the evening air felt cool and fresh on his skin compared to the sweltering confines of the hut.

For a few minutes they sat without speaking, and once more Leo took note of the jungle's unnatural silence. Without the background noise of animal sounds, the low gurgling of the lazy river reached him clearly. A loud moan came from one of the other huts, followed by the unmistakable grunting of two people engaging in intercourse. Leo frowned, and his old mentor noticed.

"It is the demon's influence."

Leo considered this. It was unusual for a demon to affect those surrounding the possessed individual. He tried to think of which ones might be capable, but the lack of information made it impossible to narrow down the possibilities.

"What else has been demonstrated?" he asked, his voice hushed, an unconscious reaction to the stillness all around them.

"Pardon?" Sanchez jumped slightly, as if startled from a doze. Knowing what the man had been through the past week, Leo wasn't surprised his old friend had nodded off.

"You wouldn't have called me all the way here for bouts of seizure and occasional levitation. To ask for my help, for anyone's help, you must have a very good reason."

Sanchez sighed and nodded. "You know me too well. Should I start at the beginning?"

Leo nodded. "That is always the best place."

"*Sí, así es.*" Sanchez took off his glasses and attempted to clean them again. With a smile, Leo handed him a clean handkerchief. "Ah, thank you. Yes, that's better. Where was I?"

"The beginning."

"Yes. Dr. Zimmerman called me a week ago, asking for my help. He studied medicine in Rome and we had met several times while I performed last rites. He said he had a patient suffering from fever and convulsions and none of his medicines had worked, just like nothing the family had tried had worked before that. In his words, 'I believe the Devil has taken this boy.' When he told me the local priest had died while ministering to Anibal—"

"What? A priest died here?" Leo's shock came as much from his having heard nothing about it, despite being in a parish only fifty or so miles away, as from the sad fact of its occurrence.

Sanchez nodded, his face grim. "Yes. Father Hector Ecchivaria. He walked out of that hut and threw himself into the river. His body hasn't been found."

"Hector? I heard he died in a boating accident on his way to visit a village."

"The local government didn't want a story about demons spreading to other areas."

While Leo digested that news, Sanchez continued speaking.

"When I arrived, the boy was as you saw him just now, shaking with fever. The first thing I did was begin a prayer for good health. No sooner did I speak the first few words than Anibal sat up and swore at me, much as he did to you before."

Leo allowed himself a small smile. "Yes, he does seem to have quite a way with words."

"More so when you find out he neither speaks nor understands English."

Despite the heat, a cold shiver ran through Leo's body. "Are you sure? Even if his family doesn't speak it, plenty of trading boats pass through here. Others in the village speak it. The boy could've picked up any number of foul words from them, or from the sailors."

Sanchez shook his head. "No, his family assured me those were the first words in English they had ever heard him utter. Even so, he has spoken in other languages as well. Tamil. Hebrew. Latin."

"So, speaking in tongues. What else?"

"He has immense strength. You saw how he pushed Zimmerman to the ground? I've seen him break free of four men at once. Then there is the levitation. And finally, he shows a complete intolerance for anything holy, including the names of God, Jesus, or any of the saints."

"All of the signs," Leo said, as much to himself as to his onetime teacher. "But that's not why you called me. Something is different this time."

Another nod from Sanchez, his dim figure more spirit than human in the darkness, an image that made Leo shiver anew.

"Besides his foul epithets, Anibal has also spoken…a name."

"What was it?"

"Asmodeus."

Leo's thoughts dissolved into nothingness. For a moment, his whole body went numb. He no longer felt the sweltering heat, the savage mosquitoes, the rough wood of his seat. He opened his mouth, but it took several seconds for the words to form.

"Asmodeus? Are…are you sure? Perhaps you misheard—"

"I didn't. He repeated it more than once. He even said it while speaking to me in Spanish. He referred to himself as Lord Asmodeus, the one before whom someday all shall bow."

Leo stared at the old priest, who'd seen so many things in his life, and saw fear in his friend's eyes. Asmodeus was more than an ordinary demon. A prince of Hell, one of the original banished ones. A fallen angel who commanded legions in the name of Satan and served as the Dark One's left-hand confidant. Many ancient writings referred to him as the many-headed beast and the demon of lust.

If he truly has come into our world....

"Wait," Leo said, as a thought came to him. "One of the first things you taught us is that demons lie. How do you know it's really Asmodeus?"

"*That* is the reason I sent for you." Sanchez gripped Leo's arm. "I have made three attempts to banish this evil from the boy, but it only grows stronger. Its foul presence is spreading through the village. You can feel it, it permeates the air like a terrible odor. For days now, the animals of the jungle have been dying and the people of this village...several have taken their own lives in the river and others have experienced episodes of unbridled lust, even rutting like beasts right in the center of the village. It has grown steadily worse since... Father Ecchivaria's visit. I fear he may have attempted to drive the demon out on his own."

"What? An untrained priest performing an exorcism?" Leo gave an involuntary shudder. "Why would—?"

"We do not know what he did or did not do. Perhaps he simply read the rites to appease the family, or test the boy. Of course, if he did carry out the rites...."

Sanchez didn't need to finish the sentence. They both knew the dangers of an exorcism conducted incorrectly. One of Sanchez's first lessons had focused on that topic.

"When a demon is not exorcised properly, the danger is magnified and you will spread the demon's influence even farther. You must always remove evil by the roots, so that nothing remains behind."

"Is there anything else I should know?"

Sanchez's frown deepened. "There have been instances of poltergeist activity as well. Objects moving on their own. Violent acts with no recollection afterward. We must end this now. Whatever it is, the thing inside Anibal is too strong for me alone. Call it luck or fate that you happened to be nearby, but I trust you more than any other to help me with something so powerful. We must drive whatever inhabits that child back to whence it came."

The grip on Leo's arm grew tighter. Although his friend's words terrified him to his core, Leo placed his hand over Sanchez's.

"Tell me what to do."

Leo struggled to remain on his feet as a horrific wind turned the inside of the hut into a miniature tornado. Clothing, bowls, and the broken pieces of Father Sanchez's wooden cross whirled around, metamorphosed into deadly missiles by the supernatural storm.

Squinting against the gale, his clothes slapping painfully against his skin, Leo raised his Bible and pointed a finger at Anibal, whose rotating body floated five feet above the ground.

"I exorcise thee, unclean spirit, in the name of God, the Father Almighty, in the name of our Lord, Jesus Christ, and in the name of the Holy Spirit!"

Across from him, Sanchez repeated the phrase in Latin. "*Exorcizo te, immunde spiritus, in nomine Dei Patris omnipotentis, et in nomine domini nostri, Iesu Christi, et in nomine Spiritus Sancti*!"

While he spoke, Sanchez waved a wand-shaped aspergillum back and forth, spraying holy water across the levitating figure.

"*Pūcāri, uṅkaḷai ēmāṟṟuṅkaḷ*!" Anibal shouted, his face twisted in pain.

Leo had lost count of how many times they'd performed the rite over the past twenty-four hours. In between, they'd prayed to Jesus and all the saints and recited passages from the Bible. They'd even bound the boy with garlands of grass woven around Eucharistic wafers, to no avail. His skin blistered and red, Anibal had torn away the strings and defecated on them, desecrating the body of Christ, all the while cursing in Latin, Spanish, English, and several other languages Leo didn't recognize.

"Leo, now!"

Earlier, Sanchez had decided they needed to add something new to the rite. As he'd often said in class, "An exorcist must adapt to the situation at hand, because every instance of possession is different." Pushing himself forward against the battering wind, Leo took a silver cross from his pocket and pressed it against the boy's chest.

"*Crux sancta sit mihi lux! Vade retro Satana!*"

Let the holy cross be my light! Step back, Satan!

At the same time, Sanchez grabbed the boy's head and poured an entire jar of blessed water into Anibal's open mouth. Blinding white light burst from the boy. Hands raised against the glare, Leo watched as the possessed child writhed in midair, arms and legs twisting into shapes that shouldn't have been possible for a thing of flesh and bone. One arm bent backward and caught Sanchez around the neck. Leo heard a *crack!* and Sanchez fell to the dirt floor. Light still streaming from mouth and eyes, Anibal turned and looked at Leo.

"This is not the end for us, Father Fucking Bonaventura! You cannot kill me, for I am eternal. We will meet again."

An invisible force exploded outward and knocked Leo to the ground. The silver cross shot toward him and he threw up his arms to protect his face. Burning pain ran down one arm and he cried out.

Manic laughter filled the air and then faded away. A horrendous howling rose up throughout the jungle, reached a deafening crescendo, and then stopped. The light disappeared, leaving charred holes where Anibal's eyes had been. With a final scream, the body dropped to the ground and lay still. The wind slowly dissipated and Leo had to cover his head as dishes and other objects fell to the floor.

With the candles extinguished and the mystical illumination gone, the only light came from the thin streams of dawn leaking through the tattered remains of the hut's walls and ceiling. Leo rose to his knees, straining to see the body of the cursed boy, alert for any signs of treachery.

Anibal's mouth fell open and a swarm of beetles flowed out, each as long as a man's thumb and black as obsidian. More of them climbed from the empty eye sockets. Within seconds, hundreds of the giant insects scurried across the dirt floor, the sound of their legs and bodies like someone shaking dozens of maracas all at once. Careful to keep his hands and feet away from the creatures, Leo grabbed an empty jar and scooped up several of the bugs. He screwed the lid on tight and backed away from the body. Screams from outside the hut told him the beetles had found their way into the village.

And then as fast as they'd appeared, they were gone.

Leo set the jar down and hurried to Father Sanchez. The old priest's chest didn't move and his head flopped loosely from side to side when Leo touched him.

"God be with you," Leo whispered. He wanted to cry, to mourn his friend, but his exhaustion had numbed him, body and soul.

Movement by the door caught his attention. Anibal's family stood there with Dr. Zimmerman, the rest of the village behind them. Their eyes all held the same question.

"*Lo siento.*" *I'm sorry*. Leo shook his head. "Anibal *es muerte,*" he added, hoping his limited Spanish was correct.

A stout woman stepped forward. "*Y el demonio?*"

And the demon?

Leo started to speak and then paused, remembering the demon's words.

"Your time will come, Father Fucking Bonaventura! You cannot kill me, for I am eternal."

Maybe they hadn't killed him, but he was certainly gone. Banished to Hell forever.

"*Adios,*" Leo said, making a waving motion with his hand. "Goodbye. No more." He tried to remember the Spanish words, but they weren't necessary. The woman offered a solemn nod and made the sign of the cross.

"*Gracias, Padre. Dios de bendiga.*"

Thank you, Father. God be with you.

Leo patted her shoulder. "*Y contigo tambien.*" *And with you too.*

The woman smiled weakly and then left, her family following her.

Alone in the tent with the two bodies, Father Leo Bonaventura retrieved the silver cross and slipped it into his pocket, then knelt and gave thanks to the God Almighty for his help and strength.

As he made the sign of the cross again, he noticed blood dripping from his arm and remembered the cross striking him. He looked at the wound and shivered as a wave of cold terror ran through him.

Carved into his flesh was a single word.

Asmodeum.

Three weeks later

"Father Bonaventura? It's Ed Oberle, at St. Alphonse University. I've identified your beetles. Can you come over here right away? This is quite amazing."

"I'll be right there." Leo hung up the phone and grabbed his jacket. St. Alphonse University was only a ten-minute cab ride from the hotel he'd been staying in since bringing the insects to one of the top entomologists in New York State. More than long enough for knots to form in Leo's stomach as he wondered what kind of news waited for him. He had a strong suspicion he'd have another unbelievable report to file with his superiors.

The short ride through the quaint rural town of Hastings Mills and then across the neat green campus of the university did nothing to quell his nerves. Any other time, he'd have enjoyed his visit.

Perhaps someday I can get an assignment at a place like this. After all, when he finished his training, he'd have to be placed somewhere. And teaching at a university would allow him ample time to continue his research.

When he arrived at the Life Sciences building, he found the Head of Entomology at his desk, his head in his hands.

"Dr. Oberle? What did you find?"

Oberle looked up, and Leo immediately knew something was wrong.

"They're gone. All seven of them. The one I preserved and the six I left alive."

Oberle pointed a shaking finger at a nearby lab table, where a glass tank sat next to a microscope and several reference books.

"I don't understand how it happened," the gray-haired scientist continued. "I never left this room except to call you. One minute they were there, and the next...."

"Gone," Leo finished. A seed of fear came to life in his belly. He felt no surprise at the disappearance, not after what he'd witnessed in the jungle. What concerned him was *where* they had gone. "Tell me. What were they?"

"*Cerambyx certo*. The Great Capricorn beetle, an extremely rare species from Europe. Extinct since the 1700s. And unheard of in Central America. So now please tell me the truth. Where did you really get them?"

"Get what?" Leo indicated the empty tank. "I don't see anything. Perhaps it's better if we just go on as if this never happened. Have a good day, Professor." Before Oberle could respond, Leo turned and exited the office.

The next morning, he was on a plane to Rome.

By then, the seed of fear had already sprouted leaves.

CHAPTER TWO

Hastings Mills, NY, forty years ago

Father Doyle Bannon descended the steps of Holy Cross Church and paused to take a deep breath of the brisk November air. It brought with it the smells of winter in upstate New York: dry earth, decaying leaves, and the metallic hardness of frigid water from the Alleghany River, which formed the south boundary of Hastings Mills and the back border of the St. Alphonse University campus.

His stomach growled and he made a mental note to go into town for a quick shopping trip after his walk. His cupboards were almost empty, and while he took most of his meals at the campus friary's private cafeteria, he liked to keep some sweet snacks around for when cravings hit.

The late afternoon sun glistened off church spires and roof shingles still moist from the morning's rain. A smattering of cars drove past, people heading home from work or out to early-bird dinners.

"*Buon pomeriggio, Padre.*" Pasquale Fromo, a neighbor and parishioner, waved as he passed by on the sidewalk. He still wore his blue coverall from his job as head janitor at Hastings Mills Elementary. Although technically Holy Cross was part of the St. Alphonse campus, it primarily served the local community, while the newer, smaller St. Alphonse Church, in the middle of campus, served the students.

"Best o' the day to you, Pasquale." Bannon smiled back. "Beautiful afternoon, isn't it?"

"Sure is, *Padre.* Gotta enjoy them while we can." He nodded and continued on his way.

Bannon watched him go, thinking that sometimes the most

profound statements came from the mouths of ordinary people. *Enjoy them while we can.* That didn't just apply to days; it applied to everything in life. People, food, being one with God. He made a mental note to include that in his next sermon.

A tickling sensation on his wrist caused him to look down. He gasped as an enormous insect crawled out from his jacket sleeve and across the back of his hand. With a cry he shook his arm, dislodging the bug, which fell to the ground and scurried toward the church steps. His disgust faded when he saw it wasn't a cockroach but just a large beetle, shiny black and easily the size of the rectangular pink erasers the kindergarten classes used. He tried to smash it with his foot but it dodged away and disappeared into a crack in the cement. Despite the fact that he didn't have a fear of insects, the sight of it turned his stomach. He hated roaches with a passion, and made sure to have the church and the small rectory behind it sprayed every three months. The damned beetle looked too much like a roach for his taste, and if beetles could live on the grounds, so could roaches.

And how did it end up in my jacket?

That thought made him pause. It was November. Shouldn't bugs be hibernating or whatever they did in the winter? And Jesus Almighty, it was huge!

All of a sudden, he wanted nothing more than to strip his clothes off and make sure no other creatures hid inside them. Or his closet. His afternoon walk forgotten, Bannon headed back to the rectory to clean his whole room and then call the exterminator company to arrange a special visit.

There'd be no vermin in the church under his watch.

"Well, that should do it, Father." The exterminator, a skinny, balding man named Ray who referred to himself as a 'pest control technician', slammed the doors of his white van – with the obligatory dead roach painted on the side – and wiped his hands on his blue uniform shirt.

"I put down dust along every wall and in every corner, and set bait traps besides."

"Thank you." Bannon signed the itemized form and handed it back. The bill would be sent to the archdiocese.

"Gotta say, though, I didn't see any signs of bugs, 'cept for a few spiders down in the basement. The quarterly treatments are doing their work. You sure that beetle you saw didn't get on you outside, like off the sidewalk?"

"I'm not sure, but I don't want to be takin' no chances." Just thinking about the creature from Monday made him want to shower again.

"Well, cleanliness is next to godliness. At least that's what my ma always said." Ray slipped his pen into his pocket and got into the truck. As he drove away, Bannon found himself mouthing the words, "Feck off, arsehole," to the departing vehicle.

Shaking his head at the unexpected eruption of what his own mother always called his Irish temper, he said a quick Hail Mary for his transgression and returned to his office, where he'd been struggling all day with his sermon for the Sunday Mass. Usually they came right to him, the words flowing from brain to pen as if the Lord himself spoke through him. He'd always had the gift of the gab, ever since his days in seminary school. But for the past four days he'd been afflicted with a writer's block the likes of which he'd never experienced. Instead of being unable to find the right words, his mind kept wandering down strange roads.

Strange and dark.

Unwholesome images kept creeping into his thoughts, visions of sexual perversion and physical violence. At the age of fifty-two, Bannon was no stranger to the sins of the flesh – any priest worth his weight in sacramental wine would admit, at least in private, that lustful urges came as part of the human condition. He'd confessed to his fair share plenty of times over the years. But having an urge and acting on it were two different things. A cold shower, a sleeping pill, and a few passages of scripture in bed usually kept the demon of self-satisfaction at bay. It had never concerned him, because his dreams and fantasies had always involved adult men and women doing what came naturally.

Not young boys.

His hand went down to the lowest drawer of his desk. His fingers brushed against the metal handle and then pulled away. Denied its recently acquired prize, the temptation roared inside him like a caged animal, throwing its invisible body back and forth until Bannon's arms shook and sweat rolled down his face.

Not now, he told the beast. *Not during the day, when someone might come in. Later. When we're alone.*

He returned to his sermon. The words blurred on the page and imaginary movies of naked, writhing flesh filled his head. Bannon sat back and rubbed his eyes. When he looked down at the paper again, the words he'd just written stood out from everything else on the page.

If the Lord didn't want us to have sex with little boys, then why are they so beautiful? The pleasures of the flesh are not to be ignored, for surely God gave us the ability to feel that pleasure. There is a reason angels and cherubs flock together in Heaven. This is God showing us that men and children are meant to share His love.

"Blasphemy," Bannon whispered. What if he'd read that aloud during Mass? His blood pounded in his temples and heat spread through his body. His clothes rubbed against skin that had grown so sensitive he could feel every hair springing to attention. His legs rubbed together, delivering waves of pleasure that caused him to moan.

This time, his hand didn't hesitate. It opened the drawer and removed the magazines hidden in the folder labeled *Liturgical Research.* The ones he'd bought that morning, at a tiny store over the border in Pennsylvania, where no one knew him. Lurid images on the covers made his heart beat faster. Naked boys on the laps of smiling men. Teenagers and adults nude in the forest, holding hands.

He opened the first one and undid his pants. This was for the best, he told himself. Eliminate the urge and he'd be able to concentrate on holy matters again. And later he'd go across town to St. Anthony's and confess his weakness.

He'd just begun stroking himself when the door opened and the new altar boy, Bobby Lockhart, walked in.

"Father Doyle, I— Oh!" The boy's face turned red and his eyes went wide.

Bannon leaped up from his chair, which only exposed his shame even further.

Why shame? There's no shame in sharing God's love. The voice in his head was low and confident. *That's your job, isn't it? To spread the teachings of God. And doesn't he teach us to love one another?*

Yes. Yes, he does. Bannon smiled at the boy, who still stood frozen, his eyes locked on the staff sprouting from its nest of red hair.

"Shut the door, Bobby. I've got a special lesson for you today."

Father Doyle Bannon stood at the front window of his office and stared at the crowd gathering in front of the church. He knew why they'd come. Knew it before he even saw the police car parked there.

I really fecked things up.

He should have expected the Lockhart boy wouldn't keep his promise of silence. Who had he told? His father? His mother? It didn't matter. Someone had believed him, had gone to the police. And now there'd be hell to pay for his transgressions.

I'm soiled. Dirty. Unclean to the very depths of my soul. For the first time, he understood his own hypocrisy. How could a man who took pleasure in the sins of the flesh, right in the house of God, carry Jesus's word to the people?

As he unlocked the window, he found himself wondering why God allowed such things to happen under his own roof. He'd never questioned the Lord's motives before, and certainly never objected to the advances of the parish priests when he'd been an altar boy, or a novitiate.

Still, he'd always known they were wrong, and he'd made sure to do his penance after. But this....

I must atone.

A firm knocking on the door turned him away from the view of the street.

"Father Doyle? Open the door, please. It's Officer Rose."

Bannon sighed. Alex Rose. Of course. A parishioner of Holy Cross, his family had deep roots in the community, from long before Bannon took over as pastor. They'd shared more than a few whiskeys on cold winter nights, both in the rectory and down the street at the Hickory Tavern, discussing everything from the church to politics to movies. He considered the officer a friend.

And now he'll be the one to put me away.

How can I possibly explain to him what happened, when I can't even explain it to myself?

"It's open," Bannon said. A second later, Rose entered, wearing his blue uniform beneath a rumpled overcoat. His graying hair stuck out at angles, as if he'd been running his hands through it. A mixture of regret and anger showed in his eyes, but when he spoke, his voice was calm.

"We got a situation, Father. You're gonna have to come to the station."

"I'm sorry, Alex. I didn't mean for it to happen."

Rose stared at him and said nothing, the silence dragging on until it became uncomfortable. Bannon wished he'd say something. Anything. An accusation, or perhaps an apology of his own for what he had to do. Even an angry condemnation for his act of perversion.

"You must respect those in authority, Doyle."

Bannon jumped at the words. *That voice! It couldn't be....* It was his old parish priest, Father Brendan Donahue. The man who'd introduced a young Doyle Bannon to the dark pleasures of sex back in Dublin more than forty years ago.

Bannon opened his mouth, but no words came out. Rose continued speaking in the long-dead priest's voice. "Take off yer trou, boy. Let Father Brendan show you how to be a man."

Memories came flooding back. Bending over the chair. The sharp pain as something entered him. Donahue's animal grunting, in time to the sound of flesh slapping against flesh.

"A good shepherd tends to his flock."

"The spirit of God flows through us all."

"Jesus gave himself up for us."

Every Friday, in Donahue's chambers. He'd teach the Bible and more.

"You know what you have to do."

"What?" Bannon opened his eyes. Rose still stood several feet away, his mouth closed, his features twisted in a manic grin. *Had he even spoken? Was I hearing things?*

The officer pointed at the window. It took Bannon a moment to understand. Then everything became clear.

It wasn't his old friend speaking to him. It was God the Almighty. Using Rose as a tool, a human burning bush. Like he'd done with Samuel, Ezekiel, and Moses, the Lord had descended to personally deliver a message to a mortal man.

And that man is me.

The time had come for him to pay the price for his sins.

A sense of peace came over him, and he knew the weight of guilt had been lifted from his soul. Rose continued to stare, his arm still extended. A sign that couldn't be ignored.

"Forgive me, Lord," Bannon whispered, "I was weak in the face of temptation." He went to the window. When he opened it, a pigeon leaped from the ledge, startled by the movement. The sounds of the neighborhood came to him from twenty feet down, the twittering of birds and squirrels, music from a nearby house, the muted growl of someone blowing leaves. A delicious odor wafted in, the mouth-watering scent of frying hamburgers from the Barton Hotel a block away.

He loved the town, and he'd tried to do right by it, despite his personal failings. Now he'd never see it again. Never get to say goodbye to his family. He turned back to look at his old friend as a new thought came to him. If he committed suicide, what would happen to his soul?

"Is there no other way?"

Rose reached out and approached him, moving swiftly across the office. Bannon's heart soared and wonder filled him when he saw his friend's feet weren't touching the ground.

A miracle! I've been forgiven. Truly this is a wondrous day and the Lord has—

The officer's hands struck him in the chest and then he was falling over the ledge, sailing through the air. As he plummeted, he saw another face superimposed over Rose's.

A twisted, evil visage with yellow eyes and a laughing mouth.

He had time for one last thought – *the Father of Lies has deceived me!* – and then Bannon's back and ribs shattered as he landed on the iron railing of the church stairs.

Dead on impact, he never saw the large, iridescent-black beetle that launched itself from the window ledge and flew away.

Boston, MA, forty years ago

Father Leo Bonaventura hung up the phone and tugged his sweater tighter around his shoulders in an attempt to ward off a sudden chill that had nothing to do with the November weather or the poor insulation in his office.

"You've been transferred, Leo. A big opportunity. Your own parish plus a teaching position at a university. This is just what you've been asking for."

Yes, it was. But when he'd heard the name of the school from the archbishop, he'd gone cold and momentarily lost the ability to speak.

St. Alphonse.

Memories of the beautiful upstate town of Hastings Mills and the terrifying events that had led him there that summer came flooding back. Fifteen years had passed and he still had nightmares.

And the scar on his arm to remind him it all really happened.

He remembered the drive to the campus on the morning he'd learned the impossible insects had disappeared. How he'd thought he'd love to settle down in a place like that.

"Be careful what you ask for," his mother had been fond of saying.

Now he understood the truth of that old adage.

Praying he hadn't made the worst decision of his life by accepting the position, he returned to the sermon he'd been writing and flipped over a new page in his notebook.

The subject of his talk would now be decidedly different.

CHAPTER THREE

Hastings Mills, NY, thirty years ago

A brisk October wind, redolent of crisp dead leaves and the first hints of winter, swirled around the small group of students standing in the night-darkened shadows of St. Alphonse University's Dallas Hall. Caitlyn Sweeney shivered and Rob Lockhart put an awkward arm around her. They'd been dating since the start of the school year but only recently gone 'all the way', as Caitlyn had phrased it that night in her dorm room. In the days that followed, he'd been struggling with confused thoughts and feelings. He enjoyed spending time with her, but the physical part of the relationship…lacked something. Something he hated to admit he needed. He'd thought this time would be better because Caitlyn was different from his other girlfriends.

Now he feared she might not be different enough.

"Are you sure we won't get in trouble?" Caitlyn asked. She kept her voice to a whisper, even though they were alone behind the building.

"Chill out." Her older sister, Lori, poked her in the arm.

"We won't get in trouble if we don't get caught," Rob said, taking a set of keys from his coat pocket and jingling them.

"That's comforting," Caitlyn muttered.

The seven of them – Michael Choi, Maggie Brown, Kylie Johnson, and Patrick O'Hare made up the rest of the group – had left the warmth and cheap beer of the Hickory Tavern to sneak up to the fifth floor of Dallas Hall and party in the supposedly haunted attic storage area that had once been a commons room for the dorm.

"Relax. Everyone's gone for the weekend. This is gonna be our best chance to do this." Rob approached the heavy metal door that would let them into the back stairwell of the massive brick-and-stone Gothic structure.

The second oldest building on campus, Dallas Hall stood two stories higher than any of the other dormitories and was something of an architectural wonder in the daylight, with expansive archways, numerous cupolas, and a sharply peaked roof done in a California Mission style. Its ivy-covered walls didn't match any of the other buildings on campus and it seemed to stand sentinel in front of the more modern gray-stone structures, its brooding presence the first thing visitors saw as they entered the campus. In keeping with the university's century-old dedication to learning, the original architects had included bas-relief plaques on the front wall representing the seven medieval arts: Tonus (music), Numerus (arithmetic), Ratio (dialectic), Lingua (grammar), Tropus (rhetoric and literature), Astra (astronomy), and Anglus (geometry).

To the chagrin of the administration, a recent survey by the school paper had shown not a single student questioned could name even one of the symbols.

In the dark, the building morphed into something better suited to a medieval monastery than a co-ed residence hall, and the bas-reliefs took on the appearance of sinister glyphs.

The idea had come to Rob after hearing a story related to him by his father, who'd worked as a librarian at the university for several years. A story about the fifth floor being haunted.

"A girl committed suicide up there in the fifties," he'd related one night after dinner. "Before my time. Rumor has it, she was pregnant. A real sin back then. The school covered it up, probably with help from the parents. After that, strange things kept happening until one day, they just stopped using the whole floor."

Now, as a resident assistant in the dorm, Rob had a master key to all the doors in the building. Including the top floor, which had been converted from a commons area to a storage room back when his father worked at the school. Aside from the six RAs in the building, only maintenance and campus security had access to the back entrance.

The open door revealed a narrow staircase leading up into a lightless void broken sporadically by small emergency lights set into every fifth stair.

"No way, I am not going up there." Lori turned and looked at Pat. "Let them go. We can wait for them back at my room."

"C'mon, babe." Pat gave her a quick kiss. "Midterm break is the only time we'll get a chance to do this. The rest of the year there's too many people around."

"I've been up there a dozen times, and it's not scary," Rob added. "The worst thing I ever saw was a mouse."

Lori frowned but followed Pat as he made his way up the stairs. Kylie, Maggie, and Michael went next, with Caitlyn and Rob bringing up the rear. They waited until Pat clicked on a small flashlight before shutting the door. In the resulting darkness, the emergency lights glowed like eerie alien life-forms beneath their feet.

"You know," Rob said, his voice echoing off the cement walls, "they say the girl killed herself up there on Halloween."

"Shut up, Rob." Lori's voice floated down to the others from somewhere above.

"She slit her wrists," Rob continued. "And now, every October, you can hear her crying for her baby in the early morning hours."

"Rob, stop it. You're creeping me out."

"Seriously. And that's not all. There were the animal sacrifices."

"Idiot." Caitlyn poked him. "Now you're just bullshitting us. Besides, Halloween is next week."

At the top of the stairs, the group gathered on the small landing while Rob unlocked the door. It opened with a loud click.

"Enter, if you dare," he intoned in a mock sepulchral voice.

Michael laughed, and then stopped when one of the girls shushed him.

They filed into a wide, open space Rob had cleared for them earlier. Pat took some candles from his pockets, placed them in a circle, and lit them. To the far left and right were stacks of chairs, office supplies, and spare bed frames. The ceiling angled from close to twelve feet high in the middle to only eight by the walls. Pink insulation filled the gaps between beams. Rob's father had told him there'd once been a plan to renovate the space and turn it into dorm rooms, but it had been abandoned back in the early 1970s. Cobwebs draped corners in gray lace, decorated with the husks of long-dead insects. Faint rustlings hinted at mice lurking amid the clutter. Rob caught a glimpse of a dark shape scurrying away from their lights, flat and low to the ground, and he hoped it wasn't a roach. If the girls saw one, the whole night would be ruined.

"Let's get this party started," Rob said, putting the giant bug out of his mind and opening his backpack to reveal a large bottle of tequila and a plastic bag filled with lemon slices.

"What's with the candles?" Kylie asked, sitting down on the dusty tile floor. The others joined her inside the circle. The flickering light made the shadows come alive.

"Atmosphere," Pat said, a broad smile on his freckled face. Rob knew the real reason, but kept silent. Their plan had a much better chance of working if everyone caught a buzz first.

They spent the next twenty minutes doing just that. The tequila traveled the circle several times, thanks to the game of 'I Never' Rob and Pat started. By the time they finished half the bottle, the girls were in full giggle mode and nobody worried about trespassing or stories of ghosts.

Judging it to be the right time, Rob caught Pat's eye and nodded to him. In response, Pat lifted the bottle and raised his voice.

"I never had a séance in an old dorm."

Everyone went quiet.

Then Michael burst into laughter.

"Man, that shut everyone the hell up!"

"Not funny." Maggie pointed at Pat. "Drink, motherfucker. You ain't had no séances anywhere."

"Wait." Rob held up his hand. "We could all drink, since that's the rule. Or...we could really have a séance."

"Séance," Pat said, just like they'd planned.

"Séance," agreed Michael, who Rob knew would pretty much agree to anything when drunk. Like the time they'd told him it would be cool to go streaking at the basketball game.

"You don't know the first thing about a séance." Caitlyn shook her head, and he imagined her giving him one of her eye rolls as well. His confusion rose up again. Sometimes her attitude grated on his nerves. Like he was a child and she the parent. More and more, he'd found himself wondering if they were right for each other. He'd thought dating a sophomore would be okay, but perhaps he'd be better off with someone else. Someone who'd be thrilled to date a senior. Like one of the freshman girls.

Or maybe someone even younger.

"Not true. We learned about them in Father Leo's class. He covered the basics." Pat looked at Rob, who nodded.

"He's right. We both took the class."

Father Leo Bonaventura served as head of the religious studies department at the university, but it was his Religion and the Paranormal class, nicknamed 'Spooks', that had made him one of the most recognized professors on campus. As an official exorcist for the Catholic Church, Bonaventura brought real-world experiences to the class, which had long been one of the most popular electives at the school. His habit of reserving the front row for 'spirit friends' was just one of his many quirks; another was steadfastly sticking to the belief that God and the Devil existed and constantly battled for souls. In an era when the majority of Christians – including priests – believed in a more abstract definition of evil, Bonaventura's opinions made him somewhat of an anachronism among his peers. That, in turn, only increased his popularity among his students.

"Don't we need, I don't know, goat's blood or a Ouija board or something?" Kylie asked.

"Ta da!" Rob reached into his pack and withdrew a square object that he unfolded to reveal a series of black letters and symbols against a white background. He placed a heart-shaped planchette atop the board.

"You two had this planned, didn't you?" Caitlyn asked.

"It'll be fun," Rob replied, purposely not admitting his guilt. "C'mon. We'll play for a few minutes and then do something else. But we'll be the only ones on campus who can say we tried to call a spirit on Fifth Dal."

"Pat, you're an asshole." Lori slapped him on the shoulder. "If you think you're getting some tonight, think again."

Pat grabbed her by the waist and kissed her. "Who are you kidding? You'll be jumping my bones later."

"La la lalalala!" Caitlyn put her hands over her ears. "I do not need to hear about my sister's sex life."

"This shit ain't right." Maggie shook her head. "This is how every scary movie starts, with a bunch of kids doin' something stupid."

"Relax. It's just a game," Michael said.

"Fine. Let's just do this and leave. I'm cold and I want to get back to the Hickory." Kylie shivered and wrapped her arms around her chest. "Cindy gets off work in an hour and we have better plans than this."

"I'll bet." Michael made a peace sign and wiggled his tongue between his fingers.

"You're such an ass." Kylie gave him a good-natured punch on the shoulder.

"How do we start?" Lori scooted closer and the rest of them did the same. Rob moved the planchette to the center of the board and placed a finger on it.

"Everyone puts one finger on the planchette and then we ask questions. It will move from letter to letter if something's here with us."

"Y'all better not cheat," Maggie said. "I didn't come all the way up here and freeze my ass off just so's you could make dumb ghost jokes."

"I'll keep you warm, babe," Michael said, putting his arm around her. She snuggled against him and kissed his cheek.

"No one will cheat," Rob agreed, surprised to find he meant it. He'd always had a fascination for the paranormal and he didn't want to ruin his one chance to try something for real.

"What do we ask?" Lori hesitated before placing her finger next to Rob's.

"You're supposed to start by asking if anything is out there. Is anything listening."

"Is there anybody out there?" Pat intoned in a decent imitation of Roger Waters.

"Dude, not like that. You have to—"

The planchette slid an inch to the left.

"Shit!" Lori jumped back.

"Who did that?" Maggie asked. "You all said no cheating."

"I didn't do anything," Rob said. Pat and Michael chimed in on their innocence as well.

"Again." Rob motioned for them to put their fingers back. Slowly, they all resumed their places. "Is there anyone out there?"

When several seconds went by with nothing happening, Rob waited a moment and repeated the question. Then asked it a third time.

The planchette jerked under his finger. Up and to the left. This time no one removed their hands, although Caitlyn gave a startled gasp.

The planchette continued to move in short increments until it stopped on the *Yes*.

"I swear, if any of you is—"

"We're not doing anything," Rob interrupted Maggie. Not that he knew if any of the others had cheated. Only that he hadn't. Either way, it didn't matter. They'd have a great story to tell later.

"Ask it something else." Pat sounded excited.

"The instructions say to ask for a name," Rob stated.

"No, you're supposed to make sure it's friendly," Kylie said. "I saw that in a movie."

"That's stupid." Michael shook his head. "Like, would an evil spirit tell the truth? Hey, are you the ghost of a student?" He raised his voice as he asked the question.

The planchette vibrated but didn't move.

Lori frowned. "Does that mean yes?"

The planchette vibrated again.

"This is wack." Maggie leaned forward. "If you're really a ghost, prove it."

"Mags, a ghost can't—"

The planchette shot out from beneath their fingers and shattered the tequila bottle. Lori screamed and everyone jumped to their feet. A frigid breeze whipped through the room, sending dust and old papers flying. All the candles blew out, leaving Pat's flashlight as the only illumination. Something fell over with a crash and Caitlyn wrapped her arms around her sister.

A rustling sound came from the far end of the room.

"Who's there?" Rob called out.

"Stop!" Caitlyn's voice sounded too loud. The acoustics in the room seemed off to Rob; he could hear everyone breathing, hear the pitter-patter of things scurrying in the eaves.

Something landed on his shoulder and he jerked back, brushing at it with his hands. A huge beetle perched there, wings spread as wide as his hand. Its eyes blazed yellow. He went into a crazy dance, trying to slap the oversized insect away. The creature skittered down his arm and disappeared. Behind him, Kylie shouted.

Pain blossomed in his cheek at the same time as something buzzed past his head. Michael cried out and then cursed. Rob touched his face and his fingers came back red with blood. He turned toward Michael, who pulled something from his arm.

The planchette.

"What the—"

POP!

The flashlight's lens shattered and the bulb went out, casting the room into total darkness. The temperature dropped even further and the wind picked up speed. Unseen objects struck Rob's back and neck and he put up his arms to protect his face.

Then the wind stopped and the only sound was heavy breathing from all around him.

"Rob?" Caitlyn's voice came from his right. He moved toward it, one hand outstretched. His fingers touched cloth and she gasped. He put his arms around her and Lori and pulled them close.

"I'm right here. Everything's fine. Hey—" he raised his voice slightly, "—is everyone else okay?"

"Yeah." Michael cleared his throat. "Yeah. I'm good. Mags?"

"Here."

"Me too," Pat said from their left. "Kylie?"

Rob looked around, trying to find her in the dark. When she didn't answer, he repeated her name.

"Kylie, cut the shit," Maggie said, equal parts annoyed and nervous.

One of the candles flickered to life, casting a dim circle of light. A pale shape appeared in front of Rob and he jumped back.

"Kylie?"

She'd removed all her clothes, exposing her thin body and small breasts, as well as the hairless area between her legs. In the faint light, she looked way younger than twenty and Rob felt himself responding in a way he'd never experienced with Caitlyn. She held out her arms and he stepped toward her. Just as her hands touched his shoulders, her mouth opened in a silent scream and her eyes narrowed to slits. Sharp nails dug into his arms and she bit his chest, growling and gnawing at his flesh like a rabid dog.

Rob shouted and pushed her away. Kylie's nails raked his cheeks.

"What the fuck?" he yelled. The only answer was the *thud* of bodies colliding and then Maggie screamed, a long wail worse than anything Rob had ever heard. He ran to the sound and stumbled over two people thrashing around on the floor. Muffled, wet grunts reminded Rob of the time he watched pigs eating at his uncle's farm. Remembering Kylie's attack, he grabbed hold of a leg and tried to separate the two bodies.

A blinding light flared in the darkness and resolved into the yellow glow of a flashlight. Patrick swept the beam around the room; it settled on Michael kneeling next to Maggie, who had her hands over her face. Blood dripped from between her fingers.

"My eyes! My fucking eyes!"

"Maggie! Ohmygod! She's hurt. We need a doctor." Michael tried to pull her hands away but she screamed and fought his efforts.

"Kylie did it," Rob said, standing up. "Where is she?"

Pat played the flashlight back and forth. "I don't see her. What happened?"

Lori and Caitlyn stood shoulder to shoulder, looking all around.

"Where is she?" Lori asked. "Why—"

"Stupid sheep."

The rough, sonorous voice came from above them. Pat swung the light up.

Kylie perched in the rafters like a giant pale spider. Her normally blue eyes glowed orange. Bloody drool hung from her open mouth. Her hair stuck out in all directions. Strange markings crawled across her flesh like swarms of insects.

With a growl, she dropped onto Lori and Caitlyn, all three of them crashing to the floor. Someone cried out and Kylie leaped up and ran for one of the small, arched windows that lined each wall.

No, she's not running, Rob realized. *She's floating!*

Her feet were inches above the floor and her legs motionless. Yet she crossed the room faster than Pat could follow with the light. When she reached the window, she stopped, still suspended in the air, and looked back at them. The gruff, deep voice emerged from her throat even though her open mouth didn't move.

"Close the door, Bobby."

The thin form spun around and crashed through the window.

Rob stood still, his brain and body frozen.

Did she really say—?

Pat pushed past him, calling Kylie's name. That broke Rob's stasis and he followed, afraid he'd see Kylie's broken body sixty feet down on the lawn. And even more terrified that she'd still be floating in midair.

Blood dripped from the daggers of glass that jutted from the windowpane like giant teeth. Something else hung there as well; Rob's stomach lurched when he saw it was a clump of her hair, still attached to a scrap of flesh.

Five stories below, Kylie lay impaled on the iron fence that surrounded one of the many gardens in front of the dorm.

"Lori's not breathing!"

Rob turned at the sound of Michael's shout, and then looked back out the window.

Kylie was gone.

On the last day of classes before Thanksgiving break, Rob Lockhart stood in front of Father Leo Bonaventura's office, wondering if he should knock or just leave. During the four weeks since the awful night in Fifth Dallas, his life had been a crazy mess. He'd run all the way down to the third floor to find a pay phone that worked so he could call the police. The EMTs had rushed Lori and Maggie to the hospital, where doctors tried in vain to save Maggie's eyes. The one time Rob tried to visit her, she'd looked like she'd been mauled by a tiger.

As soon as she heard his voice, she told him to get out and never come back.

No one had escaped without injury. Lori'd suffered a fractured skull and brain trauma, and would probably be institutionalized the rest of her life. The rest of them had needed stitches for the various wounds they'd suffered. Caitlyn had dropped out of school to help her family with Lori's care, and Pat and Michael refused to talk to him after they'd all been put on probation and forced to find off-campus housing.

Kylie had been found on the other side of campus, near the river that flowed beyond the soccer fields, her arms and legs broken, one side of her face crushed, her flesh sliced to the bone and gaping holes where the iron posts had punctured her.

Their statements to the police had all matched. Kylie had gone crazy and attacked them without warning. None of them mentioned seeing her floating or climbing the rafters.

The official report attributed everything to alcohol and possibly drugs, and the school and police were only too happy to close the case and move on.

Close the door, Bobby.

After weeks of replaying everything in his head, Rob had finally admitted he needed to talk to someone about what he'd seen, what he'd heard. He'd been having nightmares so bad he couldn't sleep, couldn't concentrate on his schoolwork. Terrible dreams of Kylie floating over his bed, her hands like claws and her face covered in blood. He couldn't tell the police, and his friends wouldn't return his calls. God knew he couldn't say anything to a shrink. He'd be locked away forever. And despite what had happened to him as a boy at Holy Cross, he'd never lost respect for the Church or the people who served it. Maybe a priest – at least a certain priest – was his only answer.

And if he doesn't believe me, at least he can't have me committed.

Father Leo Bonaventura's office looked the same as the last time Rob had seen it, at the end of junior year when he'd stopped by to get his final grade. Narrow and cluttered, with overflowing bookshelves taking up both of the long walls and a desk at the far end, a dusty window behind it. The books ranged from religious texts and translations of old scrolls to a variety of paranormal topics such as poltergeists, unexplained phenomena, and UFOs.

And demonic possession.

One shelf held volumes Father Bonaventura had written. Rob had read a couple, and it always surprised him how different the priest looked compared to the back cover photos on the book jackets. Despite being only a few years old, they showed a much younger face than the man standing before him. Bonaventura's face carried the lines and wrinkles of a man much older than his mid-fifties, his jet-black hair already turning silver and thinning at the top. He was neither too thin nor overweight for his average height. His cheeks were slightly sunken, with hollows under his eyes. Round glasses perched at the end of a bulbous nose and a cardigan sweater worn over the traditional black shirt of a priest completed the image of an elderly professor.

"Please, sit down." Father Bonaventura indicated the single plastic chair in front of his desk. His face floated above stacks of papers and books that would have hidden a smaller man.

Rob sat, and found himself at a loss for words, with no idea how to begin.

Father Bonaventura saved him the trouble. "I'm glad you came. I'm interested in hearing your story. The real one, not the fabrication you told the police."

Rob's heart slammed against his chest and he jumped a little in his chair. Before he could deny the statement, Father Bonaventura smiled.

"It's all right. I'm not looking to cast blame or get you in trouble. Whatever you say will remain within this office. No matter what it is, or how strange it sounds."

"How…how do you know…?"

"Let's just say I have a nose for the unusual." He tapped his nose and winked.

The priest's matter-of-fact answer made Rob feel like he'd made the right choice, which eased his anxiety enough so he could speak.

"I…I don't know where to start. Everything that happened…it's so messed up."

"How about the beginning? You told the police you went up there to have a little party and play a parlor game. You're not the first ones to do it, you know. Students try it all the time."

"But no one dies, do they?" Bitter guilt crept into Rob's voice.

"We can discuss the history of the fifth floor another time. For now, let's hear about your experience."

Rob looked at the priest's face and realized things had been left unsaid.

How much of the legends is true?

I don't think I want to know.

He took a deep breath and began his story. When he got to the part about the planchette moving and everyone asking different questions, Father Bonaventura pursed his lips and frowned, but didn't interrupt. As Rob spoke, the memories and feelings of that night came rushing back. The hardest part was describing Kylie crashing through the window and the last words she'd spoken, and why they terrified him. Father Bonaventura's frown deepened. When Rob finished, goose bumps decorated his arms.

Father Bonaventura leaned forward, his hands folded atop a pile of test papers waiting to be graded. "Is that all of it? She didn't do anything else?"

She climbed the ceiling like a damned spider and floated in the air. Isn't that enough? He kept the angry reply to himself, but he couldn't help reliving the scene again in his mind.

Close the door, Bobby.

Rob shivered and rubbed his arms. "What about Kylie? Was she, I don't know, possessed? Did we make it happen with the Ouija board?"

"Possession is a complicated matter, Robert. And not that common." Father Bonaventura sighed. "I hesitate to say anything supernatural happened. The police are probably correct. Group hysteria and hallucinations brought on by too much alcohol. You've taken my course. You know I discourage people from using implements of magic, such as Ouija boards. Because there are rare instances of untrained persons calling forth unfriendly spirits, including poltergeists. Is it possible something supernatural occurred? Yes. Is it likely? Probably not."

"Either way, it was my fault. And Pat's. We came up with the idea, we pushed everyone to try it."

"And I believe that's what's really brought you here." Father Bonaventura's tone should have been comforting, but Rob took none from it. "I can't absolve your guilt. No one can. But I can remind you of one thing. People have free will. Your friends chose to stay when you proposed your game. You had no intention to hurt anyone. We all make mistakes in life, and part of living is accepting our blame, apologizing to anyone we've hurt, and moving on. Hopefully a little wiser. The Lord knows what's in your heart, and He is the ultimate provider of forgiveness."

"Forgiveness. Huh." Rob knew that would never happen. What could he ever say or do to make it up to Maggie, or to Kylie's family? They would never forgive him, and he'd never forgive himself. Not even a lifetime would be enough.

A lifetime.

He looked at the man sitting across from him. A man who'd dedicated his life to God, to helping people.

Maybe he couldn't make it up to Kylie or Maggie, but he could bring peace to others. And along the way, prevent what had happened to him and his friends from happening to anyone else.

"Thanks, Father." Rob stood up. He still felt guilty as hell, but at least now he could put that shame and remorse to good use. "You've been more of a help than you know."

"God be with you, Robert," Father Bonaventura said.

Rob waved and exited the office, his new path in life already taking shape ahead of him.

He could make a difference.

No, not could. *Would.*

Leo opened the door to Dallas Hall's fifth floor and paused at the threshold, as he did every time he visited the storage area. He'd had a key for almost fifteen years, ever since a former university president, Father Gervais Carrich, had asked him for a special favor.

He shined his flashlight back and forth, his attention focused more on the atmosphere of the place than his actual surroundings. He closed his eyes and took a step forward, half afraid he'd feel something other than cool air against his skin. The palpable presence of evil, cold in its own right. Or perhaps hints of burning sulfur lingering in the air.

Instead, he sensed nothing. The room felt no different than any other on campus.

Still, he had to be sure nothing had changed. Making his way around the toppled candles left behind by Rob and his friends, the latest in a long list of students to play dangerous games in the attic space, he went to the far wall and peered beneath the insulation between two rafter boards.

A communion host sat in its wax paper wrapping, just as he'd left it the last time he'd been there. A quick check revealed all the hosts still in place, with two of the six partially eaten by rodents. The crosses he'd hidden were also right where they should be.

He replaced the hosts with new ones, blessed them, and then scattered holy water throughout the attic. He usually performed the cleansing during the Christmas and summer breaks, but this year he didn't feel comfortable waiting. Not after what had happened.

Nothing unnatural had occurred in the storage area since he'd begun performing his ritual, and he intended to keep it that way. There'd be no repeats of the manifestations that had plagued the dormitory throughout the years, even before that poor girl's death in 1957. Not on his watch. He prayed this terrible accident was just that: an accident, and nothing more sinister.

He'd learned the truth of the place in his first year, when Father Gervais told him the history of the fifth floor and asked him to cleanse and bless the building.

"Just to be safe."

Safe. He'd quickly found out the fifth floor was anything but. The apparitions Father Bonaventura encountered that day had convinced him of two things: Dallas Hall definitely housed dangerous psychic manifestations, and they could never be allowed to return.

He'd often wondered if his status as an exorcist played a role in Father Carrich personally requesting him to be transferred to St. Alphonse. Especially when he learned how the previous parish priest had committed suicide by jumping from his bedroom window after molesting an altar boy. A suicide Leo held suspicions about after experiencing the inhabitants of Fifth Dallas.

After conducting the cleansing, he'd never again felt the presence of the spirits or auras that had haunted the attic, but that didn't mean they didn't still lurk. So, even after Father Carrich had retired from his presidency and a secular president had taken over – the first of several business-oriented rather than spiritually focused head administrators – Leo had kept his master key and continued his protective actions in secret.

Soon a cleaning crew would arrive to take care of the mess left behind by the students and the police. He glanced around the room. The hosts would be safe tucked away under the insulation. It was unlikely anyone would be scrubbing the place down with cleaners, except for the bloody area around the boarded-up window the Johnson girl had leaped from. Just to be safe, he splashed more holy water across the wall and frame, and made a mental note to come back after maintenance replaced the window and bless that as well. And double-check everything else.

He was about to head to the exit when something caught his eye. A pattern of dark smudges on one of the rafters. Most likely smoke from the candles. Although as he drew closer, they looked almost like....

Letters?

He aimed the flashlight at the markings and recoiled, almost dropping the light.

Although it had been several years since he last read a text written in ancient Latin, he had no trouble translating the charred letters.

Asmodeum.

The Latin spelling of Asmodeus.

It can't be possible.

The room grew darker and Leo's heart jumped. He glanced behind him. It was only a cloud passing across the sun, but the symbolism wasn't lost on him. The dusty attic disappeared and his memories transported him back to that long-ago day in the jungle, the body of the dead boy at his feet and the demon's last words hanging in the air.

"Your time will come, Father Fucking Bonaventura! You cannot kill me, for I am eternal."

Had the creature really returned? In their drunken foolishness, could those students have let something through?

No. Common sense returned and his pulse eased. There'd been no signs of possession in any of the students, and he felt no presence of evil lingering in the area. No demon had been loosed into the world. Even if they had opened a doorway, it had only been a crack, just wide enough for a malicious spirit to momentarily enter the dimension of mankind. And whatever it had been – ghost, poltergeist – it had done its damage and returned to its own realm.

He rubbed at his arm, where the demon's name had faded to nothing but thin white lines.

"Your time will come, Father Fucking Bonaventura!"

With a shiver, he sprayed holy water across the letters and then hurried down the stairs, making sure to lock the door behind him. Even after he had left the building and the weak but bright November sunshine did its best to warm his back as he crossed the campus, he could not stop his hands from shaking.

The demon was still locked safely in Hell. He knew that in his heart and soul.

But for how long?

CHAPTER FOUR

Midway, OH, twenty years ago

Claudia woke from the nightmare with her hands pressed over her mouth to keep from screaming. A few feet away, her twin sister, Shari, sat up at exactly the same moment, her hands also muffling a terrified cry. They looked at each other in the dim glow of their matching angel nightlights, wide, terrified eyes mirroring their fear.

—*The bad thing!*—

Shari's panicked thought echoed her own, clear as the church bells on Sunday morning to Claudia. They couldn't always hear each other, although they wished they could. Often they just got a vague sense of the other's thoughts. But in times of stress, or when their emotions ran strong, then their mental voices sounded as sharp and loud as a radio tuned to a rock and roll station.

Claudia knew exactly what had her sister so frightened. They'd had the dream so many times the past week they'd almost grown used to waking in a cold sweat, choking back their cries so they wouldn't wake anyone, especially *him*.

But tonight it had been different. Instead of just a scary premonition of danger, there'd been a new component. A feeling of immediacy.

It was about to happen.

—*We have to warn her.*—

—*She won't leave him. She loves him.*— Shari's hatred momentarily cut through their shared fear.

—*Yes. But we have to try.*—

Shari scowled but nodded. She got out of bed, her movements casting pairs of diabolical shadows on the walls, dark orbs that bobbed and glided around the room like ball lightning in negative. Claudia had only recently learned about ball lightning, after it had appeared in the schoolyard a month ago, sun-bright orbs of energy zipping through the sky, leaving purple afterimages in everyone's vision. Claudia and Shari had been so terrified they'd run all the way home and then watched as the two lightning balls exploded into fireworks of white above the street. The kids who'd been teasing them before it happened had told everyone it was the Brock sisters' fault. Now everyone avoided the twins like they carried the plague.

In the space of one afternoon, Claudia and Shari had gone from being the weird, silent twins that everyone ignored or made fun of to the creepy freaks everyone feared. The Witches of Midway. The Lightning Rod Twins. The Strange Sisters. Even their teachers looked at them differently, although none of them had said anything. Yet.

Claudia shivered as the cool November air evaporated the sweat on her skin. She pulled on the sweatshirt she'd worn the previous day, the one with the purple faerie on the front. Shari's had the pink faerie. Both of them put on jeans and then heavy socks and sneakers. It would be cold outside; Claudia could see frost glittering on the grass in the light of the half-moon floating over the big apple tree in the backyard.

A sudden impulse made Claudia slide her purple backpack from under the bed. While she dumped out her schoolbooks, Shari repeated the process at her own bed. With a nod, Claudia went into their bathroom and gathered a handful of tampons and feminine napkins. They'd both gotten their first period back in October, the same time on the same day. Mother Warwick had said they were a little young at ten, but it wasn't unheard of.

"Kids grow up so much faster these days," she'd told them with a wistful smile. "Sometimes I think it's from all the chemicals in our food."

Since then, they'd noticed their abilities had grown stronger. A little research on the library computer had shown psychic powers in women were often linked to menstrual cycles, that the time of 'becoming a woman' often triggered an increase.

Neither Claudia nor Shari doubted they had psychic abilities. While it wasn't uncommon for twins to have a bond, theirs went much further. They felt what each other felt, did and thought things in perfect synchronicity, and sometimes shared thoughts.

And then there were the dreams.

Every night, good or bad, the dreams as identical as the twins themselves.

And tonight one would come true.

They both knew it. The same way they knew it wasn't a coincidence the lightning had chased them or how things on their dressers sometimes fell to the floor when they got angry or scared. The same way they knew their foster father hit his wife when he got angry, even though they'd never witnessed it. Claudia stuffed the feminine hygiene products into the backpack and felt tears running down her cheeks. Shari sobbed softly while she filled her pack with pictures and mementos.

Whatever happened tonight, they wouldn't be coming back to this house.

Sometimes she wished they didn't know things. It only seemed to make life sadder.

Outside, something splattered against their window, a soft plop that made Claudia think of the first few giant raindrops that fell right before a thunderstorm hit. Only rain never filled her with fear the way this sound did. She turned her head in unison with Shari.

A quarter-sized blob of green, glowing slime oozed slowly down the glass.

Claudia looked at her sister.

—It's starting.—

—Yes. We have to go.—

They put on their matching fall coats, swung their packs over their shoulders at the same time, and walked down the hall with its yellow and orange flower wallpaper and the antique corner table with the frilly doilies on it. In the darkness of Mother and Father Warwick's room, the bed was nothing but a vague shape in the night. Claudia and Shari moved around the curved footboard by habit and went to Mother's side of the bed.

"Mother Warwick." Claudia put a hand on her shoulder and felt the warmth of Mother's skin through the heavy flannel nightshirt. A gentle shake produced no change in Mother's breathing. Downstairs, the front door slammed.

—He's home!—

"*Edna!*" Father Warwick's bellow shook the house. "*Daddy's home.*"

His words were garbled, a sure sign he'd been drinking. Claudia bit her lip. He was always most dangerous when drunk.

How would they get past him? Their dream hadn't shown them that part, only that if they stayed, someone would die.

Green stars appeared as two thick droplets hit the window over the Warwicks' bed, their glow muted by the white gauzy curtains hanging over the glass.

—Hurry!—

The same urgency twisted in Claudia's stomach.

"Mother!" she said, using a louder voice. This time she got a response.

"What...? Claudia? What's the matter?" The old woman's voice was slurred and groggy from sleep and all the medicines she took at bedtime. The ones for her heart, her diabetes, and her insomnia.

"We have to leave. Right now, before it's too late."

"What?" Mother Warwick sat up, rubbing her eyes. "What on earth are you talking about? Shari, you're here too?"

"We have to go. Now." Shari tugged at Mother Warwick's arm. "Danger's coming."

"*Edna! What's all that ruckus, goddammit?*"

"Hurry, Mother, before it's too late. Get dressed. We have to go!" Claudia and Shari pulled at Mother's arms, trying to get her out of bed.

Heavy footsteps pounded on the stairs.

Claudia looked at Shari. Not enough time. Maybe they could—

The door swung open. Father Warwick stormed into the room, his gray hair pointing in all directions. When he saw the girls, his hand automatically went for his belt.

"What in the hell's goin' on here? If you don't git your asses back to bed right this second I'll make sure you can't sit for a week."

"They think we're in danger," Mother Warwick said.

"Danger? What kind of fool nonsense is that? And why in hell do you have your coats on?"

More glowing drops of ooze hit the window. Above them, something larger landed on the roof.

"What the hell was that?" Father Warwick looked up at the ceiling like he could see through the wood and plaster.

Several loud thuds and thumps answered him.

Outside the window, green streaks of light flashed past.

"It's too late," Claudia said.

"We can't go outside," Shari said at the same time.

Shattering glass cut off Father Warwick's next words. A grapefruit-sized ball of phosphorescent slime came through the window and landed on his side of the bed. The blankets immediately began to emit a foul-smelling smoke from around the green substance. Mother Warwick jumped away with a frightened yelp.

"Don't touch it!" Shari cried, seeing Father Warwick reaching out a finger. Claudia turned the lights on, revealing a hole where the slime had already eaten through the sheets and dissolved the mattress pad underneath.

"Jesus fucking Christ. What is that?"

Shari pointed outside, where dozens of goo-balls fell, joining the ones already littering the lawn like giant glowing mushrooms.

Thudding noises on the roof told them more landed there as well. Claudia wondered how long it would take them to burn through the shingles and attic floor.

"Downstairs," Shari said. "It's safer."

Mother Warwick hurried into her bathrobe and slippers, her eyes wide with fear. Father Warwick charged for the bedroom door and pounded down the stairs, his face angry rather than frightened. The girls guided Mother Warwick along, making sure she didn't stumble on the steps.

In the living room, Claudia paused. Where was the safest place? They had no basement. Every room had lots of windows.

—*The bathroom.*—

—*Yes.*— The guest bathroom was right off the kitchen. A long room with a toilet, sink, and a tiled shower. "The bathroom," Claudia said to Mother. "Hurry."

"Wait, what about Harry?" Mother Warwick pulled out of their grasp and turned toward the den, where they could hear Father cursing and rummaging around.

"We'll get him," Shari said. She pushed Mother toward the kitchen. "Please hurry!"

They got Mother into the bathroom and shut the door.

—*Now what?*— Claudia asked. This wasn't how the dream had gone.

Just then Father emerged from the den, dressed in his heavy hunting jacket and pants and wearing a wide-brimmed leather hat. Yellow rain boots covered his feet. Leather-gloved hands gripped his favorite shotgun.

"Out of my way." Father Warwick pushed past them and opened the back door. Sickening green light enveloped him, causing a shadow to cast into the kitchen. The deadly rain had grown so heavy Claudia couldn't see across the yard to the garage; the world was nothing but bright green streaks and miniature explosions of glowing jelly.

A loud hissing overpowered the sounds of things hitting the ground. A glop of ooze as big as a wash bucket fell through the porch roof and landed next to Father. Splatters of green hit his pants and feet. Smoke instantly arose.

The next second, Father shouted in pain and jumped back inside, frantically tearing his clothes off to expose red, blistered skin on his legs and feet.

In the living room, something burned through the ceiling and a burst of green lit up the walls. Green slime coated the kitchen windows, and Claudia saw the glass bulging inward as it softened. Father Warwick, his face locked in a grimace of anger and pain, stomped back into the living room, his gun raised and ready to fire.

—We can't wait any longer.—

Shari nodded. They ran for the bathroom. Mother stood by the sink. Tears stained her cheeks and her hands shook as she twisted the belt of her bathrobe between her fingers.

"Where's Harry?"

Claudia opened her mouth but no words formed. Shari just shook her head.

"No!" Mother rushed for the door, knocking them out of the way with her bulk. Shari cried out as Mother threw the door open and ran for the den. Several puddles of green already hissed and steamed on the kitchen floor.

Claudia moved to follow.

—No. It's too late.—

Shari shut the door. Without saying a word, she went to the shower and sat down in the tub, her knees folded up to make room for Claudia, who joined her a moment later. With their backs pressed against the tile, they waited.

And cried for the woman they'd lost, the closest thing to a real mother they'd ever had.

—We were supposed to save her.—

Seconds later, the lights went out and someone screamed, high and long. The twins clutched hands and held tight.

They were still crying hours later when the police showed up. The tiled section of the bathroom was the only place in the house where the burning rain hadn't penetrated.

The next morning found them back at St. Lucy's Home for Wayward Children. When they got inside, a new face greeted them instead of Pastor Madsen. A younger man, wearing the black shirt and white clerical collar of a priest. His brown eyes lit up when he saw them, and shivers ran up Claudia's back. Shari's hand found hers, gripped it tight.

—Bad man. He's the bad man.—

Claudia felt it too. A nasty sensation, like an invisible aura surrounded him, an aura of—

—Danger. He's the danger.—

It struck Claudia at the same time. *This* was the danger they'd dreamed of, not Father Warwick and his temper. And they'd walked right into it.

"Hello, I'm Father Rob, the new headmaster." He approached them with his arms spread, a phony smile plastered on his face. Shari wrinkled her nose and stepped back like the priest had farted. Claudia reacted too slowly and the priest put his hands on her shoulders. An image came to her. A little girl, with dark skin and tears in her eyes. Those same hands touching bare flesh, stroking it.

—Shari! The bad man has me!—

—We have to run away.—

The idea scared Claudia, but they had no other choice. Because if they stayed, one thing was for certain.

They would end up like that other girl.

CHAPTER FIVE

Hastings Mills, NY, July 6th, one year ago

"Today marks a new chapter in the history of St. Alphonse University."

Alan Duhaime, St. Alphonse's President, stood with the seven members of the university board in front of Dallas Hall. A student reporter from the school newspaper, the *Alphonse Gazette*, faced them, his phone recording each word. The morning was comfortably warm and the humidity not too bad as he and the board posed with shovels in front of the sign warning *Construction Zone*. After weeks of discussion, the board had finally agreed to his plan to renovate the top floor of the dormitory and turn it from a storage area into something usable.

The maintenance department had emptied out all the furniture and cabinets of old files stored up there and the crews were ready to begin work. By the time September rolled around, there'd be a study lounge complete with chairs, couches, and a sink and microwave, plus two separate rooms designated as 'safe spaces' where students could escape the stress of college life by meditating to tranquil spa music (piped in by the school, no outside music allowed).

Who would have ever imagined our schools would come to this? Duhaime thought, as the workers began unloading their equipment. *Colleges are supposed to prepare kids for real life, not shelter them from it. When did all that change?*

"They're all set to start." Jesse Howard, head of Grounds and Maintenance, held out a clipboard. The final go-ahead for the project. Duhaime signed it, already mentally preparing the press release that would go out on social media and be reposted on the school's website in conjunction with the newspaper article. The alumni needed to see how their money got spent, and this was two million of it. Dallas Hall had a long history; with it being the oldest dorm on campus, he'd had to assure the big donors the face-lift would be limited to the inside, that the Gothic exterior wouldn't be changed at all.

"This building is part of our heritage," he told the reporter, "and it will remain as such for as long as the university stands."

The reporter snapped a few more pictures and Duhaime made sure to stand before the ivy-covered front wall, with the classic friezes and carved heads visible behind him.

As the reporter walked away, and the crew began lugging their supplies inside, Duhaime smiled to himself.

The success of the renovation would enable him to get more money to fix up the other buildings on campus that were long overdue for restoration or makeovers.

And create a nice little retirement nest egg for him at the same time.

This could go down as one of the best days ever.

Hastings Mills, NY, July 7th, one year ago

"Leo, time to eat. They are serving pizza today."

Lunch already? Where have the hours gone?

Leo turned away from the window of his tiny sitting room and wiped a tear from his eye. He didn't want his friend Father Henri Adebayo to see him on the verge of crying.

Henri stood at the door, an eager grin on his dark, creased face. Leo was pleased to see the old priest's hands steady on the handles of his walker. Henri suffered from Parkinson's, a late onset case that hadn't expressed any symptoms until he reached his sixties. Even with his medicines, he had good days and bad, sometimes unable to get out of bed on his own. Walking to breakfast without help meant today would be one of the very good days.

Good days. Until now, I've never had to think of such things for myself. Bad days just meant these old bones ached or I had a cold. Now, every day will be measured differently.

Stop that, or you're liable to break down again. Besides, at your age, five years is a gift.

"I'll be right there," Leo said, levering himself up from his easy chair with only a small groan. He enjoyed taking his morning cup of coffee by the window. On pleasant days, he'd open the window and let the morning breeze fill the apartment with the smells of grass, flowers, and fresh air. In the winter, the view of snow-covered lawns and the distant cemetery was serene and calming while his electric heater kept the cold at bay. And on brutal summer days like today, when the temperature hit the eighties or nineties and the humidity turned the air to water, he could relax, knowing he didn't have to even break a sweat by going outside.

God, he was going to miss it.

Lately, he'd been losing track of time. And gotten forgetful. He'd chalked it up to old age, until it grew so much worse he'd gone to see his doctor.

Now he knew it was something far worse.

And for the first time since retiring, he found himself longing for the life he'd hated just a few weeks ago. Empty days. Bland meals. A lack of intellectual stimulation. He'd never wanted to retire, but now it seemed like heaven compared to what he faced.

Retirement might be boring, and often as not depressing, but it does have its perks. Like being able to live in a clean, modern retirement facility, courtesy of the Archdiocese of New York. And having free healthcare.

In the four years since he'd given up teaching and accepted the role of professor emeritus at St. Alphonse, he'd slowly drifted into a nice, easy routine, the kind he'd never expected of himself. In the beginning, he'd gone to the university every day, walking the mile from the Holy Gardens apartment complex to campus when he could, taking a cab when the weather was poor. He'd putter around his office, fill out a little paperwork that the department secretary could just as easily have handled, and have lunch with some of the other teachers and priests. Sometimes he'd go to the library and do research for articles he intended to write with all his spare time.

But that first winter proved to be a bad one, the cold and snow combining with his advancing arthritis to keep him inside the confines of the private retirement community the church had built on the opposite side of St. Alphonse Cemetery from the campus. When he finally returned to campus in the spring, he realized no one had really missed him, the department had gotten along fine without him, and quite frankly the food was better at the retirement center than the school cafeteria.

His visits grew less frequent; his interest in his research dimmed. On the few trips he took to the library, he tended to doze off while slogging through some antiquarian tome, sometimes waking up with his face on a dusty page. More and more, he found himself reading news magazines and cheap thrillers instead of scholarly books or articles, laughing at the silly political issues of the day with his fellow retirees, and just staring out the window of his apartment, cursing his fading memory and his advancing age. He used to fear losing the ability to care for himself, and ending up in an assisted living facility, or worse. He'd seen it happen to others, the phasing out from living on their own at St. Alphonse to daily visits from a nurse or aide to being unable to care for themselves at all and getting shipped off to one of the long-term care locations the Church operated around the country. He'd just never imagined it happening to him.

Now it's not a matter of if, but when, Leo mused, following Father Henri across the courtyard to the cafeteria. The smell of oven-baked pizza and breadsticks mingled well with the sweet perfume of the rose bushes growing on both sides of the sidewalk. *Once you hear those words – dementia, mid-stage – the countdown is on.*

Even though he'd had a couple of weeks to process his new reality, thinking about his own frailty and eventual passing dampened Leo's mood enough that he barely tasted his food. Despite his own firsthand knowledge that life did exist after death – he'd seen the proof with his own eyes, after all – and his rock-steady belief in Heaven, the idea of departing the mortal coil still weighed him down with sadness every time he considered it.

And knowing he was wasting his last years sitting around, doing nothing of value, only made it worse.

But what else is there? he asked himself as he buttered another breadstick, calories be damned. He'd outlived his usefulness. His days of adventure were long behind him, and neither the church nor the school required the services of an old exorcist. After all, they lived in a time now where evil only existed in the hearts of men, and malevolent spirits were Saturday night entertainment, far less frightening than the atrocities being committed on a daily basis around the world.

With a sigh, he brought his tray to the bin by the exit and grabbed a copy of the local paper, the *Times Herald*, from the rack at the door. When he saw the date, he frowned. Something about July seemed important. In past years, he'd taught a summer session, Introduction to Comparative Religion. But that had always been in June, after spring sessions and graduation. In fact, it would be ending right around now.

Maybe that's it. I'm still thinking I need to be preparing final exams. Old habits die hard.

Another sigh escaped him. He missed those days, the mental stimulation, interacting with the bright young minds of the future. And travel. How long had it been since he'd left Hastings Mills at all? For an exorcism or anything else? He fought to remember. There'd been the trip to Rome back in…when? His brow furrowed deeper. Ten years ago? Had it been that long since he'd been informed of his dismissal from the Vatican's exorcism team? That the two stents he'd needed in his heart put him at too much of a risk?

And now he needed another, on top of everything else.

A tear ran down his cheek and he brushed it away. There'd been many bitter, angry months after that. Mostly because he knew deep down it was the right decision.

First his status as a warrior of God. Then his teaching job. Now his memories, the very essence of what made him *him*, were abandoning him.

Soon there'd be nothing left.

Another tear. He cried a lot these days. For what he'd lost, for how little time remained.

"Leo. Is everything all right?" Henri stood a few feet away, his face glistening with sweat. The brief excursion had been hard on him.

Leo waved and wiped his eyes again. He'd always felt sorry for his friend, for the long, dreadful illness he faced. Now he'd received a similar prognosis, one that made his upcoming surgery pale in comparison. It almost made him wish his heart would go first and spare him the torture of losing his mental faculties.

He glanced at the campus paper, the *St. Alphonse Gazette,* sitting in the rack. The face of the current campus president smiled up from the front page. Leo had only met him once and he'd come away with the impression the man cared more about public relations than academics or values. Not interested in the latest campus doings, he left the *Gazette* in the rack, tucked the *Times Herald* under his arm, and joined his friend for their slow walk back to the dormitory.

"So, Leo. How come you have not signed up for the annual excursion to St. Patrick's Cathedral?"

Despite his depression, Leo couldn't help but smile. Even after fifty-odd years in the US, Henri still retained a thick Nigerian accent and spoke with the formal but earnest style of a British prep school student. Leo debated coming up with an excuse or telling the truth, and decided to split the difference. Henri needed to know why he wouldn't be around, but at the same time, he wasn't ready to discuss his real issues.

"I...I have to have an operation. A stent in my heart. I'm leaving tomorrow for Buffalo."

Henri stopped and his eyes went sad. "Ah. I'm sorry to hear that. But everything else is well, yes?"

"I'm afraid it's definitely Alzheimer's, Leo. There are treatments to slow it down, drugs you can take. But eventually...."

After leaving the doctor's office, he'd spent most of that night in his chair, staring out the window and crying.

"As well as can be expected, Henri. We are old, after all."

"Yes, we are." Henri chuckled. "Would you like me to come with you?"

"No." He didn't want anyone else there, in case the doctors brought up his condition. Sooner or later, he'd have to let everyone know.

But not yet.

Henri patted his arm. "Then I shall pray for you."

I'll need more than prayers, Leo thought, as they made their way back to their rooms. *I'll need a miracle.*

And I fear I've used up all of mine.

Hastings Mills, NY, July 8th, one year ago

Curt Rawlings twitched at the sound of heavy banging upstairs.

"Abby, knock it off!"

The pounding continued, a steady *thump-thump-thump* that made him think his daughter was either slamming her chair against the wall or stomping her feet on the floor.

"Dammit, Abby!" He immediately regretted his words, but working all day in the summer heat at the university had stretched his temper to the limit. And on top of that, it was his wedding anniversary….

The pounding increased in volume and tempo.

What the hell had gotten into her? He put down the plates he'd just taken from the dish rack and headed for the stairs. If this was some kind of tantrum because he'd refused to let her go to Kim's house to swim, she'd find herself grounded for a damn week. At nine, she should know better.

"Abby, you— Hey!" He threw open the door to her room and then had to duck as a book flew at his head. Prepared to give her a royal scolding, and maybe a smack on the ass to boot, he stepped into the room.

And then froze at the sight of his daughter cowering in the corner while a tornado of books, clothes, and toys whirled madly in the center of the room.

"Daddy, help!" Abby's cry was nearly lost in the drumlike thumping of her chair rising and falling all on its own. Despite his shock at the impossible scene, paternal instinct took over and he ran to her.

I can't lose her too.

In one swift motion, he scooped her up and raced back to the door. Something struck his shoulder but he didn't break stride. He went down the hall to his bedroom and placed Abby on the bed.

"Are you okay? Abby!" He had to say it twice before she responded. Still crying, she nodded and said something he took as a yes. No bruises marked her skin, no blood that he could see, so he held her tight to his chest until her sobbing slowed to just sniffles and her breathing returned to normal. Only then did he dare leave her alone to go back and look at her bedroom.

Nothing moved.

The clothes and toys lay on the floor, the chair out of place, but other than that it looked perfectly ordinary. Not much different than how Abby, who'd always been messy, tended to keep the room.

Carl found it hard to believe anything unusual had happened, despite the memory of the crazy whirlwind fresh in his mind. If he'd been drinking, he'd have chalked it up to the liquor. But except for one mad binge after Cate's death, he'd never had more than a couple of beers after dinner. With a little girl to take care of, you always had to be sober and ready for anything.

But not this. What the fuck do I do now? He considered calling Father Gilbert at St. Anthony's, but what the hell could a priest do against… whatever the hell he'd just witnessed?

Ghosts? An earthquake?

Randi Zimmerman.

The name came to him out of the blue, but he recognized it right away. Couldn't miss it. She'd been advertised in the newspaper all week. Some kind of real-life ghost hunter from Buffalo. Had her own weekly radio show and she was coming to Hastings Mills to do a book signing.

Where's that damn paper?

After checking on Abby and telling her to stay put, he went to the garage and rooted through the recycling bin until he found the paper from the day before. He flipped through to the local section.

There.

Randi Zimmerman. Appearing at the Main Street Library.

The picture showed a middle-aged woman with dark hair and a thin, pale face. Behind round glasses, her eyes were two black circles surrounded by too much mascara. Despite the fact that she wore a fuzzy white sweater, the photo made him think of a modern witch.

At the end of the article was the information he needed.

Program begins at 8 p.m. on July 8th, in the Community Center Room, 2nd Floor.

Carl checked his watch. Seven thirty. He had just enough time to get Abby into her coat and drive to the library.

As they headed across town, he found himself praying their house wasn't haunted by something more than just memories.

CHAPTER SIX

Hastings Mills, NY, July 9th, one year ago

"Jesus fucking Christ, it's goddamn hot in here." Mike Morales paused from pulling down mats of pink insulation and wiped his arm across his forehead. Despite open windows and fans blowing, the heat in the fifth floor of Dallas Hall was nearly unbearable, thanks to the lack of air-conditioning and the sweltering weather, which had climbed well into the nineties.

Wearing a dust mask and safety goggles only made things worse, but it beat getting tiny fiberglass fibers in your eyes or lungs. Bad enough you went home with itching, irritated skin, even when wearing long sleeves.

He tossed the insulation on the floor and went to pull down another piece. Something white caught his eye. Another one of the wax paper packets with a cup and cross printed on the front. Communion wafers. He shook his head and dropped it in the garbage pile. They'd been finding all sorts of things in the rafters. The Communion packets. Wooden crosses nailed to beams.

"Watch your mouth, Mikey, or you might get hit with lightning. Didn't the nuns teach you nuthin' in school?" Larry Bristow laughed at his joke and the rest of the crew joined in, including Mike.

"You kiddin'? I went to PS 20 in the Bronx. I ain't been to church since I was a kid. Now, my Aunt Carmen, she— Augh, shit! Motherfucker!"

The others paused as Morales jumped back and slapped at his clothes, doing an awkward dance across the floor.

"What the hell, Mike?"

"Friggin' bugs." He shook the front of his shirt. A dark object dropped to the floor and scuttled away, disappearing into a pile of insulation waiting to be bagged and tossed. "I think it was a fucking roach."

"We used to get big ones down south." Felipe Waters took off his mask. "Folks called 'em water bugs or palmetto bugs, but everyone knew they's just roaches on steroids."

"They fuckin' creep me out. Always hated 'em as a kid too." Morales rubbed his gloved hands down his sides and shivered. "Goddamn roaches suck."

Bristow checked his watch. "It's almost five. Let's get this shit out of here and we can call it a day." He grabbed an armful of the insulation and stuffed it into a black garbage bag. The others did the same, except Morales. He just shook his head.

"Uh-uh. Not me. I'll carry the bags. My luck that roach'll find me again."

"What, this roach?" Waters held up his hand. He had a three-inch insect trapped between his thumb and fingers, its legs digging furiously at the heavy leather of his glove. Morales took a step back. Waters peered at the bug and shook his head. "Ain't no roach, man. Just a big-ass beetle."

"I don't care what the fuck it is. Get it out of here."

Waters lunged at Morales, who jumped away, cursing. He jabbed at Morales again, his laughter spreading to the other workers.

And then he yelped in surprise and his hand opened.

"Ow! Damn thing bit me. Right through my glove."

The beetle launched into the air and flew straight at Morales. The insect struck him in the chest and he cried out.

"Get it off! Get it off!"

The other men laughed even harder. Morales ran in circles, slapping at his shirt while the beetle avoided the blows and climbed up. His shouts grew louder when the beetle reached his neck and disappeared into his hair. He tore off his goggles, revealing the beetle clinging to his cheek, covering one eye like a metallic patch.

With a scream of pain, he clawed at his face and ran forward.

Right at the open window.

Bristow called out a warning but Morales never slowed. His knees hit the sill and he tumbled forward.

His cries for help came to an abrupt stop.

By the time Bristow and the others reached the window, the crew downstairs had already gathered around the body, which lay in a slowly widening pool of blood on the sunny sidewalk. One of the men had his phone out.

A mournful howling rose up in the distance, and for a moment amazement overtook horror as Bristow couldn't believe the police had responded so quickly. Then he realized it wasn't sirens but dogs, dozens of them, all baying at the same time.

A cold chill ran down his back, and for the first time in thirty years, he crossed himself.

Leo sprang up, a scream caught in his throat.

Darkness, everywhere. And somewhere hidden in the black depths, a terrible danger. Coming for him. Coming….

The dream broke apart, the details already fading, the sense of impending doom evaporating more slowly.

Something following me, something….

He couldn't remember.

And that scared the hell out of him.

Every thing he forgot, every item he misplaced, every clue in the crossword puzzle he couldn't figure out, had him thinking his disease had progressed further. What would come next? Forgetting his own name? Losing control of his bodily functions?

On the other hand, at times like this his faltering memory became something of a blessing. Whatever his nightmare had been, he was glad he couldn't recall it.

And is it really a nightmare if it happens during an afternoon nap?

He forced his body to move, joints popping and cracking as he stood up and went to the bedroom window. Outside, the sun barely touched the tops of the Alleghany Mountains, which meant he'd only been asleep for an hour or two at the most. He opened the window to see if the heat had abated at all. Usually, in the afternoons, a nice breeze came off the river.

Somewhere out of sight, a siren wailed, the mournful howl of an emergency vehicle engaged in its sad duty. In response, a dog howled, and then others joined in. The combined wailing set the hairs on his arms to attention, a gray-and-white forest of fear. He shivered as the cries brought back unwelcome images of darkness and hidden creatures.

A knock on the door made him jump.

"Hello, Leo. Are you ready for dinner?"

"Coming." He slipped his loafers on. His suitcase sat next to the door, packed and ready. Seeing it sent a frigid pain through his stomach, like he'd just swallowed a ball of ice.

Suddenly the nightmare he'd had seemed more like an omen than a dream.

Unaware he was rubbing the pale scar on his arm, he followed Henri down the hall.

Los Angeles, CA, July 9th, one year ago

"It's coming!"

Claudia Brock jumped out of bed, her body trembling, blankets clutched to her chest, her scream still echoing in her ears.

Downstairs, Shari cried out. A hairbrush tumbled off the dresser with a thump.

"Claudia?" Next to her, Stone Graves sat up and turned toward her, his eyes wide. "What's wrong?"

She ignored him and tried to focus on the nightmare. What was coming? She couldn't see it, not then, not now. Something evil. A formless, black shape surrounded by fire. Big, bigger than anything she'd ever seen before. Malevolence emanated from it in vile waves, contaminating everything it touched. The clock on the nearby dresser cast a diffuse red glow on the walls, and for a terrifying moment she felt sure the flames from her nightmare had followed her into the real world.

—It's coming!—

Shari's voice, in her head. Claudia wished her sister could join them, or better yet, that she could go down to Shari's room. But things were already tense between her sister and Stone, and she didn't want to upset him further.

Together they might have obtained a clearer picture. Touching each other always amplified their abilities. As children, they'd always snuck into each other's beds and held hands to see through the mists and darkness that so often clouded their visions.

"Sorry. A nightmare," she said, patting Stone on the arm. "Go back to sleep."

He mumbled something and rolled over. Claudia waited until the sounds of his breathing slowed, and then got back in bed. Eyes closed, she pictured Shari propped against her own pillows. The picture gradually grew clearer, took on three dimensions.

—It's harder to do this way— Shari said.

—We have to try.—

—Fine.— Shari extended an imaginary hand. Claudia took it in hers.

They concentrated on the dark shape lurking inside the fires. Faces appeared, indistinct. Twisted, wrong.

But no matter how hard they tried, they couldn't discern any further details. After an hour, they gave up, left with nothing but vague images and a sense of impending doom.

Neither of them went back to sleep.

The next morning, Stone had forgotten about being woken, for which Claudia gave a silent thank-you. No sense worrying him, not when she had no idea what the dream-image meant.

She saw Shari's haunted eyes at breakfast and knew she had the same thoughts. Something terrible was on the way, something worse than anything they'd ever experienced. Worse than what they'd gone through in Midway as children. Even worse than Las Vegas.

And that meant certain death for someone.

Hastings Mills, NY, July 13th, one year ago

"It's getting worse, ain't it?"

Randi Zimmerman wished she could tell the man something – anything – other than the truth. But Rawlings was an honest man who expected an honest answer, even if she didn't want to give one.

"It is."

The past four days had been the craziest of Randi's life. And that said a lot. Not only had there been multiple poltergeist episodes in Abby's room, but she'd suffered one at day care, too, when she'd been forcibly thrown out of her chair. The teacher, thinking she'd had a seizure, had called 911 and the EMTs had taken Abby to the hospital. When her tests showed nothing out of the ordinary except a slight case of dehydration, she'd been allowed to come home the next night. Since then, the strange happenings at Rawlingses' house had intensified. Drawers and doors banged at all hours. Lights flashed on and off at random.

All with Abby's room as the central point.

"Daddy!"

Abby's scream cut Randi off before she could say anything else. She and Curt ran upstairs, where Abby's door swung closed and then open again.

"Make it stop! Make it stop!"

She sat on the bed, her hair in wild tangles and her pajama top half open. Red marks in the shape of human hands covered her face and stomach. As they watched, her head flew to the side, accompanied by the *smack!* of flesh striking flesh. Another red welt blossomed on her cheek. Curt scooped her off the bed and carried her into the hallway.

"Baby, it's all right. You're okay now."

She burst into tears and clutched her father's shoulders. Curt looked at Randi, who felt guilty at her own helplessness. None of the standard cleansings she'd tried had worked, and there was no explanation for why a spirit would suddenly appear.

Poltergeist? Or possession?

No. There's no such things as demons. Don't go down that road.

Still, she had to do something. She'd never dealt with anything like this.

"I think we should call somebody with more experience."

Curt opened his mouth and Randi expected an objection. Instead, the man barked out an angry response.

"Call whoever the hell you have to. I just want this to end."

Abby's door slammed open and closed. In her room, books and shoes flew through the air and hit the walls.

Randi nodded and followed them down the stairs, already searching on her phone for the website she wanted. She knew who she needed to call. Hopefully he'd respond.

Before it was too late.

Los Angeles, California, July 13th, one year ago

Stone Graves sat in his production office, reviewing raw footage for the next episode of *In Search of the Paranormal*, when one of his assistants came in with a piece of paper.

"Sir, I think you should read this."

Stone was about to chide the woman for interrupting him – they all knew not to disturb him with a deadline so close – when he saw the look on her face. A mixture of fear and excitement, not the sort of reaction you'd normally expect from fan mail or another story about a haunted house.

As soon as he saw his real name at the top of the page, he understood the assistant's breach of standard protocol. Only his family and a few old high school friends still used it.

Nick,

I'm probably the last person you want to hear from, but I'm writing to you because I'm desperate. I need your help. Something's going on here, something real bad. Not a hoax.

I tried leaving phone messages for you but no one replied. Please call me.

It's worse than Wood Hill.

Randi Zimmerman

Below her name was a New York State telephone number.

Stone had to read the note twice before all the words penetrated his shocked brain.

Randi Zimmerman.

It's worse than Wood Hill.

The memories of that afternoon, twenty-five years old but as vivid as if they happened yesterday, came rushing back.

Entering the back door of the morgue, the third building they'd investigated that day. He'd been seventeen, living in Rocky Point, New York. A high school video club nerd with zero friends hired by a bunch of college students doing a project for their videography class. An exploration of the abandoned Wood Hill Sanitarium, ending with a visit to the supposedly haunted morgue. They'd needed him because one of their camera operators got sick and he happened to have the right equipment.

One of the students had been a freshman named Randi Zimmerman, who'd been handling EVP recordings. To a young Nick Stonewell – he hadn't yet adopted his stage name – Zimmerman had been the coolest out of all of them. She'd been cute as hell, with John Lennon glasses, onyx hair that reflected all sorts of colors in the sun, and black lipstick. Total goth.

Plus, unlike most of the kids his own age, she didn't care that he was biracial and had never fit in with either the white kids or the few Black students at the high school.

He'd crushed on her the moment they met.

He'd also been excited as hell at the opportunity to explore Wood Hill. He'd always been fascinated with the place, but the cops made sure no one trespassed. The facility had a terrible reputation – illegal experimentation, crowded conditions, patient abuse, and more. The kind of place that practically begged for someone to come in and investigate the rumors of ghosts and evil spirits.

And now someone had gotten permission, and he'd get to be part of it.

One of the students had an old map they'd found on the internet, but a lot of the hallways in the main building didn't match up. After several missed turns in the dark, chilly basement, they'd finally located the double doors to the morgue, a long, empty room with some decayed wooden cabinets along one wall. Opposite them sat a series of mahogany doors, square ones, built right into the concrete.

Behind him, someone gasped, just as Nick realized what he was looking at.

Cold storage units for corpses.

Each door had a metal handle on it. While Nick filmed, Randi turned one of the handles. The exquisitely carved wood swung to the right with only a slight squeal from the metal hinges, and a steel table slid out on runners.

"Oh, Jesus." The student in charge, Chuck O'Meara, pointed at the table. "Is that…blood?"

Nick moved forward to capture the image on film. As he did, a strange hissing, crackling sound came from next to him. Glancing away from the camera, he saw Randi holding out her EVP recorder and frowning. The sounds came from the machine.

All at once, every locker flew open and the tables sprang out with a tremendous clatter. One of them hit Chuck, knocking him to the floor. Grayish-white mist poured from the storage units, accompanied by waves of cold that gnawed into Nick's flesh. A terrible odor, the reek of death and blood, worse than any butcher shop, permeated the space. People shouted. The mist twisted and turned, forming impossible shapes. A high-pitched wailing rose up, so loud it caused feedback from the microphones. Other voices joined it, creating a din that hurt the ears.

Tendrils of fog swooped down and snaked between people's legs. Faces appeared in the mist, with gaping dark circles for eyes and mouths, features twisted in rage. Leering visages composed of green liquids that dripped like melting wax.

"You killed us! You killed us all!" The evil chorus rode a blast of fetid wind that carried the stink of unearthed graves and putrefying bodies.

And then everything disappeared, leaving the group standing alone in the cavernous room.

All except Chuck O'Meara, who lay motionless and not breathing on the cold floor.

For a long time, Stone had believed nothing could top what happened in that morgue.

Until Evan Michaels.

A name that still gave Stone nightmares. It hadn't been the same as Wood Hill, but in some ways it had been worse. And just like Wood Hill, it had ended with a death.

The boy, his skin covered in weird patterns of red pustules, leaping through the window....

If Zimmerman had stumbled into something like that....

The smart thing to do would be to say no. He and Zimmerman had parted on seriously bad terms and hadn't spoken in years. If it had been anyone else but his old partner, he'd suspect an ulterior motive, like setting him up for humiliation on national television. But not Randi. She might be stubborn and lack business sense – and have good reason to hate him – but she wasn't vindictive. Besides, she'd dumped him, not the other way around.

Still, would it be worth changing an entire shooting schedule? The upcoming season of *In Search of the Paranormal* had already been set. Travel arranged. Could they really afford to mess with that? He wasn't the only paranormal investigator in the country. Randi probably knew plenty of them. Let her call someone else. Someone who didn't have ratings to worry about.

Someone else who might end up the first person to actually document a paranormal event for television.

This was what he'd wanted ever since that afternoon in the morgue. The chance to prove the supernatural actually existed. In the aftermath of Wood Hill, the police investigation into Chuck O'Meara's death had resulted in the discovery of more than two dozen unmarked graves under the stone floor of the basement. Experts eventually identified them as patients who'd died back in the 1940s and 50s from illegal medical experiments.

Stone graves yield gruesome secrets! screamed the headline in the local newspaper, a headline he still had in his files. The same one he'd eventually taken his stage name from.

Nick got interviewed by several different reporters, for both TV and print stories, besides being questioned by the police. The mayor had even brought in an actual exorcist, a priest named Bonaventura, to perform some rituals and bless the makeshift cemetery. Nick had been there, along with half the town, to watch.

Not once did he reveal what he'd experienced in the morgue.

Although only seventeen, he'd been smart enough to know he'd sound crazy. Whatever had been in that morgue had ruined all the film and sound recordings, leaving only static. He and Randi had agreed to keep the truth to themselves, to never reveal it to anyone. And he'd kept that promise, in large part because someday he intended to get back to Wood Hill and do a full-scale investigation. So far, the town had refused permission, saying they didn't want to be featured on a cheap reality show. But he kept trying. And in the meantime, he'd built himself a reputation in the business as someone who always discovered the truth, no matter what that might be.

Usually, that meant exposing phonies. Occasionally they'd come across something unexplainable, and they'd managed to release it from whatever bound it to a place. Unfortunately, they'd never had any better luck at documenting supernatural events than any of the other paranormal programs.

This might just change that.

"Fuck it." Stone stood up. "Go get Marty," he told his assistant, who dashed off to find Marty Weiss, the show's producer. Before she was even out the door, Stone was on his phone to google a town called Hastings Mills.

By the time Weiss joined him, Stone already had a rough plan in mind.

"Cancel our appointments for the next two weeks. I want a meeting with the whole team this afternoon. And book a flight to Buffalo tomorrow."

Then, ignoring Weiss's questions, he punched Zimmerman's number into his cell. As he listened to her ringback tone – 'Tubular Bells,' naturally – he couldn't help remembering how great she'd been in bed. Even during their worst arguments, and sometimes because of them, they'd shared some amazing experiences. As much as he hated to admit it, while he loved Claudia, their relationship hadn't reached that level of fire yet, mostly because of her tightly controlled emotions.

And now he'd have to see her again.

Randi Zimmerman. Holy hell. This won't be awkward at all.

Hastings Mills, NY, July 13th, one year ago

On the other side of town from where a coroner slid Michael Morales's autopsied body back into a storage unit, Pierre Telles tucked his six-year-old son, Pete, into bed for the night. His wife, Dorothy, was downstairs washing the dinner dishes, the muted clinking and clattering as much a regular part of the evening noises in the house as the soft hiss of the water heater or the creaking of the walls as the temperature began to cool outside.

"Daddy, read me a story?" Pete pointed to a stack of books on the floor, next to his Yankees baseball hat.

Pierre held back a groan. He'd read every single book in his son's collection at least a dozen times. He was so sick of the Magic Tree House adventures and Blackie the Cat's amazing escapes from danger that he sometimes found himself tempted to chuck the whole pile into the trash. But Pete would fight sleep until he heard one of his favorites, so with a sigh Pierre reached down to the accursed stack.

"Which one do you want tonight, sport?" he asked, trying hard to keep his resignation from his voice.

"How about the one where I cut your fucking throat out?"

Pierre looked up so fast he nearly slid off the bed. He caught himself against the nightstand, still not believing he'd heard the malicious words, or the deep, gruff voice they'd been delivered in.

Until he saw his son's face.

The boy's mouth gaped, his tongue hanging down past his chin like some vile parasite. His eyes bulged from their sockets, spider veins turning their whites to an almost uniform red. His fine, silky hair stuck straight up and crackled with static electricity.

Pete let out a guttural snarl and released a blast of foul-smelling breath so awful Pierre had to turn his head away. The entire bed rose into the air and Pierre tumbled to the floor. The closet door flew open and slammed shut.

Pierre got to his feet and moved toward the bed. He stopped when he saw Pete sitting cross-legged in the air, still looking like someone had slipped a Halloween mask over his face.

The boy grinned madly and held up his two middle fingers.

"Pete?"

The back of Pierre's head exploded in pain.

Harsh, grating laughter attacked him from all directions and the world disappeared as he descended into darkness.

When Dorothy Telles rushed into the room less than a minute later, she found her husband unconscious on the floor next to a broken lamp and Pete sitting on his bed with his teddy bear, holding a Blackie the Cat book out to her.

"Read me a story, Mommy? Daddy went to sleep."

Hastings Mills, NY, July 15th, one year ago

Stone stared out the window of the rented SUV and wondered if they'd taken a wrong turn and ended up in some kind of rural Twilight Zone. Each mile seemed to take them farther back in time as they sped down Route 16 from Buffalo to Hastings Mills.

With endless acres of farmland and cow pastures going by, he could see why people considered everything above Albany a different state. In the long stretches between towns, the only signs of civilization were the tall gray cylinders of grain silos and the bright red rectangles of barns, interspersed with occasional crumbling shacks. When they did see a house, more often than not an assortment of junk – broken bicycles, grime-covered toys, aging furniture – littered the yard in between junked cars resting on blocks. Trucks with Confederate flag stickers and shotgun racks sat in driveways, their presence guaranteeing the kind of vile intolerance that had pushed him into leaving New York in the first place.

As a kid, he'd thought moving from Manhattan to the suburbs the worst thing possible. That forty-mile transition had been like traveling to another world. Instead of bustling streets filled with people, there'd been individual towns with tiny strip malls and no sidewalks. Instead of schools and apartment buildings filled with people of all colors, he'd been the only dark-skinned student throughout elementary and middle school. By the time he got to the consolidated high school with its mixture of races from neighboring towns, it was too late. Everyone had formed their cliques and groups, leaving him an outcast.

It hurt, but in the end it didn't matter much. His freshman year he discovered the video club and it became his passion. So much so that being called a nerd – and much worse – didn't even bother him.

Despite the intolerance and lack of cultural opportunities that came with living in a rural suburb, none of his experiences growing up had been as 'country' as where he now found himself. More than anything, it reminded him of the remote regions in West Virginia or North Carolina. It was hard to believe they were less than thirty miles from Buffalo and only five hours from New York City.

The blazing summer sun created heat ripples on the road despite it being only an hour after sunrise, and the muggy air teemed with bugs, which made a mess of the windshield. Even with the air-conditioning on full blast, the oppressive atmosphere inside the truck had Stone's deodorant working overtime.

He'd tried starting a few conversations with Claudia but she'd been quiet all morning. For the last few days, in fact. At first he'd chalked it up to a lingering irritation about Randi Zimmerman. Claudia knew about their past together and she'd definitely been irked when he told the team to drop everything for this new case. But she insisted she wasn't upset anymore. That had him nervous, because there were really only two possibilities. One, she was pissed at him for something else. He was aware they hadn't been getting along well recently, but he'd chalked that up to his working late and being irritable and Shari's constant insistence that she shouldn't be involved with him.

The other option had nothing to do with him, and everything to do with their new case.

Claudia hadn't been sleeping well lately. Nothing unusual for her, or Shari. They went around pale and exhausted more often than not, victims of vivid nightmares and awful memories. Claudia had confided a few of them over the years, and he had a feeling they weren't the worst ones.

As sensitive as she was to the supernatural, it worried him that her current sullen state might be related to what waited for them in Hastings Mills. There'd been times when the sisters got a 'premonition' about a place or event and it freaked them out so badly they couldn't do their job properly. He hated when that happened, because it meant extra editing work to cut them from scenes.

On the other hand, maybe he'd get lucky and this would turn out to be one of those rare occasions when she and Shari actually contacted something on the other side. It didn't happen very often. Part of the twins' role on the show was to be the 'ghost whisperers'. Each episode, they would try to communicate with whatever ghost or dark energy inhabited the house. Most times, it failed.

But when it worked, the optics always produced a ratings jackpot.

The sisters would fall into a trancelike state and their eyes would roll back until only the whites showed. And they'd speak in slow, creepy monotone voices. Usually they'd talk about impressions they received, vague sensations of loss or sadness or anger. Occasionally they'd manage to communicate with whatever mysterious entity haunted the location, and convince them to move on. Or at least stop disturbing the inhabitants.

Of course, most viewers laughed it off as shtick, but for Stone and the team, it never failed to give them a good case of the willies, because they knew it was real.

Either way, she'll let me know. When she's ready. He'd learned not to push the Brock twins about using their abilities when they didn't want to. The last time he'd tried, they'd given him the silent treatment for days.

The rest of the team seemed to be dragging ass as well, but for them Stone chalked it up to taking the red-eye out of Los Angeles the previous night. Kenjo 'Ken' Webb, the tall, lanky Japanese-American videographer, and Del Vonte Hall, their equipment man and security professional, had been up late prepping everything for the flight. Since they'd landed, Webb had done nothing but complain about the weather while Hall just smiled at his husband of two years. Coming from Mississippi, the hulking ex-Marine didn't mind hot, steamy conditions. Only some random droplets of sweat on the dark dome of his shaved head indicated he even felt the heat.

With another hour to go before they reached the town of Hastings Mills, Stone mentally reviewed what Randi Zimmerman had told him on the phone.

Abigail Rawlings, age nine. Lives with her widowed father, Curt Rawlings, who works for the maintenance department at a local university. No other kids, and he's been taking vacation time since their problems started. The first event had been in the girl's bedroom. Classic poltergeist manifestations, mostly furniture moving and temperature anomalies. She'd gone to day care the next day and suffered some kind of weird seizure. Fell out of her chair and went into convulsions, then started crying. She'd been taken to the hospital, where doctors kept her overnight for observation and then sent her home with a diagnosis of dehydration and a suggestion to see a psychologist if it happened again.

God, I'd hate to get sick or hurt out here in the boondocks.

Things went downhill rapidly after that. Escalating manifestations. More flying objects. Cold spots. And a physical attack on the girl by an unseen assailant.

Zimmerman had done everything by the book, working on the notion that Rawlings, like most people, was either too superstitious or too easily fooled. Ninety-nine percent of the time, so-called manifestations turned out to be natural phenomena, practical jokes, rats in the walls, or coincidence. But she'd found no broken air-conditioning units, no signs of rodents, no underground streams or nearby caverns, nothing. And no indication that someone wanted to pull a fast one for some quick publicity.

Which left either a serious psychological condition or a supernatural presence.

And now Randi's called me. People only call me when they want to prove an unexplained event is fake. *But in Randi's case….*

Zimmerman had become something of a celebrity in upstate New York in the intervening years. She had a local radio show. Had written a series of books about local hauntings and legends, *The Spooky Southern Tier. Volumes one through three, available at your local state fairs, roadside tourist traps, and Amazon.* Stone chastised himself at the uncharitable thought. *She's doing her best. And I hope she's happy. It was her choice not to take the deal. I told her this was our big break. What did she expect, that I'd turn down a chance for my own TV show just because she thought we were selling out? She kept saying think of the future, and I did. Just not the way she wanted.*

Now look at where we both are.

Stone forced himself to focus on the case. Nothing else mattered, including old grievances. Time for that later.

Hearing her voice over the phone had dredged up all sorts of memories, some good, some bad. She'd sounded exactly the same as the day she'd left him, her voice slightly husky in a Demi Moore sort of way, her sentences peppered with foul language. In his mind, he pictured the twenty-something Randi talking, the Randi who'd rocked his world every night in bed and stood by his side during some crazy times.

Although she'd only provided a few facts over the phone, saying she wanted Stone to make up his own mind about things, a queasy feeling had sprouted in Stone's stomach and it grew stronger the closer they got to Hastings Mills.

"It's worse than Wood Hill."

Randi and I have seen people die twice. Of the two, Wood Hill was probably the most terrifying, because it had nothing to do with human fuckups.

If she thinks this is worse...what the hell could it be?

As much as he desired to capture an actual supernatural event on film, he worried about finding out.

The Rawlings house looked like all the others on the street. A typical 1940s saltbox style, with a covered porch running across the front.

"All right, everyone. This is it. Let's get unpacked." Stone opened the door and stepped out of the SUV as their other vehicle, a large van outfitted with multiple computers and editing equipment, pulled up next to them. "I want exterior shots of the house, all angles, front and back. Ken, grab a handheld and we'll film my intro at the front door, then get a shot of me walking inside. We'll do some general exteriors later."

Stone took a step forward and stopped as an overwhelming sense of wrongness came over him. He tried telling himself it was simply a reaction to what he knew about the case and his thoughts about Randi and their shared past, but deep down he knew better. An oppressive, heavy blanket of malice seemed to have settled over everything like an invisible caul, completely at odds with the idyllic scene before them.

It feels like we're in a jungle and something nasty's stalking us.

An image popped into his head, indistinct but revolting at the same time. Human and animal faces overlaying each other, twisted horns and red eyes, squirming snakes. And although he heard no sounds, somehow he knew the creatures were laughing at him.

"This is a bad place."

Stone turned and found Claudia and Shari staring at the house. Their eyes had rolled back, exposing the white sclera. His heart thumped. Not even five minutes and they'd already gone into their private world, communing with whatever unseen forces they held a connection to. *Yes!* He pulled out his phone and began filming them as he asked his first question.

"What is it?"

"Don't go in," Shari said.

"Leave." A bit of drool escaped Claudia's mouth.

"They're waiting." Shari's voice dropped to a whisper.

Stone's hand twitched but he kept the camera on them. What was waiting? Before he could ask, a familiar voice shouted behind him.

"Stone! Thank god."

The sisters gasped and closed their eyes.

"Shit." Stone turned around. Randi Zimmerman stood on the front porch.

Stone glanced back at the twins. Their eyes had returned to normal, the deep violet almost lost in the dark smudges surrounding them.

"Is it safe?" he asked.

Claudia shrugged. Shari frowned and shook her head slightly, but voiced no objections.

Stone cursed again and pocketed his phone. The whole situation gave him a bad vibe. He trusted the sisters' abilities, even if they were notoriously erratic. If they said something was wrong, he didn't doubt it. But they had to go in. They'd come to do a job. One that might just make them incredibly famous.

Worse than Wood Hill.

"Shit. We have to do this," he said to Claudia and Shari, wishing to hell Randi hadn't interrupted them. "Can you try again? Contact whatever—"

The twins turned and headed toward the van, their answer obvious. Or maybe they just didn't want to meet Randi.

Was that it? Were they just sensing trouble ahead on a personal level? My ex is the bad thing waiting for us?

Great. As if the supernatural drama wouldn't be enough.

Stone followed the cement walkway to where Randi waited at the steps. Another man came out, older, dressed in blue dickies and a t-shirt. Stone figured him to be the girl's father, Curt Rawlings. Their skin was pale and the bruised hollows under their eyes as bad as the twins'. Despite her evident anxiety, Randi looked like her photos on her webpage, still slim, still with the same jet-black hair and John Lennon glasses. She wore faded jeans and a men's-style black button-down that revealed just the right amount of cleavage. Stone felt guilty at remembering how she looked with no shirt on and he cast a quick look back to make sure Claudia wasn't close by.

As he reached the porch, Randi's frown deepened.

"Are you all right?" she asked.

"Yeah, sure. Why wouldn't I be?" Stone heard the defensive tone in his voice and told himself to calm down.

"Seemed like there was a problem back there," Zimmerman said.

"TV stuff," Stone said. He could explain later. "Randi, why don't you show us—"

Somewhere inside, a door slammed shut with a tremendous

bang! and a heavy thumping started, like a sledgehammer pounding against wood.

"It's happening again," Zimmerman said, turning frightened eyes up at the second floor.

"Damn." Stone hadn't expected they'd have to dive right in. He clapped his hands to get everyone's attention. "All right. Ken, you're with me, right now. The rest of you get your stuff and follow as soon as you can."

Stone didn't waste time waiting to see if his team listened. Years of working together had honed them into a perfect unit. He knew Ken would be right behind him with a videocam as he pushed past Randi. As he crossed the threshold, the temperature dropped a good twenty degrees, raising gooseflesh on his arms.

A jittery, anticipatory sensation filled him, that butterflies feeling he got whenever some bad shit was about to go down. Call it a sixth sense or just the subconscious at work. It didn't matter. He trusted his gut, and it invariably led him to the truth the way a dog's nose led it to food.

Stone crossed the frigid living room to a set of stairs, which he took two at a time. He paused at the top, wondering which way to go. To his left, a door opened and closed three times in rapid succession, shaking the walls with the force of its impact.

"In there!" Stone raced for the door and grabbed the knob. Looking back at Webb, he counted out loud, matching the words with the fingers of his free hand for the camera.

"On three. One, two—"

The door swung inward, yanking Stone off his feet. He landed hard on his shoulder and crashed into a heavy wooden bed.

A bed that floated three feet in the air.

"Holy shit," Webb said from the doorway. He had his camera up and filming. Stone rolled away to give the videographer a better view.

Despite the fear squirming in his stomach, Stone kept his voice even as he directed Webb to get shots all around the room. "This isn't the first time we've witnessed levitation," he reminded the cameraman.

Charlatans used all sorts of tricks. Cables, fishing line, once even a dresser mounted to a wall that had a pulley system behind it. These days all it took was some mechanical know-how and a special effects search on Google and anyone could rig a so-called haunted house.

That doesn't explain the door, though, does it?

Stop it.

If you gave in to imagination or fear then you compromised your ability to expose the hoaxes. And he hadn't gotten as far as he had by being gullible.

Stone rose to his feet just as Claudia entered the room, her thermal meter held high. Shari joined her with the EVP recorder in her hands.

The temperature dropped again, sending uncontrollable shivers up his back.

"Over here," he said to Claudia. His breath steamed as he spoke. "We have multiple temperature anomalies."

She turned the thermal meter in his direction, her face even more serious than usual. The Brock twins had two main expressions: somber and woeful. Stone could count on one hand the number of times he'd seen either of them smile in the two years he'd known them. And that included the six months since he and Claudia first started sleeping together.

"Nothing's registering." She tapped the meter. "Ambient temperature in the room shows seventy-two."

"It feels like fifty," Ken said.

The bed dropped to the floor with a loud thud, the same sound they'd heard from downstairs. Webb moved around it, filming from all three open sides and crouching down to stick the camera between the small headboard and the wall. After that, he aimed the camera underneath, careful to stay far enough away so he'd be safe if it rose up again.

"I don't see anything." He stood and waved his arm over the bed. It shot forward and struck him in the legs, knocking him into a pink dresser. He fell to his knees and an assortment of toys, brushes, and combs rained down on him. With a high-pitched wood-on-wood squeal, the bed returned to its former position.

"Ken!" Shari rushed to the cameraman's side, eyeing the bed like it was a snarling tiger on a weak chain. Stone didn't blame her; the ordinary piece of furniture had taken on an air of menacing anticipation, an unspoken threat that it might pounce again without warning.

It's not alive, Stone reminded himself. Still, as he helped Shari get Webb back on his feet, he gave the bed a wide berth. He'd never seen an effect like that before.

Either we're dealing with a mechanical genius, or something very real is happening here.

He wasn't sure which answer frightened him more.

CHAPTER SEVEN

Hastings Mills, NY, July 15th, one year ago

Stone Graves leaned over Del Hall's massive shoulders and watched the computer monitors come to life. Eight of them in all, connected to video cameras placed throughout the house: two in Abigail's room and one each in the master bedroom, the kitchen, the living room, and the guest bedroom, which Curt's wife had turned into a sewing room and he'd been using as a sort of storage room since her death. The remaining two covered the front and back of the house. According to Randi, there'd already been one incident of strange sounds on the roof at night.

"That's some setup." Randi Zimmerman stood at the van's back doors.

"State of the art," Stone said, stepping out and leaving Del to his work. A pair of orange extension cords led from the van to an outlet on the porch, supplying the power they needed for their gear. "Courtesy of EBS Broadcasting. If you want to do things right, you've got to have the best. Otherwise some bozo's gonna make you look like a fool on national TV."

"I'm not a goddamn bozo. This shit is real."

"I know you're not. That's why I'm here. But I'm not gonna change our process just because we know each other. I have to prove these things don't have an explainable cause. Prove it so goddamned well no one can deny it. I dream of the day that happens. I'll be the most famous person in the whole damned world and people will finally have to believe that what I've seen, what *we've* seen, is real."

"I remember when you didn't care about getting rich and famous. What the fuck happened?"

"Someone offered me a boatload of money to do what we were already doing, that's what. The chance to not only stop struggling, but do more investigations and do them better."

"We were fine. And we didn't have to kiss network ass."

Stone shook his head. "I've got the number one supernatural investigation show on television. You know how hard it is for a black man to get his own TV show, let alone top the ratings? Yeah, I kissed some ass. But I worked damn hard too. Twice as hard as anyone else. And now they're all kissing my ass."

"And with all that equipment, all your so-called experts, what have you accomplished? You're number one, but you haven't proven a goddamned thing. You're no different than any other reality bullshit show."

"Don't give me that." Stone's voice rose. "You know as well as I do that ninety-nine out of a hundred cases are just people trying to pull a fast one. And the one case that *is* real, what happens? Tapes end up erased. Apparitions don't show up on film. People accuse you of using special effects. Trust me, I still want to prove the supernatural exists. But the money comes from outing the fakes. Or maybe I should get a podcast nobody listens to and spend my weekends at book fairs like you."

Stone regretted the words as soon as he said them, and he'd already started his apology before Randi's eyes narrowed behind her glasses.

"Ah, hell. I'm sorry. Guess we still know how to push each other's buttons."

She glared a minute longer then she shook her head, her expression relaxing. "I'm sorry too. Maybe I'm a little jealous. My equipment's old as shit and I don't get to do many investigations these days 'cause writing the books takes up all my fucking time."

Glad for the shift in subject, Stone nodded toward the van. "It's all necessary, and the network knows it. That's our command center while we're here. One of us is always in there to monitor what's happening and make sure everything we record is backed up to the cloud. The rest of us patrol the house with the handheld equipment –

cameras, EVP, EMF, thermal cams, temperature gauges. That's why my show is different from all the others. We don't waste fifty-nine minutes spouting scripted dialog and creeping down dark hallways with only flashlights on. We film what we experience, and you hear our actual conversations. The only thing we do in the editing room is chop out the boring parts where nothing happens and add in some commentary and setup shots."

As they talked, they headed back to the house. He wanted to gather everyone together and map out his plans for the night. The wildest things usually happened in the first twenty-four hours, when whoever was behind the scenes tried to impress the 'ghost hunters'. He also wanted to spend time with Abigail, who'd been napping since after breakfast.

"All right, folks, rendezvous in the kitchen," he said, tapping his Bluetooth. Acknowledgements came from all over the house through his earbud. Curt Rawlings had already taken a seat at the table when Stone got there. A few minutes later the entire team had joined them, either sitting or leaning against the walls.

"Okay, I'm sure most, if not everyone, has introduced themselves, but I'd like to make formal introductions anyhow. Randi, Curt, I know you've already met Ken Webb, our video man."

The tall man gave a quick wave and smiled around the cookie in his mouth. Even after working with him for five years, it still amazed Stone that Webb could eat twice as much as everyone else and stay rail thin. He was like a human garbage disposal.

"This is Claudia Brock. She handles all our thermal imaging, EVP and EMF, et cetera. Next to her is Shari Brock, our photographer."

"In case you can't tell, Shari and Claudia are related," Ken said.

Everyone laughed at Ken's joke, except Claudia and Shari, who gave weak grins. The twins were like mirror images. The only thing different about them besides their clothes was the length of their straight black hair. Shari wore hers cut just below her ears, while Claudia had let hers grow almost to her shoulders. Even Stone, after knowing them for years and sharing a bed with Claudia for months, still sometimes confused them in dark rooms, when their pallid complexions turned them into ghostly doppelgangers.

"Last, but not least, our jack-of-all-trades, Del Vonte Hall. Del handles security, driving, logistics, and anything else we need."

"Yo." Del waved from the screen of the laptop, which, like their earpieces, linked to the communications equipment in the van. Just seeing him gave Stone a sense of reassurance. Hall had pulled himself out of a dead-end future in the slums of New Orleans by joining the Marines at seventeen, where he'd shown equal aptitude for boxing and electronics. He was indispensable in a fight, could carry twice as much as anyone else on the team, and repair any piece of equipment they had. Plus he had a bullshit detector as good as Stone's; more than once he'd spotted anomalies in supposedly supernatural occurrences the rest of the group had missed. He'd mellowed a bit after marrying Ken, but still carried that aura of intimidation that had served him so well in the military.

"What can I do?" Curt asked.

Stone sat down and smiled to take the sting out of his next words. This was always the hardest part. No one liked being told to stay out of the way, especially in their own home. Over the years, Stone had gotten better at how he worded things, but most people caught on quick. And that's when the trouble started.

"Curt, you're actually going to be very important to our efforts, even though you won't be using any equipment. Your job will be to keep Abigail calm when things start to go wonky. And," he added, as Curt started to object, "it'll also be up to you to let us know if something's happening that we miss. This is your house, you know every creak and moan it makes. You know which doors might swing closed by themselves and which windows don't stay open. You know where the drafts are and which room gets the hottest during the day. If something seems wrong to you, tell us right away. Can you do that?"

Curt frowned, and for a moment Stone thought he might still object. Then the rough-hewn man nodded.

"Yeah, I got it. Don't touch the equipment and stay out of your hair."

Stone patted his arm but didn't bother apologizing. He knew it would come off as insincere, and that would only make things worse. Besides, there were more important things to worry about than bruised feelings. Like getting ready for what promised to be a sleepless night.

"Okay, here's the plan," Stone said. "I'll take first watch downstairs. Del, you'll patrol the yard. At midnight, Ken will relieve Del. Claudia, you have first watch upstairs and Shari can relieve you."

"What about me?" Randi asked. "You're not leaving me out of this."

"Relax." Stone held up a hand to placate her. "You're my relief. Midnight, same as Ken and Shari. Now, let's get the rest of the equipment tested and make sure we've motion detectors hooked up. After that, we'll record a walk-through of the house with Curt and Randi while they describe what happened before they called us."

Stone picked up a small camera and motioned to Curt.

"Is it okay if I talk with Abigail now?"

Curt shrugged and headed for the stairs without a word. Stone followed, his stomach already tingling with excitement.

Could there really be a ghost haunting the house?

On the other side of the bedroom door, Abigail put down her book.

And smiled.

Santa Gomez, Mexico, July 15th, one year ago

Robert Lockhart ducked just in time to avoid a lamp that flew past his head and crashed into the wall. With his left hand, he waved a glowing smudge stick, filling the air with the sharp tang of burning sage.

"By the four winds and the sun and moon. By the light and the dark. By the hand of God and in the name of Jesus Christ, our Lord and Savior, leave this place, spirit! I cleanse the world of your presence. Depart this plane and return to whence you came. You do not belong here. You are no longer welcome. Depart. Depart. Depart!"

With his other hand, Rob squirted holy water he'd stolen from the tiny church that served the village.

Sparks flew from the dusty ceiling fan and it came on, spinning so fast the blades became a blur and the wind dissipated the smoke. Ignoring the heavy breeze, Rob approached the center of the bedroom, where the young girl's bed vibrated and shook. He sprayed it with his bottle and waved the smudge stick again while he repeated his banishing spell. The girl, Ynez Izamel, thrashed back and forth but couldn't break free of the ropes binding her hands and feet to the bed posts. She opened her mouth and screamed, her lips stretching so wide Rob expected the skin to split. Her matted, sweaty hair slapped against sickly yellow skin.

The bed lifted up and slammed down. Both lightbulbs in the room exploded. The fan increased in speed, the hum of the motor changing to a high-pitched squeal.

"Depart! Depart!"

Cracks formed in the ceiling and plaster dust fell like snow. The fan tilted, threatening to break loose and wreak bloody havoc on his scalp.

"Depart!"

Everything stopped.

For a moment, the only sound was the whir of the fan blades slowing down. The bed remained still.

Something changed in the air. An increase in the pressure that Rob felt against his skin, in his chest, and in his ears. Like being dropped to the bottom of a deep swimming pool. His sinuses ached and he readied himself for what was about to happen.

He raised the smudge stick and waved it over his head.

"Give way, monster. Give way to God. You are not welcome. Depart!"

Here it comes.

All the windows in the house blew outward with a thunderous crash. A gust of hot wind blew through the room and stole the breath from his lungs. His ears popped.

Ynez's thin form went limp and her eyes fluttered before closing.

Rob lowered his arm, which trembled from his exertions over the past hours.

Please don't be dead. Please....

The girl's bare chest rose and fell. Rob gave a silent prayer of thanks.

"You can come out now," he called to the young couple who owned the house. They'd locked themselves in their bathroom at Rob's order. "*Puedes salir ahora.*"

"*Se ha ido*?" Miguel Izamel asked, opening the door and peering out.

"*Si*, it's gone." Rob motioned around the room. Even to his alcohol-dulled senses, the feeling of dread that had previously infused the house had disappeared, banished along with the malicious spirit that had attached itself to the couple's daughter.

"*Volverá*?" Miguel motioned for his wife, Salla, to come out. Tiny rivers ran down her dusty cheeks as they stared at their sleeping daughter.

"No, it won't be back," Rob said, although he couldn't be absolutely sure. Nothing was certain when you dealt with the supernatural. Possession always left a stain – on the soul, even on physical objects like houses – which in turn made it easier for the next spirit that came along. Still, the odds of a repeat occurrence were slim to none. Not with so many other souls in the world available as receptacles. Rob gave the couple his best attempt at a reassuring smile, which they returned, the first time he'd seen them anything except frightened since they approached him after his pop-up sermon three days before. He'd been grateful at the time, since he'd gone almost two weeks without drumming up any business from his latest mini-tour through the Baja region of Mexico. Night after night preaching about Satan and God, and nothing to show for it except a rapidly dwindling bank account.

Then the Izamels had appeared, with their story of a daughter with nightmares and objects that levitated. He'd jumped at the opportunity, figuring he'd only have to deal with a simple poltergeist.

When it turned out to be a real case of possession, he'd been both elated at the financial prospects and terrified he'd screw up. Again.

The money the Izamels owed him would be enough to get a decent bottle of whiskey in what passed for the local bar in town, with enough left over for a visit to Tijuana. A good thing, because the unholy urge had woken inside him again.

Being in the presence of Ynez the past two days didn't help.

Stop it. He pushed his evil thoughts away. There'd be time enough later, back in his cheap hotel with his bottle. Then lust and shame would be his partners all night long, or until he passed out, whichever came first. An awful way to spend the next twelve hours.

But better than the alternative.

"*Gracias, Padre Roberto.*" The Izamels were holding hands so tightly their knuckles were white. Rob sighed. Another guilt-poker jabbed him. *Father Robert.* He remembered when that title actually meant something.

Get over it. Just take your money and go.

Salla let go her husband's hands and pushed him forward. The man reached into his pocket and took out a handful of colorful bills. Probably a month's salary, maybe more. Rob hated this part the most. Guilt stabbed at him as he accepted the cash, knowing where a good chunk of it would end up.

"*Dios sea contigo,*" Miguel said. *God be with you.*

"*Y tu,*" Rob replied, then grabbed his bags and headed for his truck, their words of gratitude following him down the dusty path. He didn't hear them.

He could already see that first glass of whiskey.

In his mind, a scantily dressed Ynez Izamel served it to him.

That night, his dreams tormented him with memories of foolish mistakes. When the ghosts of dead friends and a little boy finally showed up to haunt his nightmares, he welcomed them as penance due.

CHAPTER EIGHT

Hastings Mills, NY, July 15th, one year ago

Stone Graves stifled a yawn as he poured himself another cup of coffee and wondered if the night would be a total bust. In the time since they'd set up their equipment, the closest they'd come to a supernatural event was an exceptionally loud fart thundering from upstairs around ten thirty.

His talk with Abigail had been as uneventful as the tedious hours that followed it. She had no real memory of her 'spells'. After each one, she'd woken as if from a nightmare, her recollections hazy at best. The other occurrences, such as moving furniture and the physical attacks, were far more frightening. Her father and Randi, who Abby referred to as Ms. Z., had talked to her about poltergeists and ghosts, but knowing the things she'd seen in movies or on TV might be real made things more terrifying, not less, and with each event she withdrew more and more into her own silent world.

All in all, Abigail Rawlings seemed like an ordinary little girl going through a very scary situation she didn't understand.

"Stone?" Del's voice in his earpiece interrupted Stone's tired musings.

"Yeah, go ahead."

"Shift change in ten."

"Got it. I'll— Sonofabitch!" Stone yanked his earpiece out as Del's words disappeared in a wail of static. Exclamations elsewhere in the house told him all the receivers had malfunctioned.

"I've got major activity on the heat sensors!" Claudia shouted from upstairs.

Stone grabbed his infrared goggles and rushed for the staircase. Halfway to the steps an unseen force hit him from the side, knocking him over the back of a couch and onto the floor.

Shari's voice joined her sister's, something about "EVP off the charts!" Heavy footsteps pounded down the hallway and through the ringing in his head Stone heard Webb and Randi yelling for someone to tell them what was going on.

Stone tried to sit up but the invisible weight pressed on him like a heavy mattress. The pressure increased, pinning him on his back and making each breath an effort. He tried to call for help but the force constricted his throat. He swung his arms up and they passed through the empty space. Colored explosions filled his vision and he knew he'd black out any second.

"Stone!" A man's voice, from far away. Too far away to reach him in time.

Jesus, this is it. I'm going to die from—

Strong hands lifted him up. He tensed, expecting his ghostly assailant to toss him across the room. Then the terrible weight disappeared and his chest muscles relaxed. Desperate for air, he sucked in a huge breath and gasped as sharp pains filled his lungs.

"Stone? Hey, you all right?"

"I...I'm good." Stone took another breath; this one didn't hurt nearly as much. It also cleared the last of the rainbow sparkles from his eyes. Del stared at him, beads of sweat glistening on his bald head.

"Damn, boss, I thought you was dead. What happened?"

"No time to explain." Stone fought his way through a dizzy spell as he got to his feet. Above them, something hit the floor hard and one of the twins screamed. Fear gripped him at the thought of Claudia being hurt.

"Up there," he said, still breathing heavily. "Hurry!"

Del nodded and ran for the stairs. Stone followed more slowly and they almost collided with Curt as he burst out of Abigail's room.

"Abby! Something's got her!"

Adrenaline coursed through Stone's veins. Flashes of light exploded from inside the girl's bedroom.

"Stay here," Stone told Curt. He slipped his goggles on and the house came alive in various shades of green, gray, and black. A red blinking dot at the bottom of one lens told him the built-in camcorder was working.

An explosion of brilliant white wiped out his vision and brought tears to his eyes. He lifted the goggles as another burst lit up the room like a miniature lightning blast. A third one came from the other side of the room and Stone realized lamps were going on and off in rapid sequence. He moved his hand around on the wall next to the doorway until he found the light switch.

He flicked it several times but the lamps continued their crazy display.

Every bulb in the room flared and then exploded.

Stone blinked away temporary blindness and lowered his goggles again. He let his gaze travel across the room, which had become a weird alien landscape filled with murky shapes. Everything seemed in place – a small dresser, the bed, a desk, two night tables. Only one thing was missing.

Abigail.

Muffled shouts and continued banging and thumping came from the guest bedroom down the hall but he blocked it out, focusing all his attention on finding the girl. He took two steps into the room and shivered when the temperature dropped a good ten degrees.

Curt had said, "Something's got her." Had she been taken from the room? He didn't see how; nothing could have gotten past them and the cameras in that short a time.

So where...?

Something fell on his arm. He wiped at it and then paused when his hand encountered a wet spot.

Wet and warm.

Another droplet landed on the same arm.

Stone looked up.

Abigail floated near the ceiling, arms and legs spread wide. The infrared imaging distorted her face but he recognized her instantly by her body size and long hair, which hung down around her head. Her wide eyes were two dark blotches and thick strings of saliva dangled from her gaping mouth.

She fell on him with a snarl.

Stone threw his arms up but it was too late. Once again he found himself slammed to the floor, his breath knocked from his lungs. He tried to push away but Abigail clung to him with a frenzied strength. Her nails dug into his arms while she growled and barked and snorted like a wild animal. One of her elbows struck his cheek and knocked his goggles halfway around his head. Foul-smelling drool smeared his neck and face, the stink so rancid it made him gag.

The weight on his chest disappeared. He scurried to the side and scrubbed at his face, wiping away tacky spittle. He fixed his goggles and saw Abigail sitting in the center of the room, her mouth open. He started toward her but movement above them caught his attention and froze him in place.

Two black shadows emerged from the ceiling, elongated arms of pure darkness against the greens and grays of the IR rendering. Twice the size of human arms, the shapes twisted and curved as if made of smoke. The arms paused less than two feet over Abigail's head. The hands lifted up like twin snake heads, fingers spread and aimed in Stone's direction.

A chill spread through Stone that had nothing to do with the frigid air in the bedroom. He knew what was about to happen but his muscles locked in place, as much a captive of the ghostly appendages staring at him as any mouse caught by a rattlesnake's gaze.

Faster than his eyes could follow, the arms rushed toward him, palms up and fingers splayed, the impossible appendages elongating as they sped forward to deliver their death. The cold grew worse, spreading from his chest to his limbs, turning from ice to fire.

Stone closed his eyes and screamed.

A heavy wind buffeted Randi as she tried to enter the spare bedroom. She grabbed the doorframe to keep from falling and braced her legs against the gale. Part of her wished the supernatural force would just send her tumbling down the hall, through the front door, and right out of Hastings Mills, so she'd never have to see the town or the Rawlings house again.

The single bed spun in lazy circles three feet off the ground. She'd heard Stone's description of what happened in Abby's room earlier, but hearing a story and seeing it yourself....

On the other side of the room, the Brock twins stood shoulder to shoulder, their backs pressed against a wall and their hair flying in all directions. They held their equipment out in shaking hands, Claudia the thermal camera and Shari the EVP monitor.

A thunderous crash made Randi jump before she realized it was the closet door opening and closing on its own. Ken Webb and Del Hall stood on either side of it, both of them ignoring the twirling bed, their attention focused on the closet. Ken aimed a digital camcorder at the door while Del had an odd-looking box-shaped camera with four tubes sticking out the front. Each time the closet opened, Ken's camera light gave Randi glimpses of a perfectly normal interior, clothes and toys crammed inside.

"I'm getting something over the bed!" Claudia called out. She had her camera pointed toward the ceiling. "Two distinct shapes."

At her words, the bed's rotational speed slowed until it simply floated in the air.

Without a sound, all the furniture in the room rose up to join it.

Randi backed up a step and something bumped into her leg. She jumped again and then belatedly noticed she gripped a camera strap in one hand. She couldn't even remember grabbing it in her rush to get upstairs.

"Got to fucking get this," she whispered, unaware she spoke out loud. She brought the camera up and pressed the shutter button. The flash went off, lighting up the dim room.

Before her vision cleared, all the drawers shot out of the two dressers, high-speed rectangular missiles that sped across the room. Several collided with each other or the bed, while at least two struck the twins, who both shouted in pain and fell.

At the same time, the contents of the closet burst outward, filling the room with clothes and shoes and stuffed animals that moved so fast Randi couldn't see anything except blurry, colored shapes. Her finger continued to trigger photos, the rapid flashes creating a strobe effect in which the closet-born blizzard grew in size until it enveloped everything.

Jackets and shirts wrapped around Randi and pulled tight. She dropped the camera and fought to free herself from the unyielding bindings, her breathing already growing labored as the clothes constricted around her. Sounds grew muffled but she heard someone laughing right near her head. She tried to call out for help but thick cloth filled her mouth, cutting off her air. Fire exploded in her chest as her lungs fought for oxygen and her pulse pounded in her temples in time to the continued laughter that mocked her impending death.

Colored spots appeared in the darkness, each one with a screaming face. A terrible pressure built in her skull, her body's last, futile attempts at getting blood to her head. She wondered what would give out first, her heart or her brain.

Then the force vanished, replaced by spikes of pain as blood flow returned. The clothes binding her fell away and her lungs expanded so rapidly she choked as she desperately sucked air in. With the return of oxygen to her body, her vision cleared and the drumbeat in her skull faded away.

The laughter, however, remained.

Fighting a lingering dizziness, Randi used the wall to push herself into a sitting position. The furniture still floated but the clothes and toys had fallen, allowing her to see the room again. The Brock twins, Del, and Ken were either sitting or lying on the floor. Only Ken still held his camera, which was in his lap and aimed toward the center of the room.

Claudia's mouth moved but the mad laughter filled Randi's head to the point where she couldn't hear anything else. She pressed her hands against her ears. It did no good. The irrational sounds only grew louder. She watched Del stand up and approach the bed, and wondered why the incessant cackling in her skull wasn't affecting anyone else. Del grabbed the footboard with both hands and pulled down. The ex-Marine's thick muscles bulged beneath his t-shirt until it looked like the sleeves might tear apart.

The bed didn't move.

The crazy laughter rose up another notch in volume and Randi worried her eardrums would explode. The pain left her helpless while Ken documented Del's futile efforts.

All at once the deafening sounds disappeared and the furniture crashed to the floor with enough force to dent the old-fashioned planks.

Del looked down at the metal leg that had missed his foot by less than an inch and slowly backed away.

Randi got to her feet, intending to ask them if they'd heard the laughter. But the room began spinning around her.

Then everything went black.

CHAPTER NINE

Hastings Mills, NY, July 16th, one year ago

Stone Graves sat at the table, a glass of whiskey untouched in front of him. He wanted it desperately, more than he'd ever wanted a drink in his life, but he was afraid his hands would shake so hard he wouldn't get it to his mouth without spilling it. And he couldn't afford to show that kind of fear in front of the team. Not if he wanted them to stick around.

Which he also desperately needed.

They were all gathered again in the Rawlingses' kitchen, along with Randi and Curt Rawlings. Abigail had gone back to sleep, with the help of a mild sedative prescribed earlier in the week by her doctor. Stone knew they were all waiting for him to speak but he couldn't. Not yet. He needed to come to grips with everything that had happened.

Those spectral arms rushing toward him, stretching and growing, the hands that acted as if they could see him, the wraithlike fingers curved, ready to grab him, to rend him. The terrible, arctic cold accompanying them....

And then nothing had happened.

Well, almost nothing. There'd been that instant of blackness, when he'd closed his eyes and...what? Fainted? Hyperventilated?

Simply gone blank from terror?

The moment had passed and he'd opened his eyes to find Abigail on the floor, curled in a ball and crying. The room had been empty except for the two of them. No smoke monsters bursting from the ceiling, no exploding lights, no floating children. Just an ordinary room with a badly frightened girl in the center.

Although just as panicked as Abby, he'd instinctively wrapped his arms around her, telling her over and over it was all right, they were safe. Eventually, like good, trusting children always do with adults, she'd succumbed to his lies and stopped crying, content to be held and comforted until Curt could take her.

When the group gathered downstairs, they'd looked as wrung out as he felt. He'd caught a glimpse of himself in the bathroom mirror, his blue eyes dull and his skin more of a dusky gray than its usual chocolate brown. Although the whole crew appeared pale and drawn, Randi in particular looked like she'd been to hell and back, which turned out to be a pretty good description of what had happened to her.

And now we have to decide what to do next. Well, I *have to decide. My show, my team. My decision.*

Sometimes it sucked being in charge. Part of him, the terrified part, wanted to find a bar and get stumbling drunk. But the scientist in him wanted to jump for joy because he was pretty goddamned sure this wasn't a hoax. Something out of the ordinary was happening in the Rawlings house. Something supernatural.

And deadly.

"Okay," he said, and then took a deep breath. The others looked up, waiting for what he had to say. He motioned for Ken to turn on one of the videocams. A couple of people frowned. Too bad, he thought. They needed to capture the crew's raw emotions. It would be great after editing.

"Here's the deal. We've all experienced some things since we've been here. Things that seem to be—"

"Totally fucked up," Randi interrupted. Her comment drew a couple of weary smiles.

"I was going to say unusual," Stone said, "but that description's as good as any. However, I want to make sure we don't jump to any conclusions."

"Boss, you still think this is all some kind of hoax?" Del shook his head. "'Cause I gotta call bullshit. This house is haunted for sure.

Sorry," he added to Curt, who looked worse off than any of them.

"I've known it from the beginning." Curt didn't sound pleased to admit it. "That's why I called Ms. Zimmerman."

"We've felt it since we arrived," Shari said.

"The presence." Claudia stared directly at Stone as she spoke. He caught her hint. She needed to tell him something in private.

Which meant he probably wouldn't like it.

He nodded, letting her know he'd got her message.

"I'm not stupid. I've seen shit today too." Stone held up his hand, pleased to see it had stopped shaking, to forestall another comment from Randi. "This is either a serious haunting or a powerful poltergeist event. My guess is the latter. Ghosts don't attack people. However, that just makes it more important to do our job right. We have to prove beyond a shadow of a doubt something supernatural is happening here. When we go on national TV with this, I don't want there to be any chance of someone accusing us of faking things."

"So, what's next?" Ken asked. Stone looked around the table. The life was creeping back into everyone's eyes, excitement replacing fear as the significance of documenting a major paranormal event penetrated the shock they'd all been feeling.

"Ken, take the cameras to the van and download all the files to the computer. Go through them frame by frame. Del, you can help him. Shari, you and Claudia use the laptop to do the same with the thermal and EVP data. Randi, you and I will patrol the house just in case our poltergeist returns tonight."

Claudia glared at him and he mentally kicked himself for adding fuel to the jealousy fire.

"You keep talkin' about ghosts and poltergeists. I ain't much of a churchgoin' man, not since my wife passed, but what if Abby's got some kind of demon in her?" Curt asked.

Stone watched the changes in the team's expressions as they considered the question. Foul liquids. Beatings from an invisible hand. Convulsions. Levitation.

"Jesus Christ." Ken shook his head. "That would explain a lot. Are we dealing with possession?"

"A demon would only manifest around the girl, not in empty rooms," Del said.

"Ghosts and poltergeists rarely physically hurt people," Ken countered.

"Some do," Randi said, and Stone knew she was thinking about the thing – or things – that haunted the Wood Hill morgue.

And what about Evan Michaels? The unwelcome image of the boy's convulsing form appeared in Stone's memory. The young priest reading from the Bible while clothes and papers whirled around the room and the windows opened and closed on their own.

No. We were right. Demons don't exist, not then, not now. He pushed the memory down. He had to stop this line of thinking before it went too far, for him and the others.

"There's no such things as demons."

All eyes turned in his direction. He made sure to face the camera before speaking.

"The paranormal is just a word we use for things we can't explain. Psychic powers can be measured. Auras can be photographed. I'll even grant the existence of ghosts and poltergeists. When someone dies, a little of their energy might remain behind, sometimes in an uncontrolled state. Like an invisible, semi-sentient tornado. But the idea of Heaven and Hell, or evil creatures that can cross over from other dimensions and invade our bodies…now you're talking superstition. All the signs of possession can be explained by human psychosis and psychic or paranormal phenomena. So, let's forget the religious bullshit and focus on what's real. We're here to document what's happening and find a way to put a stop to it."

For a few seconds, no one spoke. Curt frowned, and Stone wondered if he'd insulted the man with his comment about religion. *Too bad.*

"I agree."

Stone gave Randi a grateful nod. One of the reasons they'd

worked so well together right from the beginning was they shared a deep belief in science over superstition or religion. Having her back him up now went a long way.

"Guess I should get started, then." Ken stood and gathered up the cameras. "The sooner the data is downloaded, the better. Del, you coming?"

The big man stood up and the couple left. Not for the first time, Stone wondered how two such different people had ended up together.

"Sometimes opposites attract." Claudia's voice held enough ice to cause its own temperature anomaly.

"Yeah," Stone said. It always freaked him a little the way she seemed to read his mind at times, but he got her point. None of his business. And a reminder that their own relationship was just as unlikely. He lifted his glass and downed the whiskey in one long gulp. "Shari, Claudia, can I talk to you for a minute?"

The twins nodded as one and followed Stone to the living room, where they took seats on the couch. Stone pulled a chair over so he could keep his voice down while they spoke.

"You felt something tonight, didn't you? What was it?"

They glanced at each other, and a little guilt-bird hatched in Stone's belly. The two women didn't like talking about their paranormal abilities. On top of that, Shari didn't like him all that much because of his relationship with Claudia. But in this situation he wanted to hear both their impressions.

Shari nodded. Claudia looked at Stone.

"Yes, and we don't know," she said. Her words confirmed his suspicions and fears all at once.

"How bad?"

Claudia shook her head. "I...we never felt anything like it. Cold. Evil. But not...complete. Like walking on a frozen river and seeing a small hole in the ice. You know the hole could open up if you take another step, and if it does...."

"You could die," finished Shari.

"So things could get worse."

"They will."

"Do you think you can...you know...?" He left it unfinished, knowing they'd understand what he wanted. *Can you try to communicate with it?*

Shari's answer was a gaze as dead as he'd ever seen it. Lithe as a cat, she stood up and headed for the hall. Claudia rose more slowly.

"What you're asking...you don't understand."

"I know. But it's important."

Claudia sighed and nodded. "I'll see what I can do."

"Thank you." Stone leaned back as Claudia left the room. He felt bad about having to ask, especially with the Randi situation, but there'd been no choice. It would look killer on camera, the two of them going into one of their trances. Viewers would eat that up. Just as importantly, he needed more information. Claudia had said they'd felt something *not complete.* What did that mean? A presence splitting itself between two places at once?

Not complete.

No one really knew where poltergeists came from. Most experts considered them ghosts that somehow gained enough strength, either through insanity or anger, to physically affect their surroundings. They typically continued to grow in power until they either achieved some mysterious goal or got banished.

If that was the case, then the Rawlingses' poltergeist might not have reached full strength yet.

I hope for our sake they're wrong. If—

Shouting from outside the house interrupted his thoughts. Muttering curses, he went out to the van, where Ken and Del stood by the open back doors. Ken's eyes were wide and his face a pale moon against the backdrop of the night. Del, on the other hand, appeared ready to tear someone's head off.

"We found it like this," Ken said, stepping aside so Stone could see.

Stone swore. It looked like a giant had picked the van up and shaken it. Racks turned over, monitors and servers strewn about. The acrid stink of charred electronics filled the air and broken glass littered the floor. Several of the monitors were cracked or broken and much of the expensive computer equipment was smashed and dented.

"This was deliberate," Del said, pointing at one of the servers. "Look how the case is crushed. You can't do that with your bare hands. You'd have to hit it with something."

Tendrils of a cool breeze snuck through the doors and Stone shivered. *Maybe not bare hands, but what about some other kind of force? The kind that can pick up a man or a heavy piece of furniture like it weighed nothing.*

"Salvage what you can," he said, knowing it would be precious little. He felt like kicking something. The equipment was insured and the network would pay to replace everything. But in the meantime, they'd lost valuable tools. And data. They'd have only the laptop for playback. Plus, the cameras mounted in and around the house would be useless until they could be brought back online.

Ken climbed in and started picking through the wreckage. They'd have to go into town in the morning and replace what they could, and then have the production company drop-ship anything else. Meanwhile, he and Del would do their best to get some of the computers working again, but it would take time.

Time that Stone had a feeling they didn't have.

CHAPTER TEN

Buffalo, NY, July 16th, one year ago

"Your time will come, Father Fucking Bonaventura!"

Leo sat up so fast his back barked in protest. For a moment he was in the Central American jungles again, a young priest filled with the fire of righteousness, facing off against evil. Then the remnants of his dream dissolved, leaving him back in the real world, surrounded by the sterile whiteness of his hospital room. A relic well past his prime, his remaining days dwindling fast.

Perhaps down to nothing.

He glanced at his watch. Just past four in the morning. He still had two hours before the nurses would come in to prep him for his stent surgery.

They won't have to worry about waking me. I don't think I'll be going back to sleep tonight.

He'd been in Tapajo again, fighting to expel the demon haunting that poor boy. Why had his subconscious chosen to dredge up that particular event? It had been months since he'd even thought about what happened in that hut. And years – decades, really – since he'd suffered any nightmares about it.

Why now?

The question nagged at him. Most of the time dreams meant nothing; they were just the subconscious working through things. Had that been it? A manifestation of his fear that he'd die on the table?

Or one of those rare instances of something more?

Tapajo was a lifetime ago; since then, he'd done so much and seen things that would give anyone a lifetime of nightmares. Exorcisms, too many to count. Mostly simple cases of mental disorder, a scattered few actually involving the expulsion of an evil entity. Nothing on the scale of what he'd dealt with in Guatemala, but frightening nevertheless. Evil was evil. Even the lowest of the lesser demons made a potentially deadly foe if taken for granted. There'd been plenty of fakes, too, scam artists hoping to cash in on the popularity of books and movies like *The Exorcist*, *The Amityville Horror*, or *The Hinsdale House*.

And then there'd been the other things, the things no one could really explain. Or see. Ghosts. Poltergeists. Random supernatural happenings. He'd investigated many of them, disproved some of them, and developed a healthy respect for the ones that remained mysteries. Along the way he'd earned more than one letter of censure from Rome. Their official stance had always been a firm denial of ghosts or psychic phenomena or anything else that couldn't be explained by science or the Bible.

Other than demons, of course.

This from an organization that worships a ghost and a zombie as parts of its Holy Trinity.

Over the years, the number of exorcisms – and the number of priests trained to perform them – had fallen and risen as the Church went through phases of traditional beliefs vs. more modern approaches. Spiritual and psychological schools of thought were always battling for supremacy.

Of course, some in the Vatican still steadfastly followed the old ways, the men who kept the records, trained the incoming exorcists, remembered their own encounters back when priests were really priests and not just psychiatrists with stiff collars. And it was only because of his relationships with those men, and the favors they owed each other, that he'd remained on as both teacher and exorcist long after he'd exceeded the usual retirement age.

But all good things must come to an end. And when that happens, you find yourself in a chair, napping in the sun until it's time for lunch. Or lying in a hospital room waiting for a bunch of people you don't know to stick a tube in your heart so it keeps working.

All so you can hopefully spend the next five years napping in your chair and slowly turning into a vegetable.

Leo rolled over on his side and let the cheap industrial pillow soak up his tears.

"Getting old sucks," he whispered, using one of his students' favorite words because it felt more appropriate than anything else he could think of.

The idea of going to Heaven no longer comforted him as it had in his youth. As much as he believed he'd be united with God and Jesus and his family on the other side, in a place of beauty and peace, the concept of death terrified him. He wasn't ready to leave this world, and for the first time he understood why so many of the sick and injured fought so hard against it. He used to think they simply lacked true faith. Now he knew better.

It was fear.

"Your time will come, Father Fucking Bonaventura!"

A shiver skittered down Leo's spine and his whole body twitched in response.

Was today his time? The way it had been Anibal's?

Thoughts of death descended on him again, and he wiped away more tears. This time it wasn't his own mortality that frightened him, but the idea of losing the ability to care for himself. To think.

When the nurses showed up two hours later and injected his first sedative of the morning, it was a relief to drift away.

Tijuana, Mexico, July 16th, one year ago

Rob Lockhart groaned in pain as blinding sunlight bathed his face.

"*Tengo que ir.*"

The girl's voice emerged from somewhere within the supernova burning his retinas. He rolled over, turning his head away from the window. Another moan escaped him, this one born from his memory of what he'd done rather than the tequila-fueled jackhammers blasting away in his skull.

Ramona. Her name came with a picture of her face. Raven hair, eyes to match. Elfin features. She'd been standing on the corner of Coahuila Street when he'd stumbled out of the bar, his blood full of tequila and his heart filled with terrible desires. He'd truly intended to drink himself into oblivion so he couldn't pursue his fantasies.

The moment he'd seen her, he'd succumbed to temptation.

He couldn't help it. She'd reminded him too much of the others, the ones who'd haunted his nightmares for more than fifteen years. The ones who still waited out there somewhere.

"*Cuánto cuesta*?" he'd asked. *How much?* There'd been no doubt as to her profession. No one except whores, thieves, and drunks loitered in Tijuana's red-light district at that time of night.

"*Veinte dolares*," she'd replied, her eyes displaying more years than her true age, which Rob guessed at no more than fifteen. Not that he cared. She was both the reason he'd come to Tijuana and the reason he'd tried to drink himself into a stupor.

Hating himself to his very core, he'd handed over the money and led her to his hotel.

Now, five hours and another twenty dollars later, regret and self-loathing lay on his soul like twin hundred-pound weights.

"I must go," Rosa repeated, this time using broken English. He sat up. She still stood by the window, her thin body glowing in the sunlight. Rob felt the demon lust awakening even as he understood she had posed *just so* to achieve her desired effect on him. He reached down and felt for his pants. Took out his wallet. Slightly more than a hundred dollars. If he spent it carefully....

He held up a twenty. Rosa smiled and climbed back into the bed.

In his mind, her body paled and her eyes turned a deep violet as he lost himself in his darkest desire.

Two hours later, Rob crossed the border from Tijuana to San Ysidro, California. At just past nine, very little was open in the border town, but he knew from experience the Jack in the Box just past the

Greyhound bus station would be doing a lively business. He ended up parking a block away and even that short walk left him drenched in sweat and his head ready to burst. The smell of alcohol and sex clung to him, constant reminders of yet another fall from grace. In his rumpled, dusty clothes, he blended in perfectly with the day laborers, homeless, and fellow partakers of the red-light district's less savory offerings. Waiting in line between a strung-out woman with two small children and a man in ragged clothes who stunk of old shit and piss, he silently said his morning prayers.

Ain't Christianity the best? his subconscious whispered, while he mentally recited the Hail Mary. *Defile your soul for what, the hundredth time? Two hundredth? But say a few imaginary invocations and all is forgiven. You're a clean slate again.*

Rob ignored the voice and moved on to the Our Father. He took a break from his devotions to order three breakfast tacos, French fries, and a soda, then repeated the cycle.

Food can't fill the hole inside you, and all the showers in the world can't wash away the stains on your soul.

As if he didn't know that. He had an addiction, one far worse than drugs or alcohol.

Addict? You're a pervert. The first step is admitting the problem.

"Shut up," he mumbled around a mouthful of egg and hot sauce. "It's a disease."

He'd read that several years ago and latched on to it like a lifeline. A disease. Diseases could be cured. And as much as he hated to admit it, the only way to control it was to give in once in a while. Fall off the wagon, release the pressure building up inside. That didn't make it right, and he feared he'd burn in Hell someday for all his transgressions, but it beat the alternative.

Rotting in a prison cell for the rest of his life.

He hoped that someday God would answer his prayers and rid him of the curse he'd carried since his teenage years. In the meantime, he'd make his periodic visits to Mexico, where what he needed might not be legal, but the authorities turned a blind eye to it.

Therapy provided by the Church hadn't worked, and eventually they'd given up on him. But he hadn't given up on himself. God would come to him, show him the way. He felt sure of it.

He just needed to figure out what kind of sacrifice the Lord wanted in return.

In the meantime, he had work to do.

He crumpled his garbage and tossed it into the bin. Outside, the dazzling sunlight jabbed tiny claws into his optic nerves and baked his skin as he walked back to his car. By the time he got back to the one-room apartment he called home these days, he was ready for a drink, his bed, and a few hours of sleep.

Then he could start planning the route for his next tour.

Hastings Mills, NY, July 16th, one year ago

Stone woke to bright, warm sunlight covering him like a blanket. He opened his eyes and frowned at the unfamiliar ceiling staring down at him before remembering he'd sacked out on the Rawlingses' couch sometime after 4 a.m.

The smell of fresh-brewed coffee teased his nose, rousing him to full wakefulness. His back, stiff from the sagging cushions, protested as he got up, but he ignored the aches and headed into the kitchen, where Claudia was pouring a cup.

"God, I need one of those," he said, inhaling the delicious aroma deep into his lungs. Claudia pointed at some empty mugs on the counter and sat down at the table, her eyes averted from his. Not a good sign. Either she was more upset from their conversation the previous night than he'd thought, or the presence in the house was really affecting her. He was about to ask when Randi joined them, her hair still shower wet and her t-shirt clinging tightly to her chest. Claudia glared and then looked away.

Or it's option three.

"Jesus, is there anything better than fresh coffee in the morning?" Randi made hers the same way he remembered, light and sweet, and sat next to Claudia, who acknowledged her "Good morning" with the barest of nods. If Randi noticed her dark mood, she didn't show it.

"So, what's on the agenda for today?" Randi asked.

"Ken and I are heading into town to see about replacing the damaged equipment. Del and the twins are going to hit the grocery store. I was hoping you'd keep an eye on Abby, since she's already comfortable with you."

"Sounds good to me."

Shari entered the kitchen, wearing the same scowl as her sister. She sat down and proceeded to sip from Claudia's cup. A moment later, Abby wandered in and stared at him. Dark circles hung under her eyes and she held a stuffed bunny in her arms.

"When will you make the bad things go away?"

An uncharitable thought crossed Stone's mind – *Jesus, kid, I'm trying my best* – and he had to bite his tongue. Claudia and Shari both shot angry looks his way. He put a hand on Abby's shoulder and leaned over.

"We're going to make the house safe for you and your dad. It's just going to take a little while."

"You promise?" she asked. Her voice quavered in a way that reminded him too much of Evan Michaels. A promise had been made to him, too, although not by Stone. A promise that in the end hadn't been kept.

I hope to god it still haunts that goddamn priest as much as it does me.

"Cross my heart," Stone said, making the motion across his chest and praying he wasn't giving her false hope. She managed a weak smile that made him feel better and worse at the same time.

"Mr. Graves never lies." Randi tossed him a 'You better not screw this up' look and took Abby's hand. "Now, how about we make you some breakfast?"

"Okay, Ms. Z.," she said, her face brightening.

Stone motioned at Claudia to follow him out into the hall but she averted her gaze.

With a sigh, he went to find Ken.

CHAPTER ELEVEN

Hastings Mills, NY, July 16th, one year ago

"Thanks for sticking around today," Curt said, as Randi handed him the last of the breakfast dishes to dry.

"Happy to," she said, and meant it. And not just because she didn't want to run errands in ninety-degree weather. Abby needed someone with her, someone she could talk to, other than her father. The poor kid was scared to death and exhausted. After breakfast, Randi had suggested they sit outside for a while, just to get fresh air and sunshine. She'd sent Abby out first, promising to join her as soon as she finished the dishes.

From the window over the sink she could see Abby sitting at a wooden picnic table, watching something on her pad. The scene evoked a sadness in her. No brothers or sisters, a mother who passed away when Abby was still a baby, and no friends to play with because Curt feared she'd freak out again like she'd done in day care. So now she was stuck in a house that terrified her with a bunch of strangers who treated her like a laboratory experiment. Not exactly the kind of summer fun a kid her age needed.

Watching her brought back memories of Randi's own childhood, the afternoons she'd spent alone because both her parents worked and she had no siblings.

Maybe we can rent some movies for her, Randi thought, wiping her hands on a towel. *Make some popcorn, have a few laughs. Try to get her mind off things.*

With the dishes done, Randi went to get her camera before heading outside. Despite the morning being uneventful so far, a good investigator had to be prepared at all times. Stone would throw a shit fit if something happened and she didn't get it on film.

Hopefully I won't need it. As much as she wanted to capture real proof of the supernatural, she'd be perfectly happy if the next few days were devoid of freaky occurrences. *Hell, with Stone here, maybe I should just pack up and leave. Let him and his spooky girlfriend find the answers and solve the case. He can have all the glory, I don't give a fuck.*

In the years since she and Stone parted ways, she'd seen her share of weird shit. But nothing like this. Furniture slamming into people, the invisible force that had attacked her and Stone. Things had moved beyond weird and into dangerous.

Like nearly being killed by flying clothes.

She couldn't shake her fear that someone would die. The episodes of paranormal activity at the Rawlingses' house kept reminding her of that day back in college, at Wood Hill. The cold spots. The odors. The chamber doors opening and closing. The body slabs shooting out....

It was all too similar.

During their years working and living together, she and Stone had talked about that day many times. Done hours of research on the sordid history of the place. Both of them agreed it had to be poltergeist activity, brought on by a concentration of restless spirits all in one location, ghosts or latent energy or whatever left behind by so many tragic deaths and so much abuse.

They'd both witnessed the faces in the mist, heard the voices. All of which seemed to confirm their theory. A theory that had been reaffirmed, for them, with the Evan Michaels case. Another death that haunted her. Mostly because she still felt that if that damned priest hadn't interfered, they might have figured out the cause of the boy's problems and saved his life. They just hadn't had enough time. Maybe if they'd been brought in sooner, or convinced Brian's parents not to listen to the exorcist....

Which brought her back to the Rawlingses' house. The whole situation had her perplexed because it didn't fit the standard ghost or poltergeist model. Curt had said there was nothing unusual in the house's history. No murders of previous owners, no cemeteries on or near the property. Nothing to explain the presence of a powerful negative force.

There has to be a reason. Something he's not aware of. Maybe I should look into the history of the house while I'm out there.

She'd just grabbed her laptop when a startled shout came from outside.

Randi's pulse accelerated as she jumped from the chair. Curt came pounding down the hall, his face mirroring the terror exploding in Randi's chest. They ran outside to where Abby stood by the picnic table, staring at something on the ground.

"What's the matter?" Curt yelled. Abby turned. She looked confused rather than frightened, but that didn't relieve any of Randi's tension.

"A frog," she said, and pointed at the ground.

"What?" Curt stopped next to her, and Randi did the same.

Did she just say a frog?

Sure enough, a frog sat at Abby's feet. About the size of Randi's hand, it looked like pretty much every frog she'd ever seen. Green on top with some darker spots, a pale yellowish white on the underside. Instead of trying to hop away, the frog flopped back and forth, kicking its legs but not going anywhere.

Despite knowing nothing about frogs other than they lived in water and ate bugs, Randi felt confident in her assessment of the animal's condition: it was not in good health.

"I was just sitting here with the dark lady and it landed on me."

Randi's hackles rose. "What dark lady?" she asked, glancing around.

"My invisible friend. She lives in the house. She told me to go inside but I didn't want to."

"How long has your invisible friend lived here?"

Abby shrugged. "I don't know. As long as I can remember. She used to be nice but now she's kind of mean. I don't like her anymore. Sometimes she throws things."

Randi looked at Curt. "Did you know about this?"

He shook his head. "First I'm hearing about it. Honey, where did you see—"

Something hit Curt's shoulder and bounced off. Randi caught a glimpse of green and white. Curt scowled and looked around.

"That's what happened to me." Abby pointed at the second frog.

Before her father could respond, a third frog hit the picnic table with a wet thud. Like the others, it flopped around in uncoordinated fashion.

"This ain't funny!" Curt shouted, aiming his gaze at the trees along the edge of the property. "Cut it the hell out."

Two more frogs smacked off the table. Another struck Randi and she jerked away.

"Daddy, I want to go inside." Abby tugged her father's hand. Several more frogs fell around them. One gave a half-hearted croak. Randi looked up.

A frog landed directly on her face.

She cried out and wiped cold slime from her nose and lips. A dozen more struck the lawn. This time when she looked at the sky, she saw them. Black dots against the blue. Dozens of them.

Hundreds.

"Go!" Her shout came just as the rain of frogs turned into a deluge. Twisting, kicking amphibians poured down, a hail of wet, cold flesh. Croaks and squawks sounded all around them as they covered their heads with their arms and ran for shelter. The bodies beat on the roof of the house and the porch like a thousand drummers playing different songs.

Randi slammed the door shut and they stood in the kitchen, eyes wide, listening to the thunder of the impossible downpour. It grew so loud that Randi had to raise her voice to be heard over it.

"Into the living room." She pointed to make sure Curt and Abby understood. Glass shattered and several frogs landed on the kitchen floor. Their broken, bloody forms contorted like fish out of water.

Curt pulled Abby deeper into the house and Randi followed, after setting up her videocam at the window and hitting record. In the living room she found two sets of frightened eyes staring at her. Despite their silence, she heard the question they both needed answered.

What do we do?

Randi could only think of one thing.

She pulled out her phone.

Stone and Ken were in the electronics section of Best Buy when Claudia, Del, and Shari found them. Ken was attempting to piecemeal a small business network out of the few computer models and home servers the store had available.

With his limited IT skills, Stone could only stand and watch, which had him frustrated to the point where he could feel his pulse throbbing in his temples.

"C'mon, we need to be up and running. Who knows what we're missing at the house?"

"I know. I'm trying." Ken muttered a curse and put down a laptop that didn't have the right kind of video card he needed.

"Well, try the fuck harder, dammit!" Stone slammed his hand against a countertop and several sets of earbuds fell off a rack. Ken jerked away and Stone instantly regretted his outburst.

"Sorry. I know you're doing the best you can." He headed down the aisle to give Ken space and found Claudia, Shari, and Del coming toward him. Del held out a can of soda and Stone took it gratefully. Despite the fact it wasn't even noon, the store's AC struggled to keep up with the heat outside.

"How's it going?" Del asked.

"How the fuck do you think it's going?" The words came out of Stone's mouth before he even knew he was going to say them. Del's eyebrows shot up and Stone shook his head.

"Christ. I'm being an ass to everyone today. To answer your question, I think he'll be able to get us up and running." Stone held the cold can against his forehead for a moment before opening it and taking a long swallow. After letting out a stifled belch and wiping the sweat from his neck, he looked at the twins.

"Did you manage to get the data off the camera chips before you left this morning?"

Claudia nodded, but she seemed distracted and kept glancing at Shari, who frowned back at her.

"I saw some of it," Del said. "Freaky shit. But, um...your visitor didn't show up."

Stone cursed. No pictures or video of the apparition in Abigail's room. He guessed that meant no images of anything in the other rooms either, things they might not have seen in the confusion or that the human eye couldn't perceive. That explained Claudia's expression. She'd known he'd be upset and—

Shari gasped and Claudia repeated it a second later.

"Something's wrong." Before she could finish, Stone's cell phone chimed. As soon as he answered, Randi's anxious voice burst from the speaker.

"You better get back something's going on something fucking weird there's frogs everywhere!"

"Wait, what? Zim, slow down!"

The only response from the phone was a muffled shout and then the connection went dead.

"Dammit!" Stone called back and got her voicemail.

"What is it?" Del asked.

"Trouble at the house. Randi said something about frogs and hung up."

"Darkness," Shari answered.

"Like the sun disappearing," Claudia said.

"You guys go." Del stepped out of their way. "I'll get Ken and we'll follow."

Two minutes later, Stone pulled out of the parking lot, praying they'd arrive before anything got too bad, and that Randi would have enough sense to get the girl and her father out of there at the first sign of danger.

In the back seat, Shari alternated between trying to get through to 'Randi's cell and the house phone. All she got were out of service messages.

Frogs everywhere. What the hell did that mean? Stone had no idea, but it couldn't be good.

He pressed down a little harder on the gas pedal.

CHAPTER TWELVE

Hastings Mills, NY, July 16th, one year ago

Despite Randi's warning, nothing could have prepared Stone for what they found when they arrived at the Rawlingses' house.

It was covered in frogs.

On the roof. On the porch. Turning the lawn into a moving sea of green. The car slid from side to side across a carpet of them as he pulled into the driveway and slammed on the brakes.

Shari jumped out of the car before Stone turned the engine off, recording everything with a camcorder. Claudia followed, taking pictures with a digital camera. Stone slipped and slid on squashed bodies and slimy backs as he hurried to the front steps. Halfway there, the door opened and Randi Zimmerman appeared.

"Thank God. Abigail's freaking out." Randi's wide eyes told them Abigail wasn't the only one.

"How long ago did this start?" Stone jumped as a large green amphibian fell off the roof and hit his shoulder. Others dangled from the overflowing gutter.

"A couple of minutes before I called you. Just a few at first, and then thousands of them, all at once. Like the house was being fucking bombed. Hitting the roof so hard you couldn't hear anything else. Then it stopped, right before you got here."

Stone looked around. Dozens of frogs had left the property, hopping into the road and adjoining yards. A few neighbors had gathered across the street to stare, the adults holding back their children from getting too close. The kids didn't look frightened, just excited. A couple of them had their cell phones out.

"Let's get everyone inside," Stone said. "I don't want any of us ending up on the news. Or YouTube."

"I think that ship has fucking sailed."

"Great." Stone followed Randi inside.

The house was dark as dusk and cold as a morgue. All the shades and curtains had been closed. Curt and his daughter huddled on a couch in the living room, Abby's face buried in her father's chest and his arms around her, holding tight to her trembling form. Curt looked up at Stone but there was nothing accusatory in his gaze, just fear and resignation. Stone understood it. Their problem had just gotten exponentially worse if it wasn't confined to the inside of the house.

"Stone!"

At the sound of Claudia's shout, Stone ran back to the door. The twins stood on the porch, staring out at the driveway, where the van had just pulled in. At first, Stone couldn't see why that would freak them out. Then he noticed it wasn't the van, it was the yard that had their attention.

The frogs were disappearing.

All of them. The ones in the grass, the ones on the steps. The crushed and smeared ones on the driveway. You couldn't see it happen – they didn't fade away or dissolve – but each time you blinked or looked away and then back again, there weren't as many as before. Del got out and approached the house, frowning as he glanced left and right at the vanishing amphibians.

"What the hell...?" Stone's words trailed off as he stared at the empty yard. Across the road, the handful of people who'd been watching looked equally stunned, their wide eyes and open mouths obvious even at a distance. One of them, a gray-haired man dressed in blue work pants and matching shirt, crossed the street and approached the house.

Halfway there, the back of his head exploded in a spray of blood and he fell over.

One of the watchers screamed and pointed. Stone took a step

forward, intending to help the man, who lay on the lawn, his body twitching. Claudia grabbed his arm and held him back.

"No!"

Something hit the porch roof with a loud *thump!*

At the same time, several fist-sized gray shapes landed on the ground in front of them. It took Stone a moment to identify them.

Rocks.

"We need to get inside," Claudia whispered. She had the camera to her eye but her hands shook.

Something the size of a toaster struck the top of Zimmerman's car with a sound like a cannon going off. The roof caved in and the windshield shattered. The thunderous crash echoed through the still air and sent the onlookers running for the safety of their own homes.

"Move!" Del ran up the steps and pushed Stone and the twins toward the door. A drumroll of impacts against the wood spurred them on. Inside the house, Randi, Curt, and Abigail stood in the center of the living room, their faces ghostly in the dim light. A heavy object landed on the roof, sending vibrations through the house. Abigail cried out. Stone's thoughts raced as he considered different options for keeping everyone safe. Rocks were very different than frogs. They could easily smash through windows and ceilings.

And kill.

"Ken!" Del went for the door but it swung shut. He grabbed the handle but it wouldn't budge. He cursed and pounded at it.

"He's okay," Randi said, looking out the front window. "He's in the van with the doors shut."

"What's happening?" Curt asked.

Stone didn't answer. "The basement. Everyone get down there, now. Del, call Ken on his phone and tell him to stay put until we say it's okay."

Stone led them into the kitchen, where the basement door stood open, the entrance a black square of mystery that made him nervous despite knowing they had to put as much wood and plaster between them and the supernatural missiles as possible. More struck the house now, the drumroll morphing into a *ratatatat* of machine-gun fire. A window shattered somewhere upstairs. Abigail burst into tears.

Stone reached into the darkness and felt for the light. As soon as it went on, he herded everyone down. At the bottom, he looked around the long room, checking for windows and feeling a bit of relief when he saw there weren't any, only a smaller set of steps that led up to a pair of angled metal panels, which he assumed opened into the backyard.

"Over here," he told the others, guiding them to the center of the basement. The cinder block walls muted the sounds of the rock deluge outside to dull thuds and thumps. "We'll be safe here until it's over." He lowered himself to the cement floor. The others took seats around him. The hard floor was uncomfortable but the cool, damp air provided a welcome relief from the outside heat.

A tremendous *BANG!* made them all jump, and several people gasped.

"The cellar doors," Curt told them. "They're steel. They'll hold."

Another projectile clanged on the doors, this one not as loud. Abigail whimpered softly.

"How long do you—"

Randi's words cut off as the lights went out.

SECTION TWO OBSESSION

Los Angeles, Present Day

Excerpt from **Good Morning with Josh and Jenny**

Jenny Durso: "Stone, was this the first case of demonic possession you've ever investigated?"

Stone Graves: "Jenny, that's something I've wondered about for the past year, the entire time I was writing this book. Because now I just don't know. The line between the paranormal and the demonic is way more blurred than I ever imagined. For most of my life, despite all the strange things I've seen, I never believed in demons. Or even Heaven and Hell. Everything weird had a basis in science, whether that was an unknown type of energy or an unknown life-form. After something like this, you find yourself thinking back to other events and wondering if you really experienced what you thought you did."

Durso: "How so?"

Stone: "Well, for instance, poltergeists and haunted houses. I always believed they were caused by different energy forces. Leftover bits of the energy that is inside our brains, which science has shown can have tremendous power and unusual abilities, like telekinesis, telepathy, astral projection. That's not supernatural stuff, although we call it that. They're simply areas of science we don't understand."

Josh Black: "The way people in the Middle Ages thought science was magic."

Stone: "Exactly. But after what happened, I learned a lot about demons and possession, and I started to re-examine everything I'd ever believed."

Durso: "Can you give us examples?"

Stone: "I never knew demons could attract ghosts and poltergeists like a magnet, and influence their actions. Or possess inanimate objects. Or that a demon can possess a body, a soul, or both. That some demons torment the body they take over, while others use that body to torment others. What we think of as psychotic episodes might be a demon revealing itself and then hiding again."

Durso: "Like a parasite."

Stone: "Yes. It's no coincidence that one of the types of possession, as classified by the Church, is termed infestation."

Black: "You mentioned in your book that it wasn't the first time you witnessed an exorcism. And that something went wrong the last time too."

Stone: (short pause) "That was a long time ago, but yes. Someone died that night also."

Durso: "It must be hard when that happens."

Stone: "Harder than anything. If I'd known what would happen in Hastings Mills, I'd have never…." *(pauses, wipes a hand across his face)*

Black: "Maybe this is a good time for a commercial."

CHAPTER THIRTEEN

Hastings Mills, NY, July 16th, one year ago

Bang!

Ken Webb huddled under one of the consoles inside the van, his hands over his ears.

He'd been about to start unpacking the new equipment when the old man had toppled over in the yard, the back of his head exploding in a spray of blood and bone. Ken hadn't needed to hear Del and Stone shouting for everyone to take cover. He dove into the van, his arms curled over his head, as more rocks fell from the sky. He'd pulled the doors shut, but not before a rock the size of a peach pit smashed into the back of his head and another caught his shoulder. Stars filled his vision but he managed to lock the doors right before something much larger hit the metal with a resounding *clang!*

He'd fallen into one of the chairs, his bruises and cuts melding into a body-wide agony that left him gasping as the gravel hail battered the van's roof with deafening force. Dents appeared in the ceiling, evidence of the storm's destructive power. His phone rang and Del shouted at him to stay inside. He tried to answer but the hammering of rock on metal drowned him out. Glass shattered as stones came through the windshield and that's when he'd scooted under the workbench, terrified the larger stones might pierce the steel of the roof.

The barrage seemed to go on forever. He screamed but couldn't hear his own voice. There was only the thunderous drumming of stones bombarding metal.

Time lost all meaning, but eventually the onslaught diminished, tapering off until only the echo of the tumult remained.

After waiting a few minutes to be sure the deluge had ended, he was about to get up when furious laughter erupted all around him and the van shook so hard it sent boxes and tools tumbling to the floor. A freezing wind swept through, ripe with the odors of putrescent flesh and raw sewage. Ken gagged and vomited up his breakfast. The reek of death grew worse despite the rising wind, causing his eyes to water and forcing him to take shallow breaths. The foul air crawled down his throat and coated his lungs, overpowering the taste of puke in his mouth. All the while, the insane laughter continued to vibrate everything until he felt sure it came from inside his skull.

Ken cried out for God to have mercy on him and curled into a ball, knees tucked to his chest.

And then something touched his neck.

Something hot.

"How long has he been this way?"

Reverend Gregory Socha stood in the hallway outside Pete Telles' bedroom. Pierre and Dorothy were with him, both of them wearing identical hollow-eyed, pallid masks of exhaustion.

"A week," Pierre said. Long enough for the lump on his skull to fade away, but not for the memory of that night to disappear. A year wouldn't be long enough. Maybe not even a lifetime.

Socha nodded and continued watching the boy. Pete sat naked on his bed, superhero coloring books and crayons spread out in front of him. According to the parents, he'd spent the whole morning using the black and red crayons to turn each person on each page into a demon. Red eyes, black horns, scowling, fanged faces. Some had clawed hands, others coiling tentacles. Then he'd use the orange crayon to cover the page in simple but realistic flames.

"The doctor said he's fine physically. A brain scan showed no tumors and his blood work came back completely normal. He also ran some psychological tests."

"And what were his thoughts?" Socha asked.

"He couldn't find anything wrong either. Pete answered all his questions exactly how you'd expect a first grader to. Nothing out of the ordinary. Of course, that was before this started." Pierre motioned at his son. "So he recommended we see a child psychologist, and we thought rather than see some stranger, maybe you could help."

Although he'd closed his practice several years earlier to focus more on youth and family counseling, his former occupation was no secret in the parish. "Yes. Well, let me see if he'll talk to me. Why don't you give me a few minutes alone with him?"

"Sure, Father. C'mon, hon." Pierre took his wife by the elbow and led her down the hall.

Socha watched the boy for another minute, mentally deciding on how to initiate a conversation. Although he knew the Telleses as parishioners at St. Luke's Lutheran Church, he'd hardly spoken more than a few words with them over the years. He also hadn't worked a child as young as Pete in longer than he cared to admit.

Time to get back on the horse.

He cleared his throat and stepped into the room.

"Hello, Pete. Can I sit down?"

The boy looked up, his brown eyes clear and focused. "Hello, Reverend Socha."

Socha paused in pulling over the small chair from the corner. How had the boy known his name? Then he remembered the Telleses had been bringing the boy to church for a year now.

He sat down. "So, what are you drawing today?"

"Friends of mine."

"Uh-huh." A shiver ran down Socha's back. He wondered what questions the child psychologist had asked that he couldn't determine the boy was obviously troubled in some way.

Don't forget, he wasn't drawing demons then. Just having bouts of angry behavior.

"Do your friends have names?"

"Of course. Mammon. Belphegor. Lucifer." Pete flipped through the pages, tapping on pictures. As he spoke, his voice grew lower, rougher. "Leviathan. Berith."

Socha's blood went cold. *Demons! He's naming demons.*

"Beelzebub. Astaroth." Pete growled the words, the vowels drawn out and phlegmy, the consonants sharp, each 's' stretched into a hiss.

"Stop it." Socha didn't want to hear any more.

"But, Reverend, you asked, and my friends so want to meet you. Verrine, Gressil, Soneillon." The pages flew by and Socha saw the boy's fingers didn't even touch them.

"Enough!"

"Satan!" Pete's shout shook the walls, his voice deeper and louder than Socha's. The reverend jumped away as Pete stood and stared at him. Red welts covered the boy's torso and legs, the angular shapes of ancient letters and symbols. A putrid stench filled the air.

"Go home, Reverend Socha. Go back to your house and pray to your god, the god of the weak. Kneel before your Christ and lick his ass like a dog."

The coloring book flew up and struck Socha in the chest. Smoke rose where the pages touched cloth and Socha cried out, beating at the smoldering areas while the names he'd heard whirled around in his brain.

Lucifer, Mammon, Leviathan, Beelzebub, Satan, Belphegor. Six of the seven princes of Hell, representing Pride, Greed, Envy, Gluttony, Wrath, Sloth. The only one missing was Asmodeus, the demon of Lust. He didn't recognize many of the other names, but he had no doubt they were just as evil.

Someone pounded on the door and rattled the knob. "Reverend! What's going on? Reverend Socha!"

The door swung open and Pierre Telles stumbled into the room, his wife a step behind. Socha turned to point at their son, to tell them the awful truth, that he'd been possessed by a demon.

Pete lay on his stomach, his skin pale but unmarked, scribbling in his coloring book as if nothing had happened.

Pierre frowned and looked at the deceptively innocent scene. "I thought I heard shouting."

Socha glanced from father to son and back again. Anything he said would sound like the ravings of a madman, even after what the Telleses had witnessed on their own. It was a big leap from mental illness to demonic possession, and the Telleses had called him for a medical diagnosis, not because they suspected a supernatural presence.

"Let me do some research," he said, his mind already making a list of what to bring the next time. Holy water, Bible, Eucharist wafers. "I'll come back tomorrow to see how he's doing and let you know what I find."

"Thank you, Reverend." Pierre shook his hand.

Socha said his goodbyes, guilt threatening to force him into blurting out what he'd experienced. How could he leave the Telleses in the house with that…thing? Fear kept him silent. The fear of being thought crazy. The fear of facing the demon without any preparation. And a new worry was already creeping in. What if he'd hallucinated the entire episode? Experienced some sort of breakdown after seeing the child's blasphemous drawings. Possibly even suffered a stroke of some kind.

By the time he pulled into his driveway, Socha found himself wondering if he should make an appointment with his doctor, or see a psychologist himself. He'd never taken the whole idea of demons, of possession, seriously. Why now? Because a child exhibited antisocial tendencies?

It seemed ridiculous when you really thought about it.

As a psychologist himself, he knew better than anyone how the mind could play tricks.

His thoughts still in a whirl, he opened the door and hung his keys on the hook. The empty house gave its usual sterile, cold greeting. *Maybe that's the problem.* A delayed reaction to Julie and the kids moving out. God knew he'd been under a lot of stress the last two months because of the separation. Not to mention trying to pay the bills and child support with his lousy salary.

"I don't need a shrink. I need a beer and a good fuck."

He couldn't do anything about the fuck – Hastings Mills was a small town and the local pastor certainly couldn't go around picking up women in bars, not if he wanted to keep his flock – but he definitely could do something about the beer.

Two six-packs waited in the refrigerator. He hadn't touched them, or any other alcohol, since Julie walked out. Part of his promise to her. No more booze, no more gambling. If he could stay sober for three months, she'd consider coming back.

"Guess what?" he said, opening the bottle. "How's she gonna know?"

The first sip went down his throat like an icy river. God, he'd forgotten how good a cold beer could taste! The second felt even better. He sighed as his tensions began to melt away. Sometimes you just needed the simple things. A couple of beers, sit in front of the TV, and watch a ballgame. Was that too much to ask?

Apparently, since she made me stop. Sure, I got out of control there for a while, but a man needs a way to relieve the pressure. Especially with what amounted to two jobs on top of having the kids underfoot all the time.

"Screw you, Julie," he said, toasting the air with a second bottle. "Tonight I cut loose. And you'll be none the wiser."

He sat down and turned on the TV. No games, of course. Just his luck. All those damned channels he paid for and never a thing worth watching. Instead, he pulled out the laptop. Might as well look into Pete's issues.

"Kid's probably just nuts. All kids are these days. Ten years from now he'll be shooting up a mall somewhere." Still, he'd made a promise. And it wasn't like he had anything better to do.

The laptop woke up and a picture of him and Julie appeared. Dressed in t-shirts and shorts, standing at the edge of Allegany reservoir. The summer after they'd been married, before Marty and Debra came along. Hard to believe it was only five years ago. They'd been so happy. Smiling at the camera. He remembered the day like it just happened. The church picnic. Walking the hiking trails.

What they'd done behind a large outcropping of rocks.

Just thinking about it made him horny. They'd gone at it like rabbits, practically tearing each other's clothes off. And she'd let him do something that day she'd never allowed again.

Take pictures.

His hand automatically moved the cursor over the file named *Sermon Ideas*. He'd promised Julie he'd delete the photos. But he'd never intended to. Over the years, he'd returned to them now and then, whenever he needed reminding of how things had been before the twins. When they'd both had perfect bodies and no worries, and she'd shared his lust for life.

Socha clicked the icon and the first of the six images came up. Julie with her t-shirt off, her bra in one hand. Her breasts, perky and firm, milky white in the afternoon sun.

She should be here right now. He slipped one hand into his pants. With his other, he clicked on the next picture. Julie leaning against the rocks, wearing nothing but plain white panties. His hand moved faster.

Click.

Naked, her smile both teasing and embarrassed.

He paused and undid his pants. Slid them down to his ankles.

A piece of paper fell out of his pocket.

He went to kick it away and it unfolded by itself, revealing a picture of Spider-Man covered in red and brown crayon, crude fangs filling multiple mouths and four horns jutting from his head. Below the picture, in orange, was a single word.

Asmodeus.

The laptop tumbled to the floor as Socha leaped up. The page from the coloring book flared brightly, crayon flames igniting, the page browning in their wake. The rotten-egg stink of sulfur and ash brought tears to his eyes and burned his nose.

The paper disappeared. Black flakes floated in the air and settled on the carpet.

All real! It had all been real.

The laptop speaker crackled and he stepped back. On the screen, the topless picture of Julie came alive. She walked closer, still smiling. In the background, the trees waved in the summer breeze.

"You pathetic loser." Julie's voice crackled from the speaker. "I knew you couldn't do it. Couldn't stop drinking. Not even for the kids. Not even for me. You could have all this." She ran her hands down her body. Shook her hips. "But you'd rather sit home with your beer and jerk off. I'm never coming home, Gregory. In fact, I'm already fucking someone else."

A naked man appeared, sporting a giant erection. He put his arms around Julie and pulled her into an embrace that became a long, deep kiss. When it ended, she turned to the camera again.

"Goodbye. Don't call me."

The last Socha saw of her was the stranger laying her down on the grass and positioning himself between her legs.

Then the screen went blank.

Socha stared at the laptop for several minutes, a single thought running through his head over and over.

She's gone. She's really gone.

It's my fault.

Eventually he went back into the kitchen. Opened the refrigerator and took out the rest of the six-pack. Poured the bottles out and filled them with bleach. Returned to the living room and sat down.

And began to drink.

CHAPTER FOURTEEN

Hastings Mills, NY, July 16th, one year ago

Stone wiped clammy sweat from his forehead and wondered how much longer he could keep everyone from freaking out.

The constant banging of rocks on the metal doors had everyone near breaking point. They'd only been trapped in the basement for ten minutes but it felt like ten hours. Even though they'd moved to the far side of the long room, the ceaseless bombardment made conversation impossible and even thinking had become difficult.

They'd gathered in a close circle around the tiny flashlight Del always carried, the dim glow acting as a weak tether to sanity for the group.

Another rock clanged off the panels and Abby's sobs grew in volume. Her nonstop crying grated on Stone's nerves. He felt like slapping the little brat's mouth shut and—

Stone rubbed his eyes. *What the hell is wrong with you? The girl is scared, for god's sake.* He looked up and found Claudia and Shari staring at him. Shari's lips puckered in disgust like she'd just caught him picking his nose, but Claudia seemed confused. He turned away and took a deep breath. The pounding in his skull had reached the point where it became indistinguishable from the constant onslaught outside. He was tempted to go upstairs, just to escape the metallic percussions, but there'd been more than a few crashes and thuds up there, a sure sign that some of the falling rocks had gotten through the windows or walls. He had no desire to end up flattened and dead.

Like that man on the lawn. How will we explain that to the police?

Something cold touched his leg and he jerked. Randi leaned toward him. Her mouth moved but Stone couldn't hear the words over the constant pounding. He motioned to his ear and she moved closer.

"...said I think it stopped!"

Stone frowned. Stopped? He could still hear the relentless beat of rock on wood and ground, a hellish drumming that....

Wasn't there.

Once he concentrated, he realized the only sounds were the thudding of his own headache and a ringing in his ears.

Had it stopped? Was it safe for them to leave the basement?

Someone had to check.

He noticed them all looking at him. Randi. Shari and Claudia. Del. Even Curt, staring at him over his daughter's head.

I guess it's me. Isn't that just great?

Stone took the flashlight from Del and stood up.

"I'm going upstairs," he said. The others stared. Del shook his head and tapped his ear. Stone pointed up and then made his way to the stairs, his muscles stiff from sitting on the damp, cold floor.

Climbing the steps filled him with mounting dread. Each one brought him closer to the potential for having his skull crushed. His free hand clutched the banister in a death grip, partly from anxiety and partly because his headache had grown so bad it was making him dizzy.

At the top, Stone put his ear against the door, listening in vain for any signs of rockfall. The thudding of his pulse and the ringing in his ears drowned out all other sounds. He gave a silent curse, knowing he'd have no idea of imminent peril unless something landed right next to the door.

Or came through it.

"Fuck it." He pushed the door open but remained in the stairwell, counting to thirty. When nothing happened, he peered into the kitchen.

Although the power was out, enough light streamed through the windows to make the flashlight unnecessary. He turned it off and made a slow inspection of the room.

The damage was worse than he'd imagined. Shards of glass sparkled on the counter and the floor near the sink from a broken window. Something, maybe the same rock that had come through the window, had smashed through the back of a chair and dented a wall. Several floor tiles were shattered.

He moved across the hall to the living room, where more broken windows let in a warm breeze from outside. Stepping around the rocks littering the floor, he approached a window from the side and peered out, ready to duck back at the slightest sign of danger.

When he saw the yard, he couldn't believe it.

Craters of all sizes, from a few inches wide to a foot in diameter, pockmarked the ground, turning it into a lunar landscape. The driveway looked just as bad, and Randi's car had been battered beyond repair.

The man who'd been struck down earlier was barely recognizable as human, his body covered in blood and most of his head pulverized.

Stone shuddered, all too aware that it could have been any one of them – or all of them – if they hadn't retreated to the basement.

"Oh god."

Stone turned and found Claudia and Shari standing behind him, their faces identical masks of horror. He knew the reason. At the age of fourteen, the Brock sisters had experienced a hail of rocks at the group home where they'd been living. And while it hadn't been anywhere near as bad as what they'd just endured, it had been bad enough. A visiting priest had lost an eye and the media had hounded them so relentlessly because of their notorious reputation that they'd eventually run away for good.

"Claudia. Shari." He approached them slowly, the way he would a terrified fawn trapped in a garage. "This isn't because of you."

They nodded in unison.

"We know," Shari said.

"We can feel the difference," Claudia finished.

"Feel it how?" Stone asked. It wasn't often either of them proffered information without being asked. Especially without entering a trance first.

"When we were young, we didn't understand that the power—"

"Came from us," Claudia completed the sentence. "We thought something wanted to—"

"Make contact." Shari chewed her lip for a moment before continuing. "Spirits. Because sometimes we saw…things. But today—"

"There's nothing but anger," Claudia finished.

"Evil."

"The bad thing coming."

"Death."

"Death? Who's dying?" Randi asked. Stone motioned for her to be quiet and then turned his attention back to the twins. It was too late, though. They both gave Randi cold stares before turning and exiting the room hand in hand.

"Dammit." Stone had hoped to get more out of them. Instead, now he had more questions and no answers.

"Ken!" Del pushed past them and ran out the door toward the ruined van.

Oh, hell! I forgot about him. Stone followed as fast as he could.

But first he made sure to get his phone out and open the camera app.

San Ysidro, CA, July 16th, one year ago

"Good morning, Father." The portly woman behind the desk of the El Dorado Apartments smiled as Rob Lockhart crossed the tiny, outdated lobby and headed for the stairs. He gave her a half-hearted smile and a wave, his thoughts already on the bottle of vodka in his knapsack and the prospect of drinking away the stinking mess his life had become.

Warm, damp air and the pungent odor of mildew greeted him when he opened the door. He turned the balky air conditioner up to high and stripped to his underwear before lying down on the bed and opening the bottle. As much as he wanted to chug the whole thing, he allowed himself only two sips and then screwed the top back on. It had to last him a couple of days.

The money he made from his tent meetings, plus the little he squeezed from the cleansings and exorcisms he performed whenever the chance presented itself, barely paid for gas, food, and the rent on his shitty flophouse. Even buying booze on the other side of the border got expensive when you drank the way he did. He wished he could stop. The drinking helped him keep his demons at bay, but he always worried he might go too far and black out again....

No, he couldn't afford that. Not when he didn't have the Church protecting him anymore. His next arrest, all his records would become public.

The prospect of twenty years in prison was awful enough to keep even a drunken sinner like him semi-sober.

The dusty TV offered twelve channels, providing him with the options of news, soap operas, or game shows. After going through the list twice, he settled for *Let's Make a Deal* and lowered the volume to background noise level. Another sip from the bottle and he turned on his iPad, with the intention of slipping into the dark web for a bit and viewing some videos he'd never dare access through a traceable connection.

Hopefully, masturbation and booze would put him to sleep until dinner. Then he could eat and repeat the process over again.

Quite a life you've made for yourself, Rob.

The voice of his college-aged self dripped with sarcasm, like always. Along with guilt, self-loathing, and depression, it had become one of his constant companions, always ready to remind him of his many failings.

He took another swig of cheap booze and went to click play on an amateur clip titled 'Asian Girl Loses Virginity at 8th Grade Dance' when his tablet chimed, signaling an incoming search result. His finger paused over the play button.

His shameful release could wait a few minutes.

Proud of his small victory over the demon of lust living inside him, he opened the message from the search alert program that ran continually in the background. He'd set up the app to seek out stories of the weird and paranormal, and over time he'd come to both appreciate and regret it. It definitely made his life easier in the sense that he no longer had to spend hours each day combing through weird news sites or rely on attendees at his preaching events to approach him with their problems, but he'd also never realized how many reports of ghosts, demons, monsters, possession, and religious miracles occurred each week. For a while he'd kept a file of the most outlandish ones, intending to publish them in a book someday, and then he'd tossed it when he finally admitted he'd never have the ambition to follow through.

Video: Rain of frogs falls from clear sky. A link to a Reddit page followed. He clicked it, already rolling his eyes. People loved to portray rains of frogs or fish as some kind of divine event, but in reality they were almost always due to freak weather phenomena, usually a miniature cyclone burst that picked them up and then dropped them a few miles away.

Posted by jules21

2 hours ago

Check this shit out! It's raining frogs in some town!

The video came on. A road, and on the other side of it a wide lawn, the grass browned by summer heat. An old house sat well back from the street, at the end of a gravel driveway. Streaks of grayish brown obscured the details of the house. Rob's first thought was a heavy sun shower.

Then the camera tilted down and zoomed in. The streaks took on a greenish cast. And there were objects hitting the ground and bouncing.

Frogs.

All sizes. Rob knew nothing about amphibians but they looked like different kinds.

Within seconds, they were piled atop each other in the grass and on the driveway. The camera aimed back at the house, where things fell off the roof and tumbled down the front stairs. From a distance, they could have been rocks, but the camera kept moving around, zooming in and out, showing first the frogs and then the image of the property caught in the bizarre rain.

A rain that stopped at each side of the yard and at the edge of the road, as if contained within invisible walls.

The video came to an end and Rob replayed it. Then watched it a third time, paying attention to the cloudless sky. Although impossible to say for sure, it seemed like the frogs just appeared out of nowhere. After saving the link, he returned to the comments.

Where did it happen?

In upstate NY. A town called Hastings Mills.

Rob sat up. It couldn't be. What were the odds?

He reread the post again.

Hastings Mills.

Just seeing the name sent cold waves of dread through him, accompanied by memories he'd hoped never to revisit again.

Kylie floating through the air….

Booze and porn forgotten, Rob typed in additional search terms, all the while hoping there'd be a logical explanation and he wouldn't have to return to the town he'd grown up in.

Yet deep down, he had a terrible feeling God had finally sent him the message he'd both prayed for and hoped would never come.

CHAPTER FIFTEEN

Hastings Mills, NY, July 16th, one year ago

The van was battered to hell, but it hadn't been crushed like Randi's car.

Stone approached it carefully, filming everything. The lawn around it looked like a missile test site, and he knew that pictures and video of it would go viral in hours, if they hadn't already. People still stood across the street, although farther away this time. And it wouldn't be long until the police showed up, full of questions and not-so-veiled accusations of publicity stunts. The dead man, along with the stones and frogs, would bring a bright spotlight on the whole team, which would give them some nice publicity but also make his job a lot harder.

Right now he couldn't worry about that. His main concern was Ken Webb. The back doors of the van hung open and he heard Del shouting Ken's name. He put one foot on the bumper and paused as frigid air washed over him.

Something's wrong here.

Every shadow seemed alive, twisting and moving at the corners of his vision but stopping as soon as he looked right at them. A peculiar sensation grew inside him, familiar and yet he couldn't put it into words. Not quite fear, not quite nervousness, although there were aspects of both. A sensation of being watched. Yet other than Del's wide shoulders, he couldn't see anyone.

Then it came to him. He'd experienced the same impression before. Twice, to be exact.

The funerals of his mother and father.

They'd died two years apart, one from congestive heart failure and the other from cancer. On both occasions he'd spent time alone with the bodies in the funeral home, before the other mourners arrived for the wakes.

And the feeling he had now was the same one he'd had when entering those viewing rooms, staring across the expanse of empty chairs to the casket on the other side.

I'm in the presence of Death.

He had no other way to describe it. Every sense felt heightened. Like a primitive man peering into a dark cave, his flesh tingled and the hairs on his arms stood up. Did Webb lie ahead of them somewhere, his lifeless body shattered and bloody, or did the phantasm that had been bedeviling the Rawlingses lurk nearby, ready to finish what it had started?

Death, yes, but he had no idea if it was past, present, or future Death.

He fought against the urge to turn and run, sprint down the driveway as fast as he could and put all the dangers behind him, just return to his nice, safe home in California and his job of exposing charlatans. The things happening around Abigail Rawlings were real, and getting stronger. It was already worse than anything he'd witnessed in the dark confines of the Wood Hill morgue or in the musty bedroom of a North Carolina boy. And just like both those places, someone had died.

Maybe more than one someone.

He didn't want to be next. But at the same time, the desire to prove the existence of the supernatural, to document it for all the world to see, still burned inside him, just as strong as his fear.

"He's here!" Del shouted, bending under a counter.

Stone Graves lifted his phone and stepped forward.

Claudia Brock panned her camera down the upstairs hallway. Rocks of varying sizes had broken through windows in several places, denting the walls and floor.

Shari emerged from one of the bedrooms, and Claudia didn't need any special powers to know her thoughts. The look on her face told Claudia that similar damage had occurred in most of the rooms.

And worse things were yet to come.

She'd seen it in their dreams, every night since they'd arrived in Hastings Mills. Vague impressions of shadowy figures, a feeling of impending danger, images of endless burning plains. Dark, rumbling laughter that dripped with malice and evil.

The smart thing would be to tell Stone. Yet she held off. He'd never give up an investigation, especially one that looked like a career maker, because of some dreams or premonitions.

But deep down, she knew that was an excuse to avoid the truth. That something seemed…wrong about him. He wasn't himself. He'd developed a short temper and he'd been giving off some nasty vibes. Shari sensed it too. So they'd decided to wait until either he started acting normal again or their dreams grew clear enough that they could see the danger.

—*What if the danger is him?*—

Claudia glanced at her sister, more than a little guilty about having her deepest fear exposed. Stone was sensitive to the other side, even if he refused to believe it. If something had taken advantage of that to exert influence over him….

No. It was just stress. Poltergeists didn't posses people.

—*Let's hope you're right.*—

Claudia frowned, annoyed at Shari's eavesdropping on her thoughts. Shari shrugged and walked away, heading downstairs. Claudia remained behind, her worries not eased in the least. She knew she should talk to Stone. Whatever was happening, it was strong, stronger than anyone realized, and totally unpredictable. He needed to know—

—*Yes.*—

Shari, still listening. Fine, then.

—*You know what that means.*— Claudia responded.

She felt Shari's reluctant nod of agreement. It wasn't a decision to take lightly, because it meant not only discussing things they preferred to keep private but also agreeing to use their abilities in a more direct and open fashion, something they loathed doing.

Using their powers often meant attracting attention, both from the real world and the other side. Rarely did it turn out well for them. They'd learned that the hard way as children and adults.

Then she remembered the man who'd died outside.

If they could do something to prevent further deaths, they couldn't turn their backs.

Memories of past mistakes weighing heavily on her mind, Claudia went downstairs, where Randi and Abigail watched Curt inspect the damage in the kitchen. Shari was shooting a close-up of one of the rocks when she jerked upright, her mouth open and eyes wide.

At the same time, a sudden urge jolted Claudia. *Go outside.*

"Everyone, outside! Now!" Claudia's shout came simultaneous to her sister's and the others looked back and forth, startled by the dual exclamations.

"Hurry!" Shari grabbed Curt's arm and pulled him toward the back door. Claudia did the same with Abigail and Randi.

"Hey!" Curt pulled back. "We ain't goin' nowhere 'til the cops get here and—"

"There's no time!" Shari renewed her urging.

The feeling of impending doom hit Claudia so hard she stumbled and almost fell. "It's not over," she gasped, still making her way to the door.

"You're wrong," Randi said. "Rockfalls related to poltergeist activity never occur more than once in a—"

"It's coming!" Shari cried out. She abandoned her efforts to herd Curt and ran out the door. Claudia tried to follow but Randi and Abigail stood in her way, forcing her to push them forward.

"Run!" she screamed at them, desperate to put as much distance between herself and the house as she could, a task made dangerous by the hundreds of holes pockmarking the yard. Across the street, a group of people stood by the road while two more climbed out of a white news van.

She'd only gotten a few yards from the porch when a high-pitched whistling noise reached her, distant at first but rapidly growing louder until she couldn't hear anything else. Several of the onlookers pointed at her. A woman in a blue suit holding a microphone shouted something but her words were lost to the deafening *screeeeEEEEE!* battering her ears.

Her foot caught on a rock and she pitched forward, hitting the ground on her shoulder and tumbling over. She came to a stop facing the house just as a gray object crashed down, sending debris in all directions. Something struck her head and the world went dark.

The last thing she heard was someone screaming.

Stone's heart clenched at the sight of Ken Webb's body curled and unmoving in the knee well of a console.

Oh no. Fuck.

He'd been right. Death had visited the van. And it had claimed Webb.

Then Webb's arm twitched and Stone's curse changed to an exclamation of surprise.

He knelt down next to Del, who ran his hands across Webb's body and muttered the man's name over and over.

Webb appeared to have no serious injuries, although Stone's medical knowledge was so poor he had no idea what anything besides a missing limb or bleeding wound would look like. He saw a bottle of water on the floor and passed it to Del, who dabbed some on Webb's face.

"Uhhhh…." Webb's groan trailed off as he opened his eyes. "What…. No!" With a sudden intake of breath, Webb covered his face with his arms.

"Ken!" Del shook his shoulder. "Hey, baby, it's over. You're safe. Are you hurt?"

"No!" Webb shivered violently. "It was here! Laughing…it wanted me dead!"

Cold fingers danced up Stone's spine. That word again. Death.

What had Webb seen or heard? Stone's memory happily reminded him of the thing he'd witnessed in Abigail's room. Had it returned? A decidedly selfish thought intruded on the others.

Did he manage to film it for the show?

In order to find out, he had to calm Webb down so the man could talk. He pushed up next to Del so Ken could see his face.

"Ken, listen to me. It's gone now." He used a soft, reassuring tone as if speaking to a child. "Let's get you up. Can you walk?"

"Gone?" Webb looked at them, his eyes nearly bulging from their sockets.

"Gone. It's just us. Me and Del."

"I'm right here." Del took Ken's hand.

"Everything's good. Let's get you out of there." Stone took Webb's other arm and gave a tug. At first he resisted, but gentle cajoling from Del got him to slide out. When he stood up, he wavered for a second and then his balance returned.

"The others?" Webb asked. "Is everyone—?"

"They're all fine," Del said. "C'mon, we'll go inside and get you cleaned up. Are you sure you're okay?"

Webb nodded. "It was awful. This thing—"

Outside, voices shouted.

"It's coming for us!" Webb pulled free and dove back under the console. Stone bent down to pull him out but a high-pitched whistling from outside distracted him. He couldn't place it, but it sounded familiar somehow, like something he'd heard—

Like a bomb falling in a cartoon.

Or a giant rock.

"Get down!" he shouted.

A thunderous explosion rocked the van.

Seconds later, the screaming started.

Buffalo, NY, July 16th, one year ago

The boy, floating above the cot. Body writhing, arms and legs twisted into impossible shapes. Blazing white luminescence shining from his eyes and mouth.

How is this happening? Leo thought. *That was so long ago....*

In his dream, Leo watched the scene unfold again. Anibal turned and grabbed Father Sanchez by the neck. Knowing what would happen, Leo shouted, "No!"

It didn't matter. Bones cracked and Sanchez fell to the dirt floor. Face aglow in unholy light, Anibal looked at Leo.

"I told you we would meet again, Bonaventura. I am forever, and your time is coming!"

No! This is a dream, not real, not real.

Not—

Just like the night in the steamy jungle, the light grew brighter and then an explosion filled Leo's eyes. He threw his arms up and waves of heat seared his flesh. The biting stink of burning hair enveloped him. Manic laughter assaulted his ears, hammered against his brain. Louder and louder. The light changed to orange and the burning sensation grew worse. The sounds changed, growing higher, as if someone had speeded up a record. Piercing now, screeching, inhuman. Leo cried out, unable to escape the torturous dream that held him captive.

"I'm coming for you, priest! Coming for you. Coming for—"

The blazing light expanded outward, wiping out everything else. It darkened to fiery red and then to the rich, deep red of blood. The crazed laughter rose in pitch, became a bestial howling. Leo shouted for God to help him, but even in his dream he couldn't hear his own voice.

A terrible pain stabbed through his head and he screamed for mercy.

"There is no mercy. Only death!"

Everything went black.

And then the dream began again.

In the operating room, Dr. Chan Ho Sing shouted orders as the machines hooked up to Leo Bonaventura's body sounded a cacophony of alarms.

"He's coding!" a nurse called out. "Cardiac arrest!"

"Pressure's dropping fast," said another.

Ho Sing's assistant slid the crash cart over and hit the charge button. Ho Sing took the paddles and shouted for everyone to, "Clear!"

Bonaventura's body bucked as two hundred joules of energy flowed through it. Ho Sing watched the EKG monitor and then called for everyone to clear again.

On the second attempt, the line on the monitor jumped and then settled into a normal rhythm.

"He's back," one of the nurses said.

"BP's one-ten over forty," said the other. "Sinus rhythm restored."

Ho Sing wiped his arm across his head. "That was close. Okay, let's give him two ccs of—"

The alarms howled.

"BP's dropping again!"

Ho Sing cursed.

This was beginning to look like one of those cases where everything went wrong.

CHAPTER SIXTEEN

San Ysidro, CA, July 16th, one year ago

"Hail of rocks damages house in upstate New York, leaving one dead. Authorities are attributing the tragic event to a rare meteor strike."

Rob dropped his slice of pizza and grabbed the television remote to turn up the volume. He'd gone out to pick up a late lunch and just settled down to continue his internet searches when the news came on.

He immediately recognized the rock-covered property as the same one where the unnatural shower of frogs had occurred. After a moment, the video switched to an overhead image that showed a huge section of the porch missing, with wood and shingles scattered across the yard. Several windows were broken and the lawn resembled a grenade testing range, pockmarked with divots of various sizes.

The reporter continued on with the story, but Rob only half-listened. He opened a new browser on the laptop and pulled up the Reddit page where he'd first read about the weird frog deluge in Hastings Mills. Sure enough, there were multiple new postings, including footage from someone's phone camera. The point of view was so similar to the frog video from earlier that he wondered if the same person had been there all day, waiting for something else to happen.

Jules21

This is no joke. Watch to the end.

Rob clicked the video.

An older man walked into the frame and slowly started across the yard toward the house. The video dipped and shook as the person holding the phone moved. Off camera, someone asked where the hell the frogs went.

Jesus, it is *the same people*, Rob thought.

Something bounced next to the man. He glanced down.

The back of his head disintegrated.

Rob's hands jumped and the pad fell off his lap. He retrieved it and reset the video, his heart pounding.

What the hell?

He hit play and watched as the unsuspecting man tilted his head.

And died in an explosion of gore.

With a shaking finger, Rob replayed the video, this time using the advance bar instead of the play button, moving forward frame by frame.

There.

Just before the man's skull burst open, a gray, tennis-ball-sized shape appeared over him. In the next frame, it was just above his hair.

Boom.

Rob hit play. The man collapsed facedown on the ground. Fist-sized objects landed around him. Several bounced off his body. The camera turned up to the sky. Streaks of dark gray appeared out of nowhere and sped through the frame. The camera veered back to the lawn and Rob's stomach tightened at the sight of the old man lying motionless in the grass. Someone screamed, "Uncle Brian!" The gray streaks and bouncing objects increased in frequency. Several of them bounced off the far edge of the road and the camera zoomed in on them. Rocks, all of them the same dull color. From pebbles to fist-sized death bringers. Within seconds, the downfall grew so heavy he could barely make out the lawn.

The video swerved around and captured several sets of legs running. Then it ended.

"Holy shit," Rob whispered. He earmarked the webpage and went back to the TV, scrolling through channels until he found another news station covering the story. He sipped at his vodka as a reporter provided commentary from the edge of the ravaged property.

"This is Lisa Morton, live in Hastings Mills. Earlier today, this same house was the target of not one but two weird events, first when frogs fell from the sky and less than an hour ago when a hail of rocks came down, killing one man. So far, the owner of the house, Curtis Rawlings, has been unavailable for comment. The deceased man has been identified as Brian Matthews of Hastings Mills. Police are not letting anyone onto the property…."

The reporter continued to speak while the camera zoomed past her to focus on two dark-haired women as they emerged from the house to stand in the shadows of the crumpled porch. One of them shifted slightly, revealing a pale face and a bandage on her forehead. Despite the distance and small screen, Rob's heart slammed against his ribs.

No! It can't be.

A memory erupted from deep inside him. Another house, long ago.

Rocks falling everywhere. Pebbles, mostly, but a few the size of marbles and even golf balls. Bouncing off the roof. Denting the cars in the parking lot. The younger children crying while the older children attempted to comfort them.

The twin girls on the couch in the sitting room, holding hands.

Staring at him with accusing eyes.

His shame had nearly overwhelmed him that day; he'd come so close to confessing his sins to the visiting auxiliary bishop. That rain of stones hadn't been a freak meteor shower. It had been a sign from God. He knew it in his heart. With the eyes of his accusers on him, he'd stood up, ready to open the box of secrets he held and accept his punishment.

And then one of the windows shattered and a large stone had bounced off a table and struck Bishop Cooper in the face. The bishop screamed and fell to the floor, blood pouring from between his fingers.

The incredible hail ended immediately and everyone crowded around the injured man. The Brock girls ran upstairs hand in hand, but not before Rob saw their stricken faces and the tears in their eyes.

In that moment, he understood. The twins had been sent by God to be his salvation.

Except, when he woke in the morning, they were gone. He'd reported them as runaways and the police had looked for them, but he'd never seen them again.

Until now.

It couldn't be coincidence. Not with their history. He went to the station's website and watched the entire clip but they only appeared in the one shot. Then he checked the other news sites. When that turned up no additional footage, he did a search for their names: Claudia Brock+Shari Brock+Twins. Nothing, not even the story from the orphanage.

That can't be. He remembered several articles in local newspapers about the ten-year-old girls who'd been nicknamed 'the Carrie Twins' because of all the weird occurrences that happened in their vicinity.

He tried different search terms, using nicknames, towns, and phrases like 'stones from the sky' along with their names.

No results.

Someone went to an awful lot of trouble to scrub them from the internet.

The internet. That gave him an idea. He logged into the dark web and within minutes found all the old articles about the twins, the ones he remembered reading. Plus one he hadn't seen before, dated six years ago.

Nevada Diner Drenched in Flesh and Blood
By Rena Mason and James Chambers
The Eureka Gazette

Even for Nevada, this one counts as strange.

Customers at the Starlight Diner on Route 50 outside of the small town of Eureka experienced a most unpleasant surprise when, just after 6 p.m., it began to rain blood.

From a clear sky.

And just when they thought things couldn't get stranger, pieces of flesh fell on the diner.

"It started with an ordinary rain," said Patrick Freivald of Missouri, who had been eating dinner with his wife at the Starlight. "Well, not so ordinary. Not a cloud in the sky. But all of a sudden it turned red. We thought maybe there was a dust cloud nearby, and the water just picked up the color. Then someone went outside and said it was blood."

Within minutes, the building and parking lot were covered in blood and fist-sized lumps of skin and muscle. According to one witness, it was a scene of chaos.

"People were screaming. Some ran to their cars, others hid behind the counter. It was awful. And the smell...like being in a slaughterhouse."

Erinn Kemper, a waitress at the Starlight for more than thirty years, said she'd never seen anything like it. "Came out of nowhere, it did. Lasted about ten minutes and then it just stopped. Seen some weird stuff out here in the desert, but never anything like that."

Police are still looking for two more possible witnesses, Claudia Brock and Shari Brock, waitresses who were working that evening. According to the owner, Peter Salomon, the sisters walked off the job right after the bloody downpour and haven't returned.

"Can't say I blame them," he said, "but I still owe 'em a paycheck. Don't want anyone saying I ripped 'em off."

The article went on to recount other weird rains that had happened in the US since the 1800s. Rob put it aside and did some quick addition in his head. When he finished, a cold chill raised the hair on his arms and made him glad the AC in the room didn't work well.

Eleven.

The number of times the Brock twins had been involved in supernatural events as children, according to his research. The most notable had been when a green slime burned through their house and killed their foster parents. That one had brought them to him.

There'd been others, though. The falling rocks. Hail on a sunny day. A swing that caught fire. Balls of lightning chasing them down the road.

By the time he'd taken over the orphanage, the Brock twins had already gone through four sets of foster parents. After they ran away, he'd visited two of them to find out as much information as he could. Two stated 'things just didn't work out'.

When he called the third couple, they'd told him they believed 'them girls is haunted'.

The Witches of Midway.

Their faces still haunted him. Young. Innocent. Alluringly beautiful. Yet filled with a knowledge beyond their years. As if they peered into his heart and saw the wickedness that dwelled there. He'd been so sure they could cure him, that their power would transform him.

Now they were in Hastings Mills, of all places.

Kylie, floating through the air.

"Close the door, Bobby."

Rob shut off the tablet. St. Alphonse University. The place where he'd made the decision that put him on the path to the priesthood, a road that ultimately led him to the darkest depths of hell and then dragged him not into the light but at least into the gray, revealing salvation as a conceivable goal. St. Alphonse was the turning point, yes, with Hastings Mills the epicenter of all his troubles. Childhood, college, everything.

Maybe this was what the Lord had in store for me all along. My redemption lies where my problems began. A full circle, and then I'll be free.

I have to face my demons in order to banish them.

The idea terrified him. Seeing the town, the school. Reviving the nightmares that had plagued him all his life. He'd avoided Hastings Mills since graduation, leaving town and never returning once in twenty-five years. Never had to, since his family moved during his years in the seminary. But if that's what it took to rid himself of his past, to shed his sins and banish the lust poisoning his soul....

He had to do it.

Twenty minutes later, he pulled out of the parking lot and turned north toward the airport. The California heat made the blacktop shimmer and drew alcohol-tainted sweat from his pores. But although his hands trembled on the steering wheel, he didn't allow fear to weaken his resolve.

It was time to put an end to things.

His deliverance waited.

CHAPTER SEVENTEEN

Hastings Mills, NY, July 16th, one year ago

Only a purple ribbon of sky separated day and night by the time the police finally departed, leaving behind yards of yellow tape, two news vans, and a warning they'd be back the next day with more questions. When an exasperated Stone asked why, he was told in no uncertain terms that if it turned out the events of the day were arranged by his production team to help his show's ratings, they'd be charged with causing a wrongful death, so no one should think about leaving town.

With the house finally to themselves, Stone and the others gathered in the kitchen to go over the plans for the night. Before speaking, Stone took a few moments to mentally review what he planned on saying. The last few hours had been hell and the team looked shell-shocked. Claudia wore a bandage on her head where a piece of debris had caught her when the final rock had crashed through the Rawlingses' porch. No stitches, but a nice bruise was already forming. She and Shari looked paler than normal. Everyone did, actually.

Del sat shoulder to shoulder with Ken. He had hardly left his side since coaxing him from the van. It had taken almost fifteen minutes and a healthy dose of whiskey for Ken to stop shaking and give them a coherent recap of what had happened to him. Stone had filmed it all. Then he'd updated his video log of the events and made all the others do the same, before they had time to relax and regain their composure. He wanted to capture everyone's raw reactions and emotions on film.

Maybe I won't even edit it, he thought. He'd already decided that the Rawlings haunting would be more than just a single episode. *Hell, with everything that's happened so far, this could be a prime-time multi-night event.*

Which meant they had to see things through to the end, and for that to happen, he needed to make sure everyone was on board with staying. He couldn't afford to have his team flake out on him now.

Although if they did, imagine the ratings. *Haunted house so frightening Stone Graves' own team refuses to finish investigation. In tomorrow's finale, he bravely faces off alone against—*

No. They were his team, and he needed them.

With that in mind, Stone tapped his glass on the table to get their attention.

"We're all exhausted," he began. "The last couple of days have been crazy and I doubt tonight will be any easier. We've got to be on our toes, ready for anything. But we need sleep too. Tired people make mistakes, and we can't afford that, not with...whatever we're dealing with here."

"It's a demon." With his bruises and frightened eyes, Webb reminded Stone of a horse he'd once seen right after it escaped a burning stable. On the edge of panic because it still didn't believe it was safe.

"Demons aren't real." Stone knew he had to nix that idea before it grew roots. The same way he'd refused to entertain it when it popped into his own head earlier. "And they don't come and go. Does she look possessed to you?"

All eyes turned toward Abby, who surprised them by responding. She hadn't spoken since the police had left.

"You're both wrong. It's the Devil," she said, her voice soft but filled with the stubborn certainty only a child can muster. "I've seen him. In my room. You saw him too."

Stone's body gave an involuntary jerk. She'd never mentioned seeing the creature. How had she managed to keep functioning?

Lord knew he'd been unable to shake the memory of the thing he'd witnessed. To a child, it had to seem demonic.

That doesn't mean we jump to conclusions. There are all sorts of spectral beings. Ghosts. Poltergeists. Shadows.

Demons don't exist.

Besides, since when did a demon cause psychokinetic events or appear in two places at once? Manifestations like that were the modus operandi of poltergeists. Which also happened to be more common than so-called confirmed cases of possession.

What about Evan Michaels? He caught Randi looking at him and knew her thoughts mirrored his.

We never had a chance to figure out what caused his problems before that priest screwed everything up. It could have been anything.

Lots of questions, when what they needed was answers. He had to get the team focused on that, not superstitious fears. He cleared his throat.

"Listen. This isn't a demon. Think about what we've seen versus the signs of possession. Demons don't appear in multiple places at once. Demons don't cause objects to fall from the sky. Demons don't manifest outside of the possessed person's immediate space. On the other hand, poltergeists and other spectral phenomena are known to do all those things. And also move furniture, cause hot and cold spots, and even create aural and visual events. It explains everything. We're simply dealing with some sort of super-poltergeist. Or maybe multiple entities. Not a denizen of some mythical alternate world. Or the Devil," he added, giving Abby a warm but serious smile.

Instead of appearing relieved, she simply shook her head.

"You'll see," she whispered. "You'll all see. She told me."

"Hush," Curt told her, and she did. Stone wanted to ask her who 'she' was – it better not be Randi putting ideas in her head or he'd send her packing – but right then Shari pushed away from the table, her lips tightened in a grimace, and left the room. After a moment, Claudia followed her. *Damn them!* Abby's words and the twins' obvious disagreement with his assessment had done their damage.

Whatever confidence he'd started to build in the group was eroding again. Their faces showed it, ranging from fear to resignation. Time to throw them a bone.

"Hey, I'm not completely unreasonable. If we can't figure this out, then we can bring in a priest."

And I'll be right here to film that shit too. Even if I have to do it myself. If someone wants to leave, they can. It's not the military.

But maybe they'll be looking for a new job in the morning.

"Let's focus on doing this the right way. We've got video throughout the house. Ken's got some of the equipment in the van working. He and I will finish reviewing the recordings from the other night. I think the rest of you should bring blankets and pillows into the living room and we'll all sleep there tonight. And no one goes anywhere alone. Pick a buddy and pair off."

After the rest of the group left, he and Ken went out to the van, where they settled themselves in front of the one working monitor.

"Stick with the outside cams and skip everything else. I want to see who or what trashed the van."

Webb scrolled through a list of video files until he found the one he wanted.

"Here." He tapped a key. "This is one of the porch cameras, the one facing the yard. It should show us anything approaching from the back or the driveway."

An image came up on the screen, showing the van plus a wide space to either side. Rendered in shades of black, white, and gray by the infrared setting, the grainy shot seemed like a still picture because of the lack of activity. Stone glanced at the time stamp, which scrolled forward at normal speed.

"Faster," Stone said, "otherwise we'll be here all goddamned night."

Webb frowned but touched another key. The time stamp moved forward at 2x. Minutes sped by and the picture remained the same. Stone rubbed his eyes. He needed sleep. And—

A shadow darted across the screen.

"Stop! Go back."

Webb reversed it and then played the video at normal speed.

At five minutes after midnight, a dark, man-shaped form appeared from behind the house and walked at a brisk pace across the yard before disappearing behind the van. For ten minutes after that, nothing happened. Then the wraith appeared again and went back around the house.

"We've got the bastard," Stone said. "Can you zoom in on his face?"

"I'll try, but the picture's already grainy." Webb reversed the video at half speed, the shadowy figure walking backward in a herky-jerky motion until at one point he glanced toward the front of the house and the cameras mounted there. Webb stopped it and enlarged the image.

Revealing Curt Rawlings.

His eyes were shut and a hazy black aura covered him like a cloud of smoke.

"Jesus." A chill ran through Stone's body and buried itself in his guts, where it turned to a piece of ice. "Is that some kind of data glitch?"

Webb shook his head. "I don't know what the hell it is."

The ice in Stone's stomach grew from a cube to a glacier.

What if demons really did exist?

And one had already possessed Abigail's father?

Pete Telles opened his eyes and sat up in his bed. A cool breeze drifted in from the open window, ruffling the curtains and filling his room with the soft, green scents of summer. The house was silent except for the muted hum of the refrigerator downstairs and the occasional rumble of snoring from his parents' bedroom.

He climbed out of bed with his favorite toy, a Build-A-Bear named Bobo, tucked under his arm. After putting on his Yankees cap, he went downstairs to the kitchen and opened the storage cabinet where his mother kept the cleaning supplies and other household necessities. One at a time, he removed a bottle of rubbing alcohol, two cans of furniture polish, and a long butane lighter, and set them on the table.

For the next few minutes, he moved silently through the house, closing and locking all the windows on the first floor. Then he sprayed a thick layer of polish on all the tables and up the steps to the top of the staircase. After closing his parents' door, he doused polish on the floor and walls of the upstairs hallway. Downstairs, he poured the alcohol along the bottoms of the curtains and on the carpet in the living room. When the bottle was half empty, he used the rest to draw a trail into the dining room, where he took the lighter from the table and held the flame to the puddle on the floor.

A pale blue line erupted and quickly raced across the house to the curtains, which immediately burst into flames. Dark smoke rose from the carpet and began to spread as orange flared up and sparks shot through the thick strands. When the growing fire reached the areas of furniture polish, it expanded in a fury, the flickering turning into a blaze that flowed up the stairs.

Pete took Bobo from the table and went out the back door, making sure to lock it behind him. He stood at the back of the patio and watched as the reddish-orange glow in the windows grew brighter. It only took another minute before the smoke alarms kicked in, their strident cries muted by the closed windows.

Almost immediately, Dorothy's voice rang out, calling for her son. Pierre's joined in.

"Pete! Where are you? Pete!"

Their shouts continued, moving from room to room, soon mixed in with coughing as smoke filled the house. Glass shattered and flames burst through the broken windows, igniting the outside walls. More screaming from inside, frantic now, filled with pain and terror.

Dorothy's face appeared at one of the upstairs windows, covered in black, hair smoldering. Her wild eyes found Pete. He waved at her. She opened her mouth and then a wall of fire enveloped her. The window exploded and ejected her outward, a flaming missile that soared through the air and landed on the patio in a hail of broken glass. Her charred body continued to burn, filling the night with the greasy smell of roasting meat.

Pete walked around to the front and sat down in the damp grass.

When the fire department arrived, they found him hugging his bear and crying for his parents.

CHAPTER EIGHTEEN

Cleveland, OH, July 17th, one year ago

Rob Lockhart shivered as he stared at the screen of his pad.

He had no doubt something supernatural – and deadly – was happening in Hastings Mills. The internet news streams buzzed with the strange occurrences devastating the town, and it wasn't only the paranormal and weird news sites. Mainstream media covered the stories as well, although nothing had made headline material yet. That would undoubtedly come soon, though.

Especially if the incidents continued to escalate.

He read through the notes he'd taken, still amazed at what had happened in such a short amount of time. Frogs falling from the sky, and then rocks. A house badly damaged and a man dead.

And now this. Another weird occurrence, although as of yet the media hadn't linked it to the others.

A boy who somehow escaped a fire that claimed the lives of his parents. At first, it sounded like a miracle. Until you read further and noticed the subtle oddities in the story. Like the family belonging to the same church where just a couple of days earlier the pastor had killed himself by drinking bleach.

The police had ruled it a suicide based on his separation from his wife. They'd even found his laptop next to him, a picture of his ex on the screen. For the police, an obvious motive. A broken heart.

But there'd been one bit of information, in the comments section, that caught Rob's attention.

The pastor's assistant had mentioned seeing in his calendar that his last appointment before downing his poison cocktails had been with the Telles family.

The same family whose house had just burned down, leaving an orphaned boy.

Coincidence? Rob didn't think so. Not in Hastings Mills. Not with the Carrie Twins in town.

Sitting in his motel room, the four-hour last leg of his journey still ahead of him, he couldn't help wondering what would happen next.

And what else had already happened that the media didn't know about?

Rob felt sure there had to be more. Paranormal activities didn't just begin with houses getting pelted by rocks or frogs on a clear day. There would be little things first. Things people didn't notice, or didn't want to notice. Things maybe they didn't think to tell anyone about. Or they were ashamed to.

He continued his research, his pizza congealing next to his bottle of vodka. Newspapers, newswire sites, blogs, cryptozoology pages, and Reddit threads.

Nothing.

Well, not quite nothing, he amended, rubbing eyes that burned from staring at the small screen. Hastings Mills apparently had a history of bizarre occurrences, going back for decades. Murders, suicides, disappearances, packs of wild dogs racing through town, even an entire church collapsing on the day of the summer carnival.

But nothing in the last few months.

Funny that I spent half my childhood there and never knew how fucked up the town was.

He took another bite and washed the greasy cheese and dough down with a slug of vodka. *Maybe I should just call it a night and get some sleep. If I leave by eight tomorrow, I'll be in Hastings Mills by lunchtime. I can swing by the college and see if Father Bonaventura is still—*

The college.

The *Alphonse Gazette.*

He hadn't checked the campus newspaper.

His hand paused in the act of closing the pad. It would probably be a waste of time. The town paper would carry anything of importance.

It all started on that campus.

He typed in the paper's name and a link to a website popped up. No surprise there; even a small, private school like St. Alphonse usually had multiple websites, including one for the paper. What did surprise him was that even during the summer, the online edition carried new stories.

Tragic accident delays dormitory renovations.

The headline jumped out at him. He scrolled down. A man working in the attic of Dallas Hall had fallen out of a fifth-floor window. Witnesses said he'd freaked out and had a panic attack because of a cockroach.

Fifth Dallas.

Kylie. Leaping through the window to her death.

The events of that night came rushing back. The smell of the candles and the musty air. The sudden wind. The flashlights going out. The planchette flying around like a UFO. And something else… insignificant at the time, but now….

Hadn't there been some kind of bug that night too? A beetle? Or maybe…a roach?

Goose bumps ran up Rob's arms.

Two deaths. In the same room. The same way.

That was no accident.

The sense of urgency inside him expanded. He needed to speak to Father Bonaventura now; it couldn't wait until he got to the school. He looked up the directory for the theology department on St. Alphonse's website and cursed when he found Bonaventura's name with the words *Professor Emeritus* next to it, and no phone extension listed.

A quick search turned up an article in the school paper about Bonaventura's retirement. Another search gave him the phone number for Holy Gardens, where a receptionist informed him that Bonaventura was out of town. When he tried to find out more, she cited privacy rules and hung up.

Rob swiped the phone off, wishing he could slam it against the wall. Now what? Something evil had returned to the school, and was spreading into the town. He knew it as sure as he knew his own sins had stained his soul.

This is your test.

Yes. God had a plan for him. Return to where it all started and put an end to the evil once and for all.

Only then would his soul be cleansed.

Stone absently fingered a string of rosary beads with a small wooden cross at the end while he watched the split screen video feeds from the previous night on the laptop monitor. He'd gotten up early to get a head start on reviewing the files. His eyes itched from lack of sleep and his stomach burned from too much coffee, but he was wide awake.

After watching Curt make his trip to the van, he and Ken had discussed what to do next and they'd come up with a way to determine if a demon had possessed Curt or if a malevolent spirit had altered the video. Both theories seemed equally outlandish. Stone had never heard of a poltergeist or ghost doing anything to electronic equipment other than erasing it or knocking it over, but he'd also never heard of a demon possessing a person without showing any physical manifestations.

Either way, the timing of it seemed too perfect to be coincidence. The damage to the van happened just after midnight, while everyone else was occupied in Abigail's room. Try as they might, neither of them could remember Curt being around after he'd called for help. Which gave him more than enough time to sneak out and return.

In the end, the video had unnerved Stone enough that he agreed to let Ken conduct a test on Curt.

Ken had gotten the rosary and cross as a gift from a priest two seasons ago and kept them for good luck. They'd waited until everyone else fell asleep before placing it on Curt's chest. A simple experiment.

Neither of them had really known what to expect. A violent reaction? Blistered skin? According to the literature on possession, there'd be some kind of reaction if a demon resided in Curt.

He'd simply continued sleeping.

That had eased Ken's mind a bit, to the point where he grudgingly agreed Stone's theory of multiple poltergeists seemed more likely.

Still, they'd both concurred that they needed to keep watch on Curt. If something had taken him over in some way once, it might very well do it again. Or any of them.

Which was why, after a couple of hours of restless sleep, he'd given up and gone down to the kitchen. He kept thinking about the idea of multiple entities haunting the house. In all his years of paranormal investigations, he'd never heard of a single verified case like this one.

Which meant he had a publicity gold mine on his hands.

At eight, the rest of the team had wandered in, all of them grateful for an uneventful night. He'd questioned the twins and Randi about Abby's comment, and they'd all denied speaking to her about demons. However, Randi brought up something else.

"Abby mentioned a 'she' to me too," Randi said. "Right when the frog attack started. A dark lady. Said it was her invisible friend. I forgot in all the commotion. I'm going into town with them for food and plywood. You want me to ask her?"

Stone hadn't known whether to kiss her for possibly breaking the case or shout at her for not telling him sooner. An invisible friend meant there might have been years of poltergeist activity going on under Curt's nose and he never knew.

"No, let's wait until you come back. I want it all on film."

Now, with the twins running temperature checks throughout the house and Ken and Del in the van setting up the cloud backups for the new hardware, he had nothing to do but wait and watch video for the third time.

As he debated a third cup of coffee, his chair shook.

He looked up from the screen and reached for his camera. If something was about to happen....

The chair trembled again. So did his cup. He stood and the floor vibrated against his feet, this time accompanied by a low rumbling he felt as much as heard. It almost sounded like a large truck passing the house. Except the street was too far away for a truck to have that kind of effect.

Earthquake! He'd lived in California long enough to recognize one. He grabbed the table as the shaking intensified and shouts came from other parts of the house. His coffee cup bounced off the table and the sound of breaking glass and objects hitting the floor told him the few remaining items on the shelves had fallen off.

The vibrations only lasted a minute or so. Once they stopped, he ran into the living room, where he found Shari and Claudia by the window, clutching hands, their mouths tight and their eyes wide.

"Don't worry," he said. "It's just an earthquake, not another rock fall."

"No." Claudia shook her head.

Shari repeated the gesture. "It's worse."

"Worse?" Stone glanced around. He certainly hadn't expected a quake in upstate New York, but he'd experienced bigger ones in California. And the twins had been through them before too. So why were they so freaked out?

Unless….

"Oh, hell. Is it—?"

Both of the twins opened their mouths but it wasn't to answer him. The house gave a massive shudder. Pictures flew off the walls and lamps fell off both end tables. The ground didn't rumble, it roared like a hungry beast. Stone fell to his knees, sure the floor was going to open and swallow them all.

"We've got to get out of here," he gasped. He climbed to his feet and staggered to the door, spurred on by his vision of the house collapsing into a fiery pit. They had to get as far away as possible. Stone pulled the door open and nearly collided with a man standing there, his fist raised to knock.

"Jesus!" The man jerked away and his hand dropped to his gun. "Stop right there."

The twins gasped. Stone raised his hands before he recognized the man as one of the cops from the previous day.

"Look out! We have to get away from the house!"

"I said stand still." The officer, whose name tag read *Sgt. Rose*, said, "What the hell is going on?"

"Earthquake. The whole place is about to come down."

"Earthquake? What kind of bullshit is that?"

Stone readied himself to barrel past the cop, gun be damned, when he realized the shaking had stopped.

"Localized transient sensory event," Claudia whispered.

Stone looked at her. She was staring past him at the van, where Del and Ken stood talking with two other officers, a man and a woman, as if nothing out of the ordinary had happened.

"Holy fuck." Stone's legs went weak and he grabbed at the doorframe.

"Will someone tell me what's going on?" The cop's voice carried a note of aggravation, but he lowered the gun.

"I think I can," Stone said, although he wasn't sure. He'd heard of localized transient sensory events but never experienced one. In theory, a poltergeist or a powerful telekinetic could release a focused burst of energy and affect the physical surroundings in such a small area that only a few people, or even just one, noticed it. Someone standing in the very next room might never know anything happened.

Although, in a way, weren't the frogs and stones variations on the same theme? One property away and not a pebble or animal on the lawn.

"Good." Rose stepped forward and Stone and the twins said, "No!" at the same time. Stone gestured at the yard.

"Out there. Just in case. You can go inside after, if you still want to." Without waiting for the man's assent, Stone walked away, wanting to put as much distance as possible between them and the house, which had taken on a decidedly sinister air.

From a safe distance, Stone took a moment to gather his thoughts while Rose eyed him with equal parts suspicion and frustration.

It always sucked when private investigations went public. Prearranged shoots were a thousand times better. His production team had everything coordinated ahead of time. The local police usually hired on as extra security guards, and the politicians fawned over Stone and his team because they brought in money. Which made everyone happy.

Not so much in cases like this, though. When property got damaged and people hurt, rarely did the police or politicians become allies. They tended to treat Stone and his crew as an annoyance at best, and an insult to their town at worst. This was shaping up to be the latter, especially since they hadn't applied for any filming permits or let the town council know they'd be around. There'd been no need to; they weren't documenting anything on public land and hadn't required permission to enter abandoned buildings or dangerous properties. They'd been hired by a private citizen who'd signed a legal contract.

Of course, that was before someone died and a house was damaged. The cops would be understandably pissed, and the public would go nuts when the news became widespread. Which wouldn't take long in a town this size.

Probably all over the 'net. Stone made a mental note to check. Should've done that already. He really wasn't thinking clearly. That had to stop now. He took a deep breath and gave the officer his best on-camera smile.

"Officer Rose, my name is Stone Graves, and I'll be happy to answer any—"

Stone never had the chance to finish his sentence as a blinding white object shot past them and hit the ground in a silent burst of yellow and blue sparks.

"What the hell?" the cop shouted, drawing his gun again. Similar cries came from the officers by the van. Another flash and explosion left colored afterimages in Stone's vision. More of the miniature comets appeared, glowing spheres of brilliance that darted and swooped across the front yard before detonating into soundless fireworks.

Someone grabbed his arm and pulled. The cop, dragging him toward the shelter of the house. The officer shouted but Stone didn't hear it. His attention focused on the twins. Their eyes had rolled back in their sockets.

And the balls of light were forming directly over their heads.

CHAPTER NINETEEN

Hastings Mills, NY, July 17th, one year ago

Even before Rob saw the sign announcing he'd entered Hastings Mills, he knew the exact moment he crossed over the town line.

The temperature didn't drop, the skies remained the same hazy gray, and the lush pastures on either side of Route 16 didn't change.

Yet he felt the difference, a heaviness against his body, as if the barometric pressure had increased or he'd sunk to the bottom of a pool. Despite the air-conditioning in the car, it seemed harder to breathe. Sweat coated his palms and his hands trembled when he took the exit that brought him into town at the north end of Main Street. He came to a stoplight and said a quick thank-you it was red. He needed a moment to gather his composure. Memories came flooding back and for a few seconds the world seemed out of focus while images from his youth overlapped the current view.

High Street Park still sat to his right, the wide lawn browned by the summer heat. On his left, Memorial General Hospital was larger than he remembered; at least two wings had been added over the past twenty years. The old supermarket next to it had been replaced by the largest car wash he'd ever seen, with both drive-through and self-service bays.

A car honked behind him and he twitched. The light had turned green but he'd been too busy thinking about how he used to ride his bike to the Shop-n-Save as a kid to buy ice pops on hot summer days like this. He took his foot off the brake and slowly cruised down Main. On the right, several shops still carried names he remembered from his youth. Angie's Restaurant, a favorite with the old-timers. Taylor's

Dry Cleaning. Golden Dragon Chinese. Others weren't familiar. An accountant. A hair salon. No signs remained of the record store or comic book store he'd visited every Saturday during his teens.

On the left, the old mall looked deserted, with only a few cars scattered through the weed-infested parking lot, despite it being close to noon. He didn't recognize any of the stores, another sure sign the mall had devolved into nothing but bargain-basement-type shops.

Another block and he reached the center of the business district. Here people occupied the sidewalks, men and women and children, running errands, shopping, or heading to lunch. Nothing out of the ordinary, just another day in a small upstate New York town. He could almost believe nothing evil had ever happened here.

With his attention on his surroundings, he nearly ran into a car crossing the road in front of him. He hit the brakes at the last minute as another change confronted him. Where there used to be crosswalks and stoplights at the intersection of the side streets, now there were traffic circles and yield signs.

"What the hell?" Rob muttered to himself, as another car whizzed past. He was about to ease into traffic when the wail of police sirens reached him. He glanced in the mirror and saw two patrol cars coming up behind him. They went around on his left and continued down Main toward State Street.

Rob hit the gas and followed in their wake, a cold knot of dread forming in his belly. There could be a million reasons for cops to be rushing across town, all of them well within the ordinary. Accidents. A robbery. A heart attack.

Not with the Brock sisters in town.

The Witches of Midway.

Their melancholy eyes. Their solemn expressions. Their waiflike bodies.

In hindsight, he should have known better than to accept the director's role at St. Lucy's Home for Wayward Children. But he'd controlled himself, controlled his lusts, for two years. Maybe it was inevitable that he'd give in to temptation; only God was perfect, that's why he provided penance and divine forgiveness. But Rob couldn't help think God had placed him there as a test of his faith.

And he'd failed miserably.

He couldn't touch them, or any of the girls. He knew better than that. But he also couldn't keep his eyes off them. He had to see more. And everything had been fine until....

Their eyes, never leaving him as the stones outside grew larger. Silently accusing him. They knew what he'd done, how he lusted after them, and the others.

They knew the sin festering in his soul.

Shari and Claudia had left the next day, but he'd never recovered. He'd been judged and found guilty. After that, the slide down into the pit became easier and easier. Until one day....

The worst part was, the moment he crossed the final line, handed his money to a little girl in Tijuana, he'd felt not only shame – his own shame and God's – bearing down on him, but the gaze of the Carrie Sisters against his neck. As if wherever they were, they knew his intentions, had known what the future held for him ever since that day he peered into the hole he'd drilled in the shower and found them staring back at him.

Up ahead, the flashing blue and red lights changed direction, turning left onto State Street. At close to noon, the traffic was pretty lively and he had no trouble keeping up. Rob let out a sigh of relief that they'd gone in the opposite direction of St. Alphonse. He wasn't ready to face those memories yet.

He caught a glimpse of Riverside Park, which looked different from how he remembered it – at some point, they'd rebuilt the dikes and the ballfields. Then the cops headed east, and for a moment he wondered if they would keep going right out of town into Weston Mills.

They didn't. Just over the Front Street Bridge – an ancient lift bridge he couldn't believe still remained standing after all these years – they turned into one of the older neighborhoods, where the houses sat an acre or more apart, all well back from the road.

Bright light flared up ahead and Rob had time to worry he was driving right into something dangerous. Gunfire, or maybe even explosives.

The cop cars turned down a long driveway and skidded to a stop next to a white van that looked like someone had attacked it with a bat. Another burst of white.

As Rob pulled in behind them, his GPS spoke up.

"You have reached your destination."

Of course I have.

The cops hadn't left their cars and a second later Rob saw why. Dozens of basketball-sized glowing orbs darted back and forth across the property. Every now and then one would detonate like a miniature supernova.

He grabbed his phone and hit the record button as he got out. Someone called out for him to stay away but he paid no attention. He had to film this.

The lightning balls paused and formed a single, arrow-straight line.

With a high-pitched whistling, they shot toward him.

Rob screamed and dove into the car. Blinding light surrounded him.

A voice spoke in his head.

"Welcome home, Bobby. Shut the door."

Stone watched from the living room window as ball lightning swooped and darted across the yard. He'd shaken the twins out of their trance and herded them back inside, following the officer, whose full name turned out to be Corday Rose. The supernatural fireworks continued to form out of thin air at the exact spot in the yard where the girls had been standing, growing larger with each successive grouping. They'd reached basketball size when two more police cruisers showed up, followed by an unmarked car. Stone had no idea who it belonged to, but his gut clenched when the driver got out. The cops in the other cars yelled for him to get back, but the idiot ignored them.

A stupid reporter. Probably heard about the rocks and frogs and came here to cover the story, and now he's stumbled into something even better.

"Who the hell is that?" Officer Rose asked from next to him, and Stone shook his head without turning from the window.

The man raised his phone just as the balls of lightning stopped their crazy gyrations and formed a line across the yard. Rose let out a string of curses and Stone gripped the windowsill, expecting the worst.

The orbs shot across the lawn, right at the stranger. To his credit, he had enough sense to jump back into his car and duck below the window. The radiant spheres exploded all around the vehicle in a supernova so bright Stone had to shield his eyes. When the light faded, the car's paint job was blistered and charred.

One of the twins let out a gasp and Stone turned just in time to see them both fall to the floor.

"Claudia!" He rushed over to them. A quick check showed they were both breathing. When he patted Claudia's cheek, her eyes opened. Shari came awake as well.

"Holy crap, you scared me," Stone said, lifting Claudia into a hug. "What happened?"

"He's here," Shari whispered.

"He's here," Claudia repeated.

"Who's here?"

"The bad man. He's come..."

"...for us," Claudia finished. "He found us again."

Stone wanted to ask them more but frantic shouting came from outside, several people calling his name.

"Dammit. Stay here. I'll be right back."

He found Ken, Del, Officer Rose, and the other cops gathered around the steaming car. Ken had a camera aimed inside the vehicle. Del waved to Stone.

"Hurry!"

Stone increased his speed, worry giving him an extra adrenaline boost. He imagined the stranger burned to a steaming crisp in the car.

Never in his life had there been two deaths at any of his investigations; in fact, since launching *In Search of the Paranormal*, there'd been none. Evan Michaels had been before the show, when it was just him and Randi.

Would the network even keep the show on the air after word of multiple deaths got out?

Cursing his bad luck, he peered into the smoldering vehicle. The driver lay on his back across the front seats, his clothes and skin unburned, his hair mussed. When he saw Stone, his eyes went wide.

"You!"

Stone gasped and stumbled back. It wasn't possible! Him, here, at this moment?

"You know him?" Officer Rose asked.

Stone nodded, trying to find his voice. He still couldn't believe it.

"Father Robert Lockhart."

"The bad man."

Stone turned. The twins stood there, wearing identical masks of hatred, their eyes fixed on Lockhart.

"The bad man has returned."

CHAPTER TWENTY

Hastings Mills, NY, July 17th, one year ago

Randi Zimmerman twitched and looked up from her sandwich at the sound of multiple police sirens somewhere in town. Over the past three hours, the wailing of emergency vehicles had been an almost constant presence. Each time, she felt sure something terrible was happening back at the house, and she had to force herself not to call Stone.

He knows how to reach me if he needs me. I will not be the panicking woman in this situation. This is just Hastings Mills having a shit day, not some kind of omen.

Still, she couldn't help checking her phone to see if there were any messages from him. And then hating herself for doing it. For even thinking about him. Seeing him again had brought back too many old feelings, both good and bad. California life had treated him well, and he looked like he hadn't aged a day since she left him. She, on the other hand, hadn't been so lucky. She'd developed age lines around her eyes and started dyeing her hair to keep any gray from showing against the black. She'd also added a handful of pounds, limiting it to that only through strict dieting and exercise classes at the gym.

Why do men have it so easy? She knew Stone went to the gym as well, he always had, but he also ate pretty much anything he wanted. No living on fucking salads all week just so he could splurge with a slice of pizza and some wine on Saturday night.

And those creepy twins were young enough that they didn't have to worry either.

I wonder if he's ever had both of them at—

Another ambulance screamed by, interrupting her jealous musing. She glanced at Abby, who seemed oblivious to the noise as she devoured a plate of fries and a grilled cheese sandwich. Being away from the house seemed to have a good effect on her. Some color had returned to her face and she'd even smiled a couple of times while they'd been shopping. When Randi suggested they have lunch before returning to the house, Curt had looked doubtful but Abby's enthusiastic, "Please, can we?" had convinced him.

The reason for her father's reticence became obvious the moment they entered the Friendly's on West State Street, at the opposite end of town from Curt's house. All eyes turned toward them and Randi belatedly remembered Curt and his daughter were currently the most famous people in Hastings Mills, for all the wrong reasons.

By the time they sat down, the tension in the room had become a palpable presence. People whispered into phones and stared over their menus. Even the waitress who took their order and filled their coffee cups had only given them a weak smile.

A police car raced after the ambulance, lights flashing. Randi automatically checked her phone again. No messages. She nibbled at a tomato slice and sipped her coffee, the silence growing on her.

"You think everything's okay?" she finally asked Curt, who shrugged.

"Them sirens could be for anything. This ain't a big city, but we got our share of people. And a lot of farms outside of town. Besides, if something does happen, I'd sure as hell rather be here."

Although Curt's explanation made sense, Randi couldn't shake the feeling the man was wrong. That the bad things happening in town were related somehow to the problems with Abby. Even though that made no sense. A poltergeist couldn't infect multiple, geographically separated places or people. Neither could demons, if they even existed. In fact, nearly all supernatural events focused pretty much on individual locations or people. That's why you didn't have haunted towns, except in rare cases of mass deaths. In a way, taking Abby out for the day made for a good experiment. If something happened at the house in her absence, they'd know she wasn't the epicenter for the problems. It meant the house, not her, was being haunted.

Wait. Haunted house.... What if they'd been looking at the wrong cause all along? Instead of the poltergeist or spirit being attached to Abby or the house, could it be some kind of haunted object? Something the girl or her father carried with them sometimes but not others?

She had to talk to Stone right away. Had the history of the house been investigated? She'd never thought of doing it. Curt had told her they'd lived in the house for years but the troubles had just started. But what if he was mistaken? What if there'd been events all along and they'd only recently gotten to the point of being noticeable? Or if he'd just acquired the object?

That would explain the spirit of the woman Abby saw too. She could be the original owner of the object. Damn, that was stupid of me. Must be getting old. Randi took out her phone and stood up. "Excuse me for a minute. I have to—"

Something hard struck her in the chest. She let out a yelp and looked down as a saltshaker hit the floor. A flash of gray and another sharp pain, this time her shoulder.

The pepper shaker joined its companion.

Abby dropped her sandwich and snarled, her face contorting. Curt pushed away from the table, wearing that deer-in-the-headlights look he'd been showing too often the last few days.

Two booths away, someone shouted.

Randi turned just in time to see a middle-aged woman stand up, her white blouse covered in maple syrup and her face turning red. A ketchup bottle took off from a table like a rocket and exploded against the ceiling, creating a red rain that fell onto several patrons.

Randi looked at Curt. "I think we better leave."

Curt nodded, but just as he stood up, the three televisions on the wall behind the counter came alive, blasting a news report at full blast.

The entire restaurant went silent when a picture of Curt Rawlings' house appeared, identified by a scroll along the bottom of each screen.

Hastings Mills, NY. Ball lightning targets police officers at the home of Curtis Rawlings.

The announcer's voice boomed through the restaurant.

"…at the home of Curtis Rawlings, police officers were interviewing famed supernatural expert Stone Graves and his crew about recent unexplained events when balls of lightning appeared out of nowhere and began flying around the yard and exploding, forcing the officers to take cover. So far there've been no injuries reported, but a civilian vehicle was burned after being struck."

"Fucking sheep," Abby said. Her plate rose in the air and smashed against the wall.

The TVs turned off.

In the resulting silence, a man in one of the booths pointed at Abby and Curt.

"It's them. They caused this."

"Whole family's evil," someone said. Another voice repeated the word.

"Evil."

People got up from their seats. Men, women, and children all staring at Abigail, who sneered back at them. Bright red cuneiform letters appeared on her face and her hair stood straight up.

"*Yamut, khuruf, yamut!*" she shouted.

A bin of dirty dishes overturned behind the counter and the contents flew across the room, smashing into booths and walls. Several patrons ducked or ran for the door.

A few of them formed a group. A coffee cup crashed to the floor next to them. Randi thought it was another poltergeist effect and then noticed one of the men picking up a dish from the floor. His companions had also armed themselves with glasses and silverware.

"Get the hell out of here. And don't come back." Their waitress glared at them from near the coffee urn behind the counter.

"Take your devil spawn with you." A burly man in chef's whites stood next to her, a large butcher knife in his hand.

Abby whimpered and clutched at Curt's waist, her face normal again.

"Let's go." Randi tossed two twenties on the table and tugged at Curt's arm. He stared at the angry mob with a blank expression.

Randi understood. These were Curt's people. Folks he'd grown up with, worked with, saw in the stores and restaurants. And now they'd turned on him.

"Curt." They couldn't stick around. Shit had gone down again at the house and Stone would need them all there. And from the looks of things, the restaurant was no longer safe for them.

"Now, Curt." She took Abby's hand and pulled her away from her father. That broke Curt's spell. He followed silently as Randi went to the door, and he didn't shake off his daze until he unlocked the truck and got behind the wheel. As they pulled away from the curb, Randi saw multiple faces at the restaurant's window, all wearing the same expression of hatred.

Curt remained silent until they were several blocks away. When he finally spoke, Randi had to strain to hear him.

"I don't understand. We're good people. Why is this happening to us?"

Randi shook her head. What could she say? It had been a week and she still had no answers for him.

Good people.

His words still remained in her head when they pulled past a charred car and two police vehicles in the driveway. Stone and his team stood on the front porch with several officers. As Randi got out to ask Stone what had happened, a man stepped out from behind the cops.

Randi came to a stop when she saw his face.

No. It can't be.

"What the fuck is he doing here?"

CHAPTER TWENTY-ONE

Hastings Mills, NY, July 17th, one year ago

The silence in the Rawlingses' living room was so fraught with tension Stone felt sure the negative energy would register off the electromagnetic scale on his EMF meter.

Stone and the twins sat on the couch, Shari and Claudia pressed tightly against each other and holding hands. Cold hatred emanated from them as they glared at Lockhart, who occupied Curt's beat-up recliner, staring back at them with a peculiar expression Stone couldn't read. Curt Rawlings had taken the love seat, Abby on his lap and Randi next to them. Ken and Del stood behind the couch, while Officer Rose and two other cops had positioned themselves off to one side, all of them wearing confused frowns.

Just when Stone was beginning to wonder who would speak first – he certainly wasn't ready to – Officer Rose cleared his throat. Randi jumped and sat up straighter.

"All right. I don't know what the hell has been going on here, but I want the full story. No more bullshit. You." He pointed at Stone. "You're in charge, right? Start talking."

The other officers, Cindy Dicus and Lloyd Cadeyona, pulled out little notebooks and pens.

"My team and I," Stone began, wondering just how much he should tell them, "investigate the supernatural, the unexplained, for a living."

Officer Cadeyona snorted then covered his mouth with his hand.

"Can it, Nick," Rose said, his eyes never leaving Stone. "I know that already. Go on."

"We were called here by a former associate of mine, Randi Zimmerman." Stone pointed at Randi. "Curtis Rawlings hired her to investigate strange occurrences happening in this house, and to his daughter."

"Strange occurrences like what?"

Stone gave a quick rundown of the events that had happened before Randi had contacted him, including the medical tests run on Abby. Rose looked at Curt.

"Is this all true?"

Curt nodded, and Stone continued, detailing the things that happened the first night, including the destruction of their equipment.

"You didn't file a police report." Officer Dicus made it a statement.

"No. So much was going on we didn't get around to it, and then we discovered who did it, so there was no point." He described the video he and Ken had watched, feeling a momentary twinge of regret for keeping it a secret when Curt's mouth dropped open. Rawlings didn't interrupt but Lockhart did.

"Possessed! Just like the girl. There's a demon in both of them."

"Quiet," Rose said, and motioned at Stone. "Finish."

"The next day things got even crazier. First the frogs, then the stones. And you know the rest."

"Yeah. So how does he fit in?" Rose indicated Rob Lockhart.

"That's what I want to know," Randi said. Her eyes blazed behind her glasses and Stone couldn't help thinking she'd always looked sexy as hell when she got pissed. "What the fuck are you doing here?"

"Evil." Shari and Claudia whispered it together.

Stone glanced at them. They'd said something similar about the priest earlier. Lockhart was a drunken wannabe who didn't know his ass from an exorcism, but evil? Claudia shook her head, cutting off his question before he could ask.

"There is evil here, yes, but I'm not to blame. I'm the cure, sent by God," Lockhart said. Shari's eyes narrowed and Claudia's nails dug into Stone's thigh.

"No one asked you to come here. Get your ass back to whatever fucking hole you crawled out of." Randi's cheeks had gone bright red. It reminded Stone of how she'd looked in the throes of orgasm and he had to shift away from Claudia's hand.

"You don't understand who they are," Lockhart said. "Those two, the Weird Sisters. They attract Satan with their very presence. Evil is drawn to them. Mark my words, whatever's happening here, they'll make it worse."

"Fuck you." The words popped out of Stone's mouth before he even knew he was going to say them. "Like Randi said, no one invited you. Get lost."

"The Lord is my messenger. As soon as I saw them on TV, I knew they were my salvation, that this place would be my road to redemption. This is where it all began and this is where it will end. I will rid this family of their curse and my soul shall be saved!"

Claudia gasped and Shari put her hand to her mouth.

"Man, you're crazy." Del Hall stood up straighter, his six-foot-four frame menacing even without making a move toward Lockhart.

"Am I?" Lockhart pointed at the twins. "Do you what they've done? Death and destruction have been their companions since childhood. The Witches of Midway stand among you. Do you think that man's death is a coincidence? The falling rocks? The plague of frogs? The lightning that attacked me? Them! All them!"

"That's it. You're done." Stone knew the Brock sisters had a murky past, and while it irked him a little that some of those secrets might now be creating problems for him, it didn't mean the twins were evil. "No one invited you, so technically you're trespassing. Officers, please send him back to wherever he came from. Arrest him if you have to."

Officer Rose shook his head. "Not just yet. Seems like this fella knows an awful lot about you all, more than I do. No one leaves until I hear the full story."

"I'll tell you the story." Randi Zimmerman looked like she might strangle Lockhart, but she remained seated, one hand gripping the arm of the sofa as she leaned forward. Stone found himself staring at her chest and had to pull his eyes away. "Father Robert Lockhart is a goddamned fraud. He claims to be an exorcist but he does more harm than good. He killed someone, a kid for Christ's sake, performing one of his bogus exorcisms. We saw it."

"Killed someone?" Rose's eyes narrowed. "And you witnessed this?"

"Officer, that's not exactly true." Lockhart turned toward Rose, who moved a step away from the long TV stand he'd been leaning against. "The Lord doesn't always—"

Lockhart paused, his gaze moving past Rose to the top of the wooden hutch, where several pictures were arranged under the flat screen TV. The color drained from his face and his eyes widened. He jumped from the chair and nudged Rose aside in his haste to grab one of the photos.

"Hey!" Rose said, and Officer Dicus's hand went to her gun.

Ignoring them, Lockhart thrust the picture toward Curt and Abby. It showed Curt Rawlings and a dark-haired woman sitting together on a park bench.

"This woman! How do you know her? Tell me!"

"That's my mommy," Abby said, pressing tighter against her father.

"You're scaring her. Back off." Stone put himself between the Rawlingses and Lockhart, who continued to wave the picture, leaning past Stone and raising his voice.

"Your wife? Is her name Caitlyn?"

Curt frowned. "My wife's name was Caitlyn, yes. How did you know?"

"Where is she? Is she here?"

"No, she passed away when Abigail was a baby."

"How did she die? You have to tell me. How did she die?" Lockhart ran a hand through his thinning hair, leaving it a tangled mess that, along with the dark shadows under his eyes and his unkempt goatee, left him looking like he'd parted ways with his sanity.

"She was very ill." Curt glanced down at Abby, who had her face buried against his shoulder. "She...she suffered from depression."

"She killed herself, didn't she? Right here in this house."

When Curt shut his eyes and bowed his head, Lockhart stepped around Stone and shoved the picture in Curt's face.

"Tell us!" he shouted. "Tell us the truth!"

"That's enough." Rose motioned to Officer Cadeyona, who pulled Lockhart away. "Get that lunatic out of here."

"I'm not crazy! Tell them! Tell them!" Lockhart raved, as Cadeyona dragged him into the kitchen.

"Wait."

Tears ran down Curt's cheeks.

"He's right."

"Up until the moment Abby was born, Caitlyn never had any problems." Curt sat in the love seat, clutching the picture of him and his wife and slumped over as if too weary to bear the weight of the past. He'd sent Abigail to her room, telling her the adults needed to talk.

"We'd been married for a while at that point. We had Abby late. Caitlyn was forty when she got pregnant. We'd figured we'd never have a baby. And then...when we got the news, we were over the moon. So happy. Cate called it a gift from God, and even though I ain't religious, I agreed. We worried about the pregnancy, 'cause of her age and all, but everything went fine. Abby came out perfectly normal. The two of them came home a couple of days later and that's when...that's when Cate's problems started."

"What kind?" Lockhart asked.

"Nightmares, in the beginning. Two, three times a week. She said she couldn't remember them, but I didn't believe her. She'd be quiet for hours after she had one, in a dark mood all day sometimes. It didn't help having a newborn in the house, with all the crying and having to feed her and change her. Not that we minded. We loved our little girl with all our hearts. But when you're already not gettin' much sleep and then someone wakes up screaming in the middle of the night...by the end of a couple weeks, we were both exhausted. Cate started crying a lot, saying she couldn't take it, she wanted to leave. To die."

"Postpartum depression," Officer Dicus said, and Curt nodded.

"Yeah. That's what the doc told us. Gave her some pills. They worked for a while. She weren't the same as before, but she stopped talkin' about killing herself and she started laughing and smiling again. Then, right after Abby's first birthday, things went to shit. Cate's sister passed away."

"Lori." Lockhart wore a haunted expression. Stone got the sense he was holding back information. Important information.

"Yep. She was in an institution. An accident in college, she got hurt real bad. Cate saw it happen. After Lori died, Cate's nightmares came back with a vengeance. She'd wake up screaming 'bout monsters, or Kylie Johnson coming to kill her. One day I come home from work and found her...she'd...." Curt's voice broke. "She did it in the bathtub. Put a knife into her own stomach like one of those Jap soldiers. Left a note. 'He made me do it. I'm sorry.' Goddamn her!"

He slammed the photo down on the cushion and wiped his eyes again.

"When was Abigail born?" Lockhart asked.

Curt wiped the back of his hand across his eyes.

"October twenty-first."

"And Lori died how many days later?"

Curt thought for a moment.

"Four days. I remember 'cause one of her friends died on the same date."

"Kylie Johnson?"

Randi frowned. "How do you know so much about it?"

Lockhart ignored the question. "And your wife? She killed herself in October as well?"

"Right before Halloween." Curt's voice was heavy with grief. Lockhart nodded.

"I should have guessed."

Stone opened his mouth but Ken beat him to the question.

"What's so important about the month?"

Lockhart ran a hand through his hair. "Everything. It all started in October. What happened to us that night. This is why the Lord sent me here. God truly works in mysterious ways, and he's brought things full circle for a reason."

He took a deep breath.

"Thirty years ago, I attended St. Alphonse University. It was midterm break. The twenty-first of October. I'll never forget the date. We went up to the fifth floor of our dorm. We were just stupid teenagers looking for some fun. Me, Caitlyn Sweeney, her sister Lori, Kylie Johnson, and two others."

Curt twitched at his wife's name but Lockhart ignored him.

"We had a Ouija board...."

Abigail sat on her bed, her collection of Glitter Kids dolls in front of her. The voices of the adults downstairs had been nothing but distant murmurs, but now they grew louder as her door slowly swung open. She went to get up but a violent force shoved her onto her back. Her body went rigid, arms and legs splayed out.

The unseen presence pressed down on her mouth so she couldn't scream. Bright red handprints appeared on her wrists and ankles. Tears flowed from her eyes. Her bladder released, soaking the comforter. Blisters rose on her skin and formed patterns of words in a long-forgotten language.

The bed rose several feet and the other furniture joined it.

The dolls grew warm and then hot. The plastic softened and the toys melted together to create a single, misshapen body with multiple limbs.

And five heads.

⛤

"Jesus fucking Christ."

Randi Zimmerman's words hung in the air like warm breath on a cold winter day.

Stone's own emotions kept swinging between confusion and anger like a pendulum. How the hell was he supposed to figure out the Rawlingses' problems – let alone stop them – when he hadn't known half the story? Even if you discounted the possibility of demonic involvement, which got harder to do by the minute, it was obvious decades of dark energies lurked in this shit-ass town, just waiting for the right opportunity to flare up again.

"You should've told us," Randi said. "Told *me*."

"Wasn't none of your business." Curt refused to look at her.

"None of our business? A family with a history of supernatural exposure? A suicide right in the house? That's like ground-fucking-zero for—"

"Enough." Stone motioned for Randi to back off, even though he wanted to get in Curt's face the same way. He was pissed at Randi and pissed at himself. They both should have done their own research on the house. Instead, he'd trusted Randi and she'd trusted Curt. Sloppy. But now they knew. Abby was being haunted by her dead mother, and something had caused her to change from a benign ghost to a powerful, violent poltergeist. Now they just had to figure out what.

"What's done is done. We know the problem now. What's important is to figure out what we do next."

"There's only one thing to do," Lockhart said. "The Lord's will. The demon must be driven out and the goodness of God restored in these people."

"First, it's not a demon, it's a ghost. Second, an exorcism? By you?" Stone shook his head. "No chance. I watched you cause one child's death, I won't let you hurt Abby."

"And exactly how have you helped her, with your toys and your science? It's only by the grace of the Almighty she's still alive. That any of you are alive. You have no idea of the forces you're playing with, Graves. All you've done is bring matches to a room filled with dynamite." He indicated the twins. "I'm the only one who has a chance of saving her soul before it's too late."

"Hold on a minute." Officer Rose stepped between Stone and Lockhart. "I think we all need to take a breath and think logically. This is some crazy stuff. Demons, suicides, ghosts, exorcisms? This isn't television."

"You saw the ball lightning with your own eyes," Stone said.

"And what about the frogs, and the rocks?" added Del.

"I'm not saying there's nothing weird going on."

"What's your point, then, Officer?" Ken asked. Rose ignored him and turned toward Curt.

"Mr. Rawlings, you seem like a smart man. These people are just reality show hucksters and apparently that fellow ain't even a real priest anymore. Do you want them messing in your life, in your daughter's life, like this? Maybe you should send them all packing."

"Well...." All eyes turned to Curt. "Why would my wife be trying to kill my daughter? What if Mr. Lockhart's right and it's something else?"

A picture of his wife flew off the TV hutch and smashed against the wall next to Officer Cadeyona. He let out a yelp and scurried away. Two more struck him in the back. The rest of the photos flew up to the ceiling, where they slid around until they formed an inverted cross.

Upstairs, furniture thudded against the floor and doors slammed. Rough laughter echoed down.

Curt pointed at Lockhart.

"Do whatever it takes to save my little girl."

CHAPTER TWENTY-TWO

Buffalo, NY, July 18th, one year ago

Asmodeus wakes. Asmodeus wakes. Asmodeus wakes.

Father Leo Bonaventura emerged from the blackness of the Costa Rican jungle into a place just as terrifying.

The fifth floor of Dallas Hall.

Instead of running from a tiny hut, he sat at a Ouija board. Four other people were with him but he couldn't see their faces, despite a candle stub burning in the center of their circle. A potent blend of rotting flesh and sulfur filled the room.

Demon stench.

Under his fingers, the planchette darted from letter to letter with dizzying speed. He shouldn't have been able to make out the words, but somehow his mind kept up.

Asmodeus wakes. Asmodeus wakes. Asmodeus wakes.

Crimson eyes appeared in the dark, one pair over each person seated around the board. Hot, steamy breath wafted against his neck but when he tried to turn around his body wouldn't obey.

Asmodeus wakes. Asmodeus wakes. Asmodeus wakes.

One of the faceless people at the board cried out and disappeared. Something laughed, a deep, guttural rumbling. Another person vanished. The rest followed, leaving Leo alone. Voices called from beyond the candle's weak glow.

"Father, help us!"

I can't, he wanted to shout, but his throat was as frozen as his muscles, leaving him helpless as he listened to the insane laughter and watched the planchette.

Asmodeus wakes. Asmodeus wakes. Asmodeus wakes.

Hastings Mills, NY, July 18th, one year ago

"Holy Gardens. May I help you?"

"Yes. I'm looking for…um…." Rob Lockhart glanced down at the name he'd gotten from the online directory. "Father Henri Adebayo."

"Just one moment. Who's calling?" the receptionist asked.

"Father Robert Hanson. We were in seminary together." Rob mentally crossed his fingers that his ruse would work. The sound of electronic clicking reached him, followed by the buzz of a phone ringing. Rob fretted as he waited. Maybe it was too early and—

"Hello? This is Henri." The deep voice held a distinct South African lilt.

Yes! "Hello, Father. I'm sorry to disturb you. I'm trying to reach Father Leo Bonaventura but they must have called the wrong person's room."

"Leo? Oh, he is not here. He's still at Buffalo General for his surgery."

"Surgery?" Rob's hopes of having Father Leo drive the demon from Abigail Rawlings crumbled to dust.

"Yes, he left a couple of days ago to—"

Rob closed the connection and slammed his fist against the steering wheel of his car.

"Dammit!" Now what? Wait for Father Leo to recover and come home? That could take days or even weeks, depending on his surgery.

There's only one thing to do, and you know it. Evil cannot be allowed to continue. Remember Isaiah 41:10.

Robert mouthed the words to passage. "So do not fear, for I am with you; do not be dismayed, for I am your God. I will strengthen you and help you; I will uphold you with my righteous right hand."

I don't need Father Leo. I have the strength of the Lord behind me. I'm doing his will.

Rob put the car in gear.

Claudia and Shari gripped hands so tightly their bones ground together through thin flesh, but neither of them let go. They stood in a dark, barren landscape dotted with dead trees and gray boulders. An oversized eclipsed moon hung in the starless sky, turned into a hazy corona by the black disc in the center of it. A slight breeze whispered secret threats through empty branches. Strange animal cries echoed across the bleak terrain.

Danger surrounded them, unseen but nevertheless real. They both felt it, down to their cores.

This wasn't just a dream, but a journey to a place that had the power to hurt, even to kill. It wasn't the first time they'd traveled in their sleep, but it was by far the worst. Never had they visited a place so alien.

So...

—*Wrong.*— Shari's voice finished the thought in Claudia's head, reminding her that in the dreamlands they could only communicate mentally. In the real world, they were both asleep in the Rawlingses' living room.

The ground shifted violently, throwing them to the gravelly soil. Claudia yelped as jagged stones scraped her skin.

Next to her, Shari sat up, her long-legged pajama bottoms torn at the knees. Claudia looked at herself and saw she wore the t-shirt and boxer shorts she'd left on her bed in LA.

Dreaming. We need to—

—*Wake up*— Shari said. —*We have to wake.* —

Rocks and dirt exploded in front of them. Claudia threw her arms up to protect her face as earth shrapnel pummeled her. The furious tremors continued in waves, accompanied by a grinding, roaring sound.

Claudia peered through her hands as a huge mountain of red-hot stone emerged from the ground. Waves of heat emanated from it, along with a sulfurous stench that turned her stomach even from more than a football field away.

—*Not a mountain.*— Shari stood, pulling Claudia to her feet with her.

Claudia looked closer and gasped.

A giant throne, easily thirty feet tall and half as wide. A massive figure sat on the burning edifice, its dark form distorted by shimmering heat waves. Evil emanated from it with such power it forced her back a step.

—*The beast!*— Shari's exclamation echoed Claudia's own thoughts.

The same thing that had appeared in their nightmares in Los Angeles, only now its features were clearer.

Ten eyes stared down at them from the five heads atop the wide shoulders. Horse, goat, lizard, lion, and human, all with fangs and horns like some ancient dinosaur. Ebon scales covered its body and its reptilian hands ended in long, knobby fingers tipped with curved talons. Its feet had no toes; instead they were blunt hooves. Bat-like wings lay folded behind its back. Between its legs dangled an enormous penis that twitched back and forth and flicked out a forked tongue like a blind snake.

"Sssissssterss."

The word appeared in their heads and in their ears. None of the creature's mouths moved. Shari squeezed her hand tighter.

"Give yourselves to me."

—*Don't listen to it.*—

Claudia bit her lip. How could they not listen? You couldn't shut out thoughts.

The human face grinned. It made Claudia think of a boy they'd known at the foster home. He'd worn the same smile while he pulled butterflies apart.

"Kneel before me. Your souls are mine."

—*No!*— Claudia shouted it in unison with Shari.

Flames erupted around them, columns of fire rising far above their heads. The heat was immediate and intense, like standing in front of a raging furnace. Sweat ran down Claudia's face and stung her eyes.

"Submit."

—*Never!*—

The temperature climbed higher. Blisters erupted on Claudia's skin and the harsh odor of burned hair assaulted her nose.

"If one of you gives themselves to me, the other will be spared."

—*You're lying*— Claudia said.

"I will have that within you," it countered. "*One of you will sacrifice yourself."*

Claudia pulled Shari close. —*Never*— they repeated. —*We refuse you.*—

The flames grew closer. Claudia's blisters popped and smoke rose from her clothing.

"You cannot. It has already been decided. One of you will be mine."

The fiery columns bent downward and expanded, became a dome-shaped inferno that sank lower and lower. Claudia's arms and legs turned black and peeled away, revealing pink muscle. Her agony was doubled by the duplicate pain emanating from Shari. They screamed and superheated air filled their lungs, charring them from the inside. The world blazed in orange and then yellow as Claudia's eyes exploded—

—and she woke up on the floor, sunlight bright on her face.

Next to her, Shari sat up. Red blotches in the shape of fingers covered her arms. Claudia didn't have to look to know her own flesh bore the same signs of abuse.

The marks of the demon.

CHAPTER TWENTY-THREE

Hastings Mills, NY, July 18th, one year ago

Rob Lockhart stood in front of Holy Cross Church, a tsunami of conflicting emotions swirling through him as he stared at the deceptively charming exterior. Old gray stone and freshly painted white wood, with tall steps and the same arched stained-glass windows he remembered all too well.

When his family moved to Hastings Mills, they'd chosen Holy Cross for their church not only because of its proximity to their house, but because they fell in love with its small-town feel, so different from the ultra-modern church they'd attended in Syracuse. It had quickly become the center of their faith. Mass every Sunday, picnics in the summer, food drives and clothing drives throughout the year. Father Bannon was like a friendly uncle, and when he'd asked Rob to be an altar boy, Rob had no hesitation in signing up.

"Close the door, Bobby."

Rob jumped at the voice and looked around. He stood alone on the sidewalk, the hot morning sun his only companion. The fresh, green smells of summer – maple leaves, newly mown grass, flowers – were no longer pleasant. The intervening years slipped away and he was a boy again, about to climb the stairs to the bad place.

Three times he'd entered the priest's inner sanctum and shut the door behind him. Three times he'd bent over and lowered his pants, felt that pressure against his—

Stop. Those days are long gone. Bannon's dead and you're a man. You're not that boy anymore.

No, you're something worse, his conscience countered. *You've fallen from grace, become the very thing you abhorred. You're far worse than Doyle Bannon ever was.*

Not for long, though. His redemption waited close at hand. He would drive the demon from Abigail Rawlings and the darkness from his soul. And in the process, learn the secrets of the Witches of Midway. For surely they were the doorway to deliverance. Why else would they have been sent to him not once, but twice, each time at a critical juncture in his life, to shine God's holy spotlight on his sins? He'd failed the first time, but it would not happen again.

The road to salvation begins with a single step.

He lifted his foot and placed it on the slate stair.

Upstairs, a window slammed closed and a chair fell over in the rectory office.

"We need to talk."

Stone looked up from his laptop, where he'd been reading about the rites of exorcism. Claudia and Shari stood at the entrance to the kitchen, their faces flushed and their eyes ringed by dark circles. Despite the heat, they both wore long-sleeved t-shirts.

Something's wrong. He sighed and closed the laptop. *Jesus, I don't need this now. Not when everything else is going to shit too.* Then he frowned, surprised by his own vehement reaction. He must be more tired than he thought. The twins exchanged glances but sat down.

"What is it?" he asked, unsuccessful at keeping the remnants of his annoyance from his tone.

"There are some things you need to know," Claudia said.

"Things about us we never told you," added Shari.

He was tempted to ask them if it could wait for later – this wasn't the time for ancient history – but he also wanted any dirt they had on Lockhart. His own searches had turned up nothing except for a couple of small stories over the past decade of a 'Father Lockhart' who conducted tent revivals and helped some families with cases of demonic possession. Both in Texas, near the Mexican border. No pictures, but he felt sure it was the same man.

"Go ahead."

"You know we lived at St. Lucy's Home for Wayward Children when we were young."

Stone remembered the name from Lockhart's story. He nodded.

"And you ran away."

"But we never told you why. We were only ten. Our latest foster parents had just died and we'd been sent back. We didn't want to be there. Not with him."

"What did he do?"

Shari opened her mouth, closed it. Claudia did the same. It made Stone think of two guppies in a fish tank. Shari pursed her lips and Claudia glanced at her. Shari nodded.

"Okay." Claudia looked back at Stone. "It'll be easier if we show you."

"Show me? How?"

She clasped Shari's hand and held her other one out to him. He took it.

And tumbled into an endless black abyss.

"What the hell?" Stone's voice echoed in the darkness. He felt his heart pounding even though he had no body. *"What is this?"*

—It's okay. Watch.—

Claudia. Or Shari, he couldn't tell. Speaking in his head.

Telepathy? Christ, I didn't know they could do that!

—You suspected. Watch.—

Tiny lights appeared in the darkness. Expanded, became brighter. Resolved into pictures. Faces. Rooms and yards and streets. All jumbled together, like someone had taken handfuls of photographs and scattered them across a table. Only instead of photos, they were movie screens, each one showing something different. They spread out in front of him and – somehow – he could see them all, comprehend them, even though it should have been impossible.

Claudia and Shari as little girls, no more than five yet easily recognizable by their dark eyes and translucent skin. Sitting on a living room floor. An older boy takes one of their toys away. Both girls start crying and all the lightbulbs in the room explode. A man's voice, angry, shouting. "Dammit, Louise, that's the last straw! Those two is marked by the Devil hisself. They gotta go."

A room filled with children of various ages. All of them laughing and playing. Claudia and Shari sit apart, shoulder to shoulder, eyeing the others, who ignore them. A gray-haired black man in priest's clothing watches the children with tired eyes.

The twins again, older now, perhaps seven or eight. Matching pink Barbie suitcases in hand, standing at the door of a house where all the windows are broken. A woman is with them, a bloody gash on her face. She's speaking to the old priest.

"Them kids ain't right. Nothing but bad luck since we took 'em in. Sorry, Father, but we can't have them around. Ain't safe for the others."

More days at the group home. No friends. Hoping for the right family to come and take them away, but their dreams tell them it won't happen.

Another house. Lightning chases them. A bad man. He hurts people. The dreams! Filled with danger. They're afraid all the time. Of him. He's going to hurt them. They don't want him to hurt them. Green rain. Hiding. Death.

The group home again. A new priest. Robert Lockhart, only younger, his beard and hair not graying, his eyes not bloodshot from alcohol. Everyone is afraid of them now. The Weird Sisters. The Witches of Midway. Father Robert is always watching. They were wrong before. The real danger is here. Lockhart is the bad man. The shower. A broken tile and a hole in the wall. Someone peeking at them. Bad man. He peeks at the other girls too. They see it in his head. Sometimes he takes pictures. When he looks at them, he does the same thing Jerome Daniels got caught doing in his bedroom.

Sometimes the bad man comes into their room at night when he believes they're sleeping. He dreams of lying naked in the bed with both of them. And then... giving them to God? They don't know what that means. But it scares them.

Ten years old. The bad priest is going to do something. They feel it. So scared! They want to tell the other priest, the one visiting for the day, but fear keeps their mouths sealed. Then the stones falling, falling everywhere, and the older priest falls down, his head bleeding...all their fault....

That night, they run away, with money they stole from the box in the secretary's desk. They take a bus. Leave Ohio. From there they find a train. There are other children, riding railcars from state to state. A boy and his sister are there. The boy is special somehow, and not just because he has a ghost with him, the ghost of a dog. He feels different from other people. Good. One of the boy's friends helps them get fake Social Security cards. "With these, you can get jobs, or go live somewhere and no one will know your real names."

Different towns, different group homes, always the same problems. The lightning, the rocks falling from the sky, furniture moving. A diner in Nevada, at twenty, the first time they've felt like they could make a life somewhere.

A man enters the diner. Shari behind the counter, pouring a cup of coffee. Claudia cleaning a table. The man hands Shari a note, motions with a hand in one pocket. The note says to hand over all the money or she dies. Claudia sees it through Shari's eyes. Outside, something splatters against the window. "It's starting to rain," someone says. Only it's not rain. It's blood. And flesh. Pandemonium breaks out. People screaming, running for the door. In the chaos, the would-be thief escapes.

Shari and Claudia in a car, driving to Los Angeles. Looking for a home again.

Stone's bedroom. Claudia is in bed. She's dreaming about evil coming for them. Shari dreams the same thing.

All the windows disappear except for one. It grows larger. A terrible beast sits on a throne, surrounded by flame. Its many heads are laughing. The flames grow higher....

And Stone was back in the Rawlingses' kitchen. Claudia no longer held his hand. Gasping, he pushed away from the table and staggered to the sink. Images and thoughts continued to swirl through his brain. The room spun around him. He fumbled with the tap and splashed cold water on his face.

"I'm sorry," Claudia whispered. Sounds seemed duller coming through his ears rather than appearing in his head.

"Jesus. You call that easier?" He wiped his arm across his face. "Is that how you two...?"

"Yes." Shari shrugged. "Since we were babies."

Stone took a deep breath. Although still jumbled, the mind-movies were starting to make more sense as his mind sorted through the flood of information.

Telepathy. Precognition. Psychokinesis. He'd thought he'd witnessed most of the twins' capabilities, but now he realized he'd never come close to knowing the true extent of their powers.

"It's not like that. We're not superheroes," Claudia said.

"Or freaks," added Shari.

"You can read other people's minds too?" Stone sat back down. For the first time since he'd known them, he didn't want to look into their eyes.

As if that would make a difference?

"Not always," Shari said. "Not everyone."

"Only if the person is experiencing strong emotions. Or if they have a latent psychic ability themselves." Claudia raised her eyebrow at him.

"Me?" Stone shook his head. "Hell, no. I'm not psychic."

"Maybe you weren't born that way. But you've been touched by otherworldly entities. Maybe that's...opened you up somehow. Broken down the barriers most people have."

"Made you sensitive," Shari said.

"Forget about me." He couldn't handle thinking about it right then. "Lockhart. Is he really a—?"

"A what?" Randi walked into the kitchen, dressed in shorts and a Cure concert t-shirt. "An asshole?"

"A pedophile."

"What? How the hell—"

"It's a long story," Stone interrupted, not wanting to reveal the twins' secrets. He was still feeling the effects of being in their minds: the creepy, frightening sensations of being watched, of getting glimpses of Lockhart's depraved thoughts, of lying in bed at night wondering if he might do more than stand at the door and watch....

Maybe he didn't touch them. But I'll bet my ass he's done something to someone. And the Church covered it up, like they do everything.

Lockhart planned on beginning the exorcism that afternoon. Which didn't leave much time to find a way to stop him. Short of having Del knock him out and drive him out of town, there hadn't seemed to be any way to do it. Until now. If they could discredit him....

Stone grabbed his cell. They needed to dig deeper. And he knew just the people. The production company had two research specialists who did a lot of the preliminary work when he pitched an idea for an episode. Not only to weed out the obvious fakes, but also to provide him and the team with a complete history of the site, sometimes going back hundreds of years and delving into family histories. Because everyone had skeletons.

And if anyone could find Lockhart's, Joe Carlo and Hoy Lee would be the ones.

"Close the door, Bobby."

Rob froze with one foot in the church. He wished Father Bonaventura was with him. The old man's knowledge of exorcisms would be invaluable. More importantly, his presence would lend courage at a time when Rob felt none. But if God intended for Rob to walk this path alone, then walk it he would.

Are you sure you're up to it?

The nagging voice had been with him since he left the Rawlingses' house, reminding him of all his past failures, professional and personal. Kylie. Evan Michaels. Banishment from the Church. The nameless girls in filthy border towns, with their nubile young bodies and sweet lips.

No matter how hard he tried, the self-doubt refused to go away.

Satan always fights hardest when he knows God has something great in store for you.

A quote from an inspirational poster that had once hung in his office at St. Lucy's, when he'd been the headmaster.

"I won't give in to your tricks," he whispered. "I walk God's path again."

Feeling braver, he shut the door.

The interior of the church looked very much as he remembered from his childhood, only smaller, the same way your elementary school seems smaller when you go back years later. The wooden pews were unchanged. The carpet was different, burgundy instead of green, but still faded and threadbare. On the altar, the tabernacle and ambo sat in the same places and the credence table still stood off to the side, next to the ancient organ with piles of sheet music atop it.

Out of habit, Rob dipped his fingers into the chill water of the font and then knelt and made the sign of the cross. The holy water brought no sense of purification or calm, and he chided himself for even half expecting a reaction. Those days were long gone, erased by his immoral acts. Only when he cleansed his soul would he feel the miracle of God's presence again. As far as he'd fallen, he had no idea if the holy water would even protect him against evil anymore.

He made his way across the back to the family prayer alcove, where he hoped things hadn't changed too much. Even small towns grew larger, and with that came the ills of modern society, including theft. If what he needed wasn't there, he'd have to find the current parish priest and lie about his reason for needing them. Which would add yet another sin atop all the others.

To his relief, for once luck was on his side. The table he'd hoped for still sat within the alcove, with its painting of the Virgin Mary and its rows of candles previously lit in prayer or memory. On it rested a donation box next to a display of blessed candles, tiny plastic bottles of holy water, and rosary beads.

Rob took six bottles, eight candles, and three rosaries and placed them in the plastic shopping bag he'd brought. He was tempted to just leave, but even his soul hadn't been corrupted enough to steal from a house of worship. He removed his wallet and cringed when he saw the few remaining bills inside.

"Seek, and ye shall find; ask, and it shall be given to you," he whispered. A passage about how Jesus favored the poor. "I'm doing your work, Lord. So please accept this humble offering, which is all I can afford."

He placed a single dollar in the donation box and hurried out of the church, not even stopping at the font.

He was more than a block away when one of the candles in the alcove fell over and the aged carpet caught fire.

On the other side of town, a shadowy form whispered in Abigail Rawlings' ear and she began to cry.

CHAPTER TWENTY-FOUR

Hastings Mills, NY, July 18th, one year ago

"I give you this blessing in the name of the Father, the Son, and the Holy Spirit."

Stone coughed as Lockhart waved a stick of pungent incense. The entire group stood in a circle around Abigail, who lay on her bed, eyes closed and panting like a dog. Stone, Ken, Del, and Curt on one side, Randi at the foot, and Lockhart on the other side, with Shari and Claudia. Corday Rose had arrived an hour earlier, dressed in plain clothes and with dark bags under his eyes. When Stone asked him why he'd come, the officer shrugged.

"Curiosity. I'm not officially here."

"Translation: your chief told you to keep an eye on us."

Rose's lips twitched, not quite forming a smile, and Stone knew he'd guessed right. Now the cop stood by the door, his attention shifting from Lockhart to Abby and back again. Stone could only imagine what the man must be thinking, but for once the presence of the law didn't annoy him. So far, there'd been no word from the office in LA, but Stone hoped his dynamic duo would come through for him soon. Until then, all they could do was watch and wait, and pray that whatever rituals Lockhart carried out didn't make things worse.

In the meantime, everything would be captured on film, which would make for great television. Especially when after, he could swoop in and banish the spirit haunting Abby, and be the hero in front of the whole world.

"Are you getting this?" Stone whispered to Ken. He wanted every second captured.

"Loud and clear," Ken said, without looking away from his camera's screen. Two other camcorders captured the scene from the far corners of the room.

Lockhart shot Ken and Stone an angry look.

"Please don't interrupt. It could be dangerous for the girl."

"You're the damned danger," Randi mumbled under her breath. Lockhart frowned but didn't respond. He placed the incense in an ashtray on the nightstand and picked up a cheap crucifix and a small plastic bottle with a faded picture of Jesus on it.

"Blessed are the sweet names," Lockhart said, and squirted holy water on the bed and Abby, who flinched and moaned. "Jesus, Mary, Joseph."

Abby twitched as more holy water landed on her. Each drop left a tiny red spot on her skin.

"Our Father, who art in Heaven, hallowed be thy name. Thy kingdom come. Thy will be done, on earth as it is in Heaven. Give us this day our daily bread, and forgive us our trespasses, as we forgive those who trespass against us. And lead us not into temptation, but deliver us from all evil. Amen."

"Amen," Curt said. Del and Ken echoed him.

Lockhart held the cross close to Abigail's face. She moaned again, tears running down her cheeks.

"See how the power of the Lord makes her ill," he said.

"Or maybe you're just frightening the hell out of her." Stone wanted to knock the cross from the ex-priest's hand but he'd promised Curt he wouldn't interfere.

"Not her, the beast within her," Lockhart replied, using the crucifix to make the sign of the cross over her body. Head, waist, shoulders. Still holding the crucifix aloft, he exchanged the bottle of holy water for a worn Bible, which he opened and began reading from.

"By the hand of God I cast you out, demon! The kingdom of the Lord claims this child! You are not welcome here! Leave this girl. Leave her!" He punctuated each sentence with a swoop of the cross and then pressed it against Abby's cheek.

She cried out and twisted away.

"Hold her!" Lockhart shouted. Curt leaped forward and pinned her arms to the bed.

"Stay still, sweetheart. This will be over—"

"Fuck you!"

Abby wrenched free and bolted upright, her face contorted with rage. Before Curt could grab her again, she landed a fist to her father's nose with a sickening crunch. He cried out and stumbled back, blood running down his face. Lockhart slammed the cross against her chest and she hissed at him, spittle flying from her lips.

"Silence, demon! You're not welcome in this house!"

"Fuck you and your Jesus!" Abby shouted. On the other side of the room, two pictures fell off the wall. Abby swatted Lockhart's hand, knocking the cross to the floor. He grabbed the holy water and sprayed her.

"God the Father Almighty, cleanse this girl!"

The water sizzled and turned to steam where it struck Abby. A fetid odor reached Stone. A smell from his childhood, from when he and his friends would wade through stagnant ponds to catch turtles and frogs. Swamp gas and aged detritus, sulfur and rot all mixed together. Smoke rose from Abby's chest, the acrid stink of burning cloth adding to the stomach-churning mélange.

"*Ebate ti sveštenik*!" she shouted.

"Begone, demon!" Lockhart pressed harder.

"I'll see you dead, priest!"

Abby fell back on the bed, panting, a cross-shaped blackened mark on her pajama top. Red spots covered her arms and face.

Lockhart squirted more holy water, but this time Abby didn't react. Shari tried to lead Curt out of the room but he shook her off.

"I'm staying," he said, wiping his arm across his nose.

Lockhart handed him a bottle of holy water.

"Use some each time you hear me say the Lord's name," he said, then raised his voice. "I command you, unclean spirit, whoever you are, take yourself and your minions and depart! In the name of God the Father, the Lord Jesus Christ, and the Holy Spirit, depart."

Stone motioned for Ken to move closer with the camera. Curt shook the bottle over Abby. She groaned and writhed. A stack of books tumbled off a shelf.

"Just as Christ baptized his followers, so do we baptize this child again. You shall not defile this holy temple, demon. You are not welcome here. Depart!"

Abby's eyes opened, bulging from their sockets. Her body went rigid and Stone tensed, prepared for another violent outburst. But instead, she relaxed and closed her eyes. Her rapid breathing slowed. Lockhart touched the cross to her forehead.

Nothing happened.

"Is that it?" Del asked. "Is it over?"

"No." Lockhart shook his head. "This is just the beginning. The demon has retreated but the doorway remains open. The girl will sleep for a while, and we should rest as well. Then we'll begin again."

"How do you know when you've driven it out permanently?" Ken aimed the camera at Lockhart, who paused before answering.

"Trust me. You'll know."

Rob leaned against the back of the house, the late afternoon sun warm on his face. Unlike the harsh, burning rays of California or Mexico, the New York sunshine didn't cause a prickly sensation on his skin. He'd forgotten how soft East Coast summers could be, even with the humidity that sometimes made you feel like you were in a sauna.

He glanced around, took his flask from his hip pocket, and downed a quick swig of vodka. The liquid courage warmed his belly but couldn't melt the frigid knot of doubt lodged in his chest. The one that had formed there after the death of Evan Michaels and never thawed. He sipped again, wishing he didn't need the booze, that God would instead give him the strength he needed for what was to come.

Except God, much like Rob's father, seemed to be a 'you made this mess, now you take care of it' kind of guy.

You're going to kill the girl too.

"You don't know that," he whispered. In response, his inner self laughed.

She's as good as dead. You're out of your league on this one.

The word *dead* stabbed at Rob's soul, reminding him of other failures, moral and physical. Just as his psyche intended.

"I've performed dozens of rituals without a problem." And there'd never been another death after Evan Michaels. Although a few had come close.

Yes, but this one is powerful. Even a drunk like you can sense it.

His hand gripped the flask tighter and he drank again. As much as he hated the voice, it wasn't lying. This time did feel different. More dangerous. Like how he imagined a lion tamer felt each time they entered the cage, knowing that if they lost focus for just one second, the beast would be on them, teeth and claws tearing at soft flesh. Maybe he should stop, wait until Father Bonaventura recovered from his surgery. That made a lot more sense than—

What are you, a sheep?

Rob frowned. The voice had changed, grown rougher and lower. Almost a growl. Filled with angry venom instead of simple mockery.

Baa, little sheep! Walk away with your tail between your legs. Let a fucking real priest solve your problem for you. All these people will witness your failure. And you'll spend the rest of your pathetic life waiting to die. You know where your soul will go, don't you?

Rob bit his lip as the voice exposed his greatest fear. He did know. Straight to Hell. He'd degraded himself for too many years, wallowed in the pleasures of the flesh.

Unless you redeem yourself. Be a man, not a fucking sheep.

Redemption. His last hope. For so long he'd believed the stains on his soul were permanent, that he'd doomed himself to an eternity of torture for his sins. But ever since he'd arrived in Hastings Mills, he'd felt that maybe God had granted him one final chance to enter his kingdom someday.

And that chance was the Brock sisters.

The moment he'd seen them, something had changed. He knew it when he met Abigail Rawlings for the first time. So young, so innocent, so beautiful.

Yet he had no desire to lie with her.

Instead, it was the Witches of Midway who held his attention, who filled his dreams with images, both as children and adults. He desired them in a way he'd never experienced before. More than physical, it felt....

Ordained.

Yes. For once, he and his inner voice agreed. If only he knew what he needed to do.

You have to kill them.

Rob straightened up and the flask fell from his hand.

Murder? For all his transgressions, he'd never—

Really? You carry the blood of many on your hands.

Images of faces came to him. Evan Michaels. Kylie. Caitlyn. Lori. The people who'd died because of his actions.

Wasn't that murder?

For you were straying like sheep, but have now returned to the shepherd and overseer of your soul.

Yes! How could he have been so blind? The words of the apostle Peter made sense. The Lord was the ultimate shepherd, and all good Christians his sheep. And now the time had come to rejoin the flock.

"The Lord is my shepherd," Rob whispered. "I shall not want. He makes me lie down in green pastures. He leads me beside still waters. He restores my soul. He leads me in paths of righteousness."

Psalm 23:1-3. God leads, God commands, and those who follow Him shall end up in Heaven.

They are evil. All of them. You, sheep, will be the sword of the Lord.

"Thus all flesh will know that I, the Lord, have drawn my sword from its sheath. It will not return to its sheath again." Ezekiel 21:5.

The sword of the Lord.

Me.

Doing the Lord's bidding.

"Yes, my Lord," he said, looking up at the sky, his heart joyous. Finally, after so many years of doubt, God had spoken to him! "Thy will be done. But how?"

A picture appeared in his head. A cabinet. In the basement. Not a sword, but something even better.

The Lord provides for his sheep.

A gentle heat wrapped him, but instead of the sun, it was God's love warming his soul.

He slid the flask into his pocket and returned to the house.

Stone peered over Ken's shoulder as they reviewed the latest report from the team in LA. So far they hadn't had any luck unearthing the skeletons in Lockhart's closet. Now Stone had them digging deeper, all the way back to when Lockhart got in trouble in college. So far, Lockhart's story checked out. The students involved had been charged with trespassing and vandalism and put on discretionary probation for the remainder of the year. Kylie Johnson's death was listed as accidental.

"Goddammit, there has to be something!" Stone's voice reverberated in the tiny space. He kicked a metal footlocker and Ken jumped in his seat.

"Boss, they're trying. We all are."

"Fucking try harder." Stone stepped out of the van and found Shari and Claudia wearing identical frowns.

"What?" He passed them without stopping.

"Is there anything we can do?" Claudia called after him.

"Yeah. Use your superpowers and talk to the bitch haunting this house." He headed for the road. "I'm going for a walk to clear my goddamned head."

Claudia watched him walk away and then turned to her sister.

—*It's getting worse.*— She didn't want to admit what that might mean, but she couldn't hide her thoughts from Shari.

—*We have to find out. You have to find out. Tonight.*—

With a sigh, Claudia nodded. With all the evil in the Rawlingses' house, it was too hard to pinpoint any one source. Whatever creature—

—*Demon*— Shari cut in.

—had possessed Abby, it also managed to affect Curt, even if only temporarily. Which meant it could be doing the same thing to Stone. In order to find out, one of them would have to read him. Which meant Claudia. *Easier said than done.* It required prolonged physical contact, something that hadn't happened since they'd arrived in Hastings Mills. Besides there being no real chance for privacy, Stone had shown zero interest in her the last few days. She wanted to believe he was just too focused on the job, but she'd seen how he looked at Randi Zimmerman. You didn't need to be a mind reader to see his thoughts. Finding a way to get him alone for a few minutes would be difficult.

And she wasn't sure she wanted to. She'd avoided doing it for exactly that reason when they showed him the truth about Lockhart.

—*You have to. We don't have much time.*—

Shari returned to the house, leaving Claudia alone on the driveway. Her sister's last comment worried her. It was almost like she knew something she wasn't telling. Shari, the older by twenty minutes, had always been the stronger of the two. She also tended to be darker, more morose, more of a loner. She'd never had a real relationship with anyone, man or woman, outside of the occasional one-night stand purely for physical release. Her one and only love affair had turned into a disaster when the woman got into bed with Claudia and then claimed it had been an 'honest mistake'. She hadn't known the twins saw right through her charade.

Claudia's relationships hadn't been much better, until she met Stone. Their initial booty calls had quickly evolved into a real romance and the sisters had moved into Stone's house. It made for some awkward moments, but being apart too long was physically and psychically painful for them, so the three of them had compromised. Despite Stone's best efforts to win her over, though, Shari still made no secret of disliking her sister's relationship, holding fast to her belief they'd both be better off without any emotional entanglements.

She can't be hiding anything. There've never been any secrets between us. We couldn't keep one even if we wanted to.

With no real plan in mind, Claudia sat down on the porch stairs to wait for Stone. If she was lucky, maybe when he returned she'd have the chance to read him.

Hopefully I won't find anything inside him.

From somewhere in the house, Shari echoed her thought.

CHAPTER TWENTY-FIVE

Hastings Mills, NY, July 18th, one year ago

"I baptize you, Abigail Rawlings, in the name of the Holy Father!"

They'd gathered around Abby's bed again. For the past three hours, Lockhart had alternated between reading from his Bible, reciting prayers, and calling for the demon to vacate Abby's body. The feeling of déjà vu was strong for Stone as he kept flashing back to the last time he'd watched Lockhart perform an exorcism.

Just like Evan Michaels, Abby thrashed on the bed, fighting the neckties that bound her to the footboard and headboard. Red blotches covered her pale, sweat-soaked flesh wherever holy water had scalded it. Her bloodshot eyes held the yellow haze of advanced liver failure.

"We who were baptized into the house of the Christ Jesus were buried with him into death. And just like him we will be raised from death with our souls cleansed and ascend into the glory of the Father and walk with the newness of life." Lockhart cast more holy water across Abby's writhing form. Rank, polluted steam rose up, causing Ken to turn his head from the camera. Shari and Claudia gagged and covered their faces while trying to hold their meters steady.

"*Esn drek* from a whore's ass!" Abby cried, the words somehow even fouler coming from her young mouth. "*Šarlatan! Zoyne*! Your words hold no power!"

"Then why do you quake?" Lockhart shouted back. He raised his tattered Bible. "I am an instrument of the Lord and his power flows through me! I command you, foul demon, obey my words and begone! You cannot harm this creature of God now, nor the bystanders, nor any of their possessions. Obey me, beast of darkness. We are immune to your treachery. Begone!"

"*Nein*!" Abby's back arched and the tendons in her neck bulged. The covers flew off the bed onto Ken's camera and Del leaped up to pull them off. What few items remained on her shelves fell to the floor. Her face swelled, cheeks expanding until Stone was positive her flesh would split open.

"*Mâtu pri:st*!" Lumps formed under Abby's skin and slithered around like alien parasites as she shouted at Lockhart. "*Irrumabo vos sacerdos*! *Lac filio vestra mater*!"

The curtains flapped and the closet door opened and slammed shut, over and over.

"See how the demon speaks in tongues!" Lockhart poured an entire bottle of holy water across Abby's face and set the cross on her chest. "In the name of God, I command you. Begone!"

Abby shrieked and fell back on the bed, gasping for air.

The room went still.

In the resulting quiet, the air took on a heavy quality. Stone found himself drawing deep breaths and still couldn't seem to get enough oxygen. He saw the others panting as well. All except Lockhart, who held his Bible up like a shield and closed his eyes. The twins took two steps back and the frightened looks on their faces warned Stone to move away from the bed. The pressure in the room grew and a dull ache formed deep in his ears, accompanied by a loud buzzing. His face grew hot. At the same time, blood surged to his groin and set his penis throbbing. Randi's arm brushed against his and the throbbing built into a full erection.

Abby's mouth opened and greenish-yellow light exploded from her. Deafening thunder filled the room. Every window in the room shattered and the closet door slammed into the wall so hard it stuck there, the knob embedded in the Sheetrock. A tremendous gust of wind whipped up clothes and papers and knocked over the camera tripods. The dresser drawers shot out and hit Ken. Del grabbed him and held him up.

Stone's ears popped and the pressure disappeared. Everything crashed to the floor.

Lockhart lowered the Bible and approached the bed. Randi gripped Stone's hand. Abby lay still, her eyes closed. A great anger rose up in Stone.

She's dead. It's Evan Michaels all over again. I'll kill Lockhart with my own hands if that bastard has—

Her chest hitched and she drew in a gasping breath. The welts faded away, leaving only pale, white flesh unmarred by swellings or burns. Other than the deep purplish shadows under her eyes, she appeared fine.

"Is that it? It is over?" Curt asked.

Lockhart moistened his fingers with the holy water and made the sign of the cross on Abby's forehead. When she didn't react, he nodded.

"The demon is gone. Your daughter's soul is once more in God's hands, and this place is free from the creature's evil." Lockhart stepped away as Curt rushed forward and pulled his daughter into a hug.

"Abby!"

"Daddy?"

She pressed her face against his neck, tears running down her cheeks. Ken moved in closer with the handheld camera, a huge smile on his face. Even Del wore a grin rather than his usual stoic expression. Randi let go of Stone's hand and gave him a sheepish grin.

"Well, it looks like we were dead wrong this time. I guess we owe—"

"It's not gone."

Everyone turned toward Claudia and Shari. Their white eyes told Stone they'd entered one of their trances.

"Witchcraft," Lockhart whispered. Stone ignored him and approached the twins.

"What do you mean?" he asked. "Is it Abby's mother?"

"No. The evil," Shari said. "It's still here."

"The darkness," Claudia finished. "Stronger."

"The beast," Shari added.

"Move away from the witches."

Someone gasped. Stone looked back. Lockhart had a pistol aimed at the Brock sisters.

"It's their own evil they sense," Lockhart said. "The Lord has shown me the path to salvation. I must rid the world of their danger. He commands me."

Time seemed to slow for Stone as the black eye of the barrel stared at him. Light flared and an unseen force pushed him aside just as a flash of silver passed him. The boom of the gun sounded wrong in his ears, too long and deep. Someone screamed, "*Noooooo!*" the word stretched out and low, like something from a movie.

Stone landed on the bed and time returned to normal speed.

Shari crumpled to the ground, a red stain blooming in the center of her t-shirt.

Claudia dropped to her knees, her hands clutched against her chest and her mouth hanging open in a silent cry.

Lockhart pointed the gun at Claudia. "May the Lord have mercy on your souls."

The bedroom door slammed closed.

Abby let out a mad cackle and rose into the air, her eyes blazing jack-o'-lantern orange.

Stone grabbed the edge of the footboard and hung on as the bed swung back and forth. Lockhart shouted something and pointed the gun at Abby, then shrieked and grabbed his hand as the pistol twisted from his grasp and floated up in the air. Furniture and clothes lifted and whirled in a circle. Books and toys struck flesh with bruising force.

The gun went off and Del stumbled back with a bellow, clutching his arm. Another shot put a hole in the dresser. Del shouted for everyone to hit the floor. Stone rolled off the bed and watched as the others dropped to their hands and knees. The pistol fired again and again until it clicked empty. Then it got swept away in the miniature tornado.

Stone crawled to the door and yanked on the knob but it wouldn't turn. Randi pressed against him and he held her tight. They watched as Abby floated above the bed, her arms stretched out and her legs pressed together like Jesus nailed to an invisible cross.

She opened her mouth and disgorged thick ropes of pulsing green slime that stunk of sulfur and rotten meat. The wind whipped the ectoplasmic material around and splattered it everywhere. Droplets of the foul-smelling sludge struck Stone's arms, where they burned like hot oil. Abby laughed again and chanted a phrase he didn't recognize.

"*Asmodeus suscitat! Asmodeus suscitat!*"

Movement above her caught Stone's eye. A roiling black cloud emerged from the ceiling, the size of a pillow but growing larger. Shapes formed within it. Arms. Faces.

It's back!

The roiling smoke coalesced, the shapes gathering definition. Otherworldly visages, monstrous parodies of animals mixed with human features. Three, then five. Some sprouted horns, others fangs. The constantly churning cloud kept the details blurry. Tiny flashes of green lightning sparked deep inside the wraith.

A peal of thunder rattled the house and the smoke-creature broke apart. One piece dove into Abby's mouth and the rest flew out the shattered windows. The lights went off, plunging the room into darkness. Voices shouted and someone pounded on the door.

The gale stopped and a rain of clothes and toys fell down. The door unlatched with a click. The lights came back on, flooding the room with sudden brightness. A pair of legs squeezed past him and out the door. Lockhart. Stone shouted for someone to stop him.

Claudia let out a keening wail and toppled over. Forgetting the priest, Stone went to help her but Randi grabbed his arm and pointed at the ceiling.

"Look!"

A series of letters was burned into the paint.

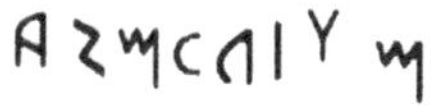

SECTION THREE INFESTATION

Los Angeles, Present Day

Excerpt from **Good Morning with Josh and Jenny**

Jenny Durso: "Would you say your time in Hastings Mills was the darkest of your life?"

Stone Graves: "Yeah, I think that's an accurate description. There were times I didn't think I'd leave that town alive. And times I felt like just giving up."

Josh Black: "What kept you going?"

Stone: (shrugs) "I really don't know. When you look back, you want to believe it's something noble. Love, bravery, a determination not to let evil win out over good. But in all honesty, I can't say any of that is true. Or at least not the whole truth. I think really it just comes down to the human spirit. We keep going until either emotionally or physically we can't. And even when I thought I'd reached my limit, when we all thought it, I guess I didn't. We didn't."

Durso: "Wow. That's so...powerful."

Black: "What you did, that's the definition of a hero."

Stone: (shakes head) "No, I'm not a hero. The real heroes are the ones who didn't make it. The people I dedicated my book to."

Durso: (holds up copy of Stone's book) "The book we're talking about is *A Town Possessed*, by Stone Graves. We'll be back to talk more with Stone after this break."

CHAPTER TWENTY-SIX

Hastings Mills, NY, July 19th, one year ago

What have I done? Rob sat in the front seat of his car, keys in the ignition. The image of the demon kept replaying in his head. The fiendish countenances forming in the hell smoke. The creature splitting apart.

Asmodeus suscitat! Rob's Latin was rusty but still good enough for him to translate Abby's words. Asmodeus wakes. Asmodeus, a name he recognized from ancient texts. One of the seven princes of Hell. Had one of its minions possessed Abigail? If so, no wonder it had been too strong for him.

I didn't drive out the demon, I freed it. I was so wrong. Wrong to think I could perform the rite. Wrong about the demon's power. Wrong to think I succeeded.

If he'd been wrong about those things, what about the Brock sisters? Maybe they weren't evil. Perhaps their power even served God in some way.

Had he even heard God's voice at all?

'For even Satan disguises himself as an angel of light.' The quote from Corinthians came to him, riding on a tsunami of remorse as he understood the truth of what he'd done. He'd killed someone, murdered an innocent because the demon tricked him.

'You are of your father, the Devil, and you want to carry out your father's desires. For he is a liar and the father of lies.'

John 8:44. Talking about Satan and those who followed him.

And what happened to murderers? Revelation laid it out pretty damn clear. He found himself repeating the quote aloud.

"But for the cowardly, the faithless, the detestable, as for murderers, the sexually immoral, sorcerers, idolaters, and all liars, their portion will be in the lake that burns with fire and sulfur, which is the second death."

Murderers. The sexually immoral. Rob groaned. Detestable. As perfect a description of him as could be written.

The sound of distant sirens reached him. Someone had called the police. It was almost time to face the consequences of his actions.

Almost.

It was too late for his soul now. Killing Shari Brock had sealed his fate. But Abigail...they still had a chance to save her. A slim one, but it existed.

Cradling his injured hand in his lap, he started the car with his left and raced out of the driveway, heading away from the oncoming police. He'd catch the highway one exit east, in Hinsdale. If all went well, he'd be back in a day, two at the most.

Hopefully there'd be a town left when he returned.

"I can't believe this shit."

Officer Cindy Dicus stood in her underwear staring at her phone, her deep scowl informing her husband, Brad, something work-related had just come through, and it wasn't good news. They'd been married for ten years, and he'd quickly learned how to decipher her various frowns. Like her mother and sister, Cindy had a portfolio of them, ranging from minor eyebrow dips when she watched the news or tried to decide on a pair of shoes to the exaggerated furrowed brow and tight lips that served as a warning to anyone nearby that the shit was about to hit the fan.

And then there were the work frowns. They happened a couple of times a month, usually when she got stuck doing traffic detail in bad weather or fixing paperwork one of her fellow officers screwed up.

Considering she'd worked late the night before and then done a day shift today, Brad had a feeling this particular frown involved more overtime.

"Bad news?"

"Goddamned ghost hunters again. Someone got shot. I'm freakin' exhausted. And now I've gotta go back there and deal with their crazy bullshit."

Brad stayed silent. Like everyone in town, he'd heard about the reality show crew and the mysterious falling rocks and raining frogs. It wasn't surprising that Cindy would get called back in if there'd really been a shooting. In a small town like Hastings Mills, with only a few officers per shift, everyone worked double time in emergency situations.

"That sounds serious." The moment he said it, he regretted opening his mouth. Cindy shot him a glare the likes of which he hadn't seen since the time his brother drank a bottle of tequila and passed out during Thanksgiving dinner. He tensed, preparing himself for the verbal tsunami about to strike.

Then her frown melted away, replaced by a sultry smile and a raised eyebrow. At first he couldn't place her expression; it had been that long since he'd seen it. Even then, he still didn't believe his eyes.

"You know what?" She crooked a finger at him and ran her other hand between her breasts. "The hell with them all. I'm gonna be late. Whattaya say?"

"Umm...." Brad motioned at the door. "The girls are still getting ready for bed."

"Read my lips. I'm horny. Are you joining me or am I taking care of things by myself?" She slipped off her panties and dropped them on the floor. That made up Brad's mind. He wasn't missing out on the opportunity, not when her crazy hours and raising two young children had reduced their sex life to once a month if they were lucky. He tried to close the bedroom door but Cindy pushed him onto the bed, climbing on top of him and pressing a hand over his mouth before he could object. With her other hand, she unzipped his fly, releasing his erection. She lowered herself onto him and he gave in to the moment, thrusting up as forcefully as she slammed down. It didn't take long for her to begin shaking, a sure sign her orgasm was only moments away. She arched her back and let out an animal growl as she squeezed his waist with her thighs. Despite his worry the girls would walk in on them, he felt his own release nearing.

Sharp nails dug into his ribs and the hand over his mouth pushed harder. Cindy continued to writhe atop him, bringing him closer to the edge. Her hand slid up from his mouth to cover his nose as well. He tried to turn his head but she leaned down, pinning him against the pillow. The tiny daggers in his side blossomed into full-grown knives and when she lifted her other hand to her lips, blood dripped from her nails. Colored spots formed in his vision and his lungs screamed for air.

She let out a long, howling cry. He moaned against her palm and she smiled, her image growing fuzzy as his eyesight dimmed. For a brief second, he saw multiple faces in a red fog, distorted images of ferocious beasts overlaying hers. Just when he thought he would pass out, she lifted her hand from his mouth and his vision cleared. He took a huge, gasping breath and went rigid as his own orgasm erupted. Cindy pressed herself against him until he finished, then rolled over and sat with her back against the headboard.

"You're welcome," she said.

"What the fuck, Cindy?" he asked, his voice hoarse and weak.

"Best orgasm you'll ever have. I guarantee you'll never have another like it."

"I don't care. I'm not into that sado-masocistic—"

She slammed the edge of her hand into his throat. Brad's body convulsed and a strangled gasp whistled through his crushed windpipe. While he clawed at his neck and fought to breathe, she took her spare pistol, a snub-nosed Smith & Wesson revolver, from the nightstand drawer and fired point-blank into his head. Blood and flesh splattered across the pillows and her breasts. She rolled off the bed as two pajama-clad girls entered the room with frightened eyes.

"Mommy! We heard a 'splosion!" Maya, six, held the hand of her sister, Lisa, who was ten months younger.

"Yes, you did, honey." Cindy pulled the trigger. Maya flew backward, a dark hole where her nose had been a moment before. Before Lisa could scream, Cindy put two bullets into her chest. She landed on her sister, red foam spilling from her mouth.

Cindy smiled at the bodies, then got her cell phone and hit 911.

"Police Department. What's your emergency?"

Cindy grimaced. Martha Plotkin, who worked part-time as a dispatcher and the rest of the time as Chief Mordecai's secretary. The bitch had been around longer than Mordecai himself, and everyone kissed her ass to stay on the chief's good side.

"Hey, Martha. This is Cindy Dicus. I just killed my family, you old cow. Tell the chief he can go fuck himself, I quit. *Asmodeus suscitat.*" She put the phone down and placed the barrel of the gun in her mouth.

The last thing she heard was Martha's voice.

"Cindy? Cindy, you all right?"

In the St. Alphonse Holy Gardens retirement complex, Father Bertrand Merkle stood up and threw his tray across the table, sending creamed corn, meatloaf, and chocolate pudding onto the shirts of his fellow diners.

"The end is near!" he shouted. The few strands of white hair remaining on his head stood straight up and his eyes bulged from his head.

The three other retired priests at the table slid back. One of them reached for Merkle's arm but the octogenarian Franciscan, who still insisted on wearing his traditional brown robe and sandals, pulled away with surprising force.

"Evil is coming and there's nothing anyone can do! The time of Satan is upon us!"

Merkle climbed onto the table, kicking food and flatware to the floor. A cafeteria worker rushed over and tried to grab his legs. Merkle slammed his foot down on the man's hand. The aide yelped and backed away, cradling his injured fingers. Another aide shouted for help while Merkle continued to stomp the table in an awkward, jittering dance and scream, "The Devil's coming! The Devil's coming!"

Several of the priests dining at the time took a few indecisive steps toward the commotion and then stopped as two orderlies rushed over. One of them jumped up and attempted to wrap his arms around Merkle. With a cry, the orderly stumbled off the edge and landed on his back, a fork protruding from his chest. His partner darted in and stabbed a syringe into Merkle's leg. Instead of collapsing, the old priest laughed and kicked the orderly in the face. Three of Merkle's toes broke with a sound like someone chewing ice. The orderly's nose exploded in a shower of blood and he joined his partner on the floor, groaning in pain.

Merkle picked up a butter knife and brandished it at the crowd.

"You've all forgotten the power of evil. Now you'll remember."

As the priests watched, Merkle rose into the air, his feet inches and then a foot above the table. He levitated another two feet and then remained there, spinning in a slow circle with his arms spread. Red lines appeared on his exposed flesh and formed arcane symbols. Bloody tears seeped from his eyes. When they touched the cryptic marks on his face, they sizzled into steam. He waved the knife and laughed.

Then he plunged the dull blade into his left eye and fell onto the table with a heavy thud.

When the police arrived, he still lay there, yellow and red fluids leaking from his ruined socket.

None of the priests had even approached him to administer last rites.

⛤

Bedlam reigned at the Cattaraugus County Department of Social Services Child Welfare Center commons room when Shelly Martin arrived from her office.

"What the actual hell is going on?" she said, panting more than a little after her sprint down two corridors. She had to raise her voice to be heard over the shouting coming from the small, glass-enclosed eating area.

"I have no idea." Leon Dawkins, her night-shift assistant, shook his head. "They were supposed to be getting ready for bed. I heard the commotion and found them like this."

The eight children currently housed at the center sat at a picnic-style metal table, staring at the ceiling and chanting at the tops of their lungs.

"Asmodeus suscitat! Asmodeus suscitat!"

The children repeated the nonsensical words over and over, their faces red and necks taut with effort.

"Where is everyone?" Shelly asked. There were supposed to be two case workers on duty every shift.

"Kasia took Selwin to the break room. One of the kids stabbed him with a pencil."

"What?" Shelly was about to say none of their children would do that, but watching them now made her second-guess that thought.

"Yeah, right in the damn chest."

"Call Dr. Rinaldi and have him get his ass over here right away. I don't know if this is some kind of mass hysteria or what, but I think they'll need to be sedated."

Shelly entered the room, wishing the county provided enough funding for them to keep a nurse or doctor on staff for emergencies. But who would've figured on something like this happening?

"Children, please, be quiet!" She could barely hear her own words over their combined voices. She approached the table and noticed one of them looking at her instead of staring at the ceiling like the others. The new kid, Pete Telles. Always wore a beat-up Yankees hat. He'd just arrived a couple of days before, orphaned after his parents died in a house fire. Tragic case. His grandparents were flying home from Europe, where they'd been on vacation, but wouldn't be back for two days.

"Pete, can you hear me? Are you all right?" She took his arm and gave it a gentle shake. When nothing happened, she shook him harder.

All the children stopped shouting.

In the sudden quiet, Shelly's ears rang like she'd spent the night at a rock concert.

"Pete?" He still stared at her.

He smiled, and something about it gave her the jeebers, as her nana used to say.

"You get the jeebers when there's haunts around."

Pete's arm grew hot in her hand and she let go. Was he feverish? Had they all come down with some kind of illness?

"*Asmodeus suscitat,*" he whispered, his smile widening.

The raucous *bang* of metal hitting metal pulled her attention away from him. On the other side of the room, every art supply storage locker door stood open and all the scissors, rulers, and pencils floated in the air. Then they disappeared. A strange humming sound reached her and her body exploded in agony.

Once more, screaming filled the room.

CHAPTER TWENTY-SEVEN

Halfway to Buffalo, NY, July 19th, one year ago

Route 219N stretched on in front of Rob, the dark macadam extending onward until it narrowed to an invisible point at the horizon. The setting sun cast elongated shadows from trees and utility poles, their shapes disfigured like reflections in funhouse mirrors. On either side, low, rolling hills mimicked the silhouettes of ancient behemoths crossing a plain.

The lightning attack of the Brock sisters had shorted out his radio, leaving him with only the droning hum of the tires and the gentle hiss of the air-conditioning. The white noise of the highway did nothing to calm his nerves.

Since leaving Hastings Mills, he'd been plagued by a nasty feeling in his gut. It started out as a nervous wriggling, the adult version of that weird tingling he used to get before a big exam. But as the miles passed, it had grown. Changed. Become something he'd never felt before, a wet, slimy eel of fear swimming circles in his stomach.

But you have felt it before, haven't you? When Evan Michaels opened his eyes and spoke to you.

"Hello, Robert. Kylie says fuck you from Hell."

That had been the moment the fear eel hatched. His pride at defeating the supernatural presence turned into soul-rending terror as Brian's body rose up from the bed and mad laughter burst from the child's throat.

The boy, floating there, while you stood frozen in terror and did nothing to stop what happened. Stone Graves shouting, "Do something!" Randi Zimmerman's video camera being yanked from her hands and thrown across the room by the invisible entity. Everything moving in slow motion while you stood there, helpless in your fear. Brian gliding across the floor, the same way Kylie did that awful night at school. Heading for the window.

Just like Kylie.

You knew it then. Knew what was going to happen. And you didn't stop it. You never even tried.

"It wouldn't have mattered," Rob said, unaware he'd spoken aloud.

The coward's excuse.

"I couldn't!" Rob's shout echoed off the closed windows, startling him. His eyes shot open and he cut the wheel right just in time to avoid hitting the guardrail on the wrong side of the road. The car swerved back into the right lane, tires screeching from his overcorrection, and then jerked the other way as he got control.

Panting, chest pounding, he let the car slow to forty. Adrenaline coursed through his body and his hands gripped the steering wheel so tight his knuckles ached. The idea that he'd dozed off, lulled into sleep or some kind of zombie-like state, scared him almost as much as the unwanted memories his subconscious had delivered. If something happened to him, all hope was lost for Abigail Rawlings. And maybe the whole town.

I need coffee. And food.

What he really wanted was a drink, but that craving, that wild animal pacing its cage inside him, would have to wait until after he spoke to Father Leo. Once the priest had all the information, the ball would be in his hands and Rob could sink back into his bottle.

Like a coward.

Ignoring the voice of his self-hatred, he slowly increased his speed, keeping both hands on the wheel. A green sign appeared up ahead, indicating an exit. No number, just the words *FOOD GAS RESTROOMS 1 MILE.*

I'll stop there. Put something in my stomach. And I can look up the number for the hospital, find out what room Father Leo is in.

The exit ramp came up on the right and he eased onto it. At the end, a road stretched to the left and right, with nothing but cornfields as far as he could see in the last rays of light. Directly across the street was a wide gravel parking lot. At the back end of it sat an old-fashioned diner, modeled like a silver Airstream with windows across the front and a pink neon sign on the roof that read *DINER OPEN 24 HOURS.*

One car sat in the lot, and Rob hoped that had more to do with the diner's location in the middle of nowhere than with the quality of the food.

How bad can it be? All I want is coffee and pie. Or maybe a buttered roll. No one can screw up a buttered roll. Still, his misgivings remained until he pushed open the glass doors and stepped inside.

His first impression was that he'd traveled back in time to his childhood. There'd been a restaurant on State Street, the Keystone Luncheonette, where he'd gone for lunch every Sunday with his family after church. A real mom-and-pop place, with Mr. Mallory doing all the cooking and Mrs. Mallory running the counter. Their two daughters had filled in as waitresses when needed.

The menu was small and the food dripped with grease and butter, but to a ten-year-old boy the place was heaven. He got the same thing every time: a grilled cheese with bacon on white bread, with French fries and a Coke. The air had always been redolent with the smells of frying meat, sautéed onions, and coffee.

The same exact odors washed over him as he entered the unnamed diner. His stomach let out a sonorous gurgle and saliva filled his mouth. His pace increased and by the time he reached the long counter he'd decided to forgo the pie in favor of a cheeseburger. Two men in dusty coveralls sat at the far end, and he caught a glimpse of people in two or three of the booths, but his attention was focused on the giant coffee urn behind the counter, and the window next to it that offered a view of a cook in stained whites flipping burgers, sandwiches, and eggs at a large grill.

He took a seat at the center of the counter just as an older woman in a starched white blouse and black trousers approached him.

"Coffee?" she asked, her blue eyes as faded as her slate-gray hair.

Even her skin had a grayish-blue tint, like when you spent too much time in cold water, and her lips had lost almost all their pink.

"Please. And I'll have a cheeseburger and fries. Make it a double burger."

The woman nodded and jotted his order on her pad. "Comin' up."

A second later a giant mug of steaming black coffee sat in front of him, the rich aroma of dark roast beans wafting up. He took his first sip and let out a satisfied sigh.

How is it the cheapest diner can make great coffee but the big-name coffee places give you burned tar, at three times the price?

"Where you headin'?" a voice asked. Rob turned and saw the two men looking his way. Both wore John Deere caps that hid their eyes in shadow. They sounded honestly curious rather than small-town suspicious, so he answered.

"Buffalo," he said. "Gotta see someone."

"Family?" The second man gave him a slight smile.

"Old friend," Rob replied. An image of Caitlyn's face appeared out of nowhere in his head and he forced it down, wondering why he'd suddenly thought of her.

"Good to see friends," the waitress said, placing napkins and silverware in front of him. A bottle of ketchup joined them. "So many memories, am I right?"

She walked away before he could answer. One of the old men nodded. "Sure are, Lori."

Rob jumped at the name.

Stop. It's just a coincidence. You've had Fifth Dallas on your mind. Plenty of people named Lori.

Still, he found himself watching her as she moved back and forth behind the counter, refilling coffee for him and the old men, consolidating the contents of two donut plates under glass domes, and adding more cream to a half dozen little aluminum pourers.

"You were a chickenshit, Rob."

"What?" Rob swung around on his stool to face the two old men. "What did you say?"

One of the men frowned. "I said, I had a chicken farm job, once. Down by Hastings Mills."

Rob's blood froze. "Hastings Mills? Why would you—"

"That's nice farm country," the other chimed in. "Good, fertile soil. Old. You need centuries of death to make soil like that."

"I don't—"

"Ain't there a college that way?" the first man asked, cutting Rob off again. "You look like a college fellow."

"Yes. St. Alphonse. I graduated from there." The rapid changes in subject had Rob's thoughts whirling and he responded out of habit.

"Here you go, college boy." The waitress slid a plate to him. He looked down.

A grilled cheese with bacon. On white bread. With a side of golden-brown fries.

"Wait. This isn't what I ordered." Rob pushed the plate back.

"But it's what you really wanted, ain't it?" Lori raised an eyebrow at him and walked away. The two old men snickered behind raised coffee cups.

Rob eyed the sandwich. Gooey American cheese oozed out from the sides, and the bacon was crisp and brown, just the way he liked it.

He *had* wanted it more. In fact, he'd ordered the cheeseburger only because it seemed silly to get a sandwich just to relive a bit of childhood. The same reason he hadn't had one in years.

How had she known?

"Lori thinks she's psychic." The men laughed and the waitress shrugged.

"Doesn't take a psychic to tell when someone's not feeling right. College boy's got troubles. Blind woman could see that." She tapped her pen on the counter in front of him and headed over to one of the tables.

Blind woman? Maggie ended up blind that night.

"Sometimes life throws a fella curve balls," one of the old men said. Rob frowned. He was having trouble telling them apart. He wished he could see their faces.

"Got that right," the man's partner said. "People get hurt. Get sick. Die. Sometimes by their own hand."

Rob's gut twisted. How the hell had they got onto the subject of suicide? Caitlyn's face rose up again, making it hard to follow the conversation.

"Hey, college boy. You married? Got kids?"

"No." He thought about telling them it was none of their damned business but starting a fight wasn't high on his list of things to do so he bit his tongue and returned to his food, which no longer seemed so appetizing. The cheese had gone cold and the bacon limp. Congealed grease covered the bottom of the plate.

"Ever fuck a blind girl?"

"What?" This time he dropped the sandwich and came halfway off his stool. Both men had their heads down.

"I did," one of them said. His voice had grown deeper, and hoarse. "She had scars all over her face. Black chick."

Bitter laughter came from one of the booths. "That's right. And then he dumped me."

Rob turned to see who'd spoken and got his first real look at the other patrons in the diner. A woman and child sat with their backs to him, with only their hair – his brown, hers onyx black – visible. Across the aisle from them were two women in a booth, one with dark skin and hair, the other with long, curly brown hair and freckles, just like—

Don't even think it.

"How 'bout a little girl?"

Rob spun toward the men. They stared at him with narrowed eyes. One of them made kissing noises and licked his lips.

"Ten goin' on eighteen," the other said, and both of them burst into laughter. Rob's stomach clenched as a different memory emerged from the closet of his past. Just as bad as the others, in its own way.

I didn't mean for it to happen. But she'd been so innocent, so beautiful, so—

"You want more coffee, Rob?"

He jumped a little as the waitress's words returned him to the present. Somehow she'd gotten back behind the counter without him noticing.

How did she know my name?

He started to ask, but when he glanced her way, she looked different. Thinner. Younger. Familiar....

Lori Sweeney. It's her, if she'd never been...hurt. Had lived a normal life.

The waitress winked at him and stuck out her tongue.

Just like Lori used to do.

"It was all your fault, you know."

That voice. The brown-haired girl in the booth. *Her.* He slowly turned around on his stool. He didn't want to see. But he couldn't help himself.

Caitlyn Sweeney stared at him. Older, but no mistaking her.

"You're the reason I killed myself." Her face was pale as milk, each freckle standing out. "What happened to Lori destroyed me. Just like you destroyed her."

"No!" He took a step toward her. Stopped when the other woman got up. She wore dark glasses, like a—

Blind woman? "Maggie?"

"How do I look, Rob? Have the years been good to me? I used to be beautiful. You never came to visit me in the hospital."

"That's not true." Rob shook his head, even though she couldn't see him. "I tried. You wouldn't let me. Then you moved away."

"You never came. None of you did. I lost everything because of you. School, a job, even my boyfriend."

"Damn straight. I didn't want no blind chick," one of the men said. Only now it was a teenager's voice. Rob recognized it right away. Michael Choi. And next to him, Patrick O'Hare. The one who'd brought the Ouija board that night. The one who'd—

"They all hated me because of you," Patrick said. "You talked me into it, said it would be fun. But after, they blamed me just as much as you. It weighed on me, Rob. Weighed on me till I couldn't take it anymore." He held up his arms. Dark blood dripped from his wrists.

"It was your idea!" Rob said. And it had been too. Pat had found the game, suggested they play.

"But you convinced everyone to do it." Lori came around the counter. Most of her hair was gone and one side of her skull was misshapen. Her eyes stared in two different directions and a line of drool hung from her mouth. "They locked me away 'cause of you. Did you know I had a baby? In the institution. Some of the orderlies like to rape the women. Fuck the dummy, they used to say. Fucked me all the time. Wanna fuck me, Rob?"

She lifted her skirt, revealing gray hospital underwear with brown stains on it.

"Go ahead." Caitlyn came up next to him. Gave him a push. Her hands were ice on his arm. "Fuck her. Fuck my sister like you fucked me. Fucked my whole family."

"Fucked us all," Michael said. He and Patrick stood only a few feet away, their faces corpse pale. Rob tried to back up, but bumped into Maggie. Her breath was warm against his neck and the sweet, rancid smell of old meat wrapped around his face. He gagged and moved forward.

Lori jiggled her hips at him and made kissing noises. Spit flew from her lips.

"Maybe we're too old for him," Maggie said. "Maybe he wants to dip his stick in a sweet young thang." She and Caitlyn moved apart, revealing a young woman with black hair and pale skin. Blood stained the front of her shirt. Shadows hung beneath her familiar violet eyes.

No. Not her too. She can't be—

"Run, Rob. Run before it's too late. I can't stay long. He's too—" Shari Brock's face twisted in pain and then her expression changed from sad to furious. "You killed me, you bastard. Ruined my life and my sister's."

"This isn't real!" Rob shoved his way between past them, got clear of the circle, only to find the little boy standing there. Blood covered his face.

Evan Michaels?

"You promised nothing would happen to me." His voice was exactly the same as the last time Rob had heard it, just before he began the rites. "Now I'm dead and it's your fault."

Rob shook his head but couldn't deny the charge. It *had* been his fault. And he'd been haunted by his mistake ever since. He should've listened to Graves and Zimmerman, should've taken their warnings seriously, should've—

"Should've died in that attic." The guttural snarl of a second voice overlaid Caitlyn's words.

The kitchen door banged open and Rob jumped. A figure came out, a woman in chef's whites, body twisted and bent, shuffling instead of walking. Head down, wet hair dangling like a mop.

"It should've been you."

Kylie Johnson.

"No, please, no." He closed his eyes. He didn't want to see her. *Body broken, skull crushed, lying on the ground....* "You can't be here. You're dead."

"We're all dead." The apparitions spoke at once, voices mingling, joined by the deep growl. "Because of you."

"Stupid sheep."

For a moment Rob was transported back to that night in the attic room, Kylie Johnson hovering over the floor, floating toward the window. She'd said those words, right before....

"Sheep." A low whisper. The stench of rotten meat stronger than before. "Look at me, sheep."

Against his will, Rob's eyes opened.

Kylie stood inches from him, her dead-gray face mottled with purple bruises. Blood dripped from her mouth, and when she smiled, her teeth were black and broken. Her knotted, wet hair stunk of mud and river water.

"Poor little sheep, you've lost your flock," she snarled, her breath so rank his eyes watered and his stomach threatened to erupt. "Likes little girls to play with your cock."

She laughed, spraying vile spittle into Rob's face. The harsh cackling echoed through the room, coming from all directions at once. Kylie's mouth stretched open farther and farther, the skin splitting across her cheeks to reveal white bone. The others crowded closer, their flesh peeling away and dropping to the floor with wet thumps.

The remains of Kylie's face shifted, lost shape, reformed. Her nose flattened and bulged outward, her lips pulled back and jagged fangs burst from her colorless gums. Her ears disappeared and her hair fell out in thick clumps. Protuberances sprouted from her skull, bony growths erupting through the thin skin like a mountain range forming on an ancient plain. When the chorus spoke again, no trace of human voices remained.

"Better go now, Father Rob. You don't want to be late for the slaughter."

The laughter grew in volume, inside Rob's head and out, so loud he thought his eardrums would burst. With a cry, he turned and ran out the door, the insane cackling following him. Glass case fronts shattered as he passed them, and the tables rattled and shook, threatening to break free from the floor.

He hit the door full speed and stumbled down the stairs, staggering as he ran across the gravel lot until momentum failed to carry him any farther and he fell to his knees halfway to his car. Certain the ghosts of his past were right behind him, he twisted around, throwing his arms up to protect himself.

Nothing happened.

Slowly, he lowered his scraped hands. A strong breeze peppered his face with dust and grit. Fifty feet away stood the ruins of an ancient Airstream, the walls rusted and dented, the roof sagging. Empty windows gaped in rotten frames and the doors hung half off the hinges. A broken sign leaned against the front, faded red letters spelling out *INER* and under that *OPE 24 RS.*

"Jesus." Had any of it really happened or had he suffered some kind of hallucination? A reaction to stress and incipient DTs?

"Bring the priest." The growling voice came from the darkness behind the doors and from inside his head. "We're waiting."

Rob got up and staggered to the car. His hands trembled violently as he pulled back onto the highway, and didn't stop until he arrived at Buffalo Memorial two hours later. Tears on his cheeks and the demon's voice still haunting him, he went to the front desk. A white-haired clerk eyed him up and down before informing him that visiting hours were over for the night. Instead of returning to his car, he went to the hospital's chapel, where he took a seat in the back, pulled out a rosary, and silently recited twenty prayers.

When he finished, he started again.

And kept repeating the cycle until the sun came up.

CHAPTER TWENTY-EIGHT

Hastings Mills, NY, July 20th, one year ago

GHOST HUNTER ARRESTED FOR MURDER IN HAUNTED HOUSE! *Stone Graves, host of* In Search of the Paranormal, *is under arrest in the upstate town of Hastings Mills after a wild shootout during an apparent exorcism left one of his crew dead and another injured. Graves and two other people, Randi Zimmerman and Robert Lockhart, are suspects in the murder, which took place in the house of Curt Rawlings, which earlier in the week was the scene of an alleged 'rain of rocks'. Graves and Zimmerman were taken into custody after reporting the shooting. Police are still searching for the third suspect, Lockhart, who left in a car and is believed to be armed and dangerous.*

"Goddamn it!" Stone's handcuffs jangled against the metal table of the interrogation room as he shoved the morning edition of the paper away. Across from him, Hastings Mills's police chief, Rick Mordecai, pursed fleshy lips under his thick mustache and stared at Stone with merciless eyes. Stale coffee breath wafted across the table every time he spoke.

"Yeah, it's some shitstorm you and your crew brought to my town. Gotta figure it was only a matter of time before it sucked you in. Sure you don't want to read the rest of the article? Take your time, bub. Not like there ain't about a dozen crimes sitting on my plate while I sit around and deal with your reality TV bullshit."

Mordecai wiped sweat from his face and Stone wished he could do the same. The tiny room had no air-conditioning vent and the temperature was steamy. A single fan on the floor sat unplugged and covered in dust.

"Fuck you. It wasn't my fault and you know it," Stone said, although deep down he didn't feel the same conviction. Maybe he hadn't pulled the trigger, or caused the rocks to fall on that man. But he'd brought his team to Hastings Mills. If he'd just ignored Randi Fucking Zimmerman's message and stuck with their original filming schedule, Shari would be alive, Claudia wouldn't be comatose in a hospital, and he'd be sitting in a nice hotel room somewhere, instead of spending the night in a jail cell that stank of old piss.

"I don't know squat, 'cept I got a bunch of Hollywood nutcases stirring up trouble all over my town. And you're the one everybody says is in charge."

"I got hired to do a job. Ask Rawlings. And I sure as hell didn't invite Lockhart. I warned your cops he was dangerous, that he'd already killed someone doing one of his crazy exorcisms. The guy's a complete mental case."

"Don't you dare blame my officers for this!" Mordecai slapped a beefy hand on the table. "One of them is dead, thanks to you."

"How is that my fault?" He'd heard the other cops talking about Dicus's suicide, but he barely remembered what she looked like.

"She was talking some sort of devil worship gibberish before she shot herself. We got it on tape. I think hanging around your kind of people caused her to have a breakdown."

"My kind of people?" Stone leaned forward. "What the hell is that supposed to mean?"

"Nutjobs." Mordecai gave him an oily grin. "Don't you try bringin' race into this. We don't see color 'round here."

Yeah, right. I haven't seen any Black cops on your force. Racist, much? Stone took a breath and forced down the words. He didn't need to end up in the hospital next to Claudia. Still, he couldn't help needling the man.

"You actually think your officer believed Lockhart's bullshit and decided to kill herself?" Stone shook his head. "Now who's the nutjob?"

"Think you're funny?" Mordecai stood up and banged on the

door. "Put this asshole back in his cell," he said when an officer came in. "He can rot there until his lawyer shows up."

"Wait," Stone said, as the officer took him by the arm. "You can't hold us. We didn't shoot anyone. I'm the one who called you!"

"Maybe I can't get you for manslaughter or murder, but I can sure as hell charge you with endangering the welfare of a minor. And destruction of property. You and your damn stunts. Hope you're enjoying your publicity now."

"What about Claudia? Is she okay?"

Mordecai gave him another nasty smile. "Still in a coma. If she dies, that'll be on you, too." The chief let out a laugh and left the room.

Stone had to fight the urge to scream after him. Losing his temper now would only make things worse.

Even so, he could still feel his rage simmering.

And he didn't know how long he could keep it under control.

Claudia floated in darkness and wept tears she couldn't feel, cried sobs she couldn't hear.

She had no body, yet her mind still existed, her thoughts still formed. And with them came the unending pain of Shari's death. She'd felt every second of it, from the burning and tearing of the bullet through her chest to the frigid stab of her heart stopping.

Worst of all, she'd seen inside Shari's head in her final moments.

Stone directly in the line of fire. The blast of energy released in a desperate hope to save him. The satisfaction of seeing his body pushed out of the way.

The knowledge that doing this thing would mean her own death.

Why? Why would she sacrifice herself like that?

—For you, sister. I did it for you.—

Shari's voice came from everywhere and nowhere.

—Shari? Is that really you?—

Even as she thought it, the warm, comforting presence of her sister joined Claudia in the endless void.

—I'm here. I'll always be here. I would never leave you.—

—But you're dead. Why...?—

—I did what had to be done.—

An image appeared in Claudia's mind, like so many other times they'd shared thoughts. The demon, on its throne.

"If one of you gives themselves to me, the other will be spared."

"One of you will sacrifice yourself."

"It has already been decided. One of you will be mine."

Understanding of what Shari had really done flooded Claudia.

—No!—

—Yes— Shari responded. *—The creature would have taken one of us in that room no matter what. All I did was make the choice.—*

—But that means—

—It has my soul.—

—Where are you?—

A quick glimpse of towering flames and oceans of boiling red lava, and then only blackness again as Shari, always the stronger, blocked Claudia from her mind.

—It doesn't matter. The important thing now is to destroy...the beast. Things are worse than we understood, but I can help. My soul might be trapped here, but the barriers aren't solid. When you need me, I'll be there. I promise to...

A jolt of pain speared through Claudia's incorporeal being.

—Shari!—

No answer. The sensation of being truly alone returned, an ache Claudia had never felt before, as if she were incomplete. She wanted to scream, to cry. Without Shari, she had nothing. Was nothing. Rather than face it, she let the endless darkness claim her again.

Better not to think or feel at all than endure the agony of permanent loneliness.

Stone paced the jail cell like a caged tiger. Back and forth, back and forth. Each time he passed the door of the cell, he paused and peered out.

"Jesus, Stone. Will you sit down? You're making me dizzy."

He gave Randi an evil glare. "So look at something else. Where the fuck is everyone? We haven't heard from Ken or Del, or the goddamned lawyer."

"They'll come when they come. Nothing we can do about it." Randi pointed at one of the three long metal benches. Stone fought the urge to tell her to go to hell, took one more look outside, and dropped onto the seat across from her.

"I'm going fucking stir crazy."

"I can tell. But you haven't been yourself for a couple of days now."

"What the hell does that mean?"

Randi shrugged. "Honestly, you've turned into a dick. You used to be nice. A little selfish, maybe, craved the spotlight, but nice. Lately, you've been a real jerk, jumping down everyone's throat, worrying more about being famous than your people getting hurt. That's not the Stone Graves I used to know. I think Hollywood's gone to your fucking head."

Stone flipped her a middle finger. "Yeah? Fuck you. You haven't changed at all. Still the same foul-mouthed bitch you always were."

"That's true. I guess that makes you a foul-mouthed bitch, now, too, since you sound just like me."

"Suck a dick."

To Stone's surprise, Randi burst into laughter. After a moment, he joined her. He realized it was the first time he'd laughed since arriving in Hastings Mills, and damned if it didn't feel good.

"Aw, hell. I'm sorry. I didn't mean it," Stone said, wiping a tear from his eye.

"I did," Randi said, but she smiled to take the sting out of her comment. "Not the Hollywood part. But the last few days."

"It's this case. Or maybe this town. It's like there's this…I don't know…."

"Big black fucking cloud over everything?" Randi finished for him.

"Yeah." He got up and sat down next to her. "I've never felt anything like it. Except—"

"Wood Hill." Now there was no trace of humor in her voice. The temporary good vibes in the cell dissipated as both their thoughts turned to the day they'd met.

Stone nodded, then shook his head. "You sound like Claudia, reading my mind. Damn, I wish I knew how she was doing."

"I'm sure she'll be fine." Randi patted Stone's leg. "She's a good one. Don't screw things up with her."

"Like I did with you?"

"I wasn't going to say that, but since you brought it up, seeing you guys together reminds me a lot of when we first met. You definitely have a type."

"A type?" Stone frowned. "You two couldn't be more different."

"Really? Have you seen your girlfriend? I could pass for her mother. Hell, I even wore my hair the same way back in college. Only difference is our eyes, and I swear like a dockworker."

Stone started to say she was wrong, but then he stopped as a memory came to him. He and Randi at the beach. Seaside, New Jersey. Only a month after what happened at Wood Hill, and they'd escaped for the day because the press still hounded them on a regular basis. With everything closed for the winter they had the whole boardwalk to themselves, except for a few screeching gulls hoping for scraps. The sky and ocean had both been gray, but the temperature was mild enough for just jackets.

They'd sat on a bench for hours, just talking about what they'd seen, what it meant, if it really happened.

The open storage units in the morgue, cold mist pouring out of them. Twisting and turning, creating impossible shapes over their heads. The screaming voices coming from everywhere. Tendrils of fog swooping down. The horrible faces... something touching him...falling. The rotten stench of death, of graves.

"You killed us! Why can't we leave?"

The crushing sense of hopelessness, of evil. Everywhere.

And then it was all gone.

And a dead body lay on the floor.

At some point, they'd stopped talking and shared their first kiss. That led to more, and by the time they went back to Randi's car they were more than friends.

What Stone remembered most now about that day was how beautiful Randi had looked. Pale skin, raven hair, dark clothes. Just like Claudia and Shari.

And she was still beautiful, just in an older, more experienced way. He wondered if she was as wild in bed as she'd been back then. He missed that, the complete lack of inhibition she'd brought to lovemaking. Claudia was good, but she always seemed to be holding back, afraid to fully show her emotions. With Randi, sex had been more than just fulfilling, it had been a total release, lust and love combined into an explosion of sensual pleasure that—

"Hey!" Hands pushed against his chest. He opened his eyes and found Randi staring at him, her expression a mix of confusion and anger. "What the fuck, Stone?"

"I...I'm sorry." He slid away. Had he really tried to kiss her? "I don't know what happened. Everything kind of went...blank."

He kept the rest to himself, the images of her writhing naked beneath him, screaming his name, the heat of their bodies—

Stone jumped up and went to the ancient sink at the back of the cell, where he splashed tepid water on his face and waited for his erection to subside.

When he finally turned around, Randi still stared at him, only now she looked more suspicious than anything. Like he might attack her again. He sat down on a different bench.

"I think the stress is getting to me," he said, avoiding her eyes. "I don't know what's gonna happen. She and Shari had this kind of bond. Like two halves of a whole. I'm not sure she'll survive."

Before Randi could respond, someone shouted upstairs and

footsteps pounded on the floor. A moment later, the wail of a police car's siren reached them through the tiny window in the wall.

"Hell, I don't know if any of us will survive this town," Randi said.

After that, neither of them spoke for a while.

The pale, emaciated figure on the bed did not resemble the man Rob Lockhart had known back in college.

He barely resembled a man at all.

Tubes and wires snaked out from under the sheets and joined various pieces of equipment that beeped and hummed next to the bed. Father Leo's arms and legs had withered to flesh-covered sticks and his cheeks formed cavities beneath the dark hollows of his closed eyes. His once-sizeable belly had shrunk to the size of a cantaloupe, which protruded like a miniature burial mound below the flatness of his chest.

The moment Rob entered the room, his hopes for Bonaventura being his savior plummeted down to zero. Even if the old priest came out of his coma, how could he possibly have the strength to banish one of the most powerful demons known to man?

Tears flowed down Rob's cheeks as he pulled a chair to the side of the bed. It was over. No hope for him, for Abigail, for the town of Hastings Mills. The evil of Asmodeus would continue to spread, infecting more and more people, until either the Church figured out a solution or the demon tired of its games.

The third possibility, one he refused to acknowledge, was that Asmodeus might fully emerge into the world and bring about the destruction of mankind. He couldn't imagine God allowing that to happen.

Then again, the past few years had delivered some pretty biblical events. Viral plagues, wars, famine...maybe they'd been signs.

"Wouldn't that be the perfect epitaph? Because of my sins and hubris, I helped trigger Armageddon." Rob placed his hand on Father Leo's arm. Loose skin shifted over aged bone.

"I'm sorry, Father," he whispered to the still form. Only a slow rising and falling of the priest's chest indicated he still lived. "I tried. I really did. But I failed God again. I've done awful things, things that condemned my soul to Hell. I don't deny my sins. But this time, this time I truly thought I was doing God's will. Only I fell victim to Satan's lies and my own pride. You were my last chance. Now I understand why the demon asked for you. It knew what I should've known. That your days of fighting are over. And so are mine."

Tears dropped onto the sheets. Rob let them fall. Each one represented his shame manifesting for the world to see. He'd ruined his life and so many others. He had willfully followed the wrong path. And now he and the world would pay the price for his transgressions. There would be no final triumph, no divine intervention. The only thing left for him to do now was turn himself in.

First, though, he would pray. Not for his own soul; it was too late for him. He would pray for Abigail Rawlings. Pray for Hastings Mills and all the people he'd wronged in his life. And most of all, he'd pray for Father Leo, that the priest might find peace and freedom from his pain, either in this world or the next.

Rob bowed his head and closed his eyes.

"He who dwells in the shelter of the Most High, and abides in the shade of the Almighty, says to the Lord, 'My refuge, my stronghold, my God in whom I trust.'

"He will free you from the snare of the fowler, from the destructive plague; he will conceal you with his pinions, and under his wings you will find refuge.

"His faithfulness is buckler and shield. You will not fear the terror of the night, nor the arrow that flies by day, nor the plague that prowls in the darkness, nor the scourge that lays waste at noon...."

Halfway through Psalm 91, Rob's exhaustion claimed him and he drifted into sleep.

He never noticed when Bonaventura's arm twitched.

CHAPTER TWENTY-NINE

Hastings Mills, NY, July 20th, one year ago

Ken Webb and Del Hall sat next to each other in the equipment van, watching the different rooms in the Rawlingses' house on the split screens.

Curt stood by the kitchen counter, pouring whiskey into a cup of coffee. His third of the day, even though it wasn't noon yet. Ken couldn't blame him. He and Del both agreed that if they'd been in his shoes, they'd be halfway across the state by now. Or locked in a mental ward.

In the living room, the sofa and chairs floated a foot above the carpet while slowly orbiting the coffee table. In Curt's bedroom, all the dressers and the closet had disgorged their clothes, which had paired up, pants and shirts, and now danced in wild fashion throughout the room.

None of that compared to the scene in Abby's room.

Dark, roiling clouds covered her ceiling. Lightning lit them from within. Each flash revealed horrific faces. Men and women, their mouths open wider than humanly possible, their eyes empty black holes. Green slime oozed from the walls and dripped onto the floor, where it disappeared into the cracks between the boards. Abby thrashed on the bed, arms and legs spasming, body writhing, head twisting back and forth. Blisters covered her skin, forming weird cuneiform shapes that constantly changed. Every so often, she'd stare at the camera with the yellow eyes and horizontal pupils of a goat, laugh, and vomit out more of the green ooze. Then she'd go back to her St. Vitus' dance.

"This is some fucked-up shit," Ken said.

Del nodded, not sure if his partner referred to the things happening inside the house or the arrests of Stone and Zimmerman. Either way, he was glad to be in the van. If Stone had been there, he'd have insisted they film by hand instead of setting up motion-activated cameras in the rooms.

Of course, even remaining on the property struck Del as pretty stupid. Only loyalty to Stone kept him and Ken from making tracks out of town. That, and the guarantee of a huge payday when everything was over and the footage got released to the world.

One of the computers beeped and a yellow light came on. Ken clicked a few keys and brought up a counter at the bottom of each screen. It showed how many hours of recording they'd made and how much storage space remained in the hard drives.

"Another forty minutes," he said. "Then we'll have to switch drives and upload these files to the cloud." Unlike their original equipment, the new backup drives had to be connected to a separate server to transfer to the cloud.

Occupied with their work, neither of them noticed the smoky tendrils creeping into the van through the open back doors. A wispy strand wound its way up Del's leg and he stiffened. A second diaphanous tentacle found Ken's foot. He went rigid as well. Both of them remained like that for a few seconds and then relaxed. Del grasped Ken's shoulders and began to massage them.

"Forty minutes is a long time. What do you think we should do while we wait?"

Ken turned his chair. "I can think of something." He leaned forward and Del met him halfway, their gentle kiss quickly growing more vigorous, lips smashing together, tongues entwining. Del ripped Ken's shirt open and slid out of his own t-shirt while Ken stood and undid his jeans. In moments they were naked and on the floor.

The hazy tendrils dissolved around them, but more slithered through the grass toward the neighboring houses.

Officer Corday Rose pulled up in front of the Motel 9 at the far end of Main Street, right at the edge of the town line. The midday sun burned his tired, aching eyes. Exiting the air-conditioned car was like being transported to a tropical jungle. Sweat broke out on his forehead and under his arms, adding to the stains he'd accumulated there during an exhausting night shift filled with some of the craziest calls he'd ever dealt with.

There'd been Mrs. Ronson throwing hot coffee in her neighbor's face during a game of Monopoly, which had led to the neighbor's husband sticking a cake knife into Mr. Ronson's stomach. Then three women at Perkins had stood up, stripped down to their birthday suits, and offered to have sex with anyone in the restaurant. By the time Corday arrived, two men had taken them up on the proposal while the rest of the dinner crowd cheered them on. After that, there'd been two robberies – the 7-Eleven on State and the Tasty Pizza right next door. Same suspects both times, a pair of teenagers who not only didn't try to hide their faces, they waved at the cameras and smiled as they left with the money.

And now this. Twenty minutes before the end of his shift, when all he wanted to do was go home and fall into bed. A call from the girl at the front desk, saying there'd been a ruckus in one of the third-floor rooms loud enough for him to hear it down in the lobby.

"All sorts of shouting, and stuff banging around," the clerk had told Martha. "Like they're rock stars trashing the place. I'm afraid to go up there."

Corday exited the car, certain this would be another messed-up situation and he wouldn't get home for hours. Not that home was any kind of haven. Every time he closed his eyes, visions of Abigail Rawlings floating in the air appeared in his head.

I need to talk to Graves. Or a shrink. Either way, I—

Three stories up, a window banged open and loud music blared out. Someone shouted, "Bombs away!"

Corday had just enough time to jump away from the car before a large rectangular object landed on it with a tremendous *crash!* The sound of glass shattering disappeared in the wail of the car's alarm going off. Corday rolled over and saw the remains of a flat-screen TV wedged into the patrol car's roof lights. Someone hooted laughter and the window banged shut.

Cursing, Corday went to the car and turned the engine off, silencing the alarm. Then he stormed into the lobby, passed the wide-eyed clerk without a word, and banged open the door to the stairwell. As he pounded up the stairs, he called in to Martha to request backup.

"It's like goddamned *Animal House* here," he shouted.

On the third floor, he had no trouble determining which way to go. Rock music screamed from around the corner to his left. He drew his gun and slowed his progress, moving carefully down the corridor. Several doors stood open, but when he glanced in, the rooms were empty.

He wondered where the guests had gone. Certainly not the lobby, it'd been empty.

He eased around the corner. The sounds of Bob Seger singing about a devil with a blue dress on blared from an open door down the hall. Not the kind of music Corday would have associated with druggies. Hugging the wall, he approached the room. The music was so loud it sounded distorted. It reminded him of the time he'd blown the speakers in his car as a teenager.

When he reached the door, he put his back to the wall and peered around the frame.

A group of naked men and women knelt in a circle around a candle on the floor, bloody hands clasped and faces turned up to the ceiling, eyes closed and mouths open. Crude symbols drawn in blood decorated their chests and stomachs. The music came from a bunch of hotel radios piled onto the bed, which had been pushed to one side of the room. Crimson letters dripped on the wall where the TV used to hang.

"—Burnin' with a fire, unholiest desires! Hellrider, comin' for you—"

The music cut off mid-verse. At the same time, all the people turned and looked at him.

With eyes of pure black.

The flame of the candle flared bright red and a tower of thick smoke rose from it, forming a dense cloud over the group. Shapes appeared in the smoke, almost like faces, except with oversized horns like a triceratops.

One of the people, a skinny woman in her sixties, stood up, her drooping breasts flopping from side to side like half-filled water balloons.

"Don't move," Corday said, aiming his gun at her.

She smiled, and the rest of the group got to their feet.

"I mean it. Not one step." He heard the wail of sirens. Two minutes away at the most. All he had to do was keep things from escalating until backup arrived.

The entire group took a step forward.

"This is your last warning." He counted thirteen of them, too many to control if they charged. They ranged from mid-twenties to definite senior citizens, including one bald, pot-bellied geezer with gray chest hair and a tiny worm dick poking out from a nest of white pubes. A pile of clothing next to the bed caught his eye, and a flash of realization hit him.

These were the people from the other rooms.

They'd all gathered together and stripped, and then...what? Decided to hold some kind of weird ceremony?

Like devil worship.

The moment he thought it, he knew it was true. And somehow related to Abigail Rawlings, Stone Graves, and that crazy priest, Lockhart.

"Fuck this." Corday turned and ran. When he reached the stairwell, he slammed open the door and took the stairs two at a time, using the railing to keep from falling. He raced through the lobby without stopping and reached the parking lot just as two more police cruisers skidded to a stop next to his wrecked car.

"What the fuck?" yelled Mitch Banks, jumping out of the lead car.

"Room three-twenty-seven." Corday pointed up at the window. "It's a bunch of devil worshippers. They're nuts."

"Let's go." Banks drew his gun. The other officer, Emil Wallace, did the same and they ran for the entrance. Corday waited until they got to the door and then climbed into Banks's squad car and headed for the station.

It was time to talk to Stone.

The sweltering darkness of Costa Rica surrounded Leo in an unending maze of terror.

No matter which path he tried, he ended up in the same place, the clearing at the edge of the village. He'd been running in circles for hours, trying to reach the river, to avoid facing the creature that waited for him.

Death.

Now he stood once again at the tree line where jungle gave way to trampled grass, his chest heaving, sweat soaking his clothes. Ahead of him, fires cast a red glow on the rounded huts. Villagers stood in small groups, waiting for him to come and cast the demon from their midst. A white man in bush clothes was with them. The doctor. Leo tried to think of his name but it refused to come.

I can't help you. It's too strong.

He turned to head back to the river. Maybe this time he'd find the right way. Make it to the boat. Then he could—

A young woman blocked his way.

"Hello, Father." She spoke softly, with more than a touch of melancholy. One look and he could tell she didn't belong in this place. Her pale skin marked her as someone who'd never spent any time in the tropical sun. And her clothes were all wrong. A plain white t-shirt and shorts made of blue denim. Sandals far too fragile for walking in the jungle.

All of this he took in with a glance before her eyes caught his attention. Upturned, slightly round. Deep violet, a shade he'd never seen before. The white of her skin made them even more prominent, almost unnatural. Like she could see into his soul. They sparkled with orange, reflecting the flames.

"Who are you?" he asked.

"We need you. The beast has returned."

Leo looked back at the village. The beast, yes. In one of the huts. His ancient enemy. He turned to the girl.

"I can't go there. Death waits for me."

"Not here. Home. I've come to take you back. We need you. She needs you." The woman held out her hand, her pallid flesh so translucent that for a moment he swore he could see right through it.

"Home? I don't understand. How—"

"We must stop it. But not here. You have to trust me."

A bestial roar sounded from the village. Someone screamed.

If she knew the way out....

He took her hand. Ice-cold fingers wrapped around his and the sparks in her eyes grew brighter. He realized she had her back to the fires.

A trick!

He tried to pull away but couldn't break free. Her ethereal flesh began to glow, the supernatural aura intensifying until it enveloped them both. Her body faded away.

The last things to go were her sad, knowing eyes.

Then there was only white.

⛤

I'm alive.

Leo knew it even before he tried to open his eyes. His left hand ached terribly, warm sweat soaked the back of his neck, and a dull throbbing filled his chest. Somewhere off to his left, a machine ticked and beeped. When he breathed, something rubbed against his nostrils.

I'm alive. I made it through the surgery.

Relief surged through him. Despite the relative simplicity of his operation, he'd been worried because of his advanced age and declining health. Anesthesia was particularly dangerous for anyone suffering cognitive issues, but his brain seemed to be working fine.

Or was it?

He did a quick memory test. The events of the past few days seemed clear enough. His ride to Buffalo. Prepping for surgery. Even the eerie dreams that had haunted him when he'd been under anesthesia. Nightmares, really. Being back in Costa Rica, and at St. Alphonse. A monstrous demon stalking him.

The ghostly young woman in the jungle....

"We need you."

The woman had disappeared in a burst of light. Light that still seeped through his eyelids. Daylight? Lights in the ceiling? He wanted to open his eyes, but when he tried, they only twitched. Like they'd been glued shut.

How long have I been asleep? Did something go wrong?

Am I paralyzed?

Sudden fear jolted him. What if his mind worked but his body didn't? The beeping by his ear sped up in time with his heart. He had to know!

He lifted his arms. They seemed to weigh a thousand pounds but they worked. At the same time, he bent his knees to make sure his legs functioned. Each movement eased the sense of terror threatening to overwhelm him. A sharp pain jabbed his left hand and he lowered it. With his right, he rubbed his eyes. His fingers came away covered in grit but he managed a quick peek before blinding whiteness forced them shut again.

The second time he tried, he succeeded in keeping them open. Tears ran down his cheeks and he had to blink several times before he could focus.

He found himself staring at white ceiling tiles and long rows of fluorescent bulbs. When he turned his head, the glare of the morning sun through a large window only made things worse. He looked in the other direction.

A man sat in a chair right next to the bed.

Leo jerked back, not expecting anyone to be there. The man's head was bowed, hiding his face, and for a moment Leo thought him deep in prayer. Then the stranger snored softly. A priest from the university? He didn't look like one. His hair and clothes were disheveled, as if he'd slept in them. A visitor who'd drifted off while waiting for Leo to wake up. But who? He reached out and tapped the man's arm.

The man rocked back in his chair with a gasp. Wide, terrified eyes stared at Leo and his mouth gaped as if about to let loose a scream. Then his expression relaxed and he grasped Leo's hand.

"Father! Thank God!"

"Do I—?" Leo lost the rest of his words as a coughing fit overcame him. The stranger grabbed a plastic cup with a straw from the bed stand and held it to Leo's mouth. The tepid water cut through the stale crust in Leo's mouth and throat and rehydrated parched surfaces. After two sips, Leo leaned back and repeated his question in a voice still weak but audible.

"Do I know you?"

The man nodded. "It's me, Father Leo. Rob Lockhart."

Leo peered at the man more closely. Lockhart…the name sounded familiar, but there'd been so many students over the years, and between the Alzheimer's and surgery, his memory….

Wait. Lockhart. His old student from St. Alphonse, the one who'd gone on to seminary. He'd passed the course on exorcism and then… there'd been some kind of scandal. Last he'd heard, Lockhart had been stripped of his clerical status. Laicized.

Why was he here?

"Well, it's kind of you to visit me. I'm sorry if I don't—"

Lockhart took his arm. "Fifth Dallas. Kylie Johnson."

Leo's heart gave a painful jump and for a moment his vision went dim. The monitor by the bed emitted a shrill squawk.

Fifth Dallas! The deaths. Asmodeus. His dreams!

"I'm sorry to bring up bad memories, Father. But you need to come with me to Hastings Mills. It's an emergency."

"What? I don't under—"

Lockhart's hand gripped tighter as the door flew open and a nurse ran in.

"It's back, Father. The demon is back."

Leo Bonaventura sat in the passenger seat of Robert Lockhart's car and stared out the window as they raced down Route 17W toward Hastings Mills. His right hand clutched the armrest on the door so it wouldn't shake, while his other hand fidgeted nonstop with the hem of his shirt.

An exorcism. The fool had conducted an exorcism on that little girl. And in the process, released…what? Could it really be the unspeakable one, the demon that had haunted him through the decades?

No. That would be impossible. The wards are in place. It has to be another. Demons lie, they don't give their true names.

But his dreams….

Some kind of premonition. Perhaps I felt the presence of evil before I left town and my subconscious automatically focused on the thing I fear most.

He glanced at Lockhart, who kept his attention on the road ahead. Tendons stood out on the man's clenched jaw and beads of sweat decorated his forehead. Together with his bloodshot eyes and pasty color, they added up to someone fighting the call of a different kind of demon. Alcohol.

Was that what brought about his dismissal? It had to have been very bad.

No wonder Dr. Ho Sing had fought so hard to keep him from leaving. He'd been comatose for almost four days and now insisted on checking out in the company of a man who looked like he'd just wandered in from a homeless shelter. A man who'd needed two broken fingers of his own set and bandaged.

"My opinion is that you should stay another day," Ho Sing had said after running several tests. "Your heart looks fine, but the complications were so unusual, I think more observation is warranted."

"My doctors in Hastings Mills will monitor it," Leo had replied. "Along with my other treatments, for my…condition. But this really is an urgent family matter I must attend to."

Ho Sing had hemmed and hawed, but in the end the surgeon agreed. It was almost noon by the time Leo left the hospital, his legs shaking but his mind clearer than it had been for months, after promising to take it easy for a few days.

If I survive what's to come, I'll have the rest of my life to sleep.

Right now, he had the Lord's work to do.

And damned if it didn't feel good to be needed again. Even if it meant cleaning up a mess that never should have happened.

Why had they done it? Lockhart, of all people, should have known better. He'd had enough training to understand the dangers of his actions. And the rest of those fools as well. Bringing obvious telekinetics in contact with a supernatural entity? In a house where a family had been tainted by a demon and a suicide had occurred? A true recipe for disaster. Hadn't any of them read his books?

Of course not, you silly old fool, his inner voice scolded. *You're two generations removed from them. Everything they know comes from the internet or TV.* On the heels of that came another thought.

What do you think an over-the-hill, doddering priest with a stent in his heart and incipient Alzheimer's can do to help?

A road sign flashed by, announcing the exit for Cuba (*Cuba Cheese Shoppe! Best in New York!*) coming up. Only another twenty minutes to Hastings Mills.

I guess I'll know soon enough.

In his head, Leo began making lists of the things he'd need.

Officer Corday Rose descended the stairs into the holding area. In the second cell, Stone Graves and Randi Zimmerman looked up. Stone immediately cursed and slammed his fist against the wall.

"We need to talk," Corday said.

"More bullshit interrogation?" Stone asked. "What's the matter, your chief can't be bothered to do it himself?"

"Stone, shut your damn mouth and let him speak."

"Screw you." Stone glared at Randi. "I wouldn't even be here if it wasn't for you."

"Oh, fuck off." The woman flipped him a middle finger and sat down as far away as possible.

"Shut up, the both of you!" Corday had no time for their petty bullshit. "Do you really believe all this demon stuff?"

"I do now," Randi said. Stone scowled and then peered through the steel bars with narrowed eyes.

"Looks like you do, too, Rose. What happened?"

Corday chewed at his lip before answering. "I saw something today. A disturbance call at a local hotel. When I got to the room there were all these people. Naked. Doing some kind of black mass or something."

"Whoop-de-fucking-doo." Stone leaned against the wall. "You came here to tell us you busted up an orgy? Or maybe you joined in?" He waggled his eyebrows.

"No. What I saw was...like the other night. In Abigail's room. Except all of them...their eyes...all wrong. And there were things in the smoke, not human...." Corday stopped as Graves's face drained of color and he stepped away from the bars.

"You know what I'm talking about, don't you?" Corday grabbed the bars. "What the hell did I see? What did you people let loose in my town?"

"It wasn't us," Randi said. "This started before any of us got here."

Cold spiders ran down Corday's back. "What do you mean?"

Stone snorted, but he still looked scared. "She means your town has been fucked up for a long, long time."

"Stop at my apartment before you take me to the house."

Robert grunted as he took the exit ramp that led into the west side of town, by the university. He'd been mostly uncommunicative during the ride, his hands gripping the wheel so tight Leo thought his bones might pop right through the skin. Sweat matted his hair and for the last fifteen minutes there'd been a muscle twitching nonstop in his neck.

As they crossed the town line, a memory hit Leo so hard he rocked back in his seat.

A warm, sunny day just like this, fifty-five years ago. Driving from his hotel to the campus, a jar of impossible yet real beetles in a box. Beetles that had come from the mouth of a dying boy. In his head, the last words that boy had spoken.

"Your time will come, Father Fucking Bonaventura! You cannot kill me, for I am eternal."

Robert pulled into the parking lot of the retirement complex and Leo told him to wait in the car. The man's grubby, wild-eyed appearance would be impossible to explain. Inside the apartment, Leo ignored the warm, musty air and went right to his bedroom closet, where he kept a small satchel filled with the essentials of his trade: a Bible, holy water, a rosary with a cross, and a packet of communion hosts. He went to shut the closet door and then reached inside again and removed a second cross, this one made of silver. The surface was tarnished and the arms twisted slightly out of shape. For more than forty years, it had remained in its wooden box.

It had defeated Asmodeus once before. It might be needed again.

After pausing to take one of the heart pills Ho Sing had given him, he hurried as fast as his aged legs would take him back to Robert's car. With each passing moment, a sense of wrongness grew stronger inside him, a sure sign that something definitely was *off* in Hastings Mills.

Heading down State Street toward the campus, Leo caught sight of yellow tape up ahead. When he saw which building had been cordoned off, he shouted for Robert to stop.

My church!

The top half of Holy Cross was gone, with nothing but charred beams poking up from the stone walls of the first story. The stained-glass windows and front door were boarded up. Black soot marred the granite.

"Dearest God, what happened?" Leo didn't even know he'd spoken aloud until Robert answered.

"I don't know, Father. It was fine two days ago. I came here for holy water and candles."

Leo turned sharply toward Robert, and then back to the ruined chapel. So many thousands of masses he'd said there over the years. So many memories. Weddings, christenings, funerals. Guiding young children on their first steps as Christians....

And it burns down right after Robert visits?

That couldn't be coincidence.

Whoever makes a practice of sinning is of the Devil, for the Devil has been sinning from the beginning. A quote from the apostle John. Robert certainly had made a practice of sinning, anyone could see that. From his alcoholism to whatever forced his removal from the priesthood, which in Leo's experience only happened in the most extreme cases of misconduct. In fact, the only three reasons he'd ever heard of were embezzlement, violent crimes, or...sexual assault.

He looked at Robert again as they pulled away from the curb. Had his drinking caused him to lose control in more ways than one?

Had his gluttony opened him to the Devil's influence?

'And give no opportunity to the Devil.' Ephesians 4:27.

Robert had said he'd spent the last several years traveling the country and performing exorcisms and banishments as a private minister. That meant a lot of contact with evil.

Oh, Robert, have you slipped too far?

Preoccupied with his thoughts as they passed the St. Alphonse Cemetery and approached the campus, Leo didn't notice anything amiss until Robert gasped and pulled over once more.

Fifth Dallas.

Construction vehicles sat parked in front of the magnificent, ivy-covered building. Dumpsters outside were filled with plaster and wood. There were caution tape and red cones around the building. The windows were missing.

God in Heaven, no! They couldn't have.

But there was no mistaking it. And in that moment, Leo understood everything. Robert, Abigail Rawlings. The fire. His own dreams.

"Your time will come, Father Fucking Bonaventura! You cannot kill me, for I am eternal."

Robert had been right all along.

They'd woken the demon.

CHAPTER THIRTY

Hastings Mills, NY, July 20th, one year ago

Corday Rose sat on the floor outside the cell holding Stone Graves and Randi Zimmerman, his thoughts spinning like a tornado from what they'd told him. He wanted to dismiss it all as bullshit but some of the facts brought back memories from years past.

The deaths at St. Alphonse. He was only a toddler at the time, but growing up he'd heard the rumors. And not just the college. His father had been friends with the previous police chief, Harry Showalter, and after a few beers he used to love telling young Corday and his sister some of the creepier stories Showalter and the other cops would share, back before Showalter disappeared the summer of the big earthquake.

"Whole area's a little weird," he said one time. *"Witches, devil worshippers, alien hunters, people sayin' they saw Bigfoot. I've seen some strange shit over the years. Something in the water. Or maybe just too many cousins sleepin' together."*

Caitlyn Sweeney's suicide. He should have remembered that, even if he didn't work the case. But he hadn't known her personally, and there'd been so many cases.

And now that Lockhart fellow had supposedly raised a demon. Two days ago, it would have seemed ridiculous. But with everything that had happened lately....

"Rose!"

The chief's voice echoed down the stairs, accompanied by heavy footsteps. Corday jumped to his feet.

"Yes, sir?"

"You just up and left your own crime scene? What in hell were you thinking?"

Corday gave a silent curse. He'd hoped Mordecai wouldn't find out until later, but someone must have radioed in from the motel.

"I, um, needed to follow up on something one of the, uh, suspects said."

"Follow up? With these assholes?" Mordecai pointed at the cell. "What did your suspect say?"

"Well, it wasn't so much what they said as what they wrote. On the wall. A single word. In Latin, I think, or maybe Greek. It reminded me of something the Rawlings girl said during the, uh, exorcism. And those people at the motel, performing a ceremony of some kind, I thought maybe—"

"You thought? You thought you had to run like a coward and leave your mess for someone else to clean up? I should fire you right now, but we're already shorthanded. The whole damn town's gone crazy. But you can bet your ass I'm writing you up and when this is all over there'll be a hearing. I—"

"Chief Mordecai, I think you should listen to your officer."

Mordecai turned at the new voice, and Corday stepped to the side to see who'd spoken.

An elderly man with fresh bruises on his arms and thick glasses perched at the end of a longish nose stood at the bottom of the stairs. Behind him lurked Robert Lockhart, who looked like he belonged in the drunk tank. Sweat stained his shirt and his hair was damp and tangled.

"Father Bonaventura?" Mordecai frowned. "What are you doing here?"

The old man gestured with a trembling hand.

"Praying to God I'm not too late to save this town."

Chief Mordecai's office hadn't changed in the five years since the last time Leo had seen it, when he'd stopped in to bless a cross for the chief's granddaughter's first communion. Papers piled high on the desk and on shelves, the same stained coffee mug next to his phone, and so much grime on the windows they barely let in any light.

Someone had brought in extra chairs so that Leo, Lockhart, and the other officer, Corday Rose, could sit. The two paranormal investigators, Zimmerman and Graves, were there as well. Another officer stood by the door. Leo recognized Graves from TV. Something seemed off about him, an angry look in his eyes like he was just itching to start trouble.

Mordecai started things off by pointing at Lockhart. "You're under arrest. Suspicion of murder. Leaving the scene of a crime. You have anything to say?"

Lockhart stared down at his hands and then glanced at Leo before answering.

"I did it. I killed that poor girl."

"Son of a bitch!" Graves lunged at him but Officer Rose held him back.

"Satan controlled my hand, but the guilt lies on my soul. I deserve whatever punishment comes my way."

"Don't give me that Satan bullshit," Graves shouted. "You've been obsessed with them for years. You're a goddamn pedophile and a murderer."

Lockhart shook his head. "My sins are many. And I will answer for them. But Abigail must be cleansed before the evil inside her spreads even farther."

"Get this nut out of here." Mordecai motioned to the officer by the door, who took Lockhart by the arm. As they left the room, Lockhart looked back.

"Please, all of you. Listen to Father Bonaventura. He's faced this demon before. Only he can save you now."

Mordecai waved his hand and Corday shut the door.

All eyes turned toward Father Bonaventura.

This was the moment he'd been dreading. In all his years with the Church, he'd never run afoul of the law before. Even in the few instances when there'd been injuries or deaths, like the house he'd cleansed for a famed husband-and-wife paranormal investigation team back in his early days at St. Alphonse. It had taken days to drive the evil spirit from that place. But the police had let him do what he needed, with a minimum of fuss.

These were different times. And Mordecai, although a devout Catholic, wasn't the type of man to believe in demons.

Still, he had to try. Lives depended on it.

"Some of you here know me, others don't. My name is Leo Bonaventura. I'm a retired priest and a professor emeritus at St. Alphonse, where I instructed theology and religion. I'm also an exorcist."

"Former," Mordecai said.

"There's never a former when it comes to that."

"Lockhart said you've faced this demon before. What did he mean?"

Leo pursed his lips at the Zimmerman woman's question. Where should he start? The events on Fifth Dallas? Or the very beginning?

They need to know what they're up against.

"We're dealing with a demon named Asmodeus. And it killed a very good friend of mine."

The Hastings Mills annual community yard sale was in full swing despite the heat. Hundreds of people had gathered in Riverside Park, most of them eager to part with a few dollars in the hopes of finding just the right knickknack for their shelf or that rare comic or piece of art at a steal. Others came out of desperation, unable to afford clothes or utensils anywhere else. Rows of tables filled the parking lot, with shoppers pressed nearly shoulder to shoulder as they browsed through mounds of clothing, outdated electronics, mildewed books and records, and rusty pocketknives for the proverbial diamond in the rough.

Wedged between a woman hawking pre-worn t-shirts and jeans, and a man selling music cassette tapes from the eighties, Ian Danziker froze in the act of handing someone change for the old St. Pauli Girl beer mugs they'd just purchased.

It's time.

The voice was back. The same one that had been speaking inside his head since the night before. It had told him the most amazing things about Heaven and the afterlife. That the end of times was coming, and only he and eleven other chosen ones would ascend to Paradise.

Like the twelve apostles? he'd asked the voice.

Yes, it had told him. A picture had appeared with the words, a long table surrounded by fluffy clouds. Jesus sat at the midpoint, his robes glowing, his halo a brilliant gold. And next to him, Ian Danziker. Only a younger, healthier Ian, without a back stooped from decades of factory work and with hair that was brown and full again. Heavenly Ian smiled, his teeth as white as snow instead of yellowed by a lifetime of smoking.

Ian turned and walked away, leaving the confused customer with her twenty plus the fifteen in change. He picked up his pace as he exited the market area and left the crowd behind. Down the slope to the dikes that had been built to keep the park from flooding when the Allegheny River rose up each spring. From there, a two-minute walk brought him to the Fourth Street Bridge.

Along the way, seven men and women joined him. None of them spoke to him, and he remained quiet, his attention captured by the promise of eternal bliss.

The remaining four waited at the bridge. All of them wore identical smiles.

As one, they climbed over the guard rail and onto the cement lip of the bridge. Thirty feet below, slime-covered rocks sat exposed by the summer drought that had lowered the water level.

"*Asmodeus suscitat,*" Ian said.

"*Asmodeus suscitat,*" the others repeated.

Ian closed his eyes. Jesus waved to come and join him.

Twelve people stepped off the edge.

The furniture in the Rawlingses' living room dropped to the floor with a tremendous crash. The same sound repeated upstairs, in Abigail's bedroom. In the kitchen, Curt jumped and dropped his cup, which by then was more whiskey than coffee.

A deep, rough voice bellowed from upstairs.

"Father."

Curt gripped the edge of the sink. He could still hear something of Abby in the bestial tones.

"Father. Come to me."

Every fiber of his being screamed at him to ignore the command, to run for help. Yet his feet moved him toward the stairs. He clung to the banister with both hands as he began climbing the steps.

"Yesssss. Come."

The guttural voice urged him on, becoming more insistent the closer he got to the top. When he stepped into the upstairs hall, Abby's bedroom door swung open. A fetid odor wafted out and Curt's whiskey-laced coffee came up in a massive eruption that splattered across his shoes.

"Come to me."

Trailing puke, he made his way down the hall. When he reached Abby's room, he wanted to scream but only a whimper came out.

She sat cross-legged in the air a foot above her bed. Her pajama top was gone, revealing a body so emaciated her ribs stood out clearly beneath her skin. Fiery red welts and purple bruises covered her flesh, some in the shape of massive hands, others depicting crude symbols he couldn't identify. Greenish-yellow fluids dripped from her nose and mouth, and more of it stained the sheets and walls.

The temperature in the room felt at least twenty degrees warmer than the rest of the house and Abby's sweat-soaked hair lay plastered to her neck and shoulders.

Abby's mouth opened and gobs of slime oozed out. When she spoke, the stench grew unbearable, forcing Curt to cover his face with his arm.

"Tell the priest." She pointed at the ceiling. He looked up and watched as smoking letters formed in the paint.

Asmodeus suscitat.

The symbols on Abby's body shifted, blending together and then reforming into crude representations of wild beasts with fangs and horns.

"*Go!*" she roared.

Curt turned and ran.

The door to Mordecai's office banged open. The chief looked up, ready to chew someone a new asshole for barging in, but the desk officer didn't give him a chance.

"Chief! We've got an emergency at the park! A whole bunch of people dead in the river."

"Shit! Send all units there now!" He headed for the door. When Officer Rose tried to follow, Mordecai held up his hand. "Not you, Rose. You wanted these nutjobs let loose, well, they're your responsibility now. You're with them, twenty-four seven. Anything happens, it's on you."

Mordecai ran down the hall to the bullpen, shouting orders as he went. A moment later, sirens wailed and then faded as five cruisers left the parking lot.

All eyes turned toward Stone. He looked back at them.

"Okay, let's do this."

Ken Webb leaped up as the back door of the van flew open and a wild-eyed Curt Rawlings jumped inside. "We have to get the priest!"

"Jesus Christ!" Ken grabbed his pants and held them in front of his crotch. Del crossed his legs and pulled a shirt over himself. "What the hell, man?"

"Abby. That thing. It spoke to me. We have to go."

"What?" Del tapped at the keyboard while Ken got dressed. The monitor showed her on her bed, masturbating inside her pajama bottoms while an invisible hand slapped her head back and forth. Del rewound the file to when Curt entered her room. When Abby/the demon shouted for Curt to go, Del hit the stop button and turned around.

"We don't know where Lockhart is."

"Then find him!" Curt said. "Before it kills my daughter."

—Claudia. You have to wake up.—

Shari's voice in the darkness. A sob rose up in Claudia's nonexistent throat. She couldn't see her sister. Would never see her again.

—No. There's nothing left for me.—

—They need you, sister.—

—I don't care.— Claudia shook her head. All she wanted to do was die. Then she'd be together with Shari again.

—Please. You can help them. We can help them.—

—No.—

—Claudia—

—NO!—

In her hospital bed, Claudia thrashed and moaned. Her EKG sounded an alarm. One of the floor nurses rushed in and checked the numbers.

"Call Dr. Ronsen!"

CHAPTER THIRTY-ONE

Hastings Mills, NY, July 20th, one year ago

In the parking lot, Stone was about to get into Officer Corday's cruiser when his phone went off.

"Hello?"

"Stone Graves? This is Dr. Al Ronsen at Hastings Mills General. You're listed as Claudia Brock's family."

"Is she okay?" At Stone's words, Randi Zimmerman motioned for him to put the call on speaker.

"Her condition has taken a turn for the worse. I think you should be here."

"No." Stone ended the call.

"Stone?" Randi stepped in front of him. "Go. The demon can wait."

Stone shook his head. "There's nothing I can do."

"What the fuck is wrong with you? This is Claudia we're talking about."

"Is something the matter?" Father Bonaventura asked.

"His girlfriend is dying and all he's thinking about is television ratings."

"That's bullshit and you know it."

"The woman whose sister was shot?" Bonaventura asked.

"Yeah." Stone nodded. "But we have to get you to the house—"

"We must go to her," the priest interrupted. "If her current state is due to the demon rather than a medical condition, I may be able to help."

Stone hesitated, guilt and anger freezing him in place. Randi was right. He should be with Claudia. Let his crew handle the exorcism. Randi would be there.

You're gonna blow your big chance? For what? You can prove to the world that the supernatural exists. That demons are real. You'll be the most famous person in the world.

He'd waited all his life for an opportunity like this. Could he really throw it all away just to sit in a hospital room while everyone else grabbed the glory?

I'll bet that's what Randi wants.

"If you're not going, I am," Randi said. "Father Bonaventura can come with me. We'll meet you at the Rawlingses'."

"Why? So I look like the bad guy? We'll all go to the hospital." That would show her. They'd check on Claudia and then perform the exorcism. And then he'd be the hero not once, but twice. He got into the back of the cruiser. The priest squeezed in next to him, followed by Randi. As Corday pulled out of the lot, the priest touched Stone's hand.

"Ow!" Stone jerked his hand away as he received a shock.

"My apologies." The old man put something in his pocket and leaned forward. "Officer, I think we need to hurry."

Rick Mordecai stood on the riverbank while three officers in a flat-bottomed aluminum boat used a gaff to pull a man's body close, so they could lift it inside. The water was shallow enough that they could have waded out to where the dozen corpses lay, but the slime-covered rocks made walking too dangerous. Instead, the officers settled for retrieving the bodies two at a time and bringing them ashore, where the coroner's team verified they were dead – as if there was any doubt – and bagged them.

Twelve suicides. It seemed impossible. That kind of thing simply didn't happen, except in one of those crazy cults you read about.

Cults.

The same word Corday Rose had used in the report he'd filed to describe the loonies at the motel.

Could there be a connection? Some Satanic group that had picked Hastings Mills for their demented rituals?

It wouldn't be the first time.

Years ago, when he'd still been a rookie, he'd responded to a call about a disturbance in the woods behind the McCrearys' farm. He and his partner, Tim Maynes, had found a full-blown black mass going on. Men and women in black robes, with nothing on underneath. A plucked chicken pegged to the ground in the center of a pentagram drawn in colored beads. A man reading from a book.

They'd all been arrested for trespassing. Over the next year, the same group got caught three more times for practicing their black magic shit. On one occasion, they'd been dancing nude in the moonlight. All locals who held respectable jobs. Said they had a right to follow whatever religion they wanted. Eventually, Chief Showalter gave them a final warning: take their bullshit religion out of his town for good or he'd release their names in the paper.

That had only been dead chickens and nudity. What he had now seemed more like total Jonestown insanity. A death cult. Maybe brought on by the bizarre falling rocks and frogs, which scientists attributed to high-level atmospheric storms bringing them from other parts of the state and then dropping them.

Whole damn town's turning into an apocalypse movie. Maybe it's good to have a priest here.

Mordecai cursed. Now he'd started thinking crazy too. And that didn't mix well with police work. Despite being a good Catholic, he'd never fallen into the trap of devout worship the way some people did. He attended masses out of habit, and to set a good example for the kids.

What he needed to do now was get to the bottom of the suicides. And that meant talking to the wackos from the motel, who'd been brought to Memorial General for psych evals.

"Hey, Lloyd," he called out to the boat. Lloyd Cadeyona

looked up. "I'm heading over to the hospital. Call me when you're done here."

The officer nodded and Mordecai climbed up the hill to where he'd parked his SUV. As he reached the top of the embankment, he saw a boy of about eight sitting cross-legged at the edge. In one hand he held a raggedy teddy bear. A dirty ball cap with the Yankees logo sat askew on his head.

Mordecai glanced over his shoulder. The bodies of the dead lay in plain sight, their crushed skulls and twisted limbs clearly visible. Not the kind of thing a child should see.

"Hey, kid. You shouldn't be here. Why don't you—" Mordecai's words stopped as the boy rose up in the air, floating a good two feet off the ground. His eyes had turned yellow, with the sideways pupils of a goat.

"*Asmodeus suscitat,*" the boy said.

The rocks shifted under Mordecai's feet and he stumbled back, losing his balance. He fell and his skull smashed into something hard, releasing red and black explosions.

A final thought registered before the darkness claimed him.

Corday was right.

—Claudia, wake up. There's no more time.—

Shari was back, her presence both welcome and torture. Each time Claudia heard her voice, it reminded her of all she'd lost.

—No. I just want to be with you.—

—It's not your time, sister. You have a job to do. The final battle is about to begin.—

—We can fight together. We're more powerful that way.—

She sensed Shari shaking her head.

—We will be together. Separate, but together. We must come at the beast from different directions. You from the outside, me the inside.—

—Why?—

—Because the priest needs you. Stone needs you.—

—What about me? I need you.—

—I'll be there when you do. Go to them.—

—No.—

—You must.—

A point of light appeared in the darkness. Although Claudia had no physical form, she felt warmth emanating from it. The light expanded and the heat grew stronger, began to burn. Claudia tried to back away but an unseen force trapped her in place as the light enveloped her, searing away the empty void. A roaring sound filled her nonexistent ears. Over the noise, she heard Shari's voice one last time.

—Be ready when I come.—

At the hospital, the front desk clerk tried to stop everyone except Stone Graves from going up to see Claudia.

"Family only," she insisted, finally relenting when Officer Rose showed his badge and Leo his Church ID.

When they got to her room, they found her doctor, a short, cadaverous man named Ronsen, by the bed. Leo's heart stuttered when he saw the young woman on the bed, her dark hair spread like nightfall across her pillow.

Her! The woman from his nightmares, the one who'd led him back to the world of the living. Even with her eyes closed and clothed in a hospital gown, he recognized her instantly. Her face was as pale as her sheets and glistening with sweat, and a dark bruise marred her forehead. Deep shadows rested in the hollows of her eyes. A machine next to the bed kept dinging an alarm and a set of lights flashed yellow. A gray-haired nurse tended to the IV attached to Claudia's arm.

"Doc, what's going on?" Randi asked.

"We don't know." Ronsen checked something on an electronic

chart and handed it to the nurse. "We've ordered a CT scan, in case it's a cerebral incident, but there's someone in the machine right now so we're just waiting until we can get her downstairs."

Leo took a deep breath to regain his composure. Lockhart had said he'd shot a woman, one of a pair of identical twins possessed of psychic abilities. Was this her, or the sister? One of them had come to him, and he needed to understand why. There was much more going on in Hastings Mills than just a case of possession.

"Doctor, can you give us a few minutes alone with her?" Leo flashed his ID again.

"I can, but as soon as that gurney gets here, we're moving her."

"Understood."

Leo waited until they left and then quickly took his cross and a bottle of holy water from his pockets. "Please, Ms. Zimmerman, Officer Rose, step back."

They did. Stone moved as well, but Father Bonaventura motioned for him to stay next to the bed. "I'll need you to hold her hand," he said.

Frowning, Stone did as he was told.

Holding the cross aloft, Leo recited:

"Christ beneath us, Christ above us, Christ in quiet, Christ in danger, Christ in hearts of all that love us. Strengthen us in the power of Your might, O God. Dress us in Your armor so that we can stand firm against the schemes of the Devil. Protect us, Lord, from the forces of darkness, against the spiritual forces of wickedness in all their forms. Be the shield that guards us."

Leo splashed the blessed water on Claudia, the bed, and Stone, who gasped and tried to back away, but Claudia's hand tightened around his, even as her moaning grew worse.

"You are our keeper, O Lord, and we your flock. Protect us from all evil and keep our souls from danger." He splashed the holy water again, this time on everyone. Stone cried out and his body went rigid.

"Guard our going out and our coming in. From this time and

forever. In Jesus's name, amen." A third spray. Stone's back arched and his mouth opened.

A puff of black smoke burst from him and disintegrated in the air. His body went limp and he collapsed to the floor.

On the bed, Claudia's writhing and moaning stopped. She opened her eyes.

"I'm still here, aren't I?" she whispered.

And began to cry.

"Any other time, I wouldn't allow this." Dr. Ronsen paused with his stylus over Claudia's e-chart. "But we've got a shortage of beds. More emergency cases in six hours than we usually get in a week."

"I'll be fine," Claudia said, but she kept her gaze averted. Stone understood completely. He still felt like he'd just come out of a coma himself.

That thing used me like it used Curt Rawlings.

The very idea of it made him want to puke. Or bathe in holy water. He remembered everything. Every snide comment, every selfish thought. For the rest of his life, he'd have to suffer the guilt of what he'd said. What he'd almost done.

What would have happened if he'd gone back to the house and left Claudia behind to die? He was afraid to ask the priest.

Worst of all, Claudia still didn't trust him. He saw it in her eyes, the way she kept glancing at him and then looking away. *Does she know what I tried to do to Randi?* What had she seen when he held her hand?

Rosen tapped the stylus on the pad and nodded. "All right. Your papers will be waiting down at the desk and—"

Randi's phone went off, playing the theme to *Ghostbusters*. Everyone turned.

"Sorry. Guess I should change the ringtone." She went out into the hall. Stone tried to help Claudia off the bed but she shook her head, adding another ball of guilt to the pile inside him.

Randi opened the door.

"Ken's downstairs. We've got problems."

"She specifically said, bring the priest."

Ken was waiting in the lobby with Curt Rawlings when Stone and the others got off the elevator. Officer Rose had gone outside to take a call from the station.

"The demon was referring to me," Bonaventura said.

Ken shook his head.

"No, she had to mean Lockhart. Abby doesn't even know you're in town."

"It knows."

The argument had been going in circles for several minutes, with Bonaventura insisting the demon wanted him, not Lockhart.

"Enough." Stone's voice carried farther than he'd intended, causing several people to glance at them. He forced himself to speak softer. "There's a simple solution. We get Lockhart and bring him too."

"And how do we do that?" Randi asked.

"We have to convince Mordecai to let him go."

"No, you don't."

Stone turned. Officer Rose had come back inside, wearing a stunned expression. Before he could speak, Claudia let out a small whimper. "Oh no."

Her eyes changed from violet to cloudy white. "Chief Mordecai is dead."

"How the hell does she know that?" Corday asked.

"Is it true?"

"Yeah. Someone pushed him off the river embankment. Witnesses… they said it was a little boy."

"Not a boy," Claudia whispered. "A beast with many heads."

"Jesus, pray for his soul." Bonaventura made the sign of the cross.

"What else do you see?" Stone asked her.

"All of us are needed. The priest. The fallen one. We must fight together. It's waiting for us. Laughing. It has—" Claudia's eyes returned to normal and she burst into tears. Randi went to her and pulled her into an embrace.

Stone turned to Corday. "Who's in charge?"

"Right now, no one. Our deputy chief has been in California for a week because his mother passed away. I'm sure someone called him, but it'll take a couple of days for him to get back. In the meantime, one of our two lieutenants will take over."

"Can you get Lockhart out?"

Corday nodded.

"Okay. Meet us at Curt's house."

"No." Bonaventura held up a hand. "Before any of us enter the dwelling, we need to be prepared spiritually and informationally. There's a church a few miles from here. St. Mary's."

"I know it," Corday said.

Stone looked around at the group. "Last chance if anyone wants to get the hell out of town. This isn't what you signed up for."

"It's my daughter," Curt said. "I'm not leaving."

"I'm in to the freakin' end." Randi gripped hands with Claudia, who nodded.

Ken cleared his throat and Stone got a sinking feeling.

"Uh, I'm sorry. I can't. Me and Del talked earlier. This is all getting out of hand. We almost died. I – we – can't take that chance again. We're leaving as soon as I get back to pick him up."

Ken's words hit Stone like a gut punch. Del and Ken had been with him since before he got his television show. They'd become almost family. Which was why no matter how much it hurt to lose them, he couldn't get angry at their decision. Forcing a smile, he nodded.

"It's okay. You guys take a cab to Buffalo. Get a hotel and wait there until you hear from me."

Ken looked embarrassed and grateful.

"Thanks, man."

Stone turned to the others.

"All right. We meet at St. Mary's Church in an hour."

CHAPTER THIRTY-TWO

Hastings Mills, NY, July 20th, one year ago

By the time Officer Rose arrived at St. Mary's with Robert Lockhart, Father Bonaventura had already spoken to the parish priest. Stone couldn't hear their conversation, but whatever the old man said, it had worked. They had the church to themselves for as long as they needed. Father Bonaventura had wasted no time, arranging the tools of his trade on the altar. Several bottles of holy water, a round censer from which pungent smoke trickled out, and a Bible.

"Please gather round," he said, motioning for everyone to join him at the foot of the stairs in front of the altar. "I am going to bless each of you."

"Uh, Father Bonaventura?" Randi held up her hand. "What if we're not Catholic?"

"Please, call me Father Leo. Or Leo. And it doesn't matter if you're Catholic or not," Father Bonaventura said. "This is to cleanse you of any dark energies and help protect your soul when you're in the presence of evil. Think of it as a temporary shield."

"Temporary?" Stone asked. "That's not encouraging."

"The demon we're facing is very powerful. Much more so than the last time he entered this world." Father Bonaventura cast a frown at Lockhart but didn't elaborate. Lockhart looked down but remained silent.

Unlike in the hospital, Stone felt nothing when Father Bonaventura sprinkled holy water on him or waved the incense his way. He thought he saw Lockhart twitch when the holy water hit him, but he couldn't be sure. Father Bonaventura read several passages from the Bible that

Stone didn't listen to, his mind already anticipating what they'd find waiting for them at the house. They'd already checked in with Del, who'd been watching Abby via the monitors. So far, there'd been no unusual activity since Curt and Ken left; she'd simply been lying in bed with her eyes closed. Even the cryptic symbols on her skin had faded to a blushing pink instead of dark red.

"Don't be fooled," Father Bonaventura told them. "The demon knows what's coming. You can be sure it's preparing itself just as we are. That's why we must protect ourselves. Please, kneel and bow your heads."

Father Bonaventura splashed holy water on each of them.

"God, Father of Light, creator of all that is good, protect your children from all evil. Guide them down the path of righteousness even as the Devil calls from the dark. Give them the strength to do your will and ignore the temptations of Satan. Protect them, Lord, in the name of your Son, Jesus, and his mother, Mary. Amen."

"Amen," Ken murmured. Curt and Officer Rose repeated it.

After they finished, Randi stood up. "Now what?"

Father Bonaventura closed his Bible and held it against his chest. "Now the war begins."

Del Hall caught the motion from the corner of his eye. He'd been uploading the backup files to a second cloud-based storage account he'd created, just in case something happened to the first one. As much as he agreed with Ken that they had to put their own safety first, bugging out on Stone went against everything he believed in. In the military, you never abandoned a post or ditched on a team member. If it had been anyone except Ken, he'd have said fuck off. But there came a time when you had to put love before work, or even loyalty to friends.

He could handle getting hurt. But dying for a TV show, or, even worse, losing Ken...those weren't options in his book.

He glanced at the monitor for Abby's room and saw she'd sat up in bed. She stared right at the camera, and it was obvious she wasn't herself. Something in her eyes shouted *evil.*

She waved and the screen turned off.

A second later, all the other monitors went black as well.

"Oh, shit." Del pulled out his cell and was about to hit Stone's number when he heard the sound of tires on gravel outside the van. He climbed out the back doors just as Curt's truck and Randi's rental car came to a stop in the driveway.

A loud electronic crackling sounded behind him. He turned just in time to see smoke rising from several of the monitors. A second later all the screens blew out with a loud *pop!*

The front door of the house slowly swung open.

In the administrative building at St. Alphonse, President Alan Duhaime looked up as something thumped against his window. He caught a flash of brown that disappeared just as quickly. Frowning, he glanced at his watch. Almost three. He'd been going over the preliminary audit findings for almost six hours, and he still hadn't found a solution to his problems.

They were going to catch him.

He'd thought he'd covered the money trail perfectly. Shifting funds, just a little here and there. Grants, donations, income. Nothing too noticeable. Just a few hundred thousand, quietly adjusted in the books as 'rebates' to the construction company for their work on Fifth Dallas. In return, a nice deposit in his personal bank account and a lower bid on the job. A win-win for everyone. He'd done the same thing for other capital projects without a hitch.

Except this time he'd forgotten to destroy some original documents when he replaced them with the falsified ones. The auditors hadn't missed the discrepancies.

Now the board of trustees had ordered a full-scale investigation. A detailed accounting of the school's financials for the past seven years. And when they uncovered all his deals, he'd be toast.

I need to clear my head. He still had two weeks to figure something out. He'd talk to his contact at the construction firm. Maybe they'd have an idea. After all, they'd be implicated too.

Better yet, maybe I can put all the blame on them.

New plan. Home, a stiff drink, and then he'd call his lawyer. He grabbed his leather satchel and headed down the stairs. He was almost at the doors when someone screamed outside. He hurried through and came to a stop when he saw Professor Marilyn Winkler standing on the cement landing, her hands at her mouth and her eyes bulging.

Hundreds of brown and black shapes littered the wide lawn and the sidewalks.

Birds.

They lay spread-winged and crumpled. All sizes and shapes. Sparrows, crows, robins, finches, and more that he couldn't identify. He even saw a large owl under one of the tall maples that lined the walkway in front of the building. A few of the birds twitched in the throes of death. Most of them didn't move.

A dark shape hit the ground by his feet. He jumped and looked up as several lifeless creatures slid off the shale roof three stories up and tumbled to the ground.

"What happened?" Marilyn asked, her hands still over her mouth. "Is it poison?"

"No." Duhaime stared at the birds. He couldn't help but feel they represented an omen of his own future.

"What is it, then?" Marilyn's voice carved through his skull like nails on a blackboard.

Shut up, you bitch. Just shut up. Shut—

"What is it? What could—"

"Shut up!" He swung around and smashed his fist into her nose. She toppled over and he followed her down, dropping to his knees next to her. "Shut up! Shut the fuck up!" With each word, he punched her again. Over and over, until she no longer moved and three of his fingers were broken.

He stared at her ruined face for several moments before standing up.

Briefcase in hand, he went to his car.

When he arrived home, he went to his study, poured a tall glass of whiskey, stripped off his clothes, and sat down in his recliner.

When his wife came to get him for dinner, she found him masturbating in front of a blank TV screen and laughing.

At the Lodge Hotel on State Street, Pete Telles put down his package of cookies and opened the sliding doors that led out to the tiny balcony. Two floors down, three children played in the shallow end of the pool while their parents lounged in chairs nearby.

"Petey, be careful," his grandmother said from inside. "Don't go near the edge. It's not safe."

"Okay." Pete leaned against the railing and peered over, watching the two boys and their sister splashing and jumping. One of the boys dove down and swam under the rope marking the beginning of the deep side. He kept going, kicking down to the bottom.

"Mommy! Martin's in the deep end!" shouted the girl. Her parents sat up.

"Martin?" The mother ran to the edge, her husband a step behind. From his viewpoint overhead, Pete watched as Martin's legs stopped kicking and a mass of bubbles rose up. A moment later, Martin's body followed them.

"Martin!" the mother screamed. The father jumped in and pulled the boy to the edge. When he lifted him out, water poured from his mouth. The mother shouted for help while the father pushed on the motionless boy's chest.

Somewhere in the distance, a dog howled. Others joined in.

Smiling, Pete went back inside to finish his cookies.

Leo watched the door to the house open. A powerful wave of evil swept over him and sucked the strength from his legs. He stumbled and grabbed the car to keep from falling. His vision blurred and his skull throbbed in time to his heartbeat.

The beast is here!

There was no mistaking the sensation. Corruption lay heavy in the air like the stench of dead flesh in a meatpacking plant. The decades fell away and he was back in the jungle, the presence of the demon fouling the atmosphere with its unholy evil.

Only magnitudes stronger.

"Father Leo, are you all right?"

Leo shook off Lockhart's hand. He needed to be strong. This was no time to show weakness; the demon would sense it right away.

"I'm fine. Is everyone prepared to enter?"

Before leaving the church, Leo had insisted they each carry a rosary. The priest at St. Mary's had supplied them, all blessed. Even the police officer, Rose, had received one, despite having to leave for another emergency call. Now Leo lifted his and indicated they should do the same. Claudia's hands shook as she placed hers around her neck. He still had his doubts about her condition but if Lockhart's information about her was correct, her abilities could be helpful.

"Then let's begin. Remember, do not listen to anything the demon says. They are all liars, and worse than that, they will twist words and facts to create doubt inside you."

With his cross hanging from his neck and his rosary wrapped around his wrist, Leo opened his Bible and led them forward, reciting from the Book of Romans.

"The God of peace will soon crush Satan under our feet. The grace of our Lord Jesus Christ be with you."

The closer they drew to the dark maw of the doorway, the stronger the aura of malevolence grew. It was far worse than anything Leo had ever experienced, and they weren't even inside yet. He wondered again if he'd have the strength to do what he needed.

If he'd even survive.

What does it matter?

The thought made him pause. Why worry about his own mortality, when it had already reached its final chapter?

I no longer have to fear death, which means it can't hold me back.

This will be my final battle.

A weight lifted from his shoulders that he hadn't even known burdened him. For months, he'd been so occupied with his own depression and fear that he'd forgotten his true reason for being.

I am God's sword, and my job is to dispatch evil in His name.

With a renewed sense of purpose, he strode forward into the house.

SECTION FOUR
EXORCISM

Los Angeles, Present Day

***Excerpt from* Good Morning with Josh and Jenny**

Jenny Durso: "Would you say the things that happened in Hastings Mills changed you?"

Stone Graves: "Changed me? Absolutely."

Josh Black: "For better or worse?"

Graves: "That's not an easy question to answer. I'm a different person for sure. Probably a better person. But am I a happier person? I don't think I can say that. I still wake up with nightmares. All of us do. And I'm more aware of the evil that lurks in our world, just waiting to destroy us. Sometimes ignorance really is bliss."

Durso nods. Black points at the copy of Graves's book on the coffee table between them.

Black: "But you did a great thing. You rid the world of some of that evil."

Graves: "Yeah. But at what cost?"

Durso: (leaning forward) "If you could go back in time, would you do anything differently?"

Graves: "Hell, yeah. I'd never step foot in that goddamned town."

CHAPTER THIRTY-THREE

Hastings Mills, NY, July 20th, one year ago

Stone watched the priest square his shoulders and walk inside. There'd been a moment where it looked like the old man wouldn't enter the house. Add that to his stumble outside and Stone was beginning to have his doubts about the exorcist. He seemed far too aged and frail for something like this.

A greatly subdued Lockhart followed Father Bonaventura. He'd changed from the manic, pompous lunatic of just two days ago. Stone still didn't trust him, but he no longer seemed to be an immediate threat to anyone.

As they entered the house, all the lights came on. A noxious odor, unlike anything Stone had smelled before, pervaded the living room. It wasn't quite wet fur, and not quite damp, moldy wood, but something close.

Randi touched his arm.

"Look."

Greenish-yellow slime oozed from the walls. Puddles of it stained the carpet. Stone turned to tell Ken to get some video of it, and then cursed when he remembered his videographer and Del were already on their way to Buffalo. He had to settle for using his phone while Randi got some shots with the small digital recorder she'd snagged from the van.

Father Bonaventura paused and glanced around the room.

"That odor. Has it been here the entire time?"

Randi shook her head. "No. This is different. Before it was kind of rotten meat and old garbage."

The priest's mouth twisted as he sniffed again. "Demon stench. That's what I would expect. Not this...."

"I've smelled it," Curt Rawlings said. "Back before all this started. Kinda musty. I thought we had some kind of water leak down in the basement."

"No. This is something else." Without explaining further, Father Bonaventura led them toward the stairs. Stone got the impression he recognized the odor, and its presence confused him.

"They're watching," Claudia said, her voice just above a whisper. Stone jumped a little. She'd been so silent he'd forgotten she was there.

"Who?" he asked.

Claudia frowned and shook her head. "The shadows. Her, and another. They're angry. And sad. I can't—"

A loud thumping started upstairs. Stone recognized it immediately. Abby's bed rising and falling. The *bang! bang!* of multiple doors slamming joined it.

"The girl's room?" Father Bonaventura asked. Curt nodded.

A picture flew off the mantel and struck the ceiling. Others followed it, glass shattering and falling like rain. The couch spun in a circle, knocking over an end table and sending a lamp crashing to the floor. A rumbling filled the room, accompanied by a vibration in the floor.

Father Bonaventura approached the stairs and grasped the banister.

The house went quiet.

"Please, all of you." Father Bonaventura glanced back at them. "Stay down here until I call for you. I need to make the initial contact without any distractions."

A picture rose from the floor and sailed across the room, causing Father Bonaventura to duck. An ashtray followed, denting the wall next to him. He murmured something and placed a foot on the staircase. When nothing further attacked him, he began to climb. The doors on the second floor slammed in synch with each footstep. A freezing wind blew through the house, bringing with it the familiar stench of dead, rotting flesh.

All the lights went out except the ones in Abby's room, which cast a yellow glow into the upstairs hallway, guiding Father Bonaventura to his destination. Head held high and Bible gripped in his hands, he strode forward.

Stone watched as he disappeared out of sight, his shadow stretching longer and taller against the wall until Abby's door banged shut and the upstairs went dark.

Randi put her hands on her hips. "Now what?"

Stone chewed his lip, wishing he'd put a camera in the room.

"Now we wait."

Leo ignored the door closing and locking behind him. The girl hovered over her bed, dressed only in pajama bottoms, her legs folded in a lotus position. Crimson marks covered her exposed flesh. Her face was sallow and drawn, her ribs prominent. The harsh stink of fresh, concentrated urine mixed with the reek of the demon emanating from her pores. A large stain on the bed showed where she'd wet it.

All typical signs of possession, and Leo felt no surprise at them. Demons – even powerful ones – tended to be unimaginative in their tricks.

On the other hand, certain details in the room cried out for his attention. The ectoplasm spilling down the walls. The stains on the ceiling. The clothes and personal items scattered on the floor, evidence of the earlier telekinetic episodes he'd been told about, which most likely stemmed from the spirit haunting the house. The same one he'd smelled downstairs.

"Hello, my old friend."

Leo returned his gaze to the girl. Her voice, low and harsh, brought him back to that tiny hut in the jungle, where a young boy spoke in exactly the same manner. Over the decades, he'd only had a few cases where a demon actually spoke through its victim; most times possessed individuals babbled nonsense or bits of different languages.

Clear speech indicated a powerful presence.

Still, he had to be sure this wasn't a lesser creature toying with them.

"Who are you, beast? Speak your name."

The closet door swung open and closed. A pile of books rose up and flew across the room like a flock of alien birds.

"I am lust. I am death. I am pain."

Leo thrust the Bible out. "In the name of God the Almighty, I command you to speak your name!"

"Leo, help me!" The voice changed, became that of an old man. A voice Leo recognized instantly. Jorge Sanchez, his old friend and mentor. The man who'd given his life in that jungle so many years ago. A frigid chill ran through Leo.

Demons lie, he reminded himself.

He reached into his pocket and removed a bottle of holy water. When he squirted some on the girl, her body writhed and she cried out. Blisters formed on her flesh and brownish-yellow urine ran down her legs.

"Your name, demon! God commands you, tell me your name!"

Clothes and books spun up and around. The bed rose and fell. All the dresser drawers opened and closed. Abigail dropped to the bed on her back, her limbs shaking.

Everything went still.

Abigail lay with her eyes closed, panting as if she'd just run a race. Leo splashed more holy water on her, but there was no reaction. The pressure in his chest eased up. Perhaps he'd been wrong. The demon of his nightmares would not have tired so easily. Which meant the root of the problems at the Rawlings household probably stemmed from the other possibility he'd considered. They'd still have a tough road ahead, but not as bad as he'd feared.

Now it was simply a matter of making the right preparations.

He turned to leave. As he reached for the knob, a line of flames ran across the wood and he jerked his hand back. The fire receded, leaving a cloud of smoke and a series of letters.

Asmodeum.

The door unlatched and opened a few inches.

His Bible clutched in trembling hands, Leo hurried for the stairs.

Childish giggling chased him all the way.

Ken and Del stood on the side of the highway and watched as the Uber driver emerged from under the hood of his SUV. The engine had died without warning just as they reached the top of the entrance ramp for Route 19, which would take them north to Buffalo.

"It's dead." The driver slammed the hood down. "Just like everyone you left behind."

"What?" Ken took a step back at the man's sudden vehemence.

"Dead, dead, dead." The driver, a twenty-something wearing a Greenpeace t-shirt, gave them a wild grin and flicked open a large folding knife. "And you're dead too. No fags in my town! Asmodeus wakes!"

He slashed at Del, who twisted away and yelped as the blade sliced a thin line across his shoulder. The driver jabbed with the knife and Del threw a roundhouse that caught him on the temple. The driver's eyes rolled up and he crumpled to the ground.

Del looked at Ken. "Did you hear him?"

"Yeah." Ken wanted to believe he'd misheard, or imagined it, but he couldn't fool himself. Stone and the others were in trouble.

And you ditched on them.

"We've got to go back."

"I know." Just saying it twisted Ken's guts in a knot. They'd both come within inches of death. Now they were thinking of putting their lives in danger again. And for what? Some stranger and his kid? Fifteen minutes of fame?

Friendship.

"Fuck me." Ken pulled out his phone to call for another ride.

The screen went black and a message appeared in bright red letters.

Deaddeaddeaddeaddead.

The glass shattered into a spiderweb of gray lines.

Del let out a curse as his phone screen cracked in pieces. The knot in his stomach tightened. Something didn't want them to leave, but it also didn't want them returning too soon. When he looked at Del, he saw the same frightened understanding in his eyes.

Without a word, they both broke into a run.

Stone and the others watched as Leo laid out a series of items on the kitchen table. Bible, holy water, rosary, candles, and incense on one side. A pile of what looked like dried weeds, unmarked bottles of clear liquid, and a lighter on the other side.

Lockhart picked up one of the bundles of stems with a frown.

"Sage and salt water? Those are for cleansing rituals."

"Yes." Leo nodded. "We're not just dealing with possession. This house is also haunted by a poltergeist. Perhaps more than one."

"A poltergeist?" Lockhart shook his head. "No. The girl is possessed. You heard the demon. Saw what it did. You even said that the construction in the dormitory most likely broke the bindings you put there."

"She is. But her possession doesn't explain everything that's happened. There is something else here. Most likely the ghost of Caitlyn Rawlings."

"A demon and a ghost at the same time? That's unheard of. More likely the demon wants us to believe something else is going on. It's a trick."

"I hate to agree with him, but it does sound kind of far-fetched," Randi said.

Leo sat down, grateful for a chance to rest. His pulse raced and his chest ached, despite the pills the doctor had given him.

"None of you really understand the supernatural. The paranormal." Stone started to protest and the priest held up a hand. "Hear me out. You've dealt with ghosts and minor demons. But you've barely scratched the surface. Are you aware the presence of a demon can make it easier for a poltergeist to manifest? It can also cause a benign spirit to become malicious. The opposite is also true. A malicious spirit can weaken the boundaries between our world and the next and make it easier for a demon to extend a piece of itself into this plane."

"Are you saying a demon can influence our world without fully entering it?"

Leo nodded. "Yes. There are different forms of possession. In the beginning, there might only be subtle signs. Changes in behavior. Or it could be physical, with only the body affected. In the later stages, both body and soul are taken over. When it reaches that point… sometimes even an exorcism cannot save the person."

"How do you know if…." Curt's words trailed off. Leo felt the man's pain. What if it was already too late to save Abby? He wished he could guarantee success, but it wasn't in him to give false hope.

"From the outside, it's almost impossible to tell. Both types can show the same stages of diabolical possession."

"What are they?"

Lockhart spoke up. "Possession, obsession, and infestation."

Leo continued. "Emotional and mental torment. Inanimate objects or lower animals acting in strange manners. Psychosis caused by the presence of a demon. Paranormal incidents. Physical wounds. Speaking in tongues."

"We've seen all of that," Stone said.

"Demons are always testing us and our world for weaknesses. Many will manipulate other forces to try and open doorways to our world. They can use the lingering energies of the dead as tools, twisting and influencing those forces just as they do living beings. And if a demon is not exorcised properly –" Leo looked at Lockhart, "– the danger is magnified even further. You must remove the beast by the roots, so that nothing remains behind."

"But it's not just here," Corday said. "It's the whole town. We've had suicides, murders, and reports of things I didn't even believe."

"Its influence is spreading. Think of a fungus or mushroom. On the surface, you see the cap and stem, one organism. But below the ground, it sends hyphae, roots, in all directions, corrupting everything they touch."

"That's not how demons work," Lockhart objected.

Leo whirled around to face him. "And now you're the expert? What do you even know of demons? Of Asmodeus?"

Lockhart didn't back down. "He's the demon of lust. One of Satan's generals. There are mentions of him well before the Bible. He's often depicted with multiple faces."

"First of all, there is no he or she when it comes to demons. And it is not just faces, it's five heads. Do you understand what that means?" The priest gave Lockhart no chance to respond. "It's a representation of the beast's true nature. That it can be in many places at once, possess multiple people at once. The more powerful it becomes, the farther its evil extends."

"I never heard of such a thing." Doubt filled Lockhart's voice.

"Of course not. You're a novice compared to me, and even after fifty years, I've only scratched the surface of all the information on Satan and his minions stored in the Vatican's catacombs."

Lockhart looked properly abashed.

"So now what?" Stone asked. "We're supposed to exorcise the entire town?"

"No." Leo pushed away from the table. "If we cast the demon from our world, the other spirits will be weakened enough so that we can banish them as well."

"If?" Randi asked.

Leo shrugged.

"When it comes to the supernatural, nothing is guaranteed."

Standing at the foot of Abby's bed, Stone suffered a wave of déjà vu. The scene was eerily reminiscent of Lockhart's failed attempt to drive the demon from Abby. Shari's glaring absence had affected Claudia badly. She looked ready to collapse, her skin pallid and her eyes barely open. He'd asked her if she wanted to remain downstairs, and she'd shaken her head. When he tried to insist, she'd slipped past him and gone into the room.

"I command you, unholy one who calls himself Asmodeus, to

leave this child of God. You and all your minions, depart this place! By the mysteries of faith and holiness, in the name of Jesus Christ, our Lord and Savior, leave!"

Father Bonaventura cast holy water across Abby. Curt had thrown a blanket over her earlier, but now her back arched and the blanket flew off, exposing her sunken chest and emaciated body. He doused her again and she screamed, twisting and turning as the liquid hit her flesh and sizzled, creating blisters between the cuneiform welts that paraded across her skin.

Stone tried to keep her in focus in his camera's viewfinder as her arms and legs contorted and she soiled herself. Next to the priest, Lockhart waved burning incense back and forth, the cloying scents of frankincense and clove struggling against the rankness of fresh shit and the pond scum odor of dried ectoplasm.

"By the light of God and the coming of our Lord for judgment, depart!"

This time the holy water evaporated into steam before it touched Abby. With a guttural laugh, she rose up from the bed and spread her arms. Fissures appeared in the walls and ceiling, and chips of paint and ectoplasmic crust rained down like snow.

"Father Bonaventura! You're too weak to save this one. She's mine now!" Still laughing, Abby leaned backward, her body bending unnaturally at the waist. Tendons cracked as she folded herself until her hands touched her feet. Then she snapped forward again. Greenish-yellow slime sprayed from her mouth.

Father Bonaventura ignored it all and splashed more holy water on her.

"Depart from here, cursed one, into the eternal fire God prepared for Satan and his followers!"

Abby fell onto the bed and Father Bonaventura rushed forward to place a silver cross on her chest. Smoke billowed up and Abby shrieked. Claudia cried out as well and clapped her hands over her ears. A second later, a chorus of voices joined in, dozens of them, all wailing in agony. Flames burst to life around Abby and her pajama bottoms disintegrated. Curt grabbed her blanket from the floor and tried to cover her but it wrapped itself around his face. He stumbled away, struggling to free himself until Randi managed to pull it off him.

When Stone looked back at the bed, the flames had disappeared.

"Let this holy cross be my light! I cast thee out, demon! Be gone!"

Father Bonaventura pressed down on the cross. With his free hand, he motioned to Lockhart, who poured more holy water on Abby's face and chest. The cross lit up with a faint blue glow, which spread to Father Bonaventura's hand.

"Be gone! I cast thee out!"

The closet door banged open and toys shot across the room. A pink softball struck Father Bonaventura in the temple and he fell sideways onto the bed. Abby lunged for him but Lockhart was faster, thrusting his cross between them. Abby hesitated and Lockhart pulled Father Bonaventura back to his feet.

"I remember this," Abby said. She took the cross from her chest and slowly ran her tongue up and down the metal. Her flesh sizzled and spat like frying bacon and more of the foul spittle dribbled from her lips. "I can still taste him on it."

She let go of the cross. It shot across the room and embedded itself in the wall. Her eyes closed and she fell back, her body limp.

"Look." Randi pointed at Abby's chest. Stone zoomed in on it. The blisters and markings moved around, forming rows of letters. Randi read them aloud.

"Alberto. Jorge. Hector. Doyle. Jonathan. Leo."

Father Bonaventura frowned at the words as he approached the bed again. Holding his Bible aloft, he read the Lord's Prayer three times and sprayed more holy water onto Abby's still form. When she didn't react, he motioned for everyone to leave the room. Lockhart had to help him down the stairs to the kitchen, where he sank into a chair with a groan.

"Father, can I get you something? Soda? Water?" Randi asked.

"Water, please," Father Bonaventura whispered. When she handed him a glass, he drank half of it down, took one of his painkillers, and drank the rest.

"It's still here," Claudia said, and they all knew what she meant.

"Yes. This is just the beginning." Father Bonaventura rubbed his eyes. "It can take days or even weeks to cast out a demon as powerful as Asmodeus."

"You're convinced of its nature?" Lockhart asked.

"Yes. Those names. I recognized two of them. Jorge Sanchez and Hector Ecchivaria. Both priests. When I faced Asmodeus for the first time, in Costa Rica, it was at the behest of Father Jorge, my mentor in Rome. That silver cross belonged to him. Unbeknownst to the Church, Father Hector had attempted an exorcism of the boy weeks earlier, and it failed. The demon killed him. To those outside, it appeared as a suicide, but Jorge knew better. And when Asmodeus proved too strong for him he called me to assist him. That night... the demon used its power to kill Jorge as well. It broke his neck and marked me with the same cross."

Father Bonaventura held out his arm, showing the faint white letters.

"What about the others?"

Father Bonaventura shook his head. "I don't know. But my name was among them. Perhaps they are all priests this foul one has interacted with, or—"

"Doyle Bannon." Lockhart's face had gone white.

"What?" Stone turned his camera on. Something about Lockhart's voice....

"Father Doyle Bannon. He was a priest at Holy Cross when I was a kid. We'd just moved here. My parents signed me up as an altar boy. Bannon...he molested me. Probably others too. They found pictures in his desk."

I knew it! Stone wanted to shout his triumph. He'd been waiting for exactly that kind of revelation. Lockhart had been abused as a kid and then followed the same path. Now to get him to admit it, to—

Claudia gripped his arm and her voice spoke in his head.

—Not now. This is more important. Later. When it's all over.—

He looked at her. A tear ran down her cheek.

Goddammit. He wanted to out Lockhart so badly. Make him pay for what he'd done.

—We will. But not now.—

Shit. He returned his attention to Lockhart. *I will get you, you bastard. You won't get away with it.*

"—when the police showed up, he committed suicide. Jumped out the window."

"I remember that," Father Bonaventura said. "That was how I got assigned to St. Alphonse and took charge of Holy Cross."

"So they're all priests." Randi took out a pen and wrote the names down on a napkin. "That just leaves two. Alberto and Jonathan."

"I can't think of any priests I know with those names who have a connection with Hastings Mills."

"Why does it have to be Hastings Mills?"

Stone swung the camera around to face Curt Rawlings. He'd been silent since leaving Abby's room, standing back from the table and staring down at his feet. Stone couldn't imagine being in his shoes, handling everything that had happened. Even if Father Bonaventura managed to somehow rid Abby of her demon and cleanse the house, how could their lives ever be the same?

How can any of ours?

"What do you mean?" Randi asked.

Curt pointed at Father Bonaventura. "You said this demon's been around forever. That you fought it in Costa Rica. Seems like them other names could be people from there. Or anywhere. Why here?"

Father Bonaventura frowned. "That's a good point. But there were no other priests in the village that night. Just us, the boy's parents, the villagers, and...the doctor." He looked over at Randi.

"Your last name is Zimmerman, yes?"

She nodded. "Why?"

"That night. There was a doctor in the village who tended to Anibal. An American. He knew Father Jorge and called him when he couldn't find a medical cause for the boy's condition. His name was also Zimmerman. John Zimmerman."

"Holy fuck."

Stone aimed the camera at Randi.

"My father's name was John. Jonathan." She looked down at the paper. "He served in Doctors Without Borders before he married my mom. I remember as a kid he was always interested in the paranormal. But he never told me why. I guess that's why I got into it, after he disappeared."

Father Bonaventura leaned forward. "What happened to him?"

"I was fifteen. We lived in Syracuse at the time. He and a friend went fishing for the weekend. They never came back. The police found their boat miles down the river a couple of days later, but no sign of either of them."

"The river?" Father Bonaventura took Randi's hand. "Do you mean…?"

She nodded. "The Alleghany. He disappeared two miles from Hastings Mills."

"Wait a minute. You're sayin' this thing's been in town for more than thirty years?" Curt shook his head. "Don't seem possible."

"Perhaps not the demon itself, but its essence. Had I known St. Alphonse and Hastings Mills already had a troubled history, I would not have brought those insects here to be identified. A town already weakened by evil…."

"Maybe you had no choice," Claudia said.

"What do you mean?"

"All of you have ties to each other. To this town. That can't be coincidence."

"But why?" Lockhart asked. "And by who?"

Upstairs, furniture thumped, accompanied by childish laughter. A heavy wind blew through the house and the back door banged open to reveal a hulking form.

The figure moved forward and Randi screamed.

CHAPTER THIRTY-FOUR

Hastings Mills, NY, July 20th, one year ago

Del Hall stepped into the light and Randi's cry turned into a shout of joy.

"Del!" She ran to him and wrapped her arms around him. Ken Webb peered around his shoulder.

"No hugs for me?"

She laughed and grabbed him. Stone joined them, squeezing them hard before moving aside so they could enter the kitchen.

"What are you doing back here?" he asked. "You're supposed to be in Buffalo by now."

"We ran into some trouble," Ken said, heading for a cabinet and pulling out a box of cookies. "God, I'm starved."

"Trouble?" Stone asked.

Del held out his ruined phone. "Car broke down. Driver went apeshit. Phones told us we were all gonna die and then they exploded. So we walked back. Took longer than we expected."

"The whole town's crazy," Ken said, around a mouthful of cookies. "People on the streets. Fighting. Looting. Heard gunshots too."

"The demon's presence grows stronger. We must put an end to it soon, or it'll be too late."

Stone took a cookie from Ken and spoke as he nibbled at it. "If Claudia's right, then we need to find out who that Alberto person is. That could help us drive out Asmodeus."

"And the others," Claudia added.

"Others? What'd we miss?" Del asked.

"I'll fill you in later. Right now, I need you to call LA and have them look into anyone named Alberto who might have a connection to Hastings Mills, exorcisms, or St. Alphonse University."

"Got it."

Stone couldn't help smiling as a new energy ran through him. Despite the setbacks, despite how frail Father Bonaventura looked and how powerful Abby's demon had grown, for the first time in days he felt a surge of positivity. He had his team back together, and even with the terrible loss of Shari, it gave him confidence that they could do what it took to drive the demon back to whatever hell it came from.

The kitchen cabinets swung open. Boxes and cans flew out.

Claudia touched his hand, her fingers ice against his skin.

"We're not safe yet."

Officer Corday Rose stood by the counter of the Fill-n-Shop on State Street and tried not to contaminate any evidence as he took pictures of the scene. Not an easy task, with four gunshot victims. The place was a mess. Blood, brain matter, and things he didn't want to identify decorated every surface. When the county crime lab team arrived, they'd have a helluva time piecing everything together, but he had a pretty good idea of the basics already.

And none of it made sense.

Near as he could tell, Desiree Watkins, the cashier, had used the shotgun under the counter to blow away two customers and the Fill-n-Shop's owner, Sanjay Nanda. Then she'd placed it against her own chest and pulled the trigger. Her ravaged body lay against the cigarette display, one hand still clutching the gun. Nanda lay by the door to the back office, his guts hanging from the giant hole in his abdomen.

The two customers, a married couple from Pennsylvania, were draped across some toppled candy racks. They'd been identified by their licenses because nothing remained of their faces.

"Someone find the security video footage," Corday said,

glad he hadn't eaten dinner yet. "I want to know what the fuck happened here."

He snapped another photo of the couple and then turned his phone on Desiree, trying to think of how he'd tell her mother, LaTonya, that her daughter had gone nuts and shot up the store. Desiree had been her pride and joy. Straight-A student, going to Buffalo State in the fall.

Now she was just a pile of meat.

He leaned over for a better angle and his radio crackled to life.

"Anyone near State and Fifteenth. We've got a report of a disturbance at the elementary school."

Corday thumbed his mic. "What kind of disturbance?"

Jeannie Klaus, the night dispatcher, cleared her throat before answering.

"Uh...the caller said there's...an orgy happening at the PTA meeting."

"Christ on a crutch." The whole town really was going crazy. As much as he hated to admit it, the idea of a demon causing all their troubles sounded more plausible than anything else he could think of.

Hoping to hell he wasn't heading for another devil worship ceremony, Corday told one of the other officers to keep the place secure until the crime scene unit arrived and then he ran for his SUV. Halfway to the school, his headlights picked out a person walking down the center of the road. As he drew closer, the figure resolved into a naked man. Cursing his bad luck, he hit the lights and pulled up next to him. When the man looked over, Corday nearly swerved onto the curb.

"Father Gager?"

The gray-haired priest from St. Mary's stared back, his expression blank, a string of drool dangling from his lip. He offered no resistance when Corday guided him into the back of the truck. He drove to St. Mary's, where he hustled the priest into the rectory and put him to bed. The moment he lay down, Gager closed his eyes and began to snore.

It wasn't lost on Corday that less than twenty-four hours ago, Gager had helped Stone and his friends prepare for their exorcism.

Outside the rectory, Corday paused by his car and then went inside the church and did something he hadn't done since childhood.

He prayed.

"I exorcise thee, unclean spirit. In the name of God, in the name of Jesus, in the names of all the saints, I cast thee out!"

Stone watched from the end of the bed while Father Bonaventura sprayed holy water on Abby, who sat against the wall, her legs crossed and her hands in her lap. The cuneiform symbols had reappeared on her skin and her face had taken on a sallow, yellowish color. Sweat soaked her hair into matted clumps. Bloodshot eyes stared out at the people gathered around the bed.

The water landed harmlessly on her, and Father Bonaventura's frown deepened.

Next to him, Lockhart waved incense around and read a passage from his own tattered Bible. "Let the holy cross be my light; let not the dragon be my guide. What you offer me is evil. You drink the poison yourself."

As he'd been doing for the past half hour, Father Bonaventura repeated Lockhart's words, but in Latin.

"*Crux sancta sit mihi lux; non draco sit mihi dux sunt mala quae libas. Ipse venena bibas.*"

Abby let out a gruff laugh and levitated off the bed.

"*Pedicabo ego crucem tuam! Verba tua et non habere potestatem super memet!*" she shouted, before dropping back down. Stone had no idea what the words meant, but from the look on Father Bonaventura's face, they weren't good.

The writing on her chest shifted again and Stone was glad he couldn't read it. Even looking at the symbols caused his head to hurt and made him dizzy.

The rest of the team looked like he felt. Ken's face was pale and sweaty behind his camera and Del had backed away until he bumped against Abby's desk. Claudia clutched Randi's arm, her eyes wide.

"Sister!" Abby's shout made Claudia jump. "Sister, come join me."

As she spoke, Abby's voice changed and became a duplicate of Claudia's.

No, Shari's, Stone realized. *It sounds like Shari.*

"Stop it," Claudia whispered.

"Sister, I did it for you. I gave him my soul. I died for you and now I'm his whore."

"No," Claudia said. "You're not real."

"He fucks me so good. He's fucking me now." Abby stretched out on the bed, hands between her legs, and began to writhe and moan.

"Stop it!"

Abby's dresser fell over with a crash. The room grew darker even though the candles still burned and the lights were on.

"Claudia, help me!" Abby spread her arms. The fiery inscriptions on her chest reformed themselves into a screaming face.

Shari's.

Abby pointed at Lockhart. "She's so good, Robert. You missed your chance."

"STOP IT!" Claudia's eyes clouded over.

A black cloud appeared at the ceiling and hail the size of marbles rained down on the bed. Abby roared with laughter as they battered her body, then her face twisted in pain and she slammed her fists against her head.

"You dare challenge me?"

Claudia yelped and doubled over. Blisters appeared on her arms. Her head snapped back and she lifted up in the air, clawing at her throat where bright red handprints formed around her neck. Her body flew backward into the hall and she landed on the floor several feet away.

The cloud disappeared and the ice storm stopped.

"Feel your sister's pain, witch! She'll burn for eternity and so will you!"

Stone ran out, Randi close behind him. Claudia got up and staggered down the stairs. At the bottom, something yanked her by the hair and slammed her head into the wall.

"Claudia—"

She waved him off and stumbled into the kitchen, where he found her bent over the kitchen sink, gagging.

Randi went to her and turned the water on. After splashing some on Claudia's face, she wet two dish towels and placed them on her injured arms. Then she led Claudia to the table and helped her sit.

"Get some ointment from the bathroom," she told Stone, giving him a look that said not to argue. By the time he grabbed burn cream, gauze pads, and white tape from Curt's medicine cabinet and got back to the kitchen, the entire group had convened there, standing around awkwardly while Claudia sobbed into her hands and Randi rubbed her back.

"Here." Stone handed the supplies over. He stayed silent until Randi finished smearing salve on the burns and covering them with gauze.

"Claudia. You can't listen to it. You know it lies."

She looked up, her eyes red and her cheeks wet with tears.

"You're wrong. It's all true. I know she's there. She told me."

Father Bonaventura turned sharply at her words.

"She told you? You've spoken with your sister?"

Claudia nodded. "In the hospital. Before I...woke up. It was like when we used to talk in our dreams. She's in Hell, and that thing... she tried to hide it, but it tortures her. I felt it."

Father Bonaventura sat down next to her. "You need to tell me everything."

Claudia wiped her eyes. Stone started to say she didn't have to but she shook him off.

"No, it's okay. He needs to know. You all do. No more secrets."

She gave them a quick version of her and Shari's troubles growing up, and their gradual awareness of their powers. When she got to their time at the orphanage, she avoided mentioning

Lockhart's spying on them but Stone saw his face go pale as she described how they could sense dark thoughts and they decided to leave. None of it was new for Stone until she mentioned the dreams about the demon she and Shari had shared, both before coming to Hastings Mills and after.

"Why didn't you say anything?" he asked her. It came out more sharply than he intended and Randi kicked him under the table.

"You wouldn't have believed us. And even if you did, it wouldn't have changed anything. You'd have insisted on coming. Because of the show. And because of her." She didn't point at Randi but he knew what she meant. And he couldn't deny it. "And then after we got here, you weren't...yourself."

"The influence of the demon," Father Bonaventura said. Curt bit his lip and went to the cabinet, where he took out a bottle of whiskey. Lockhart stared while he poured a glass.

Jesus, what a group we are. A pedophile, two drunks, and a priest two steps from the grave. And me, their leader. So full of himself he can't even see when he's putting everyone in danger. Stone wished he could go back in time and ignore the message from Randi.

Who are you kidding? Claudia's right. Your ego would never let you do that. And it was Randi...after all the years, something still remained between us. Not what we used to have, but something.

He noticed Claudia staring at him, and guilt warmed his face.

How could she ever love him again after what he'd done? What he'd thought?

"So." Everyone's attention returned to Father Bonaventura, and Stone was grateful for the distraction. "Telekinesis. Telepathy. Astral projection. I had no idea the two of you were so gifted. This is good. Please, contact her. She could provide valuable information, help us locate a weakness."

"I can't." Claudia shook her head.

"You must. I understand there's some danger—"

"No!" Claudia pushed away from the table and continued in a softer voice. "You don't understand at all. I can't contact her. She's too far away. I have to wait for her to come to me. Shari...she's always been the stronger one. I just can't do it."

"Can you at least try?" Father Bonaventura asked.

Her cheeks grew red as fury replaced sadness on her face.

"You don't think I have? Every goddamned hour since she died? I can't do it!"

In time with her shout, the cabinet doors opened and dishes rattled. The water turned on and splashed Curt, who jumped away. Stone moved between Claudia and the priest.

"That's enough. Leave her alone."

Claudia got up and left the room. Stone made to follow but Randi stopped him.

"Give her a few minutes."

He sat back down.

Father Bonaventura sighed.

"Ah, well. We must find another way, then. But not tonight. Tonight I need to rest." He got up, wobbled for a moment, and then got his balance. Curt took him by the arm and said he could use the main bedroom. Father Bonaventura thanked him and the two left the kitchen. After a moment, Lockhart followed them.

"What about the rest of us?" Del asked. "Do we take watch shifts?" His tone conveyed his lack of desire. Before Stone could answer, his phone chimed with a text message.

"Son of a bitch." He turned the phone around so the others could see. "Read this."

Ken peered down at the screen, with Del looking over his shoulder.

Robert Lockhart. Age 52. Removed from priesthood after multiple allegations of molesting underage girls. Never formally charged. Last known residence in San Ysidro, CA.

"All right. Now we send that perv packing." Del smacked one ham-sized fist into his other hand.

"No." Claudia had warned him they should wait until the right moment to out Lockhart. He had to trust that she'd let him know when. "Not yet."

"What?" Randi almost shouted the word and Stone shushed her.

"We keep this a secret for now."

"You're the boss," Ken said, although he clearly didn't understand the decision. "What next?"

"We get some sleep." Stone patted his shoulder. "We'll let the cameras do the work tonight. Maybe we'll get lucky and get some good footage."

"I'd feel a lot luckier if nothing happened at all," Randi said.

Stone couldn't disagree.

CHAPTER THIRTY-FIVE

Hastings Mills, NY, July 21st, one year ago

Alone.

Claudia drifted in the endless black abyss of death and no matter how much she cried for help, no one answered.

Shari. Her sister had to be nearby. Every time she'd visited this place, Shari had come to her.

Where was she?

—*Shari!*— She heard the words in her mind but no sound existed in the void.

She called for her sister again. And again.

Nothing.

Terror pulsed through her nonexistent form. Had something happened? Was she unconscious?

Dead?

What about Stone and the others? The last thing she remembered was brushing her teeth, her eyes still red and swollen from crying, her heart in jagged pieces at the thought of Shari being tortured in Hell because of Claudia's pitiful attempt to hurt the demon.

Then nothing.

As she contemplated the blank spot in her memory, a light appeared in the distance. For a second, Claudia's hopes soared.

Shari!

Then the glow took on an angry red cast, the unhealthy crimson of hellfire. It expanded rapidly until a terrifyingly familiar desert formed around her. Towers of flame belched up in random patterns. Her body took shape and scorching heat assaulted her flesh.

The ground ruptured and Asmodeus's massive throne rose up. The demon slouched casually, its five heads staring down at her with eyes of yellow.

"Welcome to Hell, witch." The human head spoke, but the booming voice came from everywhere. The lion head bared its fangs, the horse shook its flaming mane, and the lizard flicked a forked tongue. The head in the center, a shaggy goat, stared at her with palpable lust.

The demon flicked its hand and a human form took shape at the base of the throne. In the next instant, Shari stood there, her flesh a ruddy pink as her pale skin reflected the flames.

"Claudia—"

A stream of fire shot up and twisted around Shari's body. The burning loops constricted, squeezing Shari so tightly her arms and legs bent into impossible angles. More fiery tentacles attacked her, entering every orifice. Shari's cries escalated into agonized shrieks as her flesh blistered and peeled away.

Claudia leaped forward but the ground cracked open and disgorged a stream of lava. She could only stand and watch as Shari's skin melted and her bones charred. Claudia sank to her knees and reached out, helpless to do anything except—

Wait.

Why couldn't she feel Shari's pain? All their lives they'd shared any kind of intense physical sensation. Spankings, fights, burns, broken bones. But now, nothing. Why?

The answer came immediately.

—Because it's not real, sister.—

—Shari!—

—Hush. Come with me. We don't have much time.—

—Where?—

A vaporous hand appeared. Claudia took it and then watched in awe as she left her body behind and sailed into the darkness, an ethereal form rocketing through a starless universe. A light appeared ahead and Shari guided them to it. They came to a wall of prismatic hexagons, each displaying a different picture. Claudia had no time to focus on any of them before they entered one and then she stood before Robert Lockhart in a cheap motel room. He sat naked on a bed, his face in his hands. In the bathroom, a young girl washed herself with a cloth. He glanced at the girl and took a large knife from a duffle bag on the floor. Oblivious to Claudia's ghostly presence, he placed the edge against his throat.

—You have to stop him. His work isn't done.—

—How? He can't see me.—

—He can if you want him to.—

That confused Claudia for a moment. How was she supposed to—

Her body took on substance, not quite solid but no longer transparent. Lockhart gasped and dropped the knife.

"Don't do it." Claudia had no idea what was happening, but she trusted Shari implicitly. "It's not your time yet."

"My soul is black with sin." Lockhart looked at the girl again, who still had her back to them. "I don't deserve to live."

Claudia thought hard. She had to convince him. Her word alone wouldn't be enough.

"God sent me." She thought about Shari and a bullet wound appeared between her breasts. Lockhart's eyes widened.

"You," he whispered. He reached out and his hand passed through her. Tears welled up in his eyes and rolled down his cheeks into his goatee. "I'm so sorry for what I did to you. Please forgive me."

"That's not for me to do." Claudia saw her opening and took it. "Only God can forgive you. But not if you kill yourself."

"I won't. I swear. I'll wait for God's sign."

Something tugged at Claudia's arm. The disembodied hand again. She let it pull her back into the void. Another burst of rainbow color, and then she stood in a different room.

Where Stone Graves held a gun to his head.

It's over. There's nothing left. Stone contemplated the gun in his hand. Death surrounded him, and it was all his fault. In the bathroom,

Ken Webb reclined in a tub filled with bloody water, both of his wrists slashed open. He'd left a note blaming Stone for bringing him to Hastings Mills, where Del had been murdered by a group of homophobic good old boys who 'didn't want no fags in their town'. Rather than live alone, he'd decided to join his husband in death.

In the bedroom, Randi lay on the bed and Claudia on the floor, both of their heads blown away by the very same pistol Stone now held. Murder suicide. Claudia had put two bullets into Randi's face and then stuck the barrel under her own chin and said, "You killed my sister and ruined my life. Now you have no one."

A second later, her brains splattered on the wall.

She'd been right. He'd killed Shari by bringing her here. And all the others. None of it would've happened if he wasn't a greedy, selfish bastard.

You can fix that. Give them what they all want. What they deserve.

He stared at the gun.

Yes. You have nothing to live for. The people you love are gone. Your career is ruined. Do what's right. End the pain.

Do it for us.

Stone looked up. Claudia stood there, Shari at her side. They looked as beautiful and whole as the day he met them. Randi was with them, smiling and young again. Ken appeared with Del, their hands clasped.

Set us free.

Stone put the gun to his temple. If he could help them...why should he live when they were dead?

"No!"

Claudia shouted before she had any idea what she'd say.

Stone turned and frowned, his confusion obvious as he glanced from her to the other Claudia behind him and back again. She understood what he must be feeling. Angry burns marred her flesh and her hair hung in limp tangles. Other-Claudia wore clean clothes and looked perfectly sane. And solid.

She took a step toward him and saw his frown deepen as Shari's image appeared next to her for a moment and then vanished.

"Don't do it. None of it's real. It's a trick."

"How do I know you're not the trick?" He turned the gun so it pointed at her.

"You didn't betray me. You wouldn't. I've seen inside you. You're a good man."

"No, I'm not. I wasn't good to Randi or you. You both deserved better."

She took another step. "I love you, Stone."

"We both do." Shari's ghostly form flickered into existence and faded again, but not before Claudia felt the surprising truth of her sister's words.

"We'll never leave you." Claudia held out her hand to Stone.

The gun shook and she worried he might pull the trigger by accident. Dreamland or not, she felt sure that if either of them died here, their earthly body would perish as well.

—*Yes.*— Shari's confirmation only added to her nervousness.

"Never?"

"We promise. Give me the gun and everything will be okay."

He slowly leaned forward.

"Don't do it, Stone." Randi's harsh tone stopped him. "You have to pay for your sins."

"You have to pay for me," a new voice said. A little boy appeared next to Randi.

Shari whispered inside Claudia's head and she repeated the words aloud.

"Nick. They're lying. Death isn't the answer."

Stone's eyes widened at the use of his real name and then narrowed as he stared at the boy.

"You weren't my fault. Not you. Not any of you."

He handed the gun to Claudia.

"I trust you."

The room disappeared in a cascade of rainbows.

Stone sat up and opened his eyes. His arm was extended and his fingers bent in the form of a gun, like a child playing cops and robbers.

"Holy shit." He slowly lowered his arm and unclenched his hand. Sweat coated his face and chest. The temperature in the room had to be eighty.

Across from him, on the love seat, Claudia moaned and reached out for something. He had a feeling he knew what. Afraid that touching her might send him back to the dream world, he went around the living room turning on the lights. Ken and Del lay on the floor, both of them muttering in their sleep. Lockhart sat in one of the chairs, awake but with his eyes more haunted than ever as he stared at Claudia.

"Did she save you too?" he asked, not looking at Stone.

"Yeah. I think so." Not wanting to discuss his nightmare, Stone changed the subject. "Where's Father Bonaventura?"

Lockhart pointed at the kitchen. Stone went down the hall and found the priest at the table, pillow creases still on his cheeks and what little hair he had tousled from sleep. He was reading his Bible and marking passages with a red pen.

Stone sat and waited for him to finish and glance up. His eyes were bloodshot and worried. When he saw Stone's face, he nodded.

"It came to you in your dreams as well."

"It?" Stone asked, although he had a pretty good idea what Father Bonaventura meant.

"Tell me everything."

Stone did. Halfway through, Claudia entered the room and sat down next to him. When he finished, she told them about her experiences. As each member of the team joined them, Father Bonaventura asked them to recite their dreams. All of them had experienced something terrible. For Ken, it was reliving the day he came out to his parents, only instead of accepting him and his life choice, they kicked him out and he'd ended up hustling sex on the streets and living in a shelter. Del's involved being trapped in a cemetery where all the people whose lives he'd taken as a soldier came back to avenge their deaths. Randi said she'd been shown a future where she lived alone in a tiny apartment, broke, starving, and sickly.

All of them said Claudia had appeared just in time to stop them from committing suicide.

Lockhart didn't give any details, just said that he'd relived a dark moment from his past and he'd been near suicide before an angel of God came and saved him. He didn't mention Claudia but from the way he looked at her, Stone felt pretty sure he knew the truth.

"It's the demon's way," Father Bonaventura said. "Many times, when the despairing stand at the brink and look down, it's a demon that gives them a push. They sow darkness and despair, and tempt people to the sin of suicide so they can harvest the souls."

"Did you have a nightmare as well?" Randi asked.

The priest shrugged. "I've had them every night since the beast returned, although until two days ago, I had no idea why. But now we must put aside our fears, move past the demon's unholy persuasions. It failed to break us, thanks in no small part to the powers granted us by God." He gave a quick nod in Claudia's direction. "And today we must drive it from this world forever."

The table jumped and shook. Glasses in the sink shattered. Upstairs, Abby shrieked and doors slammed. Curt Rawlings shouted for help.

Stone ran for the stairs, the rest of the group behind him. When he got to Abby's room, Curt stood at the door, his mouth open in shock. Invisible hands tossed Abby's body through the air like a rag doll, slamming her into one wall and then the other so hard there were dents in the plaster over her bed.

"Help her!" Curt shouted. Stone tried to grab her but a nightstand smashed into his legs and knocked him over. It rose up and swung sideways, striking Curt in the ribs with a brittle *crack* like tree branches snapping in the wind. He screamed and clutched his side. Del took him by the arm and pulled him from the room. Abby fell onto the bed, her elbows raw and bleeding. She shouted at them and green spittle flew from her mouth.

"Fuck you to hell. You'll all die! Die! *Muri*! *Morir*! This town will burn and your souls will be mine."

Father Bonaventura pushed past Ken and threw holy water across Abby. She howled and bashed her head against the wall, her eyes rolling crazily.

"Bastardis sacerdos! Sus turpis! Prostituta irrumator praetor!"

Abby gasped and went limp. Her eyes closed and her chest heaved as she panted like an overheated dog.

Father Bonaventura left the room, waving for everyone to follow. He shut the door and leaned against it.

"The demon grows stronger. I must prepare myself before I begin the ceremony again."

"We need to get Curt to the hospital," Randi said. He leaned against the wall, his face white with shock and pain. Stone nodded.

"Have Del take you. The rest of us will help Father Bonaventura."

"Okay. I'll call you when we know anything." She took Curt's arm and helped him down the stairs. Del followed, after Ken hugged him and told him to be careful.

Stone looked at Father Bonaventura.

"Tell us what to do."

From the other side of the door, the rough voice of the demon shouted at them.

"Burn in hell! That's what you'll do! Burn forever with your whore!"

As he walked down the stairs, Stone prayed that Father Bonaventura could defeat the demon.

Because the alternative was too frightening to consider.

CHAPTER THIRTY-SIX

Hastings Mills, NY, July 21st, one year ago

The ER was bedlam when Randi and Del entered with a moaning Curt between them. Men and women with bloody bandages on faces and arms. Children crying. Several people wrapped in blankets or sheets who appeared to be nude underneath, their expressions ranging from confusion to embarrassment.

As they went to check Curt in, two EMTs came out a side door, talking in hushed tones.

"—Eddie heard on the scanner a bunch of people on Eighth Street were fucking right in the road."

"Town's going to shit. Probably some new kind of drug, like Molly or—"

"Can I help you?"

A middle-aged man with harried eyes behind old-fashioned black-framed glasses looked up at them from the admissions desk. He took Curt's name and insurance information, and told them it would be at least an hour. They found seats and Curt closed his eyes, his lips pressed tight.

Del leaned toward Randi. "What the hell is going on?"

"Remember what Father Bonaventura said? Violence and lust are the demon's tools." She thought back to Stone's actions in the jail cell and said a quick prayer that Father Bonaventura's protections over them would hold. She didn't want to end up rutting in the street like some animal.

Or worse.

Del sat back, frowning. He didn't speak again until the desk nurse called for Curt.

Stone was at the kitchen table watching Bonaventura bless containers of water when his phone buzzed with an incoming text message.

Just emailed you that info you wanted. What the hell is going on there?

"It's Joe in California," he said, in response to Ken's raised eyebrow. "I think they found out who Alberto is."

"What did they say?" Bonaventura asked.

"Give me a sec." Stone opened his email and scrolled down to the message from the office. "Here."

He held out the phone so the others could see.

Father Alberto Gianpolo founded St. Alphonse University in 1867. Served as the first president and father superior. In 1885, a series of disappearances happened in Hastings Mills and the nearby area, beginning with two girls from a passing Romani clan. Five other children went missing that summer. In October, Gianpolo hung himself in one of the buildings. He left a note in his chambers that read, 'My sins have grown too great. My heart has been tainted by the Devil's touch and the beast calls to me from the water. God no longer speaks to me. May he have mercy on my everlasting soul.' No charges were ever made and no evidence found. But most scholars believe Gianpolo killed those children, because the disappearances stopped after that. Hope this is the same Alberto you asked about.

"Good Lord." Father Bonaventura took the phone and read the message again before handing it back. "I should have recognized that name. Damn this brain of mine."

He rubbed his eyes. "There's a plaque commemorating Father Gianpolo right at the entrance to the university's administration building. But nothing I ever read about him mentioned any of this. Only that he founded the school and died here."

"I guess even back then, the Church covered things up. I wonder if he killed himself in the same dorm where Lockhart and his friends had their séance?"

"I wouldn't doubt it at all." Father Bonaventura leaned back in his chair. "This town, this land, has been tainted for much longer than I imagined. No wonder Asmodeus gained a strong foothold so easily. He sensed it the moment I was stupid enough to bring a physical manifestation of his power here, all those years ago. And he's been manipulating me ever since."

"All of us," Claudia said.

"Yes. Exploiting our weaknesses until it could gather us all together."

"You make it sound like some kind of cosmic chess player."

"You could think of it that way," Father Bonaventura replied to Stone. "Time means nothing to an eternal creature. It can wait for decades, biding its time, waiting for the barriers to weaken a little more...."

The aged priest's voice trailed off and his brow furrowed.

"What is it?" Stone asked. Behind him, dawn fought against the darkness outside the window. Somewhere in the distance, a siren howled and others answered.

"I've been a fool. The answer has been right in front of us, of me, all along. Abigail houses the demon but the school is the gateway. It's been tainted by evil for more than a century. Gianpolo unlocked the door and each successive act of evil or perversity has opened it a little more. Driving the demon from the girl won't be enough. We have to close the door and ensure it never opens again."

"What does that mean?"

"It means our task just got a lot harder."

Officer Corday Rose entered the police station and found it empty.

"What the hell?" He paused as the door clicked shut behind him, the automatic lock engaging to separate the lobby from the rest of the building. Even the sergeant's desk, which protocol required to be manned at all times, was empty. A quick look into the dispatch area showed neither Martha nor Jeannie on duty.

He checked the break room and Mordecai's office, which no one had used since his death. He was about to head downstairs to the holding area when he heard a noise from the women's bathroom.

"Hello?" He knocked on the door, and then rapped it harder when no one answered. Muffled sounds came from the other side, and a thump like a stall door closing. He repeated his call twice more. Thinking about all the strange shit that had been happening in town, he got a sudden picture of someone tied and gagged in a stall while vandals looted the evidence room or weapons lockers.

Praying he wasn't barging in on one of the ladies suffering from a bad dinner, he drew his gun and opened the door.

Martha Plotkin knelt on the tile floor in front of Lieutenant Parker, who leaned back against a stall door while Martha sucked his dick. A set of dentures sat next to her. The wrinkled, liver-spotted skin of her neck flapped loosely as her head bobbed up and down. Parker opened his eyes and gave two thumbs up.

"Yo, there's room for two," he said, a wicked grin turning his lips up under his thick mustache.

Unable to even find words, Corday backed out of the room.

"Pussy!" Parker's shout followed him. "See you in Hell. You and the priest!"

Father Bonaventura. He needs to know what's happening. Corday headed back out to his truck, detouring only to grab a shotgun and some ammunition from the weapons room.

Something told him the worst was yet to come.

Del and Randi crossed the parking lot as the morning sun peeked over the treetops and ignited the first eye-piercing glare on windows and chrome. As they neared it, Del pulled out the keys and then let out a curse.

All four tires were flat and two of the windows broken.

He glanced around. None of the other vehicles parked by them had been damaged.

"This was fucking deliberate," Randi said. She pulled out her phone to call for a ride and Del told her not to bother. Sure enough, no signal.

"Same as what happened to me and Ken. We'll have to walk."

"This is bullshit." Randi shoved her phone into her purse and paused when a Hastings Mills PD SUV pulled up next to them. Aware that anyone could be under the demon's influence, she felt around for her pepper spray as the cop's window went down.

Revealing Officer Corday Rose.

"Looks like you need a ride." He wore a serious but normal expression.

Randi took a chance and left the spray alone. "We sure do."

"You're lucky I saw you. I just came from the station. Every single cop is MIA except for one who's currently getting a goddamned BJ from our seventy-year-old dispatcher. Sorry," he added, giving Randi a sheepish grin.

For the first time, she noticed just how attractive he really was. About the same age as her, with soft green eyes and the first hints of gray beginning to peek through his dark brown hair. His haven't-shaved-in-a-day stubble only added to his rugged handsomeness.

Trickles of moisture ran down her ribs and made her aware that she was sweating like a horse. And probably smelled like one, too, she thought, remembering that she hadn't showered since.... *Oh, god. It's been two days!* She clamped her arms against her sides, hoping he wouldn't get a whiff. Corday's own pit stains, darkening his blue uniform, didn't bother her.

It's manly.

Wait. What the hell is wrong with me?

"You okay?" he asked, frowning. She realized she was staring at him like a high school girl with a crush on her teacher.

"Fine," she said, ignoring the heat in her cheeks. "Can we get that ride?"

"Hop in." He unlocked the doors. "It's like the whole town's going nuts."

"No shit. Father Bonaventura thinks he knows why. I'll tell you on the way."

"Good." He motioned at the passenger door. She almost said no and got in the back with Del, but she feared that would look rude. Instead, she settled for sitting as far from him as she could and praying the air-conditioning didn't reveal her stinking armpits. Luckily, the interior already carried a distinctive smell from all the unwashed bodies that had occupied it before them.

It's Asmodeus. His influence again. That's why I feel like this. Even so, she couldn't help admiring the muscle definition in his arms as he put the car in drive and spun the wheel.

Demon or not, I'd fuck him.

Afraid she'd blurt out something inappropriate, she let Del do the talking while they drove.

"Confession is the sacrament of penance, where a person is absolved of their sins by God."

Father Leo Bonaventura stood in front of the entire group in the living room. He'd informed them that in order to cleanse the campus and house of any evil spirits while also protecting themselves from demonic influence, they would first need to purify their souls.

"Father, what about a Jew like me?" Randi asked.

"This isn't about religion. It's about having confidence in the power of God. Just like the blessing of protection I did yesterday."

Officer Rose patted Randi's hand and she took it in her own. Stone wondered what had happened during their car ride.

"Normally, confession is performed in private," Father Bonaventura continued. "For our purposes, you will all silently admit your sins to God. For those of you who've never been to confession, concentrate on failings that have affected other people. Lies, greed, lust, adultery. You probably know what you've done wrong."

A picture flew off the wall and struck Father Bonaventura in the shoulder. Another followed it but he twisted out of the way. It hit the floor and the glass shattered.

Upstairs, Abby howled with laughter.

Father Bonaventura adjusted his glasses and lifted his hands, palms out.

"May the Lord be in your heart and help you to confess your sins with true sorrow."

Lockhart bowed his head. "Lord Jesus, Son of God, have mercy on me, a sinner."

As they'd been instructed, the others repeated his words. Father Bonaventura closed his eyes, which Stone took as the signal for them to recount their sins. He tried to think of where to begin. The priest's mention of lies and greed in particular struck a nerve. Living in LA, trying to build a media empire, you couldn't help lying in order to succeed. And that paired nicely with greed; hell, as much as he hated to admit it, Randi was right about him being selfish when it came to getting his own show. The opportunity of a lifetime, but it had cost him so much. Randi. Friendships. Shari.

Where does ambition end and greed begin?

He still couldn't answer that, even after all these years. But he did regret many of his actions. Hopefully that'd be enough for God.

Look at me. The one who never believed in religion, waiting for God's forgiveness. How fast things change when you're confronted with undeniable truths.

Father Bonaventura let the silence drag on. Stone saw Lockhart fingering a rosary and reciting something under his breath. He still wanted to wring the degenerate's throat for what he'd done to Shari and Claudia, and all the other girls he'd abused, but if the man had also been under the influence of the demon all those years, how could anyone fault him for his actions? If he blamed Lockhart, then he had to blame himself as well. That line of thinking only agitated him, and he was glad when Father Bonaventura cleared his throat.

"God, the Father of mercies, through the death and resurrection of his Son has reconciled the world to himself and sent the Holy

Spirit among us for the forgiveness of sins; through the ministry of the Church, may God give you pardon and peace, and I absolve you from your sins in the name of the Father, and of the Son, and of the Holy Spirit."

"Thanks be to God," said Lockhart.

"Thanks be to God," the group echoed.

"Glory be to the Father, and to the Son, and to the Holy Spirit, as it was in the beginning, is now, and ever shall be, world without end. Amen."

"Amen." This time they all said it in unison with Lockhart. Father Bonaventura sprinkled holy water on each of them while he recited a final blessing.

"May the Passion of our Lord Jesus Christ, the intercession of the Blessed Virgin Mary and of all the saints, protect you in whatever is to come. May they watch over you and help you grow in holiness, and reward you with eternal life."

Father Bonaventura then had them recite the Lord's Prayer three times and the Hail Mary four times. When they were done, he closed his Bible and let out a deep sigh.

"I must meditate on my own now. We will begin in one hour."

Alan Duhaime stared at his phone. The text message was short but its meaning unmistakable.

The board needs to speak with you regarding an urgent matter. The meeting will be at 10 a.m. tomorrow in your office.

He'd received the text the previous night. *An urgent matter.* Their way of saying they'd made their decision. He knew what their answer would be. By this time tomorrow, his name would be all over the news, his career dragged through the mud and plastered across TVs, computer screens, and newspapers so everyone could see his shameful deeds. He'd be lucky to get off with only a few years in some white-collar prison.

He only had one option left. Call his lawyer and see about negotiating a deal.

It doesn't have to be like that.

Right, he told the voice in his head. What else is there?

Take control. Don't let them win. There is a way....

Duhaime looked at the bottle of whiskey on his desk. He'd finished most of it during a long, sleepless night. Was it the booze talking, or had his subconscious discovered a way out of the mess?

"What is it?" His whisper seemed too loud in the emptiness of his office.

The voice grew deeper, stronger. It oozed a confidence he didn't have.

Show them they don't own you. Make a statement. Something they'll always remember.

A picture appeared in his head. His own face, but younger. Virile. And smiling. The kind of smile that told people he didn't give a fuck what they thought, he wouldn't bow down to them or their fake news.

The smile of a winner.

"Yes."

Good man. Now, there's one last thing you need.

The picture changed to an empty room with a podium. On it lay a speech. He couldn't read the words, but he knew he had to say them in order to clear his name.

To win.

A ten-minute walk brought him to Dallas Hall, the tallest structure on campus except for the bell tower behind the library. The perfect place for him to deliver his momentous speech. He used his master key to enter and climbed the stairs to the fifth floor, his footsteps echoing off the tiles. An empty space greeted him. The entire level had been gutted down to the studs, plywood sheets the only flooring.

A noose hung from one of the beams, dangling above a single chair. Duhaime's conviction faltered at the sight of it.

This will be your greatest achievement.

The image appeared again, this time with him standing in front of a crowd of people. Once more, he wore his victory on his face. As he climbed the podium, the crowd stood and clapped. Someone handed him a necktie, maroon and black stripes representing the school colors. He held it for a moment, unsure of what to do with it.

Do it. Do it. DO IT!

Duhaime stripped off the tie he'd been wearing and slid the new one under his collar. Over, under, through. Tighten the knot.

He cleared his throat and stepped up to the mic.

Yes!

The ground fell away and the crowd disappeared into an endless pit of fire. A beast with five heads arose, mouths open and fangs gleaming.

He had time for a single scream before the rope tightened around his throat.

CHAPTER THIRTY-SEVEN

Hastings Mills, NY, July 22nd, one year ago

"Is everyone okay with this?"

Although Stone spoke to the whole group, he let his eyes rest a little longer on Claudia, who looked like she might pass out at any second. Her eyes were sunken almost as badly as Abby's and her complexion was gray as death. Pairing her with Randi and Del to go cleanse the dormitory at St. Alphonse didn't sit well with him at all; he'd have preferred she stay at the house where he could keep an eye on her. But Father Bonaventura felt her abilities would give them a better chance of completing the ritual at the school.

"Good to go," Del said.

Randi held up her camera.

"For better or worse, we'll have a record of the whole thing."

Claudia gave a desultory nod. She'd tried to contact Shari earlier but all she'd gotten was a brief impression of endless fire and terrible screaming, and then everything went dark. Afterward, there'd been blisters on her hands again, which had faded away like the others in the hours since dawn, leaving only faint red blotches in their wake. Between those, her bruises, the lump on her head, and her general lassitude, she looked like a disaster zone survivor.

But then, that's all of us, Stone thought. Hard to believe they'd only been in Hastings Mills for a week. They'd experienced more paranormal events in that time than in the last five years, and everyone was battered, scared, and exhausted. Including Father Bonaventura, who appeared on the verge of collapse. Yet each time he wavered, each time he had to pause and catch his breath or take a pill, he rallied with an internal strength beyond anything Stone had ever seen. He'd returned from his meditation or nap or whatever with renewed energy and quickly gone about assigning everyone their tasks for the impending exorcism.

Lockhart had picked up Curt, who'd suffered a broken rib and dislocated shoulder, from the hospital. They would assist Father Bonaventura during the rite. Lockhart's experience as a former exorcist would be vital, and Bonaventura felt Curt's presence might help lend Abby strength to fight the demon infecting her. It would be Ken and Stone's job to keep a steady supply of holy water and incense at hand and also hold Abby down if necessary. Stone had already gone over the camera layout with Ken. This would be quite possibly the most important event ever captured on film, and he wasn't leaving anything to chance. He'd already recorded his intro to the exorcism, standing at the bottom of the stairs while feral grunts and howls emanated from Abby's room. At one point, all the pictures on the staircase wall had simultaneously dropped to the ground.

Watching the replay on the camera, Stone couldn't help feeling a quivering anticipation in his belly. There was a good chance that in the next few minutes he'd fulfill his lifelong dream of proving to the world the existence of the supernatural.

In that moment, everything they'd gone through seemed worth it.

Then he remembered Shari, and his fear that not everyone would survive the impending encounter came rushing back.

Del gave Stone a fist bump, hugged and kissed Ken, and went out to the car. Randi gave everyone except Lockhart a hug and whispered, "Be careful," in Stone's ear. He told her the same. Claudia was the last to leave. She hugged Stone, her flesh ice cold against his.

"Claudia," he said, but she cut off the rest by putting a finger against his lips.

"I know," she whispered. At the same time, words appeared in his head.

—I love you too. Don't worry. One way or another, everything will work out.—

Then she slipped past him, a ghost trailing after her human counterparts.

He watched through the window as they climbed into Officer Rose's cruiser. He'd already had Randi's car towed from the hospital to a garage to have the tires fixed. He'd drop them off there after a stop at St. Mary's to get more candles and incense, and check on Father Gager.

"Now it's time for us to pray," Bonaventura said. He'd changed into a black, long-sleeved shirt and black pants, and wore his white clerical collar. Stone turned away from the window as the car disappeared down the road. He bowed his head and closed his eyes while the priest began. "Our Father, who art in Heaven…."

The rest of the words were lost to Stone as he focused on his own prayers.

Please, God, keep Claudia and the others safe. I don't want to lose them too.

Corday Rose was about to open the doors to St. Mary's when someone gasped and said "No!" in a hoarse voice. He turned and found the spooky girl, Claudia, staring at the church. Her eyes had rolled back and the whites had turned cloudy gray. "Something bad inside."

Corday's body twitched as what his mother used to call invisible centipedes ran up and down his back. He looked at Randi. "Now what?"

Randi shrugged. "If she says it's bad, it's bad. At this point, that could mean anything."

"Great." Corday drew his gun and grabbed the door handle. Del took the other and nodded. They flung the doors open at the same time. Corday entered, gun ready.

Everything appeared normal. Then Del cursed and pointed.

At the far end of the church, the massive wooden crucifix had been turned upside down and leaned against the altar. A naked Father Gager was nailed to it, mocking Jesus's pose. Drying blood crusted a gaping wound in his throat. More of it coated his chest and the carpet.

Corday motioned for the others to stay put and made his way to the altar, checking between the pews as he went. He doubted whoever had killed the priest would stick around, but considering how crazy the town had gone, better safe than sorry.

When he reached the steps, he noticed several sets of footprints in the puddled blood. They led across the altar to the side exit next to the confessionals. Based on how much had dried, he figured the perps had done their deed hours before.

Maybe even right after I dropped him off.

Sudden guilt stabbed at his guts. If he'd taken Gager with him to the Rawlingses' place, or even to the hospital, he'd still be alive.

"We're ready," Del called out, his words bouncing off the walls and pews. He held up a grocery bag. Corday looked at Gager once more.

I will find whoever did this. Find them and then maybe they won't make it to jail.

No one spoke on the way to the garage. When they arrived, Randi thanked him for his help and tried to hand him money for the repairs.

"Keep it," Corday said. On impulse, he took her hand. Her eyebrows rose but she didn't pull away, giving him the confidence to blurt out, "You can take me out to dinner instead, when this is all over."

She surprised him again by smiling. "It's a date."

Before he realized what was happening, she leaned up, kissed his cheek, and then hurried to her car, where Del and Claudia waited. They drove away, leaving him standing like a dork with his hand on his face. He might have stayed there all day if the strident yowl of a fire siren hadn't broken the spell.

His emotions awhirl, he headed back to St. Mary's.

"Amen."

Father Leo Bonaventura lifted his head and opened his eyes. Four faces stared at him, all displaying varying degrees of fear. Stone Graves chewed at his bottom lip. Ken, the lanky Japanese cameraman, had a deer-in-the-headlights look as if he might turn and run at any moment. Curt Rawlings had developed a muscle tic in his left eye, the lid and brow twitching in random bursts, and he flinched each time Abigail swore or something in the house moved.

Out of everyone, Lockhart appeared the calmest, which Leo hoped stemmed from his faith and his experience with exorcisms, and not liquid courage. Drunken people made mistakes, and they couldn't afford any.

The final battle was at hand.

"When we enter the room, I'll go first. Robert will be behind me and to my right. Mr. Rawlings to my left. Mr. Graves and Mr. Webb, you'll come in last and move to the end of the bed."

Leo grasped the railing. As he mounted the first step, he recited a protection prayer.

"St. Michael the Archangel, defend us in the day of battle; be our safeguard against the wickedness and snares of the Devil. May God rebuke him, we humbly pray and do thou, oh Prince of the Heavenly Host, by the Power of God, cast into Hell Satan and all the other evil spirits, who prowl throughout the world seeking the ruin of souls, amen."

"Bonaventura! Your fucking prayers mean nothing! You cannot defeat me!"

The stairs shook and the walls vibrated with the power of the demon's bellow. A dozen voices overlapped Abby's, all of them deeper than a baritone singer and rough as if forced through a damaged throat. Leo gripped the rail tighter and pulled himself along while the steps fought to shake him loose and send him tumbling to his death. Cracks appeared in the plaster and dust fell like snow.

A sonorous rumbling rose from the ground, forcing Leo to raise his voice.

"...cast into Hell Satan and all the other evil spirits who prowl throughout the world, seeking the ruin of souls, amen!"

Lockhart shouted "Amen!" behind him.

Leo raised his Bible with his free hand. "In the name of the Father and of the Son and of the Holy Ghost, Jesus Christ defeats Satan!"

Crack! The railing fell away, pulling Leo off balance. He teetered over the floor ten feet below and insane laughter filled his ears as the rail landed spindles up, waiting to impale him when he fell.

Strong hands yanked him back from the edge. He hit the wall and his teeth clacked together. His heart gave a painful jolt and his knees buckled. Someone gripped his arm and kept him upright. Voices filled his head, accompanied by the twisted, sneering faces of a young boy and an older woman. Behind them lurked a horned goat with yellow eyes.

"You will die today!"

"Your God is weak!"

"Are you all right?"

Leo opened eyes he hadn't realized he'd closed. Purple stars floated in his vision, fading as he sucked in a deep breath. The pain in his chest diminished to a dull ache.

"Father? Are you okay?"

Lockhart held him, his face etched with worry.

"I am." Leo was happy to find no trace of weakness in his voice. "Let us continue. The demon and its minions are trying to stop us. That's a good sign. It means they're afraid."

"They're afraid?" Ken Webb said. "I nearly shit myself."

Leo held his Bible forward. *Can you hear me, demon? I will send you back to the pits of Hell where you belong.*

"St. Michael the Archangel, defend us in the day of battle; be our safeguard against the wickedness and snares of the Devil. May God rebuke him, we humbly pray...."

In Abby's room, the guttural laughter changed to a growling scream of fury. All the pictures in the upstairs hall flew off the walls. Glass shattered. Leo reached the top of the stairs and headed for the bedroom without hesitation. He heard the others behind him, their shoes crunching on the broken glass. Lockhart continued to repeat "Amen" at the end of each recitation of the protection prayer.

When they reached the door, it slammed shut in their faces.

Prepared for the possibility, Leo motioned to Lockhart while he continued to pray. Lockhart splashed holy water around the entire doorframe.

"By the power of God, cast into Hell Satan and all the other evil spirits who prowl throughout the world, seeking the ruin of souls, amen!"

White fire ran along the path of the water and the door swung open.

"Bonaventura! Welcome, old friend."

Abby floated above the bed, her arms stretched out and her feet pressed together, mimicking the crucifixion of Christ, her hair behind her like a peacock's tail. Bright red marks covered her naked body, some in the shape of human hands, others hoof prints and paw prints, as if she'd been trampled by a herd of beasts. Green slime ran down her legs and her yellow eyes had taken on the horizontal pupils of a goat.

Rawlings moaned and tried to leave the room but Stone grabbed his arm.

"You need to be strong for her," he said. Rawlings pulled away but didn't bolt. He looked ready to puke and kept his eyes averted from his daughter.

Leo motioned for the others to take their assigned places around the bed. He noticed Stone had his cell phone out and Webb held a small videocam. Lifting his Bible, he faced the girl.

Abby hissed and spat at him. Globs of burning-hot slime struck the Bible and dripped down onto his sleeve. He shook them off and launched into his first prayer while Lockhart placed several candles on the nightstand and lit them.

"Holy Ghost and the Trinity, God the Father, we command thee unclean spirit, depart! God the Son commands thee! God the Holy Ghost commands thee! By the majesty of Christ, the eternal Word of God made flesh, depart!"

A series of cold and hot winds tore through the room, strong enough to flap the curtains and bed coverings. The candle flames blew sideways but didn't extinguish. Abby growled and belched ectoplasm onto the bed.

"He who has built His church on the firm rock of love and declared the gates of Hell shall never prevail against the light of God commands thee to depart! We will dwell with the Blessed Mother Mary for all days, even unto the end of the world, and evil shall have no foothold in this place."

"The end of the world is upon you, priest! Do you not remember when last we met?" Abby folded her arms and legs and lowered herself onto the bed in a lotus position. Her lips pulled back into a mad grin, revealing pale gums and a tongue too large for her mouth. Her voice changed, became that of an older man with a distinctly Spanish accent.

"He referred to himself as Lord Asmodeus, the one whom someday all shall bow before."

Leo twitched as the words of Father Jorge Sanchez emerged from Abby's mouth. He remembered them as clear as if it was only yesterday they'd stood outside the Costa Rican village.

The voice from beyond the grave continued.

"I have made three attempts to banish this evil from the boy, but it only grows stronger. I fear I cannot do this on my own. It is too strong for me. For anyone. That is why we failed. That is why you will fail, Father Fucking Bonaventura!"

Abby sprang into the air and kicked Leo in the center of his chest, sending him stumbling backward. Curt tried to catch him but missed. He ended up on the floor, only the grace of God saving his life as his head missed the doorframe by inches. Gasping for breath, he watched Stone and Curt pull Abby down onto the bed and drape themselves over her. Lockhart poured holy water over them and held up his crucifix while he called out for protection.

"Let the Holy Cross be my light! Step back, Satan!"

Abby twisted and fought, growling and snapping like a wild beast trapped in a net. She clawed at Curt's face and he shrieked as her nails left bloody furrows across his cheek. The plywood that had been set over the broken window rattled violently. The nails shot out, zipped across the room, and embedded themselves so deep in the wall they disappeared. The plywood followed, striking Lockhart on the arm before sailing into the hallway.

Leo struggled to his knees and held his Bible up like a shield.

"In the name of God, the Father Almighty, in the name of our Lord, Jesus Christ, and in the name of the Holy Spirit, I command thee, leave this place!"

Abby's body went limp and the winds ceased. A terrible stench filled the room and Stone jumped back, gagging. Curt doubled over and vomited next to the bed. At first, Leo thought Abby had soiled herself. Thick, black liquid oozed from under her. Then it appeared on the walls as well, seeping from the cracks in the drywall. Ken covered his face with one arm but continued filming everything, his eyes watering. A coughing Lockhart lit incense and waved it over Abby's prone form.

"Our Father, who art in Heaven, hallowed be thy name. Thy Kingdom come, thy will be done, on earth as it is in Heaven. Give us this day our daily bread and forgive us our trespasses, as we forgive those who trespass against us. And lead us not into temptation, but deliver us from evil. Amen."

Abby's eyes closed and although she panted like she'd run a marathon she didn't move.

"Amen," Leo said, regaining his feet. He made the sign of the cross and kissed his Bible before approaching the bed again. When he touched the book to her forehead, she remained still.

"Is it gone?" Ken asked.

Lockhart shook his head and Leo answered, "The demon is preparing its next move."

Leo repeated the Lord's Prayer and opened the Bible to a new page.

"I command you, evil spirit, to leave this girl and depart this place, in the name of the Lord Jesus! You are not welcome here. I renounce you and all spirits that stand beside you."

The house shook and another wave of black ooze dripped onto the floor. As he continued to read, Leo couldn't help wondering what tricks Asmodeus had in store.

And who they would be used on.

CHAPTER THIRTY-EIGHT

Hastings Mills, NY, July 22nd, one year ago

Officer Corday Rose stood in the back parking lot of St. Mary's Church and kicked the blacktop in frustration.

He'd followed the bloody footprints from the altar to the side door and then the sidewalk, where they'd faded to random specks of red before disappearing entirely when he reached the parking lot. Now he had no idea if the killers had continued walking or if they'd gotten into a vehicle. As far as he could tell, there had been at least six distinct prints at the scene, and possibly more. At least one of them had been a child.

His mind kept returning to the ceremony he'd witnessed at the motel. The sense of evil emanating from the people there.

Their eyes turning red....

Had he really seen that? As much as he wanted to ascribe all the unexplained events in town to something logical – mental illness, a toxin in the air or water – rather than the supernatural, it was getting impossible to avoid the realities of the situation.

Nine-one-one had been busy each time he tried it, and neither the station nor the medical examiner's office were answering their phones. With no idea of what to do next, he decided to circle the building. A long shot, but maybe he'd find more prints. If not, he'd head back to station and figure out what—

Something caught his eye and he stopped. A box of matches against the curb. He bent down and picked it up.

Georgie's Riverside.

He recognized it as an old-timers' bar on the outskirts of town.

The owner, Georgie Biggs, ran illegal poker games in the back but every time they raided the place all they found were a few ancient geezers watching Fox News or the races. The place stunk of stale beer and body odor, much like Georgie and his younger brother, Eddie.

Who just happened to be a Hastings Mills cop.

Eddie also smoked cigarettes, and always had a pack from his brother's place in his pocket. Everyone believed Eddie tipped off George to the raids, but they'd never been able to prove it. Still, the matches could have come from anyone.

He turned the matchbox over. A bloody fingerprint was smeared on the cardboard.

Corday stuck the matches in his pocket and hurried back to his car. The department's computer system tracked all the vehicles, meaning he could find locate Eddie Biggs' cruiser just by typing in his name.

It only took ten seconds for the computer to ping the car.

St. Alphonse University.

Sudden dread churned Corday's stomach.

Randi.

He threw the SUV into gear, tires squealing as he sped out of the parking lot, hoping he wasn't too late.

Claudia fought the urge to leap from the car and run, run faster than she ever had before, run and not stop until Hastings Mills didn't exist.

The deep-seated dread she'd felt ever since arriving in town had been growing steadily over the past week, but now it had gone from a nebulous foreboding to imminent peril.

Something very bad was going to happen, and soon.

She sunk down in the back seat and closed her eyes.

—*Shari.*—

Concentrating on her sister's face, she repeated her name over and over. The movements of the car faded away and she was alone in the dark place again.

—Shari! Can you hear me?—

Sudden fire surrounded her, the intense heat forcing her to her hands and knees. Crazed laughter filled her head, accompanied by thousands of voices all screaming at once. People appeared in the flames, features twisted in agony, mouths open. Black sockets where eyes should have been. One of the figures grew larger than the others.

Shari.

Her skull-like visage gaped at Claudia. It had no hair, no ears, no teeth. Two empty slits instead of a nose. Her skin melted and ran like hot wax, only to reform and dissolve all over again. Behind her, a crow-faced demon attacked her with its teeth and claws while it brutally violated her.

A stentorian voice roared in the distance.

"Your souls will be mine!"

"No!"

Claudia's eyes opened and she was back in the car. Her hands gripped the edge of the seat, nails digging into the cloth. Sweat covered her body, dripping between her breasts and under her arms. The harsh stink of burning hair filled her nose and her red arms told her where it came from.

"Oh, fuck."

Randi's voice brought Claudia's attention to the scene ahead of them. Del had turned into the campus and at the end of a long drive a crowd gathered in front of a tall, ivy-covered stone building. A pulsating black aura surrounded the structure. Her skin broke out in goose bumps and she knew instantly they'd reached their destination.

This is it. Shari, I can't do this without you.

She found herself wishing her sister had never woken her from the endless void of her coma. Better an eternal nothing than the never-ending tortures of Hell. Better still, Shari should never have sacrificed herself in the first place. They'd both be alive now. Maybe Stone would be dead, maybe not. In a way, shouldn't he have been the one? It was his fault they were here.

No. She had to stop thinking like that. She could lay blame

forever. Randi's fault for calling Stone. Curt's for calling Randi. Go back even further, when Bonaventura brought the demon's seed to the town in the first place. Or the priests before him who'd abused those in their care.

Whose fault really? Satan's? God's?

Are we all just pawns in some stupid cosmic game?

"I don't like this," Del said, slowing the car as they neared the building. Close to thirty people stood at the bottom of the wide cement steps that led to the front doors. Above them, the smirking faces of gremlins peering out from the ivy, but the words carved over the entrance were clearly visible.

Dallas Hall.

Del turned off the car and got out. Randi joined him and Claudia followed more slowly, her heart pounding and the premonition of death a cold block of ice in her gut.

The group was a mix of young and old, men and women. A small boy stood to the front, a Yankees hat perched on his head. He said something she couldn't make out, and pointed. In response, the crowd surged forward. Several grabbed rocks and threw them. One struck Del on the arm.

A sudden rage rose up in Claudia, fueled by her anger with Shari, with Stone, with everything. She pushed past Del and shouted at the crowd.

"Leave us alone!"

Thunder boomed and the boy's hat flew off his head. Several of the thrown rocks lifted up and flew back, striking members of the mob. More thunder detonated in the clear sky and the front two rows of attackers stumbled to their knees. Claudia gasped as for the first time in her life, she actually felt the power inside her rise up, an invisible force that shoved the mob away. People fell over; others held their arms out as they retreated.

The boy shouted at them, his face contorted in fury. "*Asmodeus suscitat!*"

Claudia concentrated on him and he flew off his feet to collide with the people behind him. She continued walking and the throng backed away, all of them glaring but unwilling – or unable – to approach closer. When she reached the steps, the front doors swung open so hard the glass shattered.

She had no idea if she or the demon caused it.

"Damn, girl, that was some badass shit. Now, let's get this the fuck over with," Randi said. She sprinted up the stairs, Del right next to her.

The moment Claudia entered the building, the sense of evil struck her like a fist. She doubled over, fighting to breathe. The air dripped with malevolence. It seeped from the walls and floated up from the floor like some wicked fog. When she put her hand against the cold stone to keep from falling, the mere touch of it sent shudders of revulsion up her arm.

Del grabbed her arm. "What is it?"

She shook her head, unable to form words. But the warmth of his flesh gave her the strength to stand up. "This place," she gasped finally. "You don't feel it?"

Del shook his head.

"We don't have to," Randi said. "We know it's bad. C'mon. Fifth floor. Let's end it before the creeps get their nerve back."

Claudia needed Del's support as they hurried down the wide hallway to the staircase, but then she shook him off and climbed them on her own. By the time they reached the fifth floor, all of them were panting, and she knew the noxious atmosphere had affected them, even if they couldn't feel it.

"It's locked," Randi said, yanking on the handle.

Claudia nudged past her and gripped the lever. Concentrated on the door opening.

Nothing happened.

Frowning, she took out the master key Curt Rawlings had given them and unlocked the door. Del nudged her aside and led the way in. His flashlight revealed an empty expanse. All the walls had been torn down, leaving only a series of cement support columns. Most of the windows had plywood nailed over them. Stacks of wooden beams and bundles of insulation were piled at the far end.

Something moved in the center of the room and Del cast the light on it.

A body hung from the rafters.

Randi let out a surprised curse. A man in a business suit, with short-cropped graying hair. His eyes bulged above mottled cheeks and a swollen tongue protruded from purplish lips. A toppled chair rested a few feet away. Next to it was a piece of paper.

Randi made a wide arc around the body and picked up the note. Del joined her and shined the light on it.

"To my wife and family, I'm sorry for everything I've done. Asmodeus wakes."

She dropped the paper with another curse.

"Now what do we do?" Del asked. "Can we perform the ceremony with…." He aimed the light back at the body.

The legs jerked.

Randi screamed and Claudia's brain shouted *Danger!* at the same time. The body turned, limbs twitching. Its mouth opened and a choking *Hnnck-hunnchk-hnnk* sound crawled from its throat. The movements grew more hectic, became a St. Vitus' dance of death accompanied by a squeaking as rope rubbed against wood. The arms lunged out at Claudia, fingers clawing the air as it tried to reach her.

In her mind, she saw the rope snapping and the corpse leaping for her, hands tightening around her neck, cutting off her air—

"*No! Stop it!*" She tried to fight it off but it was too strong, it was going to—

The corpse's head exploded with a wet *pop!* that sent blood and brain matter in all directions. The body fell to the floor and went still.

Claudia wiped cold gore from her face.

Did I do that?

"I guess that solves our problem. Do me a favor, girl. Warn me the next time you decide to blow someone the fuck up?" Randi stepped around the body and opened the bag of supplies she'd dropped. Inside were the items Bonaventura had given them. Six blessed candles, a bundle of sage, a lighter, and several bottles of holy water. He'd also written down the prayers they needed to say.

Claudia went to help her light the candles and then fell to her knees as a psychic blow slammed into her skull.

Something's coming!

The door swung open and two men entered the room. They wore the blue uniforms of Hastings Mills police officers and had their guns drawn. Black auras shot through with red streaks surrounded them.

"They're not—" The rest of her words disappeared as one of the officers fired his gun. Del cried out and fell to the floor, clutching his arm. The men turned their weapons at Claudia. Another explosion, and she flinched, waiting for the pain of the bullet to strike her, remembering all too well the agony of metal tearing through flesh from when Shari had been killed.

One of the cops toppled over.

The second one turned and shot at someone in the stairwell. A shout, and the unseen person returned fire. The officer ducked down and pulled the trigger again.

The image of Shari's bloody corpse returned and Claudia felt the power rising in her. A piece of framework tore away from a wall, the ends bristling with nails. It struck the cop in the chest and stuck there. He let out a gargling cry and blood sprayed from his mouth. The gun fell from his hand and he crumpled to the floor next to his partner.

Corday Rose peered around the doorframe. A dark stain covered the side of his shirt.

"Everyone okay?"

Del sat up. Blood seeped from between his fingers as he pressed a hand against his upper arm. "I'll be fine. You?"

Corday grimaced but nodded. "Nicked my ribs. Whatever you need to do, do it fast. There's more coming."

Randi went to him and hugged him. She whispered something Claudia couldn't hear, but it didn't take a psychic to figure out they had feelings for each other. He kissed her and then went back to the door to keep watch.

With the immediate danger gone, Claudia helped Randi with the candles while Del used his good arm to pour a large circle of salt around them. Randi lit the sage bundles and placed four of them just inside the circle, one at each compass point. The fifth she held in her hand. Once Rose joined them inside the protective ring, Randi began the first cleansing prayer.

"Father God, we come to you in Jesus's name. Putting on your full armor, we take our stand against the Devil's schemes. For our struggle is not against flesh and blood, but against the powers of darkness, against the forces of evil in all their realms."

Randi waved the sage back and forth as she spoke, filling the air with its aromatic scent.

"I put on the full armor of God so that on this day I may stand my ground against evil. With my feet firmly planted and the readiness that comes from the Gospel of the Lord, I take up the shield of faith so that I may extinguish the flaming arrows of those who would do evil."

A foul smell wafted through the room, ripe with the odors of death and rot. The floor rumbled under their feet. Claudia braced herself for the building to begin shaking but Officer Rose looked at the doorway.

"They're coming."

CHAPTER THIRTY-NINE

Hastings Mills, NY, July 22nd, one year ago

Stone shivered as the temperature in Abby's room dropped from sweltering hot to so cold his breath steamed when he exhaled.

A charnel-house stench filled the air, reminiscent of his youth when the local dump would burn the garbage. Green slime had replaced the black ooze on the walls, and Stone couldn't tell if the malodorous stink came from the supernatural sludge or if it emanated from Abby as she verbally assaulted Bonaventura and Lockhart.

"Look at the mighty priests, how low they've fallen," she said, her voice coarse and deep. "One whose flesh is weak and the other losing his mind."

"Lord God, by the power of Christ and the sacred sign of the cross I command thee to depart!" Bonaventura waved the Bible up and down and then left and right. Lockhart, his face a mix of emotions, repeated the gesture.

"So many deaths, and all your fault."

"By the power of the Virgin Mary, the glorious Mother of God, I command thee to depart!"

Abby's voice changed back to that of a young girl.

"*Mirame, Padre Roberto,*" she said in Spanish. "*Tan joven y bonita?*"

Lockhart shook his head and stumbled over his words.

"Look at me, Father." Abby spread her arms and legs. "*Lamer mi coño*, Robert. You know you want to."

"Focus," Bonaventura said. "Don't listen to it."

"*Follame, Padre.*" She wiggled her hips at him. "Fuck me hard. *Mete tu pene en mi.*"

"No!" Lockhart held his rosary over her face and intoned, "Lead us not into temptation, but deliver us from evil, amen."

"Get back, Robert!" Bonaventura tried to pull him away, but it was too late. Abby spat a mouthful of yellow phlegm that struck Lockhart's hand and the rosary. The string began to smoke and he cried out as it burst into flames and the beads scattered across the floor.

"Join me, Robert. We can fuck her together." Abby's hands moved down between her legs and Curt let out an anguished cry.

"Stop it!"

"Be silent, demon!" Lockhart threw holy water on Abby. She laughed and then pointed at Bonaventura.

"Leo knows the truth. He opened the doors and let me in." Her voice became that of an old man. "You let me die, Leo. Let me die in that jungle."

Bonaventura hesitated and then continued his prayer.

"The faith of the holy apostles Peter, Paul, and John commands thee! The blood of all the martyrs and the faith of the pious saints commands thee! Leave this place!"

The lights flickered and then went off, plunging the room into a dusky twilight. Stone looked at the windows. Outside, the sun still shone midday bright but its rays no longer penetrated into the room.

Abby turned her sickly gaze toward Stone. He wanted to look away but her depraved, yellow eyes with their horizontal, rectangular pupils pinned him in place, froze his muscles. Her features shifted and a ghostly image appeared above them. Shari's face took shape in the mist and settled over Abby's like an opaque mask.

When she spoke, it was Shari's voice.

"He did it, you know. Put it in me. When we were children."

Stone's stomach flipped over. He knew she lied, but he couldn't help looking at Lockhart. Imagining him taking the nine-year-old Shari against her will. Even if he hadn't done it, he'd wanted to. And she'd seen it in his head. Which was just as bad.

"Remember, the beast lies," Bonaventura said.

"I hid it from my sister. He raped me. Right in my bed."

Doubt creeped into Stone's mind. Hadn't Claudia said Shari was always stronger? She'd hidden her abilities. Hidden her plan to sacrifice her soul to the demon.

Why not this?

"It's not true!" Lockhart's face had gone red. Anger or guilt?

"I don't believe you!" Stone lunged at him. Curt blocked his way, pushed him back.

Abby roared with laughter.

"Stop it, both of you!" Bonaventura glared at them. "Out in the hall."

Stone followed him from the room. Lockhart joined them, glowering and clenching his Bible so tight his knuckles drained of color.

"You're letting its words distract you from the task at hand. You must keep your thoughts pure or it will gain the upper hand."

"Don't blame me. I'm not the goddamn pedophile." Stone poked Lockhart in the chest.

"I never touched them!" he responded.

"Them? What about the others? How many girls did you rape?"

"It wasn't my fault!" Lockhart swung his fist and clipped Bonaventura's shoulder. The priest grunted and stumbled against the door. Stone leaped forward and slammed Lockhart into the wall. He got in two jabs to the stomach before Lockhart pushed him away and threw a punch that caught Stone in the temple. He retaliated with a flurry of blows and managed to bloody Lockhart's lip.

An ice-cold wind blew past and yanked Lockhart away. The invisible force slammed Lockhart's head into the wall three times and then dropped him. A stack of books flew from one of the rooms and pummeled Bonaventura until he sank to his knees, arms over his head. Through the ringing in his ears, Stone heard the demon's laughter.

Then frigid hands grasped his neck and tightened.

Something's wrong.

The thought burst to life in Claudia's head, reverberating around and around, gaining power with each echo until she wanted to claw it out.

Something's wrong! But what? Randi still recited Bonaventura's prayers and Corday had his gun aimed at the doorway. The crowd from outside the building stood in the hall. So far, they hadn't made a move to enter the space.

Was that it? Were they about to attack?

She tried to concentrate on the psychic warning but her head wanted to explode. If Shari had lived, she'd have been able to pierce through the wall of danger and—

An image came to her. A giant arrow plunging into a gray, amorphous wall. The moment it punctured the featureless expanse, the wall deflated like a cosmic balloon and fell away.

Revealing Stone Graves.

He stood next to Lockhart and Bonaventura, who read from his Bible, unaware of a shadowy figure of a woman standing right behind them, a wicked-looking knife clutched in one hand. In the background, Asmodeus's bestial faces bellowed laughter. As she watched, the entity plunged the knife into Stone's back and twisted it. A second, smaller specter attacked Lockhart. The scene faded, the demon's evil howling the last thing to go.

He's in trouble!

That had to be the source of her premonition. She had to warn him. She pulled out her phone but got no signal.

That left only one option. She had to leave.

But how? She'd never make it through the mob alive, and a huge pile of construction materials blocked the fire exit. She didn't even know if she could safely leave the circle they'd made.

Do something!

Every second she wasted meant more of a chance Stone would die and Bonaventura would fail. And then nothing they did here would matter.

What would Shari do?

She pictured Shari standing next to her. Her sister would be angry. She was always tightly wound, her emotions simmering, just waiting to boil over. Even as children, afraid of the things waiting for them in the dark. In their dreams. Always the strong one. When it got too bad, Shari would take her hand and use her power to protect them.

—Not my power. Ours.—

—Shari!—

—I told you I'd be with you when the time came. Now it's almost here. And you have to do your part.—

—I can't. I'm not strong enough.—

—Yes, you are. Downstairs. That was you.—

—I don't know how I did that. You were always the one. I—

—Sister. The only difference between us is that I never held back. All that was inside me waits in you. Together, we can do anything. You just need to believe.—

An invisible hand took Claudia's and her arm lifted up. She felt the familiar energy building. She'd always pictured Shari's power as a mighty river, and hers a trickling stream. This time it appeared differently. Twin torrents of liquid gold, flowing together, twisting around each other to form a living cable, elemental strands entwined and woven to create something stronger than the individual parts.

—That's right, sister. Now, set it free.—

Claudia closed her eyes and imagined a door within herself opening. Her body thrummed with the power of the release. Wood and metal clanged and crashed. People screamed. When she opened her eyes, the fire exit was clear and the building materials scattered across the room. On the other side of the main doorway, several of the people lay on the floor, covered in dust and debris. The others had backed away.

—Now, go. They need you.—

—What about you?—

—Bring Stone to me.—

—What? How do—

—Trust me, sister.—

The connection cut off but the urgency in Shari's voice remained.

Claudia tugged at Del's arm. "I have to leave!"

He looked from the door to her and nodded. Randi had paused in her recitation but now she started again.

"We command every evil spirit to leave this place now in the name of Jesus. You cannot stay here. You have no place in this world. We renounce you and any other spirits that come with you!"

Claudia jumped over the line of salt and raced for the fire exit. Behind her, people shouted from the hallway. Corday's gun went off but she didn't look back. They would have to handle things as best they could.

Outside, she found one of the police cruisers still running. Thanking all the gods for their favors, she jumped in and headed for the Rawlingses' house.

Please, don't let me be too late.

"Holy Lord, Almighty Father, everlasting God and Father of our Lord Jesus Christ, who once and for all consigned that fallen and apostate tyrant to the flames of Hell, who sent your only begotten Son into the world to crush that roaring lion. Hasten to our call for help and snatch from ruination and from the clutches of the noonday devil this family, these friends, and myself, all made in your image and likeness."

Father Bonaventura held the Bible in one hand and gripped the doorframe with his other. As Stone watched, he tried to rise up from his knees. His back bent and his body shook as if a great weight lay over him. Stone had a feeling he knew what it was; the same force that had nearly strangled him just moments before, but then it had suddenly disappeared, leaving him gasping and his throat aching, but still alive.

Fighting against a gale-force wind that roared up and down the hall in random patterns, Stone fought his way to Bonaventura, using the wall for support. He grabbed the priest's arm and hauled him up. Together, they entered Abby's room.

She floated cross-legged over the bed. Above her, the dark, roiling clouds had returned, filled with the terrible faces of Asmodeus and a host of other creatures too horrible to even look at. Ken Webb had backed away from the bed but somehow still had his camera aimed at it. The other lay by the closet, the tripod twisted out of shape.

Curt Rawlings stood by Abby's nightstand, unaffected by the cold and wind. He stared at Abby with a look of pure adoration. When they stepped inside, he turned and Stone saw his eyes had taken on the same yellowish cast as his daughter's.

Curt growled and leaped at them. He clawed at Stone's face and snapped his teeth like a wild animal. Stone managed to get his arms under Curt's neck and shove him away. Instead of renewing the attack, Curt slammed into Bonaventura and knocked him down. He crawled up the priest's body and wrapped his hands around this throat.

"This is the end, priest. Time to meet your god!" Abby shouted.

Stone rolled over and pulled at Curt's legs but the heavier man didn't budge. He turned to shout for Ken to help but a dark form separated from the cloud and struck the cameraman in the chest. Ken went down. The gaseous shape, which had the vague face of a man, grabbed the rosary from around Ken's neck and pulled it tight. Ken fell back and hit his head against the wall.

Lockhart staggered into the room. He pulled Curt off Bonaventura and punched him once, twice. His pulled back his arm for a third when a voice called out.

"Come here, Bobby!"

Lockhart froze, fist poised in the air. The new face emerged from the cloud, an older man with a clerical collar.

"Father Bannon?"

"That's right, Bobby." The spirit's smile dripped evil and its voice took on a decidedly Irish brogue. "Time for confession. You've been a bad boy."

Ken's camera tripod rose up and shot across the room. The legs struck Lockhart in the stomach and he doubled over. The tripod flipped around and smashed across his back. He fell to the floor and the camera went skidding across the room.

Bonaventura got to his knees and recovered his Bible.

"Strike terror, Lord, into the beast now laying waste to your vineyard. Fill your servants with the courage to fight against this reprobate dragon. Let your mighty hand—"

Something yanked the book from Bonaventura's hands and carried it out of the room.

"You're nothing without your toys, priest!" Abby shouted.

"I need nothing but my faith," Bonaventura countered. "God, let your mighty hand cast the demon from your child, Abigail Rawlings, so she may no longer be held captive! Redeem her through your Son, Jesus, who lives and reigns with you in Heaven, in the unity of the Holy Spirit, God, forever and ever, amen!"

Bonaventura made the sign of the cross and stood up.

Something cracked overhead. Too late, Stone tried to shout a warning. A section of the ceiling came down on Bonaventura's head. He collapsed again, fresh blood dripping from his scalp.

Lockhart pulled him up. Curt Rawlings started to rise and Stone kicked him in the face. He fell over and didn't move. Stone went to Ken and helped him over to the priests just as Lockhart shouted in Bonaventura's ear.

"It's too strong. We have to get help."

"No. We finish this today."

Everyone turned at the voice from behind them.

Claudia stood there, bruised and dusty. There was a fire in her eyes, a set to her face that Stone had never seen on her, but he recognized it just the same.

The same way Shari looked at her most defiant.

Claudia held out her hand and Stone reached for it.

Their fingers touched and his world disappeared.

CHAPTER FORTY

Hastings Mills, NY, July 22nd, one year ago

Corday Rose aimed his gun at one of the people that had the group trapped in a corner of the room.

When he pulled the trigger, all he got was the click of an empty magazine.

"That's it, I'm out," he said to Del.

"Then we're fucked," the big man answered.

Randi continued reciting from the paper she held, but to Corday it looked like the words had no effect. A black cloud had formed in the rafters, a twisting, swirling nebula that emanated arctic cold. Flashes of red lightning illuminated horrific creatures within the storm, things that made Corday think of gargoyles and aliens. After Claudia's escape, the crowd had broken through the circle of protection and forced him, Randi, and Del to the far end of the room. Moving like some kind of hive mind controlled them, the people had slowly but surely penned them in.

"It's too late." The small boy stood at the front of the mob, grinning like a madman. Under his baseball hat, his hair was matted and sweaty and dirt covered his skin. As he spoke, he levitated up until his amber goat's eyes were level with theirs. "Your friends are dead. The priest is dead. They're all going to burn in Hell and so are you. *Salvete Asmodeus*!"

"Fuck you." Corday raised his fist and Del grabbed him.

"Don't separate," he reminded him.

Corday cursed again and forced himself to calm down. Not easy when surrounded by dozens of Satanists and a kid with mutant eyes who floated like a goddamn X-Man. He'd put down eight of them, plus the two officers who'd shot Del. Now he had no ammunition left – there'd never been a need to carry extra magazines in a town like Hastings Mills – and the loonies were edging closer.

And that kid is seriously freaking me out.

As much as he couldn't imagine killing a child, he wished he'd saved one bullet to put in the little fucker's head.

"Time to die."

Corday expected them to charge, but instead they came to a stop and split into two groups, leaving an open area in the middle. New shapes emerged from the shadows at the far side of the room. Objects floating in the air. Pieces of wood. Tools.

No, not floating. Held aloft by some of the gargoyle creatures from the storm cloud.

One of the creatures flew at them with a hammer. Corday jumped in front of Randi just in time. The hammer struck him in the shoulder and a burst of pain ran down his arm and across his back. His hand went numb and his gun fell to the floor. A length of wood slammed into his ribs. He covered his head and curled up on the floor while wood and steel battered him. Cries of pain behind him told him it wasn't just him. Hot blood ran down his face and hands and he knew the devil child had been right.

They were going to die.

Stone opened his eyes to an alien landscape of hardened lava and towers of flame. The sulfurous reek of rot and demon assaulted him and he fell to his knees, coughing. Intense heat seared his flesh wherever it touched the ground. Only when Claudia tugged his hand did he realize their fingers were still entwined.

"Where are we?" he asked, getting back to his feet. The air was thick and heavy, like breathing in a superheated oven, and he had to fight to fill his lungs.

"Hell," she answered. Before he could say anything else, the ground quaked and the rumble of untold tons of rock grinding together drowned out all other sounds. Claudia's eyes went wide and Stone turned to see what had frightened her.

A giant pillar of superheated stone rose from the ground. The same one he'd seen while in Claudia's and Shari's minds.

Asmodeus.

Brightly glowing red faded to a dull yellowish orange and revealed the demon seated on its throne. The five heads – reptile, lion, horse, goat, and hideously deformed human – bellowed laughter. Tufts of flame burst from their nostrils.

"Behold! The witch brings me two presents." The demon's voice reverberated through Stone's head, as much felt as heard.

"I bring you nothing," Claudia said.

"Not you." Asmodeus lifted a massive hand like the claw of some prehistoric bird, covered in pebbly scales and tipped with onyx talons.

Several figures stepped out from behind the throne. Repugnant creatures that walked upright but bore only the slightest similarity to human form. Some scaled, others furred or feathered. Their faces mixtures of various beasts, as if they contained all the different genetic material of their master.

Then another came into view and Stone's heart jumped.

Shari!

Claudia's fingers tightened on his. Fear and sorrow seeped through them and he understood they were her emotions.

"Hello, sister," Shari said. Burnt flesh surrounded her empty eye sockets. Ragged scars covered her pale skin. She wore no clothes, but all signs of her sex had been taken from her, replaced by intricate whorls and symbols in patterns that made Stone dizzy.

Asmodeus brushed its talons across her hair. It burst into flames that burned white hot and then disappeared, leaving a bald skull in their wake. Patches of skin peeled off and floated away. As Stone watched, new hair sprouted through the wet tissue.

Shari looked up at the enormous beast.

"I kept my promise."

The quintet of fiendish beings laughed again.

"Yes. And you shall have your reward."

—No! It wasn't her. She would never betray us.—

Stone heard Claudia's thought as clear as his own. The image of a shadowy figure stabbing him in the back appeared in his head. He turned toward Claudia and saw tears in her eyes, which evaporated from the heat before they could reach her cheeks.

"I did what I had to do, sister," Shari said, revealing a mouth empty of teeth. "You will, too, after our lord has his way with your soul for a while. You'll do anything to stop the pain."

"Claudia, get us out of here. Wake us up, end the dream, do whatever." Stone tugged at her hand.

She looked down, unable to meet his eyes.

"It's not a dream," Shari said. "Didn't you know? Your lover brought you both to Hell. And you'll never leave. She's the betrayer."

"I told you I'd have your soul." Asmodeus rose from his throne and pushed Shari aside. The ground vibrated with his steps and giant crevices opened, revealing molten rock that erupted in spurts.

"I'm sorry," Claudia whispered, her sorrow a physical pain that reached him through her fingers. "It wasn't supposed to be like this."

The demon leaned down, claws extended, their tips glowing red hot. Stone's skin blistered as the temperature rose and droplets of lava rained down.

This was it, They were going to die and—

—Now, sister!—

A surge of energy enveloped Stone, coursed through his nerves to his very core. Claudia's eyes went wide and turned purest silver. She lifted her arm, bringing Stone's with it. A third hand, unseen yet as familiar as his own, joined theirs.

A bolt of dazzling white burst from a point just in front of Claudia and Stone and pierced the demon's chest. Asmodeus jerked up straight and let out a deafening cry.

"You dare?" it thundered.

Shari darted around its legs, ignoring the lava and fire burning her, and grasped their hands with hers. Silver orbs glowed in her sockets. The laser-bright energy beam doubled in size.

Asmodeus bellowed and its throne exploded into a thousand boulders that transformed into nightmare creatures with tails and wings and fangs. Stone tried to duck as the hellish imps descended on them but something held him fast, his body paralyzed.

The flying spirits disintegrated in bursts of white.

With a roar, Asmodeus charged them. Gigantic spikes of glowing crystal shot up from the ground and pierced its scaled flesh. The demon howled but kept coming. Clouds formed above it and white rain fell, the droplets burning through its wings and singeing the fur around the heads of the lion, goat, and horse. Cries of pain joined furious snarls.

And still it kept coming.

—Now!—

Leo Bonaventura watched as Stone's eyes changed from brown to silver. Next to him, Claudia's did the same. The hair on his arms stood up and the temperature in the room rose until he thought the walls would ignite. The air grew heavy and charged with electricity.

Abigail Rawlings went rigid in the air above her bed and let out an unearthly howl. The house trembled. Above them, the supernatural cloud by the ceiling grew darker.

"Father, what's happening?" Ken asked.

"Now!" Leo heard it simultaneously in his ears and in his head, and in that moment, he knew God had sent him a sign.

"Robert, pray with me! I command every evil spirit to leave this home now, in the name of Jesus! You cannot stay. You are not welcome. I renounce you and all spirits that come with you!"

The vibrations grew louder. The walls cracked and plaster rained down. Curt Rawlings screamed and grayish smoke billowed from his mouth. It formed into a terrified face that rose up and joined the others in the bilious cloud. Leo repeated the prayer, Lockhart echoing his words. They cast holy water onto Abby's levitating body and Leo led them into the next passage.

"Demon, I renounce thee! Only the spirit of the Lord can dwell in this place. God and the Holy Trinity guide me. Send all your angels to aid me in the removal of these spirits, and to fight on our behalf against any demonic powers we cannot handle alone."

Red and orange lightning flashed down. Several bolts struck Leo's arms and left blisters but he didn't falter.

"We exorcise thee, unclean one, satanic power, infernal invader, wicked legion, in the name of the Lord and by the power of God, Jesus Christ, and Mother Mary! Most cunning serpent, thou shalt depart this place forever and return to the bowels of Hell for all time!"

Abby fell onto the bed. The faces in the cloud wailed, a thousand voices crying out in despair and frustration. One of them exploded in a flash of blinding light. Then another. Bursts of white filled the cloud, which shrank as each spirit disappeared. On the bed, Abby rolled back and forth, her limbs twisting in impossible positions.

"Hold her down!" Leo commanded. Curt crawled up to the bed and threw himself across her. After a moment's hesitation, Ken grabbed her legs. Leo draped his rosary over her neck and pressed his silver cross against her chest. Lockhart held a smaller cross to Abby's forehead. The skin blistered and turned black and she shrieked.

"Fuck your Jesus! *Harq fi aljahim*!"

"Holy Lord, Almighty One, everlasting God, and Father of our Lord Jesus Christ, who consigned all the fallen and apostate tyrant to the flames of Hell, hasten to our call for help and snatch from ruination and the clutches of the Devil the soul of this girl, Abigail Rawlings! Strike terror into the beast that lays waste to your vineyard. Let your mighty hand cast him out of this child so that she is no longer held captive by evil!"

With his free hand, Leo emptied a bottle of holy water on Abby's chest. Green fire rose up and the red symbols on her skin split open, releasing yellow fluids that stunk of sulfur.

Abby's mouth opened so wide her chin touched her chest and her lips stretched back almost to her ears. Brown and green slime spewed out, accompanied by odors so foul Ken vomited onto the bed. Her screams were deafening in the small room but Leo raised his voice and kept praying.

"Redeem this soul through your Son, Jesus Christ, who lives and reigns with you, in the unity of the Holy Spirit, God, forever and ever! Amen!"

"Amen!" Lockhart repeated.

"In the name of God, I exorcise thee, demon. Asmodeus, be gone! I close this vessel to you. I close this place on earth to you. No longer shall you use it as an access. From here on, only the angels of Heaven are allowed to enter this home."

Abby's eyes bulged and her black tongue flopped over her cheek.

"I consign thee to the depths of Hell, Asmodeus, for now and all eternity, and I mark you with the sign of the cross, in Jesus's name." Leo used holy water to draw a cross on Abby, from head to waist.

Glowing white flames burst up and smoke poured from her mouth.

Asmodeus fell to its knees, green ichor dripping from a thousand wounds. Two of its heads, the horse and the lizard, hung limp, eyes staring lifelessly at nothing. The other three howled and moaned as it clawed at the ground, attempting to reach Stone and the twins. Orbs of glowing energy joined the neon rain. Everywhere they struck the demon, more flesh melted away, revealing a shining black armor underneath.

The human head lifted up, one horn missing, the other melting. Its eyes burned with hatred, and when it spoke, the eternal evil living in the demon reached Stone despite the weakness in its voice.

"You think you have won. But I can never die."

Shari led their circle a step forward, their hands still clutched. Much of her skin was burned away, revealing raw muscle, but the vivid silver of her eyes hadn't diminished.

"You don't have to die. You just have to go away."

Dozens of the energy balls coalesced into a single sphere as large as a small car. It descended onto Asmodeus, whose cries reached deafening levels. When it struck, arcs of electric blue and gold raced across what remained of the demon's skin, dissolving the flesh to reveal the creature beneath, a titanic beetle of purest ebony, with giant protuberances on its head and huge, multifaceted eyes. The colossal insect shook itself, casting away the remains of its former faces.

"You cannot defeat me!" it roared. "I will eat your flesh and your souls will suffer for a thousand millennia! I am Asmodeus. I rule—"

The ground gave a massive quake and an enormous chasm opened beneath the demon. It struggled for a moment, clawing at the edges, and then fell into the flaming depths. The edges of the fissure ground together, sealing the gap.

But not before a final cry echoed up from the abyss.

"Nooooo!"

"Noooo!" Abby's back arched so high only her head and feet touched the bed. The force of it threw Ken and Lockhart to the floor.

With the last of his strength, Leo held his cross against her chest and poured a bottle of blessed water into her mouth.

"I close this door to any evil spirit. Let the holy cross be my light! Step back, Satan!"

The house shuddered and all the windows shattered. The floor creaked and moaned, and a section in front of the closet bulged up and then collapsed into the living room below. The dressers fell over and huge cracks shot up the walls and across the ceiling.

Blinding white light exploded from Abby's mouth and eyes.

Lockhart called out for God to protect them and Ken turned away, shielding his face from the intense radiance.

The light faded and Abby's head lolled to the side. She stared at Leo with empty sockets. A sharp pain jolted Leo's chest and he collapsed to his knees, powerless as his worst fears materialized and a stream of beetles poured from Abby's mouth. The swarm covered the bed and descended to the floor.

He swatted at the creatures climbing up his arms and his mind flashed back to that long-ago night in Costa Rica.

"Your time will come, Father Fucking Bonaventura! You cannot kill me, for I am eternal."

We failed. The demon will return and—

Two pairs of legs stepped past him. Whispered words reached him through the chittering of the insects and the sound of his own heartbeat pounding in his ears.

"...go away."

The beetles disappeared in a display of sparks like a thousand fireworks going off in the sky.

Enjoy Hell, Asmodeus, Leo thought, staring at the galaxy of red stars. In the center of it glowed a yellow sun. *You cannot die, but we will not meet again.*

Then his chest hitched again and the sun expanded until nothing else remained.

"Nooo!"

Corday opened his eyes and watched in amazement as the young boy put his hands to his head and stumbled backward. Behind him, the other attackers dropped their weapons and fell to their knees. He tried to get up but his legs refused to work. Del, his face battered and bleeding, reached out and shook Randi's leg.

"Finish it," he said.

She groaned and rolled over. In a voice hoarse from shouting, she read the final words Bonaventura had given her.

"We beseech thee, Lord, hear, our prayers! Shutter this place against all evil and drive away all those who would do harm against your flock! Deliver us, oh Lord, from the hand of the Devil and by the most sacred light of Jesus, make this place holy again!"

Dazzling bursts of white light exploded from the rafters. Everywhere they appeared, flames flickered to life across the aged wood. The townspeople tumbled over, their eyes burned away. Swarms of beetles emerged from the sockets and skittered across the floor. Del let out a hoarse shout and Corday slapped at the advancing insects.

With the sound of a thousand corn kernels popping, the beetles disintegrated into rainbow-colored sparks that merged with the ashes of the burning wood and showered down like psychedelic rain.

Something creaked and snapped. A piece of a rafter fell, trailing flames. The ceiling moaned and all the windows shattered.

"The whole place is coming down!" Del pushed to his feet, pulling Corday with him. He pointed at the exit and grabbed Randi's arm. "C'mon. We gotta get the hell outta here."

They stumbled for the door, the blaze expanding behind them as if the walls had been soaked in gasoline. Cement and tile blazed up impossibly fast and formed a tsunami of flame that chased them down the stairs. By the time they reached the car, the whole building had been consumed. From a safe distance, they watched as the bell tower collapsed in a cascade of smoke and sparks. A moment later, the entire roof followed it.

"Holy shit," Randi said. "What about all those people?"

"Fuck 'em," Corday responded, clutching his ribs. Randi glanced at him.

"Anyone ever tell you, you curse too much?"

He looked back at her and even though it hurt like hell, they both burst out laughing.

⛤

Dr. Avis Fromm jumped away from his autopsy table as Shari Brock's body lit up in flames and then disintegrated into a pile of sparkling ash that whirled up into the air-conditioning vent and disappeared.

At the police station, the suspects arrested at the Motel 9 collapsed to the floor. When Martha Plotkin returned to work the following day – with no memory of the last forty-eight hours – she found their desiccated bodies in their cells.

Only charred holes remained where their eyes had been.

In Abby's bedroom, Stone and Claudia cried out as silver flames ignited on their wrists.

Selwin Ammoun knew something was wrong the moment he opened the door to the Child Welfare Center. The sickly-sweet odor of burning flesh billowed out, bringing back unwanted memories of the bombings in Beirut and Lebanon before he'd come to America. He moved quickly through the halls and common rooms before moving on to the bedrooms.

At first, he couldn't figure out where the seven boys currently residing there had gone to.

Then he saw the piles of ash on each bed.

When Kasia arrived for her shift, she found Selwin sitting out front.

Crying.

Stone stared at the destruction in the room and tried to process everything that had happened.

Ken had gone downstairs to call an ambulance. A sobbing Curt sat on the bed, cradling Abby's lifeless form against his chest. Charred flesh surrounded her eyes and the damaged sockets leaked bloody fluids. Lockhart knelt next to Father Bonaventura, frantically trying to find a pulse.

We did it. We really did it.

"No."

Stone turned at Claudia's statement. Her eyes were silver again. A tingling sensation prickled Stone's skin and a sudden intuition of foreboding coursed through him. Movement at the door caught his eye just as Claudia spoke again.

"They're still here."

In time with her words, a shadow materialized in the doorway. The specter rapidly coalesced into a human form. A woman's face appeared.

Lockhart gasped.

"Caitlyn?"

The spirit glared at him and its lip curled up in a silent snarl. The temperature in the room dropped again and frost formed on the walls. Two more figures took shape next to her. A second woman, with a misshapen skull, and a small boy.

Evan Michaels!

Stone's feeling of doom grew stronger.

Lockhart whimpered and shook his head.

"Caitlyn. Lori. No. No, please. I'm sorry."

Caitlyn took her sister's hand, and Lori took Brian's. The vaporous forms melded into a single body with three heads and glided toward Lockhart. He shouted "No!" again and jumped up, but the nightstand slid around to block the door. Abby's dresser scraped across the floor and the two pieces of furniture crowded him back across the room with the ghostly trio following in their wake.

Stone saw their plan at the same time Lockhart figured it out. Abby's shattered window was right behind him.

Lockhart glanced at it and then back to the approaching spirits.

"Please. I never meant to hurt anyone. I've paid for my sins."

His hips hit the window ledge and the furniture slammed against the wall to either side of him, obstructing any escape. The bedroom door swung shut and the lock clicked.

A smoky tentacle emerged from the center of the manifestation and touched Lockhart in the chest. His mouth fell open but no sound came out. He stood frozen in a silent scream as his flesh turned bluish gray and the color drained from his eyes. His breath steamed in the frigid air and then his body lifted up and tumbled over the ledge.

The spectral mass turned and floated back to the bed, where Curt pulled Abby tighter. Tears ran down his cheeks and turned to ice as the temperature in the room dropped further.

Caitlyn's face twisted in pain. The other two ghosts grew indistinct, their images blurred. A wispy hand reached out and Curt turned away.

Stone moved toward them. He had no idea what to do, but he couldn't let anything happen to Abby or her father, not after all they'd been through to save them.

Claudia touched his arm.

"Wait."

Caitlyn's hand stopped just above Abby's head. A tiny bolt of blue arced between them and Abby's body twitched. She sucked in a deep breath and moaned.

"Abby!" Curt looked up at Caitlyn. "Thank you."

She nodded.

"I'm sorry. I didn't want to. It made me...." The words whispered through the room, everywhere at once. Curt burst into tears.

"Goodbye, my love."

The apparition broke apart into puffs of mist and faded away.

A moment later, Ken opened the door.

"The ambulance is on the way." He looked around. "Where's Lockhart?"

Stone looked at Claudia, whose eyes were once again their normal violet. He shrugged.

"Where he belongs."

CHAPTER FORTY-ONE

Hastings Mills, NY, July 25th, one year ago

The summer sun was warm and friendly on Stone's shoulders as he placed a red rose atop Leo Bonaventura's coffin. The funeral at St. Alphonse Cemetery had been a sizeable affair, with former students and co-workers from around the world in attendance. Now the mourners were gone and only Stone and his team remained. One by one, they said their goodbyes and set flowers on the casket returning to their cars.

Randi wiped her eyes. "I hope he's with Corday's dad and mine. They can catch up and swap stories."

Stone nodded. "How's Corday doing?"

"The doctor said there's no internal damage. Two broken ribs that will hurt like hell for a few weeks and some bruises, but he can go home tomorrow."

"That's good," Claudia said.

There was an awkward silence, and then Stone looked at Ken and Del and brought up the subject he'd been dreading.

"Claudia and I are heading back to LA tonight. Randi's joining us after Corday's on his feet again. You sure you won't change your minds?"

Ken shook his head.

"We're done with the supernatural. From now on it's the boring but infinitely safer life of videoing weddings and birthdays for us."

"Besides, ain't like you'll be short-handed." Del squeezed Randi's shoulder. "You got this bad bitch to keep you safe."

"Got that fuckin' right!"

They all laughed, and then Stone gripped Del's arm. "We're still gonna miss you guys."

"It's all good. And we'll still be around. LA's not so big that we can't grab a beer now and then."

"Right," Stone said, although deep down he wondered if he'd ever see his two old friends again. Separate paths had a habit of leading in different directions. As much as he hoped it wouldn't happen, he couldn't help feeling a sense of finality as he hugged them goodbye. He saw it in Claudia's eyes, too, when they leaned down to kiss her.

"Well, I guess I'll see you in a couple of weeks," Randi said, as they watched the rental car drive away. "I hope the studio isn't too pissed at you. I would really hate to fly across the country and find out I've got no fucking job."

"You and me both." Stone still held out a desperate hope that they'd be able to salvage something from the hours of video files they'd uploaded. Everything on the camera chips and in the van's computers had been wiped clean, and all of their phones had been fried during the final confrontation. "But it is what it is. Suddenly ratings don't seem so important."

Randi raised an eyebrow.

"Wow, listen to Mister Maturity. What's got into you?"

"Let's just say I've seen the light." Stone touched his right wrist where the blisters had faded, leaving a white scar behind. Claudia bore an identical one on her left wrist.

Both of them spelled out *Forever.*

"Well, whatever happens, I've got your back. Claudia, take care of him until I get to LA."

The two women embraced and Claudia whispered something in Randi's ear. They both looked at him and laughed.

A tingle in his wrist let Stone know he could hear them if he wanted. Although he'd never be as good as the twins, he'd already improved at divining thoughts and emotions. Especially now that he had a little help from the other side.

This time he didn't bother. Some things were better left unknown.

A few minutes later, as they pulled onto the highway at the edge of town, the throbbing returned, only stronger. With it came a memory of something Father Bonaventura had said to him one day in the Rawlingses' kitchen.

"Evil never truly dies. All we can do is banish it temporarily."

He glanced at Claudia, who stared out the back window with a frown.

"What is it?"

"Nothing, I guess." She took his hand and looked forward again.

—*Nothing.*— Shari didn't sound any more convincing than her sister.

He checked the rearview mirror and watched the Hastings Mills sign recede into the distance behind them.

Only when he couldn't see it anymore did his anxiety fade away.

EPILOGUE

Los Angeles, Present Day

***Excerpt from* Good Morning with Josh and Jenny**

Jenny Durso: "Stone, some people have said that this is all just a way to keep your name in the spotlight. After all, there's no proof any of it happened."

Stone Graves: "They can say whatever the hell they want. I can't explain what happened to all our data files, but I have my suspicions. What I – what we – experienced in Hastings Mills, at the Rawlings house, has made a believer out of me. Demons do exist, and they're out there."

Josh Black: "So, what's next for Stone Graves now that you don't have your show anymore?"

Graves: "I don't know. The last year's been so hectic, with the book and getting married, I haven't thought about the future. After what happened, do we really want to put ourselves in danger again? Maybe it's time to take it easy."

Durso: "Well, whatever you decide, I'm sure it could never be as exciting as what's in the pages of your book. This has been fascinating. (Jenny holds up a copy of the book) A Town Possessed.* Get it now in your favorite bookstores or online. Stone Graves, thank you for joining us today and have a Good Morning."

Graves: "Thank you, Jenny and Josh."

Black (looking at camera): "Coming up next, chef Alan Abercromby will show us how to make twenty-minute meals that will amaze your friends."

"Aaaand, cut!" The segment producer clapped her hands. "Mr. Graves, that was great. If you could follow me, we'd like you to sign a couple of books as giveaways for some contest winners."

Stone followed the woman to a small alcove, where the couple of books turned out to be a dozen. After he signed, an assistant showed him to the green room, where Randi and Claudia waited with excited looks. His wrist gave a sharp quiver before they even spoke.

"We just got a call. The mayor of Rocky Point wants us to do a full investigation of Wood Hill," Randi said.

"Corday's bringing the car around," Claudia added.

"Whattya say?" Randi asked.

Wood Hill. Where it all started. Did he want to face that again?

Stone looked down at the book he held. With a smile, he tossed it onto a nearby couch.

"What the hell. Let's go."

Hastings Mills, NY, Present Day

Curt Rawlings placed an ice cream bar in Abby's hand and fixed her oversized sunglasses. The town park was filled with people enjoying a beautiful summer morning, with groups of teenagers playing Frisbee or just sitting on blankets, couples strolling hand in hand, and senior citizens chatting on benches.

As he guided her through the park, describing what he saw, a baseball cap tumbled by in the breeze and came to a stop in front of them. The hat was blue, with the Yankees logo on the front. Dark smudges stained the material. He picked it up and looked inside. A name was written in faded marker on the brim.

P. Telles.

He looked around for a garbage can but there weren't any in sight.

"Daddy? What is it?"

"Nothing, sweetheart." He stuck it in his pocket, intending to toss it out later.

"Can we go to the swings next?" Abby asked.

Curt's body gave a twitch and he stopped. A large black beetle crawled out of his pocket and up his shirt.

"Daddy?"

"I've got a better idea," he said. "How 'bout we take a walk along by the river?"

"Okay!"

He took her hand and led them down the path.

"I hear the current's really strong this summer."

ACKNOWLEDGMENTS

As always, I have to thank the people who were invaluable in making this book possible. My wife, Andrea, for all her support of me and my writing. My mother, who is also a tireless supporter of mine. My friends and family, who provide much-needed smiles and encouragement. Bruno, our rescue pup, who gets me up from my desk when I lose track of time.

The world's best beta readers: Rena Mason, James Chambers, Erinn Kemper, Patrick Freivald, Chris Marrs, Peter Salomon, Lisa Morton, and Brian Matthews. They're also great writers in their own right, so you should check them out.

The people at Flame Tree who make the magic happen. Don D'Auria, my editor. Gillian Whitaker, Maria Tissot, Molly Rosevear, Josie Karani, Nick Wells, and the fantastic editing and art teams, who do such a great job of getting the books in shape. You are all a huge part of this, and I thank you.

Father Alphonsus Trabold, the real-life inspiration for Father Leo Bonaventura. His stories while I attended St. Bonaventure University have stuck with me throughout the decades and now I've finally been able to (hopefully) do them justice.

The good people of St. Bonaventure University, Olean, and Allegany in New York, where I spent a good chunk of my formative years and had some amazing adventures. Unlike the fictional St. Alphonse University and the town of Hastings Mills, Allegany and Olean are not demon-infested communities, and St. Bonaventure was actually a great place to go to school. Although, some of the historical events in this book are based on real stories. I'll leave it to the readers to figure out which ones.

FLAME TREE PRESS

FICTION WITHOUT FRONTIERS

Award-Winning Authors & Original Voices

Flame Tree Press is the trade fiction imprint of Flame Tree Publishing, focusing on excellent writing in horror and the supernatural, crime and mystery, science fiction and fantasy. Our aim is to explore beyond the boundaries of the everyday, with tales from both award-winning authors and original voices.

•

Other titles available by JG Faherty:
Hellrider
Sins of the Father

Other horror and suspense titles available include:
Snowball by Gregory Bastianelli
Thirteen Days by Sunset Beach by Ramsey Campbell
Think Yourself Lucky by Ramsey Campbell
The Hungry Moon by Ramsey Campbell
The Influence by Ramsey Campbell
The Wise Friend by Ramsey Campbell
Somebody's Voice by Ramsey Campbell
The Haunting of Henderson Close by Catherine Cavendish
The Garden of Bewitchment by Catherine Cavendish
The House by the Cemetery by John Everson
The Devil's Equinox by John Everson
The Toy Thief by D.W. Gillespie
One By One by D.W. Gillespie
Black Wings by Megan Hart
The Playing Card Killer by Russell James
The Sorrows by Jonathan Janz
Will Haunt You by Brian Kirk
We Are Monsters by Brian Kirk
Hearthstone Cottage by Frazer Lee
Those Who Came Before by J.H. Moncrieff
Stoker's Wilde by Steven Hopstaken & Melissa Prusi
Slash by Hunter Shea
Ghost Mine by Hunter Shea
Misfits by Hunter Shea

•

Join our mailing list for free short stories, new release details, news about our authors and special promotions:

flametreepress.com